Black Tide

A LEWIS COLE MYSTERY

BRENDAN DuBois

OTTO PENZLER BOOKS

NEW YORK

**OTTO
PENZLER
BOOKS**

Otto Penzler Books
129 West 56th Street
New York, NY 10019
(Editorial Offices only)

Simon & Schuster Inc.
Rockefeller Center
1230 Avenue of the Americas
New York, NY 10020

Manufactured in the United States of America

1 3 5 7 9 10 8 6 4 2

Library of Congress Cataloging-in-Publication Data

DuBois, Brendan.
Black tide: a Lewis Cole mystery/Brendan DuBois.
p. cm.
1. Journalists—New Hampshire—Fiction. I. Title.
PS3554.U2564B53 1995
813'.54—dc20
94–28920
CIP
ISBN 1-883402-58-1

For Mona Pinette

ACKNOWLEDGMENTS

The successful completion of a book often depends on other people. For this one, the author wishes to express his deep thanks to the members of his family, Ernie Connor of the N.H. Port Authority, Dan Chartrand, Tom Raynor, Ron Sher, and special thanks to Michele Slung and Kate Stine of OPB, editors extraordinaire.

Black
Tide

CHAPTER
ONE

On this late July Sunday afternoon the great gray waters of the Atlantic Ocean were rolling gently onto the shores of Tyler, New Hampshire, not causing much surf or foam to break upon the rocks and sand. I was sitting on the rear deck of my two-story home, overlooking a private cove of mine that's probably one of the most inaccessible parts of the eighteen miles of this seacoast which stretches from the Massachusetts border to the shores of Maine. The day was hot and the air was still, and to the north, beyond the woods of the Samson State Wildlife Preserve, a bank of thick gray and black clouds was moving out to sea. Every now and then I would hear the distant rumble of the storm, sounding like some pile-driving machinery out there in the sky.

It was a muggy day and all I wore was a tattered pair of gym shorts from the University of New Hampshire. At my elbow was a round wooden table and a pair of binoculars, and an empty bottle of Molson Golden Ale. Another bottle was sweating cold ice in my hands, and as I watched the waves roll in, I thought some about the passage of time and its odd little mileposts. More than three hundred and fifty years ago some Englishmen in two leaky wooden boats—the *Beaver* and the *Resolute*—made their way from England to these shores, and the town and its beaches were named for their leader, the Reverend Bonus Tyler. Over a hundred years ago, fearful of a new Spanish Armada, the land on which I now lived was converted from a lifeboat station to a Coast Artillery installation, and the home in which I slept and drank and wrote once belonged to some junior officers in the U.S. Navy. Now the home is mine and the concrete bunkers to the near north are part of a wildlife preserve and belong to the woodchucks and rabbits.

I rubbed the cold bottle of beer against my forehead and looked down to my left side. A month ago I was in a hospital bed in Cambridge, Massachusetts, and now I was back in Tyler, and at my side, the angry red of the skin where the thirty-two stitches had gone in had now subsided to a bright pink. The healing of the flesh and the changing of its color was a process as dependable as the rising and setting of the sun, and it was a process I was intimately familiar with.

But that didn't mean I was happy about it.

I picked up my binoculars—which were just slightly younger than my scar, its predecessor currently resting on the bottom of Tyler Harbor—and I looked south, to Weymouth's Point and the narrow stretch of beach which was called North Beach. To the near south was a pile of broken rocks and rubble that discouraged most sightseers and blocked the view of all but a tiny portion of the sands of North Beach. The main beach of Tyler—which on this Sunday was no doubt filled with tens of thousands of sunbathers, tourists and assorted (and sordid) hangers-on—was a couple of miles further to the south, but from the number of tiny figures visible in my binoculars, it looked as if North Beach was holding its own. It didn't have the arcades or fried-dough stands or bars or pizza joints or T-shirt emporiums that were crammed into the main beach, but it did have reasonably clean sand, which was pretty good, considering all that had gone on some weeks ago.

In moving around my fake-redwood chair, I took a deep breath, and the tug at my side was not as painful as it was last week. I was doing all right, just like the beaches. In taking that deep breath, I caught the faint stench of petroleum. Lifting up my binoculars again, I remembered how the beaches had muddled through that disastrous night a month ago, when I was flat on my back in another state and was wondering why hospital dietitians couldn't design a better way of serving scrambled eggs than from a scoop fashioned from an ice-cream spoon.

I scanned the ocean and stopped for a moment at the rocky islands of the Isles of Shoals, about eleven or so miles out on the ocean. On a moonless evening last month a small tanker carrying tens of thousands of gallons of home heating oil had run aground on a ledge near Star Island, one of the nine rocky outcroppings making up the Isles of Shoals. Despite the White Island lighthouse, the well-marked charts and the size of the islands themselves, the crew of the *Petro Star*—those few who weren't sleeping or who weren't getting ready for a night ashore at Porter or who weren't drunk—had put the tanker aground. And in the fine tradition of those ship captains who are ruled by budgeters rather than common sense, the master of the *Petro Star* had tried for a half hour to pull the vessel free before contacting the Foss Island Coast Guard station. In the space of those thirty minutes, he had torn out the hull of his ship.

Thousands of gallons of oil began washing ashore the next day on the beaches of Falconer, Tyler and North Tyler, New Hampshire, and there was I, far from home, watching the news on the television in my hospital room with my hands twisting the sheets in disgust and fury. In a while I stopped with the sheets and I scribbled some thoughts on a notepad a friendly nurse had given me. A couple of weeks ago, I had come home. By then the bulk of the *Petro Star*'s cargo had been pumped into another tanker, and the vessel had been taken to Portland, Maine, while the inquiries had begun. And in my fine Puritan traditionone I'm sure would have impressed the Reverend Bonus Tyler—I began work the day after I got home.

First I walked along my stretch of shoreline. Volunteer cleanup crews had been up and down the coast, no doubt ignoring my homemade and quite illegal "No Trespassing" signs, but the stink and remnants of what one writer has called "the devil's excrement" were still there on the rocks and the sand. I walked slowly, for the stitches were still in my side, covered by a gauze bandage. I used an oak walking stick to help me move along the rocks and boulders, and wore thigh-high rubber boots over my trembling and weak legs. And though the volunteers had done their best, there was still the stench of the oil, so thick that I could actually taste it, and I was slipping and sliding on the rocks as I walked, trying to convince myself that the tears in my eyes were from the smell.

In just a day I went through a half dozen trash bags, picking up dead seagulls, cormorants, plovers and terns, as well as cod and bluefish and perch, and oil-sopped masses of seaweed and chunks of driftwood. When I was through for the day the clothes and boots and gloves I wore went into another trash bag, and I washed myself down with a sponge, not wanting to get the bandage soaked by taking a shower.

In a few days I stopped the cleanup, since I had done about as much as I could. It was up to the waves and the storms and the weather to finish the job. And I went to work on other things, by using my phone, my computer and my modem. Some years ago I had been trained by people who received light green U.S. Treasury checks each pay period and who were the very best in ferreting out bits and pieces of information for the Department of Defense, and now I was using those wonderful skills to find some answers, about who owned the *Petro Star* and who had sent it out that evening to Porter, the state's only major port. It was a hunt that I knew was going to be long and difficult, and so far, my predictions had been painfully accurate.

Other work and other cleanups continued, done by other people, and the news media blitz began to drift away. And in what was politely called the "global view," Tyler and its neighboring beaches had done fairly well. The oil had at least been refined, and wasn't the sticky crude horror that Exxon had so thoughtfully deposited in Alaska's Prince William Sound some years back. Only a few weekends were lost to the tourist season, and a long stretch of hot weather had brought them back. They had to be careful, though. While some beaches were littered with tampon dispensers or hypodermic needles, these sands were soiled on occasion by the smell of oil. Still, the tourists came. Just the price to pay for living in our wonderful modern society.

So I had been busy these past weeks. But on this July Sabbath day, no work was to be done. The hours were hot and I was tired, and the beer tasted just fine, thank you. From the north came another rumble of thunder. I turned and looked and saw a flash of lightning flare through the dark clouds. Rain this afternoon, maybe in less than a half hour. I scanned the waters again and saw a couple of sailboats and a charter fishing boat, out from Tyler Harbor. Near the shore I made out a dark lump just under the surface of the ocean, washing in to the beach. In the binoculars it looked like another lump of seaweed, or maybe a petroleum souvenir from the *Petro Star*, jostled free from the sandy bottom near North Beach. Marvelous. Something else for the tourists to take pictures of, and something that I was sure wouldn't make it in the Chamber of Commerce's advertising campaign for next year.

The binoculars came down and the bottle of Molson came up, and as I took another swallow I kept an ear open for the telephone. For the past few weeks I had screened all of my calls through my answering machine, for while I was in the mood to sit in my office or on the deck, I wasn't in the mood for playing Mr. Conversationalist. There had been a couple of calls from Diane Woods, detective in the Tyler police department, and I had returned one of those and had lied about wanting to have lunch with her soon. There had also been about a half dozen from Felix Tinios, a resident of North Tyler and a former resident of the North End in Boston, and one whose job was listed on his tax forms—or so he told me—as a "security consultant." I had returned a few of those, and made similar promises about noontime meals sometime in the future.

There had been no phone calls from the Tyler *Chronicle*, the town's daily newspaper, or its best reporter, Paula Quinn. And though I knew Paula's home and work numbers by heart, I had made no moves to punch out those numbers on my phone.

Instead, I sat. Here on my deck and upstairs in my office.

I checked the moving blob again. It was getting closer, and seemed to be more defined. Not like a lump of seaweed.

The binoculars felt heavy for a moment and I put them down, and then I lifted up the Molson and finished it off. I eyed the empty green bottle for a moment. This afternoon there were many things which could be done, from continuing my *Petro Star* project to thinking about writing my next monthly column for *Shoreline* magazine to emptying the trash. But emptying the trash meant a drive to the town landfill (read: dump) and I was at a momentary dead end on the *Petro Star*. The column was due in a few days, and although the terms of my employment were quite secret and quite liberal, I would hate to miss that deadline. I had never done it before, and I didn't want to start a trend.

Or so I hoped. While the column should be worked on, another beer did sound pretty good. I replaced the empty with the binoculars and looked south again, to the outcropping of land that was Weymouth's Point and where an old friend had once lived, and out to the ocean. The black object was about fifty or so feet from shore, and as I was getting up the energy level to go inside for another Molson Golden Ale, the dark shape was caught in a rolling swell that was heading to the sands, and a fin popped up.

In a second or two I was standing at the south end of the deck's railing, resting my elbows against the stained wood. The fin was black and distinct, a triangular shape, and I was thinking: A shark, a shark attack at North Beach? And were there lifeguards there at the beach, to sound the alarm? And did those swimmers to the north and south of the shape see that it was even there?

Those thoughts and others tumbled through my head as another rolling swell came by, tossing the black shape, and a pair of fins popped up, and I realized two things at once: that the fins were made of black rubber, and that they were attached to a pair of legs.

TWO

Within a few minutes I had parked my dark green Range Rover illegally on Atlantic Avenue, having stopped in front of a fire hydrant, and I went across the street and through a stairwell built into the shoulder-high concrete seawall and down to the sands of North Beach, with binoculars in hand and a coil of rope around my shoulders. I had expected the beach-goers to be curious about what was going on, about why a tall thin man with brown hair was scanning the waters with binoculars while muttering to himself, but no one paid me any attention. In a small way I was almost disappointed. There were families and couples and groups of young men and women, lying on blankets and chairs, drinking and eating and reading, and many of them were lined up like a grove of sunflowers, all facing the sun to the southwest, their eyes and thoughts hidden by dark glasses, and all listening to metal noise from their radios and tape decks. No one seemed to see what I saw, and no one seemed to care about the darkening clouds and the sound of thunder to the north. For a moment it made me wonder if the shapes were even human.

As I looked across the waters I made out the twin fins poking up again through the swells, and I recalled the quick phone call I had made to the Tyler police dispatch. Even with sirens and lights blaring and lighting the way, it would take ten or so minutes for the first cruiser or fire truck to fight its way through the Sunday beach traffic to get here. And what might be here when they arrived? He might disappear by then, be tossed back under the waves or caught in a fast-moving current, and that was not acceptable.

Having gotten dressed a few minutes ago back home, I now got undressed, dropping my worn topsiders on the sand, placing the binoculars on top of them and covering it all with a T-shirt that said NASA in red and blue letters. I started running into the ocean and grimaced as my feet went into the cold salt water. I tried not to groan as the water splashed up my legs. This is one of my deepest and darkest secrets: though I love living by the ocean, and love the sights and sounds of the seacoast and the ever-changing weather, I can count on the fingers of a half hand the number of times I've actually gone swimming here. The water is too damn cold, and today was no exception. Within seconds the nerve endings in my feet there had gone to sleep, and it was as if I were walking on two granite blocks. Even in the shallow stretch, it was hard going, for the bottom was littered with rocks and stretches of gravel, and I stumbled a couple of times, the weight of the 3/8-inch rope on my shoulders not helping one bit.

I think I yelled three times as I plowed into the water. The first time was when the cold water reached that nether area above the knees and below the waist. The second time was when a wave broke upon me and the cold salt water soaked the healing

wound on my side. And the third time was when I immersed myself and began swimming awkwardly to the black shape.

There were strands of seaweed floating about me and I
smelled something thick and pungent as I approached the dark
shape. The flippers rose up again from another passing swell, and
I saw that the legs were enclosed in a wet suit. A diver, no doubt,
who was out here drunk or alone or inexperienced, and who had
drowned less than a hundred yards from shore. A not too un-
common story, and even as I swam toward the diver, puffing and
cursing at the weight of the rope on my shoulders and the weak-
ness of my legs and the sharp pain in my side—the old phrase
"rubbing salt in a wound" seemed appropriate at that moment—
I thought that this might end up as a column in *Shoreline*.

When I reached the diver I was well over my head and I
treaded water as I tugged the rope coil free. I made a quick slip-
knot of a noose, and as I got closer to the diver's body, the sound
of sirens to the south became louder. I paddled closer and another movement of water came by, and in a slight panic, I realized I
was too close. I bumped into the stiff rubber flippers just as they
were rising up, and one of them caught me in my mouth. I nearly
gagged from the smell and taste of the rubber, and my hands
were shaking as I passed the rope around the two flippers and
pulled it tight. I then looped the rope a few times around my right
arm and began paddling back to shore.

By then some people were standing at the water's edge,
shading their eyes from the glare in an odd type of salute, and as
I swam in, I tried to do it at an angle, for the flippers were striking my back with each push toward shore, and the slimy touch of
the rubber against my skin almost made me drop the rope a few
times. The odor was of rubber and salt and decay, and I saw the
flashing lights of a fire truck and a police cruiser, on the street side
of the concrete seawall, and the movement of people.

In another minute or two my feet touched the rough bottom
and I began wading ashore, pulling the soggy rope now with
both hands. I looked back quickly and saw that the diver didn't
seem to have an air tank on him, which made sense. In times of

panic, when a diver believes he or she is only seconds away from drowning, they tend to drop everything in a desperate attempt to reach the surface.

This one's attempt hadn't succeeded.

I was coughing and shivering as I walked past the surf line and onto the moist sands of the beach, dragging the diver behind me, and the crowd of people there came toward me, hands outstretched, a couple of them carrying cameras, all of them wearing bathing suits. There was an old man with dark, leathery skin, and a white fringe of hair around his sunburned skull. A fat woman in a pink suit with a skirt, holding the hands of a boy and a girl, both looking about age four or so. And a group of three teenage girls, huddled together, wearing sleek black one-piece suits, whispering at each other from behind manicured hands held up to their made-up faces.

And in a brief moment, they scattered, and some of the women—and even a couple of the men—started screaming and yelling. Up on the seawall a couple of cops and some firefighters began jogging toward me across the sand. The police had radio microphones in their hands and the firefighters were carrying a Stokes litter.

I dropped the rope and looked behind me, and then quickly looked back up at the seawall, knowing that I didn't want to get sick in front of all these people, though it seemed to be a marvelous idea.

For the diver had no head.

Or hands.

In about twenty minutes I was sitting against the concrete seawall, still on the beach side, and the overhanging curve of the concrete provided some shade. I had my T-shirt back on but my shoes were at my side, next to my binoculars. I was hot and my legs and feet were crusted with beach sand, and I could feel sand working its way up the wet openings of my shorts. The body of the diver was at the water's edge, now covered by a blanket, and a group consisting of Tyler police officers, firefighters, Diane Woods and another guy I didn't recognize were down there. One of the uniforms was busy taking pictures as another lifted up the blanket, and two other members of Tyler's finest were holding back the crowds. I was by myself, which was fine. I had talked a bit to the first uniforms at the scene and I waited for Diane Woods, the sole detective for Tyler, to come over to talk to me.

In the north the clouds were quite dark and I made out a bright flash of lightning. I started counting to myself, one one-thousand, two one-thousand, three one-thousand, and when I got up to ten, the low and long rumbling of thunder seemed to echo along the sands of the beach. About two miles away, and the clouds seemed to be heading south, toward these people and my resting place. I looked over and Diane was coming toward me, along with the guy in civilian clothes. She carried a clipboard in her hands and so did the guy. Diane had on black workout sneakers and was wearing light green shorts which I guess were long enough to be called culottes. She had on a white pullover shirt and she was wearing her detective's shield on a chain around her neck. I knew without asking that underneath that shirt and against her slim body was a holster and her revolver, a Ruger .357. Her thick light brown hair was cut shorter than its usual wedge shape and her skin had tanned nicely over the summer, except for the short white scar across her chin. That came from when she was a uniform and a drunk banged her head in the booking room at the Tyler police station.

Diane once told me that when no one was looking later that night in the police station, she had broken one of the drunk's fingers, and although she later laughed and told me that she had made the story up, I didn't believe her. Didn't believe her making the story up, that is.

When the guy came closer I realized who he was. Roger something. A State Police detective from Massachusetts, up to Tyler for a few weeks to see how their little neighbor to the north handles crime. For the first time in a long time, the governors of New Hampshire and Massachusetts were actually cooperating with each other—instead of snarling about tolls, border liquor stores and out-of-state taxes—and this detective's trip was one of the little exchange programs that were going on between the Granite State and the Bay State. When I last talked to Diane she had said, "The selectmen didn't like the idea of another detective coming aboard, Lewis, especially one from Massachusetts, but when they found out he was going to work for free, they practically offered him a full-time job. And don't laugh, but he's told me he likes it in Tyler so much he's thinking of applying for the chief's job. Jesus."

It could be true, I thought. The police chief was away on medical leave, being treated for cancer, and if anybody knew when and if he might come back, they weren't talking. This boy was fairly smart then. Show the local yokels a good job and they'd think twice of him if the applications started coming in for the chief's position.

"Lewis," she said when she got close to me. "I want you to meet Roger Krohn. He's the detective with the Massachusetts State Police I told you about."

Roger looked about thirty-five, which made him my age, and he was a couple of inches taller than me and wearing a short-sleeved blue-and-white-striped shirt and tan chinos. His face was angular and his nose was just a tad too large, and he had light brown hair that was thick and parted on the side, the type of hair that dries in about five seconds and looks perfect for the rest of the day. His smile was tentative, for like all cops, he wanted to know what was going on, and he wasn't sure who I was and how I was connected with Diane. His eyes seemed blue and were squinty, as if the sun off the beach sands disturbed him.

He held out a beefy-looking hand. I reached up and grabbed it, and his grasp was dry and firm. I said, "I'm sure you don't mind that I don't instantly jump up."

His smile became less tentative. "I can see why. Not a problem."

Diane said, "Lewis is our resident writer in this town. He writes for a magazine out of Boston, called *Shoreline*."

Roger looked slightly impressed. "Really? A magazine writer. But Lewis, I'm sorry to say that I've never heard of *Shoreline*."

"Don't worry," I said. "It seems like no one has."

Diane smiled at me and squatted down and said, "I've read over what you gave the first guys on the scene. Fairly straightforward, Lewis. Anything else you can add? Anything more since you've been here?"

The taste of rubber was still strong in my mouth. "Nope. Just taking it easy on my rear deck and spotted something black floating off North Beach. Figured it was a lump of seaweed or a large tar ball until I saw the flippers poke up."

Roger said, "You have good eyesight."

"I was using binoculars. Seven-by-fifties."

He smiled. "Checking out the babes on the beach, right?"

I decided then that Detective Roger Krohn had a wonderful career ahead for him in Massachusetts, where he and I would probably never meet again.

I said, "I'm sure it might come as a surprise to someone from the big city, but when you live by the ocean, you like to look at the ocean. Sailboats. The Isles of Shoals. Birds."

Diane said quietly, no doubt trying to defuse the situation, "Then what?"

"Then I called Tyler dispatch and grabbed some rope and came down here and went into the water. Damn near froze everything I'm proud to own. And then I snagged the body with the length of rope and dragged it in, and when I saw what happened to it, I nearly lost the day's meals, and then I started talking to your comrades."

"Why did you do it, Lewis?" Roger asked, also squatting down next to me.

"Do what?" I said.

"Go into the water like that to retrieve the body," he said. "It wasn't like the guy was in trouble or was drowning. You could have waited."

I thought of what I should have said to him. That some years ago friends of mine had died in the high desert of Nevada, and that all their families knew was the lie that they had died in an aircraft accident, that the bodies were burned and charred beyond recognition, and that no remains were retrievable. That somewhere, somebody would want this poor body in the ocean back, and I wasn't going to allow it to drift away.

Instead I said, "It seemed to be the thing to do."

Roger nodded and got up and brushed some sand from his pant legs and said, "Pretty ballsy move."

"I beg your pardon?" I asked.

By then he almost looked shy, and I noticed that he was developing a bit of gut, and he didn't seem so perfect after all. "Listen, Lewis, I didn't mean to jerk you around like that. Place I come from, the only time someone wants to retrieve a body, they want to see if it's carrying a fat wallet. Know what I mean? So I didn't mean to come on to you that strong. And I meant what I said—going in after this floater was a pretty ballsy move."

I decided then that I was tired and felt miserable and that Roger Krohn probably didn't kill puppies for a living. I said, "Not a problem."

He shook my hand again and said, "Diane? Will you excuse me for a minute? I want to see how the photos are coming along."

She said that was just fine and when Roger was out of earshot I said, "Is he as good a detective as he is a politician?"

Diane was balancing the clipboard on her knees, which were tanned. "What do you mean?"

"After giving me the big smart detective routine, he remembered that you and I were friends. And then he was Mr. Apologies."

She laughed and said, "Stories he's been telling me about Boston, Lewis, would curl your hair. And I mean stories about the politics and the work. So cut him some slack. He's not too used to the slow pace of this town."

I nodded over at the people standing around the body. "Some slow pace, Diane."

"Yeah, I know."

"I never did take forensics or animal science in college, but I would say that the poor diver did more than drown, and I don't think his body was nibbled on by sharks or tumbled around by a boat's propeller while he was in the water. Someone took off his head and hands, Diane. Nice and clean."

She looked down at her clipboard. "That's a fair observation. Someone did take care of this guy, wanting to make it hard for him to be identified, and they did a pretty good job. Oh, we'll check his wet-suit gear to see if it was rental, and we'll do a canvass of the dive shops up and down the coast, see if that works. But I doubt it. If there's anything traceable on that wet suit, I'll give you good odds that it's already gone. Starting the job to ID this guy means we're already starting from a deep hole."

By now Roger Krohn was back with the small group of officers around the body, clipboard in hand. A few yards away a young Tyler police officer in his dark green uniform was talking to two young ladies in black-and-white bikinis. Their skins were oily and slick and even with that horror only some feet away, they were smiling at the officer. I guess his presence had a calming effect.

I said, "But without an identity, what's the point?"

She got back up on her feet. "What do you mean?"

"Without word getting out that this guy is dead, what's the point?" I asked. "The only people who'll know that our diver is dead are the guys who did it. So maybe they left the wet suit on as a message, so someone reading tomorrow's paper will know that his or her husband, brother or father—who's also missing from a trip up here involving skin diving—has just turned up at Tyler Beach with his head and hands missing. They get the message. And it'll be interesting to see what kinds of calls you get, once this hits the papers."

"Not a bad thought," she said, and when I decided to stand up and go home, she said quietly, "You intending to write a column about this one?"

I brushed the sand off my hands and looked at her. She didn't look mad or angry. Just curious. Each month I have a

2,000-word column in *Shoreline*, called "Granite Shores." I have the freedom to write about practically anything I want, so long as it has something to do with this state's eighteen-mile coast, the shortest in the United States. *Shoreline* covers the New England coast, from Eastport in Maine to Greenwich Point in Connecticut, and what with the boating industry, the U.S. Navy and the hundreds of years of history along these New Hampshire shores, I've not yet tired of having to come up with a monthly column.

Then there are my other projects, my other "columns." One was my current attempt to find out the parties responsible for the *Petro Star*. Other columns I've done in the past in Tyler have led me down some paths that have also been trod upon by Diane Woods, and over the years we have come to an agreement on what I do. So I knew that my answer to her one question would cause her to make some decisions and assumptions about her investigation. I decided then to make it clean and clear.

I said, "Diane, I'm tired. I've been tired for a while. I think I'm going to pass on doing a column on this one."

She put the clipboard under her arm. In the dark clouds approaching from the north, there was a flash of lightning, and a boom that came only a few seconds later. Less than a mile away and closing fast. "You still feeling down from your operation?"

I shrugged. "I'm doing better. Honest. And I appreciate the cards and visits last month, you know that. And if this had happened last summer, yeah, I'd probably be doing a column. But right now, well, I'm not particularly interested in looking up the names and addresses of people who can sleep at night after cutting someone's head and hands off."

She nodded. "I know, I know," she said, almost sighing, turning to look down at the group around the body and then turning back to look at me. "This past summer's been rough, Lewis, real rough. And with the chief's condition up in the air . . . The department's in a shambles, with the two deputy chiefs practically pounding on each other over who sets policy and controls the budget. I just try to do my job, but it doesn't seem like I've been winning that much, Lewis. There's too much going on with too many tourists and not enough cops, and then this diver washes up ashore. And now I'm going to have to try to look up those names and addresses you mentioned."

For a moment her face was troubled, as though she had gone many hours without sleep and seen many awful things with thick smells, and she said with a bleak tone, "At least you have a choice, Lewis."

And then she went back to the body.

When I made my way up the short concrete stairs that led to the opening through the seawall that was next to the sidewalk on Atlantic Avenue, a young woman was coming through, wearing loose black slacks, white sneakers and a plain white T-shirt. She had a black handbag over her shoulder and a reporter's notebook in her hand, and she had on dark aviator-type sunglasses. Her long blond hair was tied back in a ponytail and her ears stuck out at a slight angle. Paula Quinn, reporter for the Tyler *Chronicle* and second-best writer in Tyler, stopped at the bottom of the steps as I came closer.

And then she surprised me. She actually smiled. "Lewis Cole. I guess the story is true. You were the one who discovered the body."

"My reputation precedes me," I said, conscious that she looked as if she had just stepped away from a beach party, while I looked as if I had spent the night inside the North Beach rest rooms. My shorts and NASA T-shirt were soaked and crusty with beach sand. I carried my binoculars in my right hand, and I was happy to leave behind the rope I had brought to the beach.

"Maybe your reputation does precede you, but the cop directing traffic up there told me you were here."

"How did you hear?"

"Came over the scanner, Lewis. We started something where we rotate weekend duty, and I have to check with the local cop shops. I also have to stay within ten miles of home in case a story breaks, like this one. It really stinks. But tell me what happened."

I said, "Off the record?"

"Off the record." She nodded, and I told her. She took a few notes, and even with what had happened—or hadn't happened—I trusted her not to use me in her story. There are many times I like to keep a low profile, and this was one of those times. Being publicly ID'd as the guy who discovered a headless and handless diver would definitely not contribute to that fine effort.

Then she looked up at me and said, "How are you feeling, Lewis?"

A lot of things and phrases came to mind, and I just said, "I'm doing okay. And thanks for your cards. Both of them."

The minute I said those last three words, I regretted it. But her smile didn't waver. She nodded and said, "That was a good one. I guess you are doing better."

"I guess." She just stood there, and I said, "It's been a while, Paula. Haven't seen you since you spent the night at my place, back in June. Before I went into the hospital. How are you doing?"

She shook her head and said, "I'm doing all right."

I said nothing and she returned the favor, and then she sighed and said, "Lewis, I'm sorry but this conversation is like being in a dentist's chair without Novocain. I've got to get to work and talk to Diane Woods and find out what the hell is going on. Look, I know we've got some things that need to be cleared up but I've got to get this story. I'll give you a call."

Paula went by and I said nothing else, because with my wet clothes and what I had seen on the beach sand and other things, I was in no mood to talk. I just nodded my head and walked across the street to my Range Rover.

And through it all, she kept her sunglasses on, which I found disturbing. I had wanted to see her eyes, to see what they were saying to me.

I drove north along Atlantic Avenue, which is also known as Route 1A. There are a lot of roads in this part of the world that have two and even three names. Some of the old maps show this road being called Ocean Boulevard, but that was changed sometime in the mid-1920s. From what I've been able to figure out, some investors building a hotel at the beach wanted something to mirror Atlantic City, and Atlantic Avenue was as good as they could get. The investors soon went bust and their hotel was never completed. I have a feeling their ghosts knew what had happened to the real Atlantic City and they probably decided they got off easy.

Atlantic Avenue is twisty and follows the New Hampshire coastline, and in this part of the coast the east side is bordered by the North Beach seawall and the beach itself, and the west side has condos, some motels and a couple of convenience stores. It's been spared the development and the cheek-by-jowl construction that was dumped upon the main beach, Tyler Beach. As a result, it's popular with families who want to bring their kids to the beach without having to put down their blankets and chairs next to a gang of young boys who constantly use the F-word as a noun and adjective.

In a minute or two of driving, the sands of North Beach disappeared into a collection of rock ledges and boulders, and the road rose up some and curved to the right. Then I came upon a large, Victorian-style hotel, called the Lafayette House. Local legend has it that the Marquis de Lafayette stopped there for a quick drink in 1825 during his famed tour of the United States. Once Betsy Tyler, a selectman in her mid-seventies and a descendant of the Reverend Bonus Tyler, told me that if the Marquis de Lafayette had stopped at every watering hole that claimed him in this country, then no doubt he died of cirrhosis of the liver.

Most of the original tavern was either burned or torn down, and the current Lafayette House was built in 1902 in the old, Victorian-hotel style. It's near the border of Tyler and North Tyler, and even when business is slow, it always does well from those middle-aged people who want to spend a week at the beach but who don't want to rent a room next to a mill worker from Manchester. Across Atlantic Avenue from the hotel was a tiny parking lot with a sign that said PRIVATE PARKING FOR LAFAYETTE HOUSE ONLY. I turned into the lot and went to the north end, passing the parked BMWs, Porsches, Volvos and Mercedes-Benzes. One Mercedes caught my eye. A red convertible, with its top up. A good decision, for by now the rain had started, big fat raindrops that splattered on the Range Rover's windshield, or windscreen, if you want to be entirely accurate.

At the north end of the lot there was a low stone wall and a place where some of the rocks had fallen free. There was a path there, wide enough for a bicycle or a four-wheel-drive vehicle. I took the dirt path as it went down and to the right, past two homemade "No Trespassing" signs, and my house came into view. It's a two-story cottage that's never been painted and which has a dirt crawl space for a cellar. The lawn is just some faded green tufts of grass that have managed to poke through the rocky soil. The lawn rises up to a steep rocky ledge that hides my home from Atlantic Avenue. In the time I've lived here only a few people have clambered up the steep ledge and tried to come down to visit me, but my brusque manner quickly induced them to leave. I have no doubt they were helped along by my "No Trespassing" signs and the habit I have of answering the door with a 12-gauge shotgun in my hands.

But today was the exception. Standing in the open shed that serves as my garage was Felix Tinios of North Tyler. He politely moved to one side as I pulled the Range Rover in. Thunder was rumbling as I got out and stepped onto the packed-dirt floor. Felix's dark skin had been made even darker by his tanning marathon over the summer, and his thick black hair looked like it had just been caught in the rain. He wore a padded black leather windbreaker and open-necked white shirt, and had on baggy light gray trousers and matching light gray leather shoes.

I closed and locked the Range Rover's door and said, "Where's the gold chain around the neck, Felix? Are your standards slipping?"

He laughed and I only wondered for a moment why he was wearing a jacket in this weather. "Carrying, right?"

His smile was wide and even. "Very good, Lewis. Someone's trained you well."

"Problems?"

He shrugged, opened his hands. "Every day, someone's got problems. Today just happens to be mine, I guess. Listen, can I come in for a minute? I got something to ask you."

I hesitated for a moment, since I felt grubby and my wet and sand-encrusted shorts were riding up some, making it feel like I was wearing a jockstrap made out of soggy sandpaper. But Felix's face looked earnest, which was an odd description for Felix, since earnest isn't a word that comes to my mind when I think of Felix. Direct, maybe, or even deadly. But not earnest.

But he had sent me flowers every week I was in the Cambridge Hospital, and had visited a half dozen times and sent cards and chocolates. Once he had sent something extraordinarily thoughtful which still made me feel slightly warm every time I thought about it. And so far my response to that and his phone calls to my house hadn't been equally thoughtful.

He rubbed at his chin, lightly scraping the blue-black stubble. "You haven't forgotten about Christy?"

"No," I said, giving in with a smile. "Haven't forgotten one bit. Yeah, come on in, Felix. But I've got to take a shower first."

I walked past him and started running to the front door as the rain tumbled forth. He followed behind me and yelled, "What's the matter, you been swimming?"

"Fishing," I said as I scrambled through the rain and to my front door, key in hand. "And you wouldn't believe what I caught."

CHAPTER

THREE

Behind us came a flash of light and that awful crack-boom that seems to flutter up your heart valves, and which means that a lightning bolt has struck close, very close indeed, and Felix murmured, "Jesus Christ," as I slammed the door behind him.

We were in the living room of my house, which has an old and slightly murky history. I've gone through old maps and deeds at the town hall in Tyler and in the county courthouse in Exonia, and have learned that my house was built about a century and a half ago. It first served as a home for the supervisor of a Lifeboat Station that was operating at Samson Point sometime in the middle part of the 1800s. When the War Department took over the land and built the Samson Point Coast Artillery Station, the house became junior officers' quarters. Over the succeeding years, it was expanded and contracted, parts of it torn down and added on, until it was turned into a residence and ended up still being owned by the U.S. government, when the mistake of a dead man in Nevada brought me here to own it.

"I'm going to grab a shower," I said. "You're welcome to root around and get a beer."

"Thanks," Felix said, heading for the kitchen. "I'll just make myself at home."

Making one's self at home or not, I noticed that he kept his leather jacket on. Something was disturbing him, and I hoped whatever it was hadn't followed him here. Felix's problems usually came well armed and angry. I went through the small living room and ran upstairs to the second floor. Before me was the door to the bathroom, and to the left was my study and to the right was my bedroom. The rain was hammering down fairly heavily and I hesitated for a moment before going into the bathroom. I felt cold for a moment, and I thought of the weapons that I had here on the second floor and which were within easy reach: the 12-gauge Remington pump action with extended magazine under the bed, the 8 mm FN assault rifle in the closet, and the 9 mm Beretta in my study.

Other weapons were downstairs, but these would certainly do. I was tempted for a moment to go into the study and bring the Beretta with me into the bathroom, but there was no reason to do it. I was home. I was safe. The doors were locked. And although our relationship certainly couldn't be easily explained through a *Cosmopolitan* magazine survey, I knew that Felix would come to my aid if need be.

Another rumble of thunder.

"Stop being a chickenshit," I said aloud, and so I went to take my shower.

The sneakers and the clothes came off and all were dumped in a blue plastic garbage pail that served as a clothes hamper. I flipped on the shower, and in a few short seconds I started feeling better, just letting the warm water wash away the sweat and grit of the sand that seemed to settle in each fold of my skin. In my infrequent trips to the beach, I'm always amazed at the number of people who wallow around in the wet and sticky sand, building intricate castles, tossing mud balls at each other or letting themselves get buried by children. And this type of sandy misery is called fun?

As I showered, I was careful washing on my left side, just above the kidney, for the skin there was still sore, and I remembered.

One day last month, I was reading the Boston *Globe* and taking notes on the *Petro Star* spill. I was in a private room on the second floor of the Cambridge Hospital, and all things considered, it was a hell of a lot nicer than the last hospital I had been in, some years ago, in Nevada. For one thing, weak as I was and with an IV tube running into my hand, I could get up and walk out onto the tiled hallway and shuffle my way to an elevator, and head for the streets and Cambridge Square. Oh, I'm sure I would have made the nurses and a doctor or two upset, but they couldn't have held me. By signing a disclaimer and leaving the IV apparatus behind, I could leave if I wanted to. In Nevada, it was different. Quite different. I'm certain that some people wanted me to leave that Nevada hospital as ashes and bone chips in a steel container. Instead, thanks to some luck and timing and good bluffing, I left on my own, breathing and with most of my body intact.

Not a bad record, considering where I had been and what I had been doing for a living.

I put the *Globe* down when a man a few years older than me stepped into the room: Dr. Jay Ludlow, wearing green hospital pants and a white jacket with the obligatory stethoscope hanging around his neck. He had tan skin and dark curly hair which was receding some, making his forehead shiny, and he was wearing half-glasses, the type favored by this state's senior senator in Washington, when he's not sailing or drinking. He leaned against a pale green radiator and started looking at a couple of papers attached to a clipboard he was carrying.

"Good news, Lewis," he said. "The lab reports on the tumor came back negative. It's benign. But you know as well as I do that there's no reason you won't get another tumor sometime in the future. It may be next week, it may be next year. I just don't know."

"That's like telling me the Red Sox need pitching, Doc," I said, resting the *Globe* on my bed. "It's something that's not really news."

"Probably not," he agreed, holding the clipboard against his chest with both hands. "Still, I want to keep you for another week or so. We did some major cutting and I want to ensure you make a good step forward in your recovery. Then you can go back north and I'll see you in a month for a follow-up. Anything you need in the meantime?"

"Better food," I said, with a joking tone in my voice, but Dr. Ludlow didn't seem to take it as a joke. He scribbled something on a piece of paper and passed it over. It was a man's name, Brett, followed by a four-digit number.

"Brett works in the cafeteria," Dr. Ludlow explained, "but he also does some outside work. You call and mention my name and he'll take care of you. Even if it means driving up to Saugus to get you a piece of beef from the Hilltop Steak House."

I thanked him and placed the piece of paper on top of a pile of magazines—about the only positive thing about a hospital stay is that you can catch up on your reading—and Dr. Ludlow shifted his feet and said, "I have something to ask you."

"Go ahead," I said.

"I'd like some information," he said, not looking at me. "The report on your tumor was an odd one, and it would be helpful if I could learn more about what might have triggered it. What medical records I do have on you and your past history are pretty incomplete . . . You know that. If you could give me some family history, some type of exposure or occupational hazard that you might have faced . . . Information like that could be helpful."

I held the *Globe* in both of my hands and said, "Sorry, Doc. It'd be a hell of a story, but I can't do that, and you know it."

He just nodded and said, "Well, I knew you'd probably say that, so I plan to send some tissue samples to the CDC in Atlanta and—"

"Doc, if you do that, it'll be a hell of a mistake."

"Lewis, I—"

I didn't let him finish. "Doc, we both have an agreement with men with long memories down in D.C. Remember? Guys who have a very focused way of doing business. And our agreement means keeping our mouths shut. Have you forgotten? I haven't. And I like my new life, and I don't feel like passing away in a mysterious car accident the next month or two."

I thought he was going to argue with me but instead he looked over his shoulder, at the afternoon June sky in Cambridge. His fingers rubbed at the edge of his clipboard and he looked sheepish and said, "You're right. It's just that your case raises questions and I'm one to poke at questions until I get an answer. Your file is quite interesting, Lewis, but there's a lot of blacked-out pages. There are times I want to find out what's hidden behind those black marks."

He turned away from the window and smiled and said, "That's a pretty good attribute for a doctor, but not for someone involved in whatever the hell I'm involved in with you."

"Fair enough," I said, and deciding I needed some humorous reading right about then, I opened up to the *Globe*'s editorial page. As Dr. Ludlow was leaving, he said, "One more thing, Lewis."

"Yes?"

"I won't do it again. I don't feel like getting into a mysterious car accident either."

I nodded and buried myself back in the *Globe*. At least in those pages were people who thought they had all the answers.

When I was done with my shower I stepped out and rubbed myself down with a big white towel and then I looked at myself in the steamy mirror. My short dark brown hair had a few more flecks of gray, and there were a few more lines around my blue eyes. I dried myself off and then checked my skin, as I do every day. There's a faded scar along my left side just above my kidney, on my back near the coccyx and on my left knee. And above the faded scar on my left side was the new and bright one, pink and fresh-looking, with the suture marks still quite visible. Eventually the scar would fade away to a dull pink and so would the suture holes, and then the suture holes would close up, and for all intents and purposes, I would be considered healed.

Yeah. Right.

In my bedroom I put on a fresh pair of light blue gym shorts and a T-shirt that said "Glavkosmos," which is the civilian space agency for whatever's left of the old Soviet Union. My bed is an old four-poster oak antique, and I have a matching set of bureaus to go with it. In one corner, sitting on a black tripod, is my reflecting telescope, and in another corner is a bookshelf. Near the bookshelf is a sliding door that leads out to a smaller deck on the south end of the house, and which has great views of North Beach and Weymouth's Point. I could check the beach with my reflector telescope and see if Diane Woods and Roger Krohn were still there, laboring in the rain, but since I had company, I let it slide. Besides, I had seen the headless and handless diver up close. I had no urge to see him again, even if it was from a comfortable and considerable distance.

I padded back downstairs in bare and slightly wet feet and found Felix leaning against the counter, a glass of water in his hand. "Thought I'd just have some ice water," he said, swirling the ice cubes around. "It's too early for a beer." He looked down at the glass. "Too bad there's no limes. Lewis, your refrigerator is damn near empty."

"I hate to shop," I said, joining him in the kitchen, which is always clean because I hardly ever cook in it. That's probably not a philosophy that would go over well with certain PBS home-cooking hosts, but it worked for me.

"Maybe so, but it seems you like to buy some things," and with that, Felix tapped his foot against a light green plastic bin under the counter that had "Tyler Recycles" on its side in white letters. With each tap of the foot came a *clink-clink* of empty beer bottles striking one another.

"Is that a week's worth?" he asked, and I didn't feel like telling him the truth, so I said, "I haven't been to the recycling center for a while, so it adds up."

"Yeah, well, other things can add up too, Lewis, and I don't want to see you get fat and sloppy."

"Thanks for your concern," I said, moving past him to get to the refrigerator, and for a moment I thought about getting a beer just to egg him on, but instead I poured myself some lemonade. Outside, the rain was still coming down in thundering gray-black sheets and I was sure that North Beach was probably now empty, save for Diane and Roger and the cops and maybe even Paula Quinn. What a way to make a living.

Though it was warm, Felix had kept on his jacket and he said, "What were you up to this afternoon, Lewis? You said something about going fishing?"

The lemonade was sharp and cold and wonderful, and I said, "About an hour or so ago, I saw something floating in the water. This something turned out to be a diver. I got to North Beach and helped bring him to shore, and when he got there, it seemed pretty sure that his death wasn't accidental drowning."

"Oh?" Felix said, raising one eyebrow.

"Unless drowning divers are in the habit of cutting their hands and head off while they're dying. Sound like anything you might have run into, years back?"

Then it seemed as if I had insulted him tremendously, for his face flushed and his eyes narrowed down and I saw that the skin on his hand was turning lighter as he squeezed the water glass. But instead of cursing at me in his favorite Italian phrases, he just shook his head and said, "Lewis, I don't know much but I do know this: you do not want to write a column about this one. This is heavy, quite heavy. Sounds like some of our South American brethren had a point to make with that guy. Up in these woods at least, if you're taken care of, it's just you and maybe an ally or two. But some of those groups down south . . . Lewis, they'll take you and your family and your maid and your dog and your first-grade teacher if they can find her."

I took another swallow of lemonade. The rain was plastering itself against the windows, making a sound like the glass was being slapped with wet towels, and I said, "Relax, Felix. I'm in no mood to track this one down. I'm going to let Diane Woods and the Tyler police and the State Police have everything on their own. My column this month is probably going to be on the new fisheries bill."

He seemed to relax a bit at that. He placed the half-empty water glass on the counter and said, "Good. That's why they get paid tax dollars. To shine flashlights in dark places and find out things other people would rather not know about."

"Nice point of view," I said. I raised my lemonade glass up in a salute and said, "A few minutes ago you said you had problems, and that you needed to ask me something. Well, ask away, Felix."

"Well," he said, hunching himself up a bit in his jacket. "It's sort of complicated."

"With you, Felix, I'm sure it couldn't be anything but."

He motioned to the living room. "Mind if we sit down?"

I nodded and followed him into the next room, which was an open living room and adjacent to the kitchen. He sat on the couch and I took one of the two nearby chairs. Near us was a stereo and GE television with VCR unit, and in the large room were three bookshelves, crammed with hardcovers and paperbacks. Against the open stairs leading up to the second floor was the cold and quiet brick of the room's fireplace. Behind me were the sliding-glass doors that led out to the first-floor deck, where I had been earlier that day, dreamily drinking a bottle of beer and getting ready for another one, when I saw the black shape moving across the water. The day's events had quickly burned off whatever alcohol I had consumed, and though I was tired, I was ready for whatever Felix had to say.

Above Felix's head and mounted on the wall was an old photograph of the White Fleet, the naval fleet that our second President of the twentieth century sent around the world in 1907 to prove that the United States was now a great power to be dealt with. There's also a framed picture of the space shuttle *Discov*ery taking off on the other wall, and in both of their journeys, they circled the globe and spoke of United States power and prestige. One fleet was now only scrap metal, and the other, smaller white fleet was still alive, and that suited me fine.

Then Felix surprised me by saying, "I need your help."

"You need what?"

"Your help." He stretched out his feet on the hardwood floor of my house, which was covered by oriental rugs purchased at estate auctions throughout the state. "I'm involved with something tricky, something complex."

I held the glass of lemonade in both hands and said, "What are you trying to do, write a magazine article?"

Outside, the rain was still roaring down, and there was a hard *slap-slap* sound of the rain falling on the first-floor deck. Another rumble of thunder came from the south. This storm was taking its time in moving through.

Felix tugged at an ear and said, "I'm not joking, Lewis. Look. I'm dealing with something that's interrupting my regular business. It's become a hassle, and I need your company and your good graces, along with your calming influence, as I handle things. I need an outsider's point of view. Otherwise, I'm afraid that I might lose it, might lose it bad. And I want to walk away from this one nice and happy and resume my career."

"It must be a weird and tough time when you come see a magazine writer for help," I said.

He eyed me for a moment and said, "You may say you're nothing more than a writer, Lewis, and that's like me telling everyone I'm just a security consultant. Wordplay, that's all. What counts is what's there, and what I know about you and your background makes you more than just a writer. You had some years at the Department of Defense, and from what little I've learned, you were up to your eyeballs in some sort of black work. Then something happened in Nevada to put you in a hospital and that's it, nothing else. And then you ended up here with a habit of getting into stuff that's right on the border. So don't try to play spin doctor on who you are and what you can do, Lewis. I know what kind of pay there is in magazines, and unless you own one, I don't think you could afford this place and the wheels you drive around in."

I nodded at him and said, "Thanks for the philosophy lesson. Give me some background, Felix, and words on why you came here."

Felix sat back and tossed an arm across the couch and the leather of his shoulder holster became visible. "Some old history is coming back to bite me, that's what's wrong. I've been getting calls and mail these past couple of weeks, people asking me the address of one of Jimmy Corelli's safe houses. Jimmy's been dead for a couple of years—he died in Leavenworth, in his sleep, if you can believe it—and he had a couple of safe houses that he used whenever he needed to get away from Boston. These houses were in false names and Jimmy dealt with some real estate firms through third parties that kept the taxes and utilities and landscaping paid. Where these houses are located is about as deep a secret as you can get."

He rubbed the fabric on the rear of the couch. "There haven't been that many firefights and feuds here in New England—at least not lately—but it's always made sense to have a base or two where you could lie low until things quieted down."

"So you worked for this Jimmy Corelli?" I asked.

Felix shrugged. "Yeah, for a while, when I was younger. I was sort of a utility player back then. Passed around to whoever needed something done at the time. And for a bit I was a soldier for Jimmy Corelli."

"And when you worked for him, you found out where his safe houses were."

He held up a finger. "Only one, Lewis. Only one."

"So who's asking you about the safe house now?"

Felix managed a slight smile at that one. "Nameless and gutless wonders who leave odd messages on my answering machine and send me nasty notes. Threats that say horrible things will happen if I don't reveal the location of Corelli's safe house. They want me to send a note to a post office box in Porter with the safe house's address. So the fact that people are asking me about the house's location made me think that maybe now I'm the only one who knows where it is. Which can happen, the way they keep secrets." He laughed. "Like I have to tell you about keeping secrets."

"I imagine you weren't in a hurry to come right out and write that note about where the house is."

"You imagined right."

I shifted in my seat. The sounds of the rain started to slow down, and the rumbling of the thunder seemed to quiet some. I said, "Sounds like something important's stashed at the safe house. Money. Drugs. Jimmy Hoffa."

Felix's smile was wider. "My thoughts exactly. So one afternoon I went up there and the house was still where I remembered it, looking nice and neat. I let myself in with a key that's hidden on the property, and it only took me about five minutes to find out what the fuss is all about."

"And what's the fuss?"

Felix crossed his legs and his pant leg rolled up, exposing a length of black sock. Felix is the type of guy who would never have socks short enough to expose his shins while crossing his legs. He said, "My secret, for now. Let's just say that what's at the house is something that was stolen from this state five years ago, and which made tremendous news at the time. You were probably still working in D.C. five years ago, right?"

I held up my near-empty glass. "Like you said, that's my secret, for now. So what's the big deal? Tell them where the house is and let them be on their way."

Felix shook his head. "That's against my principles, to give away something for nothing, and especially when they've been so rude to me. They want the location of the house and what's in there, then it's going to cost them some money."

"They might not want to give you any money, Felix."

He replied harshly: "They might not have a choice."

I looked at him and said, "It must be something quite valuable, then."

He nodded. "Quite. And in addition to wanting some money, I want some guarantees. The value of what's there . . . Well, let's just say that it's a great incentive for someone to take care of any loose ends. My mamma didn't raise me to be a loose end, Lewis. So I'm looking for money, and I'm looking for guarantees."

The rain had nearly stopped, and the sky was growing lighter, as the dark clouds moved south. I said, "So why in hell are you here, looking for me?"

He uncrossed his leg, smoothed out the fabric of his pants. "Like I said before, I need your calming influence. Eventually there's going to be some discussion, some sort of negotiations. They're going to do their best to upset me, to make me fly off the handle. Okay, that comes with the turf. But I'm looking for you to help me out, to make me see things clearly."

I finished the lemonade and started crunching on the ice. "Nope."

Felix said, "Look, don't say no or yes, okay? Just think about it for a day or two."

"I already said no."

"Yeah, but I didn't tell you what's in it for you."

"Let me guess. Going on a one-way trip out to Hampton Shoals on a boat with guys named Guido and No Neck, with a length of anchor chain wrapped around my body, all because I decided to help you out."

He smiled and shook his head and said, "Look, I'm going to be the lightning rod here, okay? You'll be fine. No danger. And besides, you help me out, I'll give you 10 percent of what I'm going to demand for the location of the safe house and its contents."

"Which is what?"

Felix told me and the ice in my mouth damn near melted of its own accord. "That's a healthy amount."

"Yeah, pretty robust, ain't it?" He slapped his hands on his thick thighs and said, "Look, I'll let you be, Lewis. Give me a call in a day or two, and we'll go on from there."

He got up and I walked him to the door. Before he went outside in the wet and gray afternoon, he slapped me on my side—the good side, the one without any scars—and said, "Whatever you decide, do decide one thing, Lewis. Lay off the beers for a while. They're making you fat, and they're slowing you down. Not a good prescription for one just out of a hospital."

"Thanks, Doc."

He slapped me on the side again, softer, and said, "If you don't be nice, I'll sic Christy on you."

"You do that, I'll send Diane Woods in your direction. She has a nasty habit of playing with handcuffs."

That brought another laugh and I watched for a minute or two as he trudged up the dirt path that led up to the parking lot of the Lafayette House, where his Mercedes was parked. I rolled the figure that he had mentioned around in my mind for a bit, before closing the door. A lot of money. Enough to help me do some other things.

I closed the door and went upstairs to get to work, and for the rest of the afternoon, all I drank was ice water. Not because of any health reasons, but because the damn taste of rubber was still strong in my mouth.

CHAPTER

FOUR

On the Sunday evening of June 23, when I was sleeping in my private and free room at the Cambridge Hospital, the *Petro Star* was heading up the Atlantic coast, heading for the harbor at Porter, New Hampshire, and the Piscassic River, which leads upstream to a complex of terminals and oil farms at Lewington. The 30,000-ton tanker was 550 feet long, with a 90-foot beam, drawing a 35-foot draft. It carried a load of fuel oil, and as the single-screw tanker headed north, it was not a happy ship. As with most cargo ships these days, it had a mixed crew, and communications among the crew members were equally mixed. The captain was an old German, a year or two away from retirement, and his first officer was from India. The deck officers were Filipino, and the deckhands were Chinese.

There had been difficulties with the *Petro Star*'s loran navigational system and the steering mechanism was balky.

On the evening of June 23, the captain was drunk and asleep in his cabin. The first officer was ill with a stomach virus, and the ship's wheel was in the hands of a young Filipino man who was inexperienced and unaware of the treacherous waters around the Isles of Shoals. At about 10:40 P.M. the steering mechanism began a slow failure that led to the ship being off course, and the scared and unskilled Filipino sailor brought the *Petro Star* right up on a ledge off White Island. The force of the grounding even woke the captain, and panicked at what was going to happen to him and his retirement, he tried to get the ship off the ledge without contacting the Coast Guard.

It didn't work.

The *Petro Star* was single-hulled, and soon its cargo began spilling into the waters around Porter and the Isles of Shoals. When the Coast Guard came—alerted from its base at Foss Island—there wasn't much to do except try to begin the cleanup and start finding out what the hell had happened. Even with the fuel oil coming ashore the next day, the very first session of a Coast Guard hearing began in a courthouse in Porter. Within a couple of days, after its cargo had been off-loaded into another ship, the damaged *Petro Star* was taken north, to a dock facility in Portland, Maine, to be repaired while the other players in the drama continued their activities.

So there it rested. After the black tide washed up on the shores and the cleanup commenced and the newspaper stories were written and the lawsuits were threatened, all I cared about was the man who ran the show: and this man, like myself, seemed to have a well-hidden past.

The *Petro Star* was owned by a corporation—Petro Associates—that had registered the ship in its supposed homeport of Monrovia, Liberia. The corporation was based in Burma—or Myanmar, depending on your geography teacher—and its officers were from Thailand. Petro Associates also had a business office in New York City, run by one Dmitros Skarvelis, who had a

3 percent ownership in the company. Whoever owned the other 97 percent of the shares was a secret, except that in reading and rereading the pages of testimony from the preliminary hearings on the grounding and the oil spill, I had learned one interesting fact: Petro Associates had a majority owner, a man who made the decisions, and this man was an American.

So he was in this country. He was "gettable." But investigators with the U.S. Coast Guard, the Department of Transportation and the Department of Justice had been unable to locate him. Usually the United States had a cooperative working relationship with shipping investigators in Thailand and Burma, but this year—due to a border dispute between the two countries and the current Administration's policy on the matter—Thailand and Burma were both politely telling the United States to go to hell. Dmitros Skarvelis had smiled a lot when he was not answering questions, and then one night he left his New Jersey apartment and was now believed to be back in Athens.

I leaned back in my chair and rubbed at my neck. My Macintosh Plus was on, its friendly gray screen setting up a glow in the late evening twilight of this July Tuesday. It had been more than a day since Felix Tinios had left me, and except for sleeping and eating and a bit of recreational reading, I had spent most of the past twenty-four hours in this room on the second floor of my house. The study has windows that overlook the ocean and my tiny beach to the east, and the jumbled rocks and wooden hills of the Samson State Wildlife Preserve to the south. Years ago, when the place was called the Samson Point Artillery Station, two batteries of giant twelve-inch artillery pieces were maintained and hidden in concrete bunkers that were covered with dirt and growing grass, to masquerade them as benign hills, and to hide them from the eyes of the Spaniards, and then later the Germans and even the Soviets.

But years later the masquerade was over, the hidden guns were pulled away, and tourists and picnickers now walked the previously forbidden grounds of what was once a sealed military installation.

So some masquerades get pulled away. But the man I was looking for had a very firm mask, one that was proving difficult to displace.

"And what do you do when you find him?" I announced to my empty study. "Arrest him?"

I swiveled some in my chair, enjoying the faint squeaking noise that I'm sure would drive others crazy but which soothed me and made me think. The study was about as large as my bedroom, and in addition to the Macintosh Plus and an office-surplus desk that shared its paint style with battleships, there were floor-to-ceiling bookshelves. Among the biographies and history books and astronomy texts, there were also some bound back issues of *Shoreline*. Black filing cabinets held scraps of information and newspaper clippings and bills, and there was one oriental rug in the center of the polished hardwood floor.

And among all the books in this room, I had not picked up one in the past twenty-four hours in my quest for the man behind the *Petro Star*.

The reason for that was my Macintosh Plus, my modem and my telephone. If one didn't care that much about long-distance telephone charges—which I didn't—one had entire libraries, newspaper morgues, encyclopedias, clipping services and reference materials available just by dialing up phone numbers. There are thousands—maybe even tens of thousands—of computer bulletin boards and on-line services—including the information superhighway known as the Internet—that can serve practically any purpose, any need. There are computer bulletin boards where you can enter and play sex games over your keyboard with someone in a different time zone. There's a bulletin board that, if you give your longitude and latitude, will tell you when the Mir space station will go overhead. And there are bulletin boards that, well, offer some unique and strange interests. Coon hunting, for example, or comic book collecting. And in my own hunt over the past day, I had gone through a dozen or so of the boards, doing what was called "info surfin" just setting up word and program searches about the *Petro Star* and Petro Associates. It had taken some time, and besides helping increase the net worth of AT&T's long-distance division, there hadn't been much out there.

So far, I had about a handful of sentences' worth of information. The man with the 97 percent share in Petro Associates was quite deep. I had not been very successful, and I was almost depressed at the lack of information I had managed to retrieve. All I knew was that he was male, he lived in the United States, he was a businessman who owned the majority shares of Petro Associates, and he had other business interests. For all the work I had done, I had garnered information which could have been connected to about half of the mailing list for *The Wall Street Journal*. Not much progress.

And yet . . . well, there was one more phone number . . .

"Nope," I said, speaking again to the empty room. "Not tonight, and not ever."

I shut down the computer and switched off the modem and went downstairs. In the living room I turned the television on, then turned it off, and sat down on the couch. On the coffee table was a copy of yesterday's Tyler *Chronicle*, and the lead story had been written by Paula Quinn. The headline said, DEAD DIVER RECOVERED AT NORTH BEACH, and I wondered how the New York *Post* or the *Daily News* would have reported it: HEADLESS DIVER COMES ASHORE? CATCH OF THE DAY: DISMEMBERED DIVER?

Her lead: "Tyler and State Police are investigating the death of a man clad in a wet suit who washed ashore at North Beach on Sunday and whose body had been mutilated."

Not bad. In the second graph, she mentioned the lack of head or hands, and she had quoted Diane Woods by the fourth paragraph. And throughout the entire story, not once had she mentioned how the body had been recovered, how a columnist from *Shoreline* had gone in and had swum out, and had dragged it ashore with a rope.

The man was between twenty and thirty years of age. No word on any identifying scars or tattoos, which made me think that there had to be some evidence there, which Diane Woods and the State Police were keeping secret. No word of any missing divers, nor was there any information about diving equipment being overdue from any of the rental shops on the coast.

There also wasn't any information about anybody witnessing a headless body being tossed overboard from a passing boat or fishing vessel, but I guess that was too much to hope for.

Along with the story was a photograph of Diane Woods and Roger Krohn of the Massachusetts State Police, standing around and looking at a blanket-covered shape on the beach. I thought for a moment of calling Diane, knowing that she'd probably be at her condo at this hour, but it was fairly late, and if she had any time to herself right now, she was probably sleeping. I had nothing to offer, nothing except a word or two of encouragement, and that wasn't worth getting awake for.

Besides, I really didn't want to know any more about the diver. I had brought him in. It was up to others to give him a name and to send him home.

I got up from the couch and headed to the kitchen, and remembering with a wince what Felix had said the other day, I skipped the beers and threw some ice cubes in a glass and drew some water from the sink. I slid open the door to the rear deck and stepped outside. The sounds of the waves were quiet, just a gentle hush, like some distant soft breathing, and luck was with me this evening, for the night sky was clear and the stars were quite bright.

The teapot shape of Sagittarius was tipping to the horizon to the south, and over my head I made out the constellations of Cygnus, the swan, and Cepheus, the husband of Cassiopeia, captured forever in their flight across the sky. Within two weeks, the Perseid meteor showers would begin, and I would not get much sleep, for this yearly show promised to be a good one this summer, with no moon to glare away the streaking light of the meteors, and with the possibility of clear and crisp weather to cut down on the haze. At least for a few nights then, I would spend the dark hours out here on my deck, on a mattress and with a blanket, counting the shooting stars and looking for the steady movement of satellites across the black sky.

I drank the water in one gulp and sat down and propped my feet up on the railing. Though the stars were bright and clear tonight, there was still something dirty out there, something distorted, like a puddle of urine before a garden statue. With every breath and movement of air, the stench of oil came to me. There was still cleaning to be done, though the volunteers and the state and the Coast Guard had given up and had passed on that responsibility to nature and her waves. The natural cleansing action of the ocean, I saw it called in one of Paula Quinn's newspaper articles about the spill.

Natural cleansing. Some time ago a man had made the decision that sent the *Petro Star* to these shores and its cargo to my home, that had sent the *Petro Star* here understaffed, with faulty equipment and a single hull and a crew that couldn't have handled a car wash. One man had done that, and I was not going to allow him to think that it was now only a problem of insurance agencies and repair bills.

I made a tossing motion with my right hand and the ice cubes flew out of the glass and headed to the oily and salty water below me.

Except that so far he was doing a pretty good job of keeping himself hidden, and that did not make me happy.

So. In a month or two there were going to be congressional hearings in Porter on the spill, and maybe the mystery man's identity would be revealed then. And in the meantime . . .

Well. There was that matter Felix Tinios had brought up.

I set my empty glass down, brought up my knees and looked out to the lights of the Isles of Shoals on the dark waters, and I tried to think, though that oil stank so damn much.

CHAPTER
FIVE

In the basement of the Tyler *Chronicle*'s offices, the floor was damp and covered with mildew, and in one corner was a sump pump that clicked on every now and then as I worked. In another corner was a room with a closed door with a sign that said, "Knock Before Entering or You'll Let All the Dark Out!" That door belonged to the *Chronicle*'s darkroom, and whoever was the newspaper's chief photographer this summer was in here this early Wednesday morning, listening to rock music and banging things around.

There was a smell of chemicals from the darkroom and wet paper and decay from the basement, and before me were home-made wooden shelves, which held bound copies of past issues of the Tyler *Chronicle*. Each volume was bound in blue leather, with gold lettering identifying the months and the year. Being here was silly in a way, for I'm sure I could have done a good enough job from home with my Apple Macintosh and its modem. Or I could have gone to the town's library—the Gilliam Memorial Library—and spent some time in the microfilm room, sitting in a comfortable chair instead of standing on dirty and wet concrete. And if I wanted to go to the very best at hand, I could have made the half-hour drive to the University of New Hampshire's library in Durham.

But I convinced myself that I was tired of looking at a computer screen, and I also convinced myself that I didn't want to race through blurry microfilm. I wanted the old newspapers in my hand, to look through the stories and get a feel of things, without having the barrier of a computer screen or a microfilm reader in the way.

Sure. Basically, I was doing what was called in my previous life a two-track search, back when I read for a living and wrote reports that had a circulation of less than a dozen. One track was what I was currently involved with, looking through the musty and heavy volumes of the Tyler *Chronicle*. The other track had occurred earlier, when I arrived at the paper's offices, intent on seeing Paula Quinn, but ending up only seeing her boss, Roland Grandmaison. Rollie had been at his deskup to his elbows in paper as usual—and there was a scent of sour breath mints about him as I walked through. He had on a stained white dress shirt that was getting thin at the elbows, and a striped tie that was undone a bit at the frayed collars. What was left of his light brown hair was plastered to his freckled skull, and he looked up at me with moist eyes behind heavy black-rimmed glasses as I came by and asked permission to look in the morgue.

Rollie had said yes and then, with pencil in hand, said, "You're looking for Paula, aren't you?"

"That I am."

He shook his head. "Girl's been keeping her own hours here lately." He marked up a piece of paper and looke at me and said, "Something's poorly with her, and I don't know what it is. I think she's getting dull here, but she don't give me the sign that she's ready to move on. I don't know. All I do know is that I hate dealing with other people's problems when I got a paper to get out. It makes a lousy job even worse."

"Just the joys of being an editor, Rollie," I said, and he grunted and I gathered that our conversation was over.

With that bit of cheery news, I went down the threadbare carpeted stairs to the basement-cum-morgue, where I started going through the first bound volume from five years ago. Felix had said his concern was connected with a theft five years ago, and the *Chronicle* was as good a place as any to begin the search. While it mostly covered the eastern end of Wentworth County it also carried stories from the Associated Press bureau out of Concord, the state capital. If the news had been as big as Felix had indicated, then it would have been reported in the *Chronicle*.

Five years. I flipped through the pages, half remembering the old stories that popped up, about countries and political crises and obsolete borders that now belonged in the history books, remembering where I had been and where reading the newspaper every morning was a secret and fun ritual. Secret because newspapers weren't usually allowed at your desk—except when it was specifically connected to a special project—and fun because there was a tingle of joy in reading the stories and knowing how close the reporters were to getting the truth, or knowing with a smile how far off they were.

Old pleasures, now gone. I turned another page and found what I was looking for.

At the time five years ago my office was in a side basement, in a building in Virginia with five sides, and the office came with issue furniture, cubicle walls and no windows. The cubicles did not reach to the ceiling, so if you stood on a chair, you could see how your neighbor was doing. I had a computer terminal and an electric typewriter, and four special locked black filing cabinets that were supposedly rated to withstand the blast of a ten-kiloton battlefield tactical nuclear weapon from one mile away. No personal decorations were allowed in our cubicles, but the people in my section managed to get around that in various ways. Calendars were allowed, and mine was a gorgeous one from the Planetary Society, with each month showing a color picture of a planet or moon in our solar system, the photos taken by either satellites or ground-based telescopes.

On the right side of my cubicle was another bank of black filing cabinets, and my neighbor to the left was Carl Socha. I had just completed a research project on Indian and Pakistani civil defense agencies (with a special focus on how they were prepared to handle a nuclear exchange during a three-week ground war) that had taken almost a month, which was done in preparation for a meeting between someone in our department and someone across the river in D.C. However, I had learned an hour ago that the meeting had been canceled due to some tiff over policy. There was little chance of it ever being rescheduled during this current Administration and the four numbered copies of my work had entered a shredding machine that morning. By now they were being converted into ash in another basement office in the same building.

I wasn't in the best of moods.

My desk was clear of work for the moment and I felt antsy, so I pulled my chair back, climbed up on it, and poked my head over the cubicle wall. Carl Socha was there, leaning back in his chair with his feet propped up on his desk, flipping through a magazine that had a smiling Soviet soldier on the cover. The magazine's title was in Cyrillic characters. Carl had on a tight red polo shirt and designer jeans, and in the fluorescent lights, his black skin looked smooth and polished. He had taken off his shoes and socks and was letting a small electric fan cool his feet. He claimed that cooling his feet helped him to think, and since he was one of the best in our section, George Walker—our section leader—pretty much left him alone.

We were definitely an odd section compared with the other

ones in this part of the building. Each of the other sections had an easily assigned title and task. There were Soviet experts and Soviet republic experts, people who could tell you the history of each Communist Party in Central America, and bright and earnest people in sections on Far East affairs who could talk to you for hours about the economic and military links between Malaysia, Indonesia and Singapore.

Every now and then, though, there came through a research project that fell between the cracks, and that was the job for our section. George Walker, our section leader, didn't like his job and didn't particularly like us, and one reason was the name for our section: we didn't have one. We were just known by the letter and number that designated our room. We called ourselves the Marginal Issues Section, which suited us but didn't suit George Walker.

The people who made up the section were the ones who didn't quite fit in. I, for one, was bored after doing a project or two on the same subject. I needed to root around and try something different each time. My neighbor, Carl Socha, knew his Soviet history better than that of his home country, yet he kept butting heads with the orthodoxy in vogue during the current Administration. They thought they were punishing him by placing him here and making him my neighbor, and I think we confused them by becoming friends.

He was chewing gum as he flipped through the magazine and said, "What are you looking at, farm boy? Ain't you never seen someone read before?"

I rested my chin on the cubicle's metal top. "Ah, such a life," I said. "Remember how it was during orientation? After they swore us to secrecy and made us sign all those forms? A relaxing job, they said. Like spending all day in the library, the best library in the world. Do some writing here and there. Make a contribution to national security in the process. Grow and develop as a unique individual."

"Man didn't force you to do anything, son," Carl said, still looking at the magazine. "You entered on your own two feet. You knew what you were gettin' into. Me, when they told me how much I was gonna get paid for reading and writing, why I damn near had to change my underwear. Would have to be a moron not to take it up, and stay in it while you can."

"That's right, and I did the same thing," I said. "Reading and writing for a living. Almost sounded too good to be true. And what they didn't tell you was that after you spend days and weeks researching and preparing a report, your hours of effort can get trashed because one D.C. bonehead doesn't like the voting record of another D.C. bonehead. All for nothing. Carl, I could have submitted a hundred and twenty pages of cookie recipes for all the good it did."

"Still pissed?" he asked.

"Still pissed," I said.

Carl looked over his magazine, but didn't look at me. He glanced out into the central area of our offices, which had additional computer terminals, television sets continuously tuned to the four networks, plus monitors for—among others—the Associated Press, United Press International, Reuters and English-language translations of Agence France-Presse, Tass, New China News Agency and the All India News Service.

"Well, then," Carl said. "Something's approaching which might change your attitude, son. Time to get down off your chair."

I did as he suggested, just as Cissy Manning came in, smiling and giving me a furtive wink. Her hair was long this summer, and since I liked red hair, I'd told her teasingly that it gave me more fun things to play with. The petty rules which ran our section went fairly deep and wide, but so far, thank God, they hadn't yet gotten down to the fashion level. Cissy wore a pleated black skirt that was a couple of inches above her knees, charcoal-gray stockings and black high-heeled shoes. She also had on a dark green silk blouse that highlighted her green eyes, and which was unbuttoned far enough so that when she bent down to kiss my nose, I made out the faint spread of freckles across her chest and the lace cup of a white bra. Remembering the last weekend we had shared together, on the Maryland coast, I blushed. That recent evening, fueled with a half-bottle of champagne, I had gone on a freckle hunt and after a lot of laughs and shrieks, I had lost count and shared an entirely pleasurable post-hunt repast with her.

"What are you up to?" she asked, sitting on the edge of my desk, swinging one shoe free from her foot.

"Trying to maintain my enthusiasm for this section, and having a hard time doing it," I said, sitting back in my chair.

"A lack of enthusiasm, Mr. Cole?" she asked in mock surprise. "You've always had a reputation in this office for a lot of enthusiasm."

And with every word of her last sentence, and with a wicked smile on her face, she pulled up the hem of her skirt until I could see a garter belt snap, holding up the charcoal gray stockings. Then she winked and dropped the hem of the skirt, and leaned forward again. By then I could have used Carl's fan for my face.

"Heard that your latest work has been de-atomized," she said, her voice low.

"You got it."

She looked behind her—no doubt checking for eyewitnesses—and then turned again and kissed me on the forehead and said, "I've got the latest Victoria's Secret catalogue at my place. Care to browse through it with me tonight, after a sinfully delicious meal? You know, in a couple of weeks, we're going out to Nevada for our field re-qual training. This might be our last chance for some decadent living before we're out tramping through the sands."

"Is there a modeling session included?"

She jumped down from the desk. "What do you think, that I'm a tease? Seven o'clock?"

"Seven it is."

Cissy winked and left my cubicle and I took a deep breath, thankful that the gods and the fates had put the two of us together. As she bent over to check one of the wire service terminals, Carl's voice came drifting up from the other side of the cubicle: "A lingerie fashion show, how sweet."

In a moment I was back on my chair, looking down at his smiling face, and I said, "You got big ears, Socha."

That made him laugh. "Been accused of having big body parts before, but never ears. You go on and have yourself a good time tonight, Lewis. I'm tired of havin' a grump for a neighbor."

I didn't answer Carl, but I looked over the cubicles of my working group, smiling at them all, at Carl and Cissy and Trent Baker over by the Reuters wire, and even the damnable George Walker, sitting in his office (a supervisor's one, it had a real door), peering out at us with distaste. Though I was in a job that could never be discussed with family and friends—except for those who shared the same clearance level—it was a job that I enjoyed very much. I was where I wanted to be. I fit in. I was content.

Within two weeks, everyone in this room—except for me— would be dead.

When I got back upstairs, Paula Quinn was there, sitting at her desk and typing on her Digital computer terminal. Her blond hair was curled back from the front in a sort of half-flip, and she had on a short denim skirt and a plain black T-shirt that had a pocket over the left side. The desks at the *Chronicle* are a collection of wooden and metal antiques, and about the only modern things in the office were the Digital computers, with terminal cables leading up to the ceiling. The computers looked out of place in an office where holes in the carpet had been repaired with gray duct tape, but Paula had confided in me one night that the only reason management had purchased the computers was that it allowed them to fire a staff of typesetters and to save money on wages and future retirement benefits.

I sat in a folding chair next to her desk that had "Property of Spenser Funeral Home" stenciled on the back. She looked up at me, gave me a quick smile, and said, "It's a busy morning, Lewis."

"I'm sure it is. What are you working on? Our headless and handless diver?"

"Nope," she said, eyes staring ahead at the glowing screen of the terminal, her hands click-clicking on the keyboard. "State liquor store got robbed about an hour ago, out on I-95."

"Got a minute to talk?" I asked.

She was quiet, not saying anything, just typing along, so I reached up to the rear of the Digital terminal and found the power switch and clicked it off.

Her hands froze in mid-motion and then she looked up at me, her eyes fixed and unyielding. Then she turned and yelled out at Rollie, "I'm taking a five-minute break, Rollie. I'll be back in time for deadline."

She reached behind her, pulled out her black leather handbag and swung it around, and then stormed out of the office. I followed her and looked over at Rollie, who was popping another breath mint into his mouth and rolling his eyes.

When we got outside we walked in silence for a moment or two, heading to the Tyler Town Common, which was adjacent to the office building that contained the *Chronicle*. Park benches were set up under the birches and near some flower beds maintained by the Tyler Garden Club. We sat on one of the green benches, which faced out to downtown Tyler and Route 1.

She folded her arms and said, "Well, if you wanted to get my attention, Lewis, you certainly succeeded."

"Thanks," I said. "Seems like I haven't been able to do that the past few weeks."

"Hunh," she said, staring out at the traffic going by, lost summer people no doubt, knowing that they were in Tyler but surprised at not finding the beach in the downtown area. "Suppose you think I owe you an apology."

"Maybe so," I said. "Or maybe some words, Paula, about what's going on here."

She attempted a laugh and refolded her arms and said, "Well, since we both make a living in words, I suppose this should be easy to do. Here's the condensed recap, Lewis. One day in June, you and a prominent citizen of this resort town enter the marshes near Falconer. You come out and they find this citizen dead with a slashed throat. Story comes out, linking our prominent person to a couple of murders. You give me some great background info about what happened, and I probably write the best series of stories I've ever done. Then I come over to your place, to celebrate and thank you and, I guess, to see how you were doing."

I started to speak and she held up a hand. "Please, let me go on. So I spend the night, Lewis, and yes, it was quite enjoyable. In my own little heart, I'm thinking, well, maybe this is the start of something. Not talking commitment or marriage or any of that crap. Maybe it's just the start of something that I haven't had in a long while. Well, that particular thought lasts a few hours, when I get woken up by you cursing and yelling at some guy named George who isn't even there. You won't tell me shit about what's happening and so I leave a nice warm bed and some nice warm fantasies behind, and the next thing I learn—and not from you, but from Diane Woods, which gives me pause—is that you're in the hospital. I get not one word from you about what put you there, or why you're there. Not a word. And you begrudge me the cards I send you. Not bad, Lewis. Maybe I didn't do so hot, but you weren't exactly too forthcoming."

We sat for a while, not saying anything, while a robin scampered along the grass, cocking its head, until finally it struck and something squirming and alive was in its beak, and it swooped up, triumphant in its kill.

She said, "So while all that crap is going on, I put together a package of my very best stories about the murders here and such, and I start mailing them out to newspapers that have more weight and more money than the poor little *Chronicle*. And even though Rollie has the heart of a true newspaperman—'What you did yesterday was great, honey, but what do you have for me today?'—and even though I'm doing stories about third-graders going on field trips to Boston, I'm giggling inside 'cause I know that pretty soon the replies are going to be rolling in, and that I'll spend this summer somewhere else than Tyler. Doing real stories, stories that I can spend a couple of days working on. And I can move away and start forgetting about a certain night with you, Lewis."

I reached over and put my hand on top of hers, and I sensed a small victory, with her not pulling away. "No replies, right?" I asked.

"Oh no, there were a lot of replies, and they all said the same thing. Nothing. No jobs, no openings, no chance of future openings. Here I am, working on my second newspaper job, trying to climb that damn career ladder. But someone's up on top, pulling it away from me. You understand?"

A boxy gray Chevrolet had pulled up near us, with Massachusetts license plates and a couple in the front seat. The backseat was filled with three or four kids—it was hard to tell—and one young boy was leaning out the window, dumping potato chips on the ground. The driver's-side door opened and a heavyset man wearing bright yellow shorts and a T-shirt that said "Professional Muff Diver" ambled out, carrying a road map in his thick hands. He started walking over to us until I nailed him with a look that made him glance down at the map and head over to the Common Grill & Grill.

I said, "Labor Day's only a month away, Paula, and you're not looking forward to doing another bunch of back-to-school stories."

She moved her hand against mine. "Right. By now I thought I'd be in a new office, in Boston or Hartford or maybe New York, learning the names of my co-workers, and instead I got Rollie chewing on me about not getting the school bus schedules in on time."

I squeezed her hand. "I came back from the hospital, hoping to find you on my rear deck sporting a string bikini, and instead, my home smells like a gas station and I feel like you're about ready to slip a knife into my ribs."

For a moment she giggled and she said, "Your imagination's too much, Lewis." Then her voice softened and she said, "This hasn't been the best of summers, and it started going downhill right in June, right after that night. I thought I was the best then, being with you and scooping every news organization in the region about the murders here, and then in a couple of weeks, I was doing a story about Miss Tyler Beach and wondering what in hell had happened to you. And you haven't been much help, being the secretive guy you are. Still won't tell me who George is—or was."

Somewhere hundreds of miles away from this sunny spot was an office with a filing cabinet and in that cabinet was a signed agreement that allowed me to be here, to live in relative comfort and to live in silence. It wasn't an arrangement that I particularly liked, but it was the only arrangement available.

I said, "George was my boss, once. He did something stupid that ended up, well, it ended up hurting me. And when I found out that night that I was sick again, his was the first name that came to mind. His stupidity was a curse, one that's always going to be with me, Paula. And I'm sorry, but I can't say any more."

"I know," she said, moving her hand to the safety of her lap. "And I also know that I want things right, and I want them back to where they were. I'm going to have to buck up and do what it takes to stay at the *Chronicle*, even if it means having a smile on my face when Rollie asks me to rewrite the school lunch menus for the week."

I turned to her and said, "And you want things back to where they were with us, before June."

She nodded. "For now, Lewis. For now. Give me some time to get things back and we'll see. But in the meantime, well, I'm going to consider your house a dangerous place to be. For a while, other neutral spots are okay, and I hope you understand, Lewis. It just has to be this way."

I didn't want to get into a fight or a quarrel or a discussion that was laden with words such as "commitments" or "feelings" or whatever, so instead I touched her hand again and I said, "You should probably get back in, do that story about the liquor store robbery, Paula. Rollie's no doubt wondering if any of his favorite brands were taken."

I was rewarded with a smile and she said, "You're probably right."

"I am right. And I'm sorry about shutting your terminal off."

She shrugged. "That's all right. I was only into the second sentence." She got up, started to turn and said quietly, "And I'm sorry I didn't visit you, Lewis. As mad as I was, I should have visited you when you were sick."

As she started to walk across the closely trimmed grass, I called out to her. She turned and I said, "I read your story the other day, about the diver. You know, there's not one mention in there about how his body was recovered."

"Yeah, I know," she said, her hands in the front pockets of her short denim skirt. "I wrote it that way on purpose."

"Thanks," I said. "I like my privacy."

"So I've noticed." She smiled and went back to her office. I sat on the park bench and looked over at the gray Chevrolet with the woman and three or four screaming kids. I guessed I was doing better than most. I sat out in the sun, not feeling particularly angry or sad, just feeling all right, in knowing what was going on. A holdover from my old job. I hated secrets.

And I remembered what I had learned down in the basement of the *Chronicle*, and I whispered, "Felix, I got you."

But I was in no hurry to move. I liked the feeling of the sun on my face, though I had one more place to visit before the day was over.

CHAPTER

SIX

In New Hampshire there are only a handful of communities large enough to be called cities, which is nice if you like to live in a state that's holding on—hand and fist—to its rural traditions and backgrounds, but which isn't so nice if you like to live in a state that's on the cutting edge. Which isn't to say that New Hampshire relies on horses to deliver its rural mail or doesn't have its share of the latest high-tech industries: it's just that some of our newest immigrants get a shock when they arrive here and find out that in many towns the agricultural fair is the biggest cultural event of the year. These people do one of two things: they move back to where they came from, or they move to one of the few cities in the state and try to adjust the best way they know how.

New Hampshire's largest city is Manchester, which was named—like so many of the places in the state—after a town in Old England. To get to Manchester from Tyler takes about an hour, going west on Route 51, which then transforms itself into Route 101 just outside of Exonia, the county seat. The road is two-lane for most of the way and is quite dangerous, with accidents on it every week and a fatality or two at least once a month. The road is twisting and the speed limit is fifty miles per hour, and almost everyone traveling on the road exceeds the limit by about ten miles.

Manchester was built up around the banks of the Merrimack River, and like most of the few cities in this state, its life started as a mill town, with tall red brick buildings along the riverbanks, the flow spinning the turbines that milled cotton into cloth, and which also powered the machinery for making leather hides into shoes. From 1838 to 1846, when the mills arrived, the town's population went from less than 100 to more than 10,000. There is still a large French-Canadian population in Manchester, made up of the descendants of many of those first workers in the city's mills, who came here from southern Canada or the towns in the northern part of the state, such as Berlin. In some of the city's bars and taverns, the term "Canuck" still guarantees the start of a brawl.

While the French-Canadians sweated and bled in the mills, a number of families became quite rich, and the smart ones spread their wealth around into shipping and timber and banking. The not so smart ones suffered and crashed when the mills closed during the first part of this century, when the competition from Southern mills proved to be just too much. An old story, one that's still being written today in places such as Juárez and Guadalajara.

One family which prospered was the Scribner family, and one of their foundations set up the Scribner Museum of Art, located only a few minutes away from the downtown of Manchester. While the downtown has some high-rise buildings—high for New Hampshire—it's only a matter of a few blocks in either direction before you come to residential neighborhoods, and it was in one such neighborhood that I located the Scribner Museum of Art this late Wednesday morning.

I parked my Range Rover across the street from the museum and walked over. There was hardly any traffic and the day was hot, with a heavy haze in the air. I wore shiny new brown loafers, a short-sleeved white shirt and pressed chinos, and there was a tan reporter's notebook sticking out of my back pocket. The Scribner Museum was two stories high and made of stone and exposed brickwork. The grounds were landscaped with some trees and shrubbery and crushed-stone paths. There were long Roman-type columns at the front entrance to the museum. On each side of a pair of great wooden doors at the entrance was a stone mosaic showing medieval knights, swords in their hands, the points aiming downward to the soil.

Inside the Scribner Museum was a coffee-table-sized box of glass and wood that had a sign asking for donations, and I slipped a five-dollar bill into an opening at the top. I was about fifteen minutes early for my appointment, so I made a quick walk through the two floors of the building, and even though I felt the museum was probably just an attempt by the Scribner family to resolve its guilt over how they had treated their mill workers, I was fairly impressed at what I saw.

While there wasn't much space to be offered on its two floors, the museum did give a quick read of some major artists and epochs. There was a room of French Impressionists, including two Monets and a Matisse, and there was also a gallery on the second floor devoted to early New England furniture, from Chippendale chairs to some massive hutches and clothes chests. Another room showed early American portraits of stiff-necked men and women who lived in this state at the turn of the nineteenth century. One long display of silver showed some items from Paul Revere and his descendants, and there was even a wing of modern art and sculpture, with two Picassos and a portrait by Georgia O'Keeffe and a small mobile by Calder.

I'm sure that anyone with a passing interest in art who's

been to Paris or New York or even to Boston would have a fit of giggles about spending some time in the Scribner Museum, but in a state with a single major daily newspaper and only one commercial statewide television station, I thought it did a fairly respectable job of giving a brief overview of what art had to offer. The museum this day held a mixed bag of visitors: a few elderly ladies walking through and spending ten minutes in front of each painting, earnest young art students dressed in black clothing and with sharp haircuts and a couple of young mothers and their children, perhaps spending a day away from the heat, perhaps even spending a day here to see what was out in the world besides tabloid newspapers and tabloid television.

When I had passed through my fifteen minutes, I went downstairs past the gift shop to a small office that had a sign over the door that said "Administrative—Private." The office was carpeted and there were two desks and a woman who looked to be a few years older than me sitting behind one of them, typing away at an IBM clone. She swiveled in her chair and gave me a big smile as I walked in. Her desk was fairly neat with the usual Rolodex and appointment calendar and a few open files, and near her telephone was a vase with a single rose and a miniature statue of Michelangelo's *David*. The nameplate on the desk said Cassie Fuller.

I gave her my business card and said, "I have an appointment with Justin Dix."

She looked at the card. "So you do. Hold on for a moment and I'll see if he's free."

Instead of picking up the phone, she smiled again, got up from her desk and walked to another office door, at the other end of the small room. She had a thick mane of black hair, tousled back down to her shoulders, and she was wearing a tight black dress that was a few inches above her knees and which was kept together by a couple of metallic zippers. It looked like something from San Francisco, definitely not from Manchester or even Boston. Her legs were enclosed in clear nylons, and she wore red high heels. It looked like the dress was a size too small as she walked away, and somehow, from the smile she gave me, it didn't seem she minded that one bit.

She leaned into the doorway, said something quietly, then turned her head and said, "He'll see you now, Mr. Cole." As I walked across the office she lowered her head and gave me a "I may be working at a stodgy museum but I'm something else out of work" look. I wondered if she practiced her moves and her hooded-eye gaze at home in front of a mirror.

Her perfume tickled at me as I walked into Justin Dix's office, past the open door that said "Security" on a metal plate, and I had to remind myself to get into my role as I reached over to shake his hand. Justin was in his forties, edging closer to being fifty, and he was about twenty pounds or so overweight. He had on a blue blazer, gray slacks and white shirt with a striped tie that probably belonged to some New England prep school, but his handshake was firm and had nothing preppy about it. His ears were a bit too large for his head, a double chin was developing, and there were faint acne scars along both cheekbones. With the black-rimmed eyeglasses and the thick brown-and-gray hair combed to one side, he looked like a mortgage officer at a bank, ready to ask you why you were ten days late in making a MasterCard payment nine years ago.

But he seemed gracious enough as he pointed out a chair for me to sit in, before his desk, which was neat and uncluttered. "You know, just before we start, I went to the trouble of verifying who you were, even though I only had a couple of hours since your call this morning."

"Really?" I said, taking out my notebook and placing it in my lap as I sat down. The office looked out over a courtyard behind the museum and there was a small fountain there, endlessly sprinkling water in an arc to a stone basin. It was well lit and had a few plants, and there were framed prints of Van Gogh hanging from each of the four walls. It seemed to be the type of place where you could spend most of the morning sipping a cup of coffee and browsing through the day's New York *Times* before getting down to work, all the while listening to classical music from WEVO-FM in Concord.

Justin hitched up his belt some and sat down, and then picked up a copy of this month's *Shoreline*. "Interesting magazine," he said. "I had Cassie pick it up at the news store down the street. Gave it the once-over and I liked your column this month, about the yearly battle between the townspeople and tourists of a resort area. You know, I spent a few summers playing in those sands, going to Tyler Beach when I was a kid. Growing up in Boston, there wasn't much chance for outdoor stuff."

"Get back to the beach much?" I asked.

He shook his head. "Nope. Those times are good kid memories. I don't want to ruin them by going back to Tyler as an adult and seeing what's changed. You shouldn't futz with your memories like that." He flipped through *Shoreline* and said, "Mind telling me again why you're interested in coming here today? After all, it's been five years."

I crossed my legs and thought, well, here we go again, preparing to perform the Great Lie that is the secret of all journalists, reporters and magazine writers. The Great Lie that you're deeply interested and concerned in what your source is telling you. The Great Lie that everything told in confidence will remain in confidence. And the Great Lie that says the source and the reporter will remain the best of friends, even after the story is finished and the reporter goes on to something else.

Of course, I have my own personal Great Lie: that I was actually doing a real story about the Scribner Museum, and it would appear in a future issue of *Shoreline*.

Some work. I don't recommend it.

Putting on my most sincere and interested face, I said, "Like I told you on the phone this morning, I'm trying to convince my editor to do a piece about the number of New England landscape artists that had an interest in the shores and harbors of the region. Besides the main story, I thought what happened here would be a good sidebar."

Justin said "Hmmm," flipped through a few more pages of *Shoreline*, and then looked up at me. He gave me a rueful smile and said, "You know, I mentioned to the museum director that you were coming up here and wanted to do a story, and he was against it. Didn't see any use in dredging up old news, and especially old news that put the museum in an embarrassing and bad light. You understand that?"

I kept the reporter's notebook closed. "I do."

He nodded. "Knew you would. And you know what I told him? I said, look, even though it's been five years, I want to keep it alive. I still want it out in the press, on the off chance that someone will remember something, that someone will recall an incident five years ago. Some clue, some tip. I don't want this to die, not like this. So that's what I told him."

From the outer office I could hear Cassie Fuller humming and typing on her IBM clone. I said, "So the director changed his mind?"

"Nope," Justin said, smiling again. "He's still against it, and I could give a shit. He'd have to convince the board of trustees to fire me, and that's not going to happen. Not for this. Come on, let's go for a little walk."

He got up and I followed him through the outer office. Cassie looked up from her keyboard and smiled at me. I smiled back, feeling a little foolish. Her red fingernails made loud clicking noises on the keyboard as she typed. We went past the gift shop and out to the main lobby, and then to the west gallery, which had the modern art and sculpture. Our footsteps were loud on the polished hardwood floor. Two older women with long black skirts, their gray hair in braids, were talking in whispers at the far side of the room, standing before an enormous painting that showed a desert landscape at night, with an animal skull as the rising moon. At one corner of the room Justin stopped and I stood next to him. Before us was a sculpture that looked as if it was made out of crushed copper piping and black lava rock. I didn't recognize the name of the artist on the little nameplate which was set on the wall.

Justin folded his arms and started talking, his voice almost dreamy, as if a part of him was woken up that had been asleep for about five years.

"Back then we didn't have that much of the modern works, so we could make room here for that summer's exhibit. We were excited, you know. Newspapers were interested and we had a film crew from Channel 9 show up. We even had lines of people trying to get in here—the first time that's ever happened at the Scribner."

Even though it seemed to sadden him, he smiled. "This was one of the largest shows we ever put on, containing highlights of late-nineteenth-century American art, and it took a lot of convincing for the other museums to lend us their works. Almost as hard as convincing a woman to go to bed with you, Mr. Cole. It's the same type of seduction. Whispered promises and agreements, and a special understanding. And my God, the scandal that broke later on, and the screaming I had to put up with, over the phone . . . The three paintings were right here, Mr. Cole. Right here before me, and I can close my eyes and still see them there. Tell me, what do you know about Winslow Homer?"

What I did know I had picked up from a quick visit to the Gilliam Library. I said, "He was born in Boston in the 1830s and became one of the best-known illustrators and painters in the United States. Lived at Prout's Neck in Maine for most of his life, and was highly regarded for his paintings of the ocean and the men and women who worked from the sea. Also did a lot of etchings and engravings, and many of his works had no people in them—just nature. Traveled abroad and to the Caribbean, and made a rather comfortable living doing what he did. Died in the early 1900s in Maine, I believe, and never married."

Justin nodded, as if pleased that a student of his had done unexpectedly well. "Yes, that's true, and much, much more. He started out as an exceptional illustrator during the Civil War, and his works appeared in *Harper's Weekly*, the most popular illustrated magazine in the country back then. He did his works in oils and watercolors, and though he's known for his New England works, a lot of his better-known paintings were inspired by his trips to the Caribbean and to the Adirondacks. And on this particular day in July, five years ago, we had three of his best, on loan from the Museum of Fine Arts in Boston, the Metropolitan Museum of Art in New York and the Addison Gallery from Phillips Academy in Andover."

He still had his arms folded as he turned to look at me. "We had a clipping service that kept track of the stories after the theft. There were hundreds of them. You wouldn't believe the number of those that said we were a backwoods gallery, with no alarm systems and rent-a-cops as guards. Not that I'm going to tell you any secrets, Lewis, but the night of the theft, we had one of the better security systems in this region. Motion detectors. Break alarms on all the doors and windows. Infrared detectors. Monitoring cameras and videotape recorders."

"Still didn't work, did it?" I asked. By then I had pulled out the reporter's notebook and was making notes, though I trusted my memory more than my notes. Pen and paper can't quite capture the mood and tenor of a person's voice, or how one's face looks like when telling a story. But the reporter's notebook and pen were necessary for the Great Lie.

"No, and you know why?"

I looked back at the wall space that was covered by a twisted hunk of metal, and I tried to imagine what it might have been like to have been here that night, five years ago, to stand before those paintings, breathing heavily and sweating, knowing that in a few moments they would belong to you and no other.

I answered by saying, "The part of the system that doesn't come with a warranty failed you. The human factor."

"Exactly," he said, still in that schoolteacher voice. "The humans. We had two guards on duty that night, a Ben Martin and a Craig Dummer. Ben was a retired Manchester cop looking to earn a little extra money to flesh out his pension and his Social Security, while Craig was a student at New Hampshire College studying criminal justice and looking for some experience he could use after he graduated."

"How much were they paid?" I asked.

He eyed me, arms still folded. "Not a bad question, Mr. Cole. That was something else that we got hit with from news reporters who became instant art experts after the theft—that we had millions of dollars' worth of art being guarded that night by old fat guys making minimum wage. Which wasn't true. Both Ben and Craig were making a fairly decent salary, and they both went through a good training program and an extensive background check. You know, I'd rather hire a couple of bright, trainable people than Ph.D.s who think they know everything."

The two older women came closer, and the nearest one made a show of trying hard not to listen to us. I thought we were going to have to move until a young mother came in, chewing gum, pushing one of those collapsible strollers that's the size of a U-Haul trailer and which was carrying a set of twin baby boys. They were gurgling enough to drown out whatever we were saying.

I asked, "So what happened?"

Justin said, shaking his head, as though he still couldn't believe what had occurred, "At about eleven at night on July 6— during the long Fourth of July weekend—two men dressed as Manchester cops came to the front door, where there's an intercom and a closed-circuit television monitor. Ben and Craig were on duty that night and had completed their rounds. They were at a security station that was set up near the front door, and they saw the cops as they rang the buzzer. The cops said that they needed to talk to them about a reported disturbance on the museum property."

He turned again to look at me, and the eyes behind his black-rimmed glasses were practically brimming with tears. "Against all training, instructions and just plain damn common sense, they let them in. They didn't call to verify who they were, they didn't ask for more information, they just damn let them in. You know, a reporter from the Boston *Globe*, I believe, asked the Museum of Fine Arts in Boston if their guards would have let them in, and the spokesman said, 'We wouldn't open up for God.'"

"Did both of the guards agree to let them in?"

He turned away, and I think he was embarrassed at his display of emotion. "At first Craig didn't want to do it, but Ben thought he recognized both of them, and so he sent Craig to undo the door. They came in and drew their guns and in a couple of minutes Ben and Craig were in one of the offices, handcuffed and with masking tape around their mouths and eyes. They worked quick, Mr. Cole, and they knew what they were doing. The first thing they did was to go to the VCR, and they took the tape that showed them entering. They disabled the alarm systems and went to work, and they knew exactly what they were looking for: the three Winslow Homers. Nothing else was touched. It was like they had a shopping list to fulfill and they did it, and then they left. This is a fairly active Manchester neighborhood, and none of our neighbors saw anything untoward."

By then a couple of teenage girls had wandered in, and the gallery was getting full. Justin motioned with his head and I followed him back to his office. Cassie looked up from her machine and smiled at the two of us. Something gave me a little tingle as her gaze stayed with me about three seconds longer than necessary. But if Cassie had any effect on Justin, he didn't show it.

He went back behind his desk and I sat down and said, "So how did you find out about the robbery?"

Justin tapped his hands on the desk's surface. "Morning shift couldn't raise anyone on the intercom, and the door locks were unlatched. I live twenty minutes away, and when I got the call that there was a break-in, I got here in ten. You know," he said, again with that wistful look, "my wife and I owned two cars back then, a Ford and a Toyota, and to this day, I couldn't tell you which one I used to come here. It was a madhouse, simply a madhouse, for a couple of weeks after the theft. Phones rang off the hook. We had calls from all over the country and even England and Japan. Wire services, newspapers, radios, television stations. The Manchester police and the FBI practically camped out here for days. I think I got home maybe twice during that time, and only for showers and naps."

The tone of his voice reminded me of another time, in my old job, how a phone call one early morning, about an unexpected invasion of another country many thousands of miles away, had sent me and the others scurrying to the five-sided palace for days on end, sleeping on cots and eating from vending machines. Long hours of scanning the news wires, reading declassified reports, answering demanding phone calls and questions, trying to read, trying to interpret and make sense of it all, trying to write reports. To this day, I cannot eat a ham and cheese sandwich, or eat a bag of potato chips from a vending machine, and I hate the sound of a ringing phone late at night.

I said, "I'd imagine that the first thought that came to you that morning was that this was an inside job."

Justin didn't say anything for a moment or two, and it felt odd, since he had been so open in the past half hour. He just gazed at me through those glasses, chin in one hand, and then he slowly said, "This is still an open investigation, so I can't really comment on that, Mr. Cole. But I'll tell you that from that day forward, we always knew where Ben Martin and Craig Dummer were living and what they were doing."

"And what are they doing today, Mr. Dix?" I asked.

Again, that eye-piercing pause. I felt like I was skirting close to the edge of something that Justin didn't want me to see or to look at, and then he surprised me by smiling a bit.

"I suppose I could tell you it's none of your business, but if you dug a little bit, you could find out," he said. "So I'll save you some time. Craig Dummer's living in Bainbridge, a couple of towns over. Completed college and got his criminal justice degree, but I don't think he ever got a real police job. Last I heard, he was back doing security work, and was considering going back to school to get his law degree. If you can believe that."

"You don't know?"

Justin shrugged. "I don't care. He could be the president of Amoskeag Bank for all I care. Just so long as I know where he's living and if he's spending his money on Porsches or Caribbean trips. That's all we care about."

From the other office, Cassie was humming something. I knew that I could never work in this office, for the distractions were too many and too attractive. "How about the other guard, Ben Martin?"

The little smile came back. "Well, the job's considerably easier now, you see. Ben Martin died of a heart attack two years after the theft, and he's up in the Manchester Memorial Cemetery. His kids live out on the West Coast and wouldn't know a Winslow Homer if it was hanging over their living room couch."

"So the focus has been on Craig Dummer."

He leaned back in his chair. "I didn't say that. You did."

"How did the investigation go, at the beginning? I don't expect you to give me any secrets, but . . ."

"But you want some details, right?"

I nodded. He went on. "Like I said before, it was like they had a shopping list. The two fake cops came in and took those Winslow Homers, and nothing else. The FBI and others found this to be very strange, since we had other paintings worth more than those three. Hell, some of the silver work upstairs is extremely valuable, and other items. I mean, well, just one of our Chippendale chairs is worth nearly a hundred thousand dollars. Which told us one of two things, Mr. Cole."

"Someone has specific tastes, or they were spooked and had to leave early," I said.

"Exactly," Justin said, his voice returning to its previous pleased-professor mode. "But I would tend to think that they had a specific order to fill, and that those three Winslow Homers were it. They had done quite a good job on the alarm system, and both Ben and Craig were well put away."

"Any leads?"

"None of which I can share with you, but I'll tell you that for the first year after the theft, we were flooded—literally flooded—with phone calls and mail and visitors who said there was a trembling in the cosmic conscious and that they'd be able to find the paintings."

"For free?"

He snorted. "They may have been strange but they certainly weren't fools. There's a price for everything. We even got the oddest items." He reached into a desk drawer and pulled out a sheet of paper in a clear plastic folder. "Like this one, for instance. Take a look and tell me what you think."

He passed it over and I gave it a quick read. It was column after column of letters, numbers, exclamation points and other symbols from the top row of someone's keyboard. They had been written on a light green piece of graph paper with what looked to be a No. 2 pencil. Both sides of the graph paper were covered.

"A secret message?"

Justin smiled. "Of sorts. The letter that came with this secret message said that if we could decipher the code, it would tell us where the paintings were. And the funny part was that the FBI actually made a photocopy of this letter, and I hear that they sent it over to the National Security Agency."

With those last three words we had slipped into an area of conversation that I really didn't want to explore, so I passed the sheet back and said, "Do you mind if I ask you a rude question?"

He seemed surprised and faintly amused. "Go ahead, so long as you don't use any foul language."

I looked around the office and out at the well-groomed, clean courtyard, and I said, "How come you're still working here?"

His eyes seemed to focus right in on a spot an inch below my jaw. "You mean, why wasn't I fired?"

I nodded. He tapped his fingers again and said, "It certainly wasn't for lack of trying on the part of some of the trustees, and for a few days afterward, I really thought that I would spare them any debate and give them my resignation. And then maybe go home and put the car in the garage and turn on the engine."

Justin tugged at his tie and coughed and said, "But I got angrier and angrier, at what had happened, at what those two men had stolen and the incredible lapse of judgment by Ben and Craig. I went before the trustees at a special meeting and laid everything out, from the alarm system to the training and background investigation that I used before hiring Ben and Craig, and I threw the question to them: What more could I have done, with the budget and the resources that were available to me? What was broken in the alarm systems that could be fixed? What could have been done to stop this, outside of locking the guards in every evening?"

"It looked like it worked," I said.

"I'm still here," he said, grinning.

I made a show of flipping through my notes. I looked over at Justin and saw his hand beginning a tap-tap dance with a pencil, and I knew it was time to go. Sources and people you interview always tell you a lot, even if they don't say a single word. I could always come back or call later. I told him I was finished. He nodded and said, "I want to show you one more thing before you head out."

We went through the office again and Cassie looked up at me with a wide smile and said, "I do hope you get up here again, Mr. Cole. And I'll make sure to check on your magazine the next time I'm at a newsstand."

I gave her my "polite-but-I'm-interested-against-my-common-sense" smile and said, "Buy a subscription if you can. Believe me, the magazine could use it."

I was still hearing her laughter as Justin brought me into the gift shop. The two older ladies were in there, going through a rack of postcards, and there were a couple of kids with their noses pressed up against a display case. He stopped before a poster stand, one of those metal contraptions with cardboard backing that show posters that are for sale.

Justin said, "The director and trustees want to think the theft is behind us, and that we have to look forward to the future, but I know better. The public knows better."

He started flipping through the poster display, the metal rods squeaking as he went past posters that showed a Monet, a Picasso and a photograph of the antique furniture from the second-floor gallery.

"Here," he said, stopping for a moment. "Look at these. These are prints of those paintings, done to exact size."

Even as posters, their colors were vibrant, and if I had been standing some distance away, they might have looked real. Justin's voice became dreamy again as he described each print, and his hands practically caressed the slick paper. The first showed a fisherman alone in a dory, out on a wide ocean, looking over his shoulder at a schooner on the horizon. He shared his dory with fish and gear. The sky was dark and menacing, with a cloud bank of sorts heading toward the distant schooner.

"*Fog Warning,*" Justin said. "Painted in 1885. You know, you can't really see the fisherman's face, but you can sense the danger, the tension. The fisherman is alone out on the ocean, and fog is heading to his schooner. He only has minutes to reach the schooner before it disappears. There's a race on, a race for life. Events like this happened every day out on the Grand Banks."

"So I've heard," I said. "Many of those fishermen didn't even know how to swim, and in those waters it wouldn't have taken long to die of drowning or from the cold."

"A lonely death," Justin said.

Another print came into view. Two men stood on the deck of a ship wearing foul-weather gear. In their hands they held navigation instruments, sextants or octants, I wasn't too sure. In the gray sky, heavy storm clouds were breaking up and the sun's rays were just bursting through.

"This was painted in 1886," Justin explained. "*Eight Bells.* It's been called one of the finest portrayals of men on the sea ever made. See the story here, Lewis? Two men 'shooting the sun,' trying to determine the exact position of their ship. That's the apparent story. But look beyond that, Lewis. Look at the weather, their hunched shoulders, the shape of the clouds. They must have survived a terrible time of it, out on the open sea during a terrible storm, and now, only just now, do they have a chance to breathe and take stock, and the first thing they do, they try to find out where they are."

"Sounds like someone's life philosophy," I said, and Justin rewarded me with another smile as he flipped to the next poster, and even I recognized this painting. A black man on the steep sloping deck of a dismasted sloop. The waves were high and threatening, and off in the distance was the curving funnel of a waterspout. In the foreground, traipsing through the waters as if waiting for their meal, were a school of sharks. One of the sharks had its head breaking the surface, the cold eyes showing a very long patience.

"*The Gulf Stream*," I said. "Considered one of his best."

He nodded, gazing at the figures on the print. "Painted in 1889, it took years of preparation and work. Homer spent a lot of time in the Caribbean. You know, it must have been so different from his years in Maine, being in such an exotic place, all that heat and hot sand. When this was first exhibited, people were shocked at how strong, how vital it was. Homer even ran into criticism for depicting this man in such desperate danger without showing some conclusion or hope."

"And what did Homer tell them? To go to hell?"

Another smirk. "Close enough. What he said was so funny that I've even memorized it. He wrote back once, saying, 'The criticisms of *The Gulf Stream* by old women and others are noted. You may inform these people that the Negro did not starve to death. He was not eaten by the sharks. The waterspout did not hit him. And he was rescued by a passing ship which is not shown in the picture.'"

I laughed along with Justin and said, "Sounds like a guy I'd like to share a beer with."

"Well, Homer would have gone along with that. He did like his drink."

Justin then shook his head as he let the poster display slap back into shape. "Such art, such artistry. Before the theft sales of those posters were only so-so during our special exhibit, but after the theft, they just kept on selling and selling. Those three prints are our bestselling posters in the gift shop and every few months we have to restock them. Can you believe that?"

I remembered a trip from two years back and said, "I can. Once I went to the Kennedy Space Center in Florida, and the most popular photograph they sold in their gift shop was one that showed the crew members of the *Challenger*. Sometimes people like souvenirs of bad times, Mr. Dix. Makes them feel indestructible."

"Maybe so, maybe so," he said, shaking his head again as if he couldn't believe he lived in a country such as this. "Here, let me walk you out."

The center lobby had about ten or fifteen visitors, and their voices echoed against the tall ceiling and the pillars. I shook his hand as he opened the entrance door and I thanked him again for his time, and then he stood erect, gazing out to the street, as if he were looking for two men dressed as Manchester cops.

"I want them back, Mr. Cole," he said, the sudden strength in his voice making me take another look at his expression. "Some days I don't care what it takes. I just want those Winslow Homers back."

He looked at me as though he was almost shocked at his outburst. "But please don't put that in your story, all right?"

As I walked out the door and into the warm July day, I headed to my Range Rover. Crossing the street, I thought again of what Felix had told me a few days ago, about his problem, and I thought of how much emotion Justin Dix had put into those words, about wanting the Winslow Homers back.

There was something odd there, and it didn't strike me until I had been driving for five or six minutes.

When he told me how much he wanted those paintings back, I believed him.

But from the tone of his voice, I wasn't sure if he wanted them back for himself or for his museum.

CHAPTER

SEVEN

It was early afternoon by the time I left the Scribner Museum. I drove to downtown Manchester, which is built around a long main thoroughfare called Elm Street, and is one of the oddest avenues in the world: start out from the downtown and head north, and you'll go from twenty-story office buildings to businesses to residential homes in a space of five minutes, and then you'll come to a dead end. Travel that distance about two and a half miles in the other direction, and you'll also come to a halt. I believe it's the only main street in a large city in America that stops at two dead ends.

On this hot day I wasn't in the mood for measuring distances or dead ends and instead I stopped at a restaurant called Book-Binder's. It had a bookstore in the corner, and after lunch I spent a pleasant ten minutes or so there, just browsing through the shelves, seeing what new history books were available. For some reason books feel and smell better in bookstores than they do at home, with their pages stiff and crisp and that fresh smell of ink and paper that promises so much.

On my way out of BookBinder's, I passed a pay phone in its tiny lobby and underneath its shelf a Manchester phone book was hanging from a metal cable. From looking at the inside cover, I saw that Bainbridge was one of the towns contained in the directory and it took me a moment only to find "Dummer, Craig 57 Mast Road Bainbridge." I wrote down the phone number in my reporter's notebook, and then, just as I was putting the book back underneath the pay-phone counter, I looked again and saw this listing: "Fuller, C. 12 Trenton Lane Bedford."

I wrote down that number, too.

Bainbridge was ten minutes from Manchester and was a town that reminded me of the real New Hampshire, not the idealized towns you see in Hollywood movies or on the evening news every four years when there's a presidential primary being conducted in our snow and ice.

Through the help of a wonderful gazette I keep in my Range Rover that had road maps of every one of New Hampshire's 269 cities, towns and land grants, it was an easy drive, though I'm sure it's not one that drivers in vehicles with Massachusetts or New York license plates have made that much. It's off the main highways, so it's probably bypassed by the tourists in the summer, the leaf-peepers in the fall and the skiers in the winter and spring. The downtown consisted of a branch of the Fleet Bank, a few shops and two gas stations, and the mandatory town common with the Civil War statue in the center. Though it was a hot and steamy day, I drove with the windows down and the air conditioner off. Air conditioners in moving vehicles give me a headache.

I could tell from the size of many of the homes and their lots that this was a bedroom community for those people fortunate enough to be doing well in a state with low or nonexistent state taxes and whose property taxes were among the highest in the country. The homes I saw in this part of town were large and well groomed, and many had the obligatory Volvo or Audi in the driveway.

Driving my Range Rover, I knew that at least the vehicle I owned would fit in, but I had serious doubts about its sole occupant.

After another five minutes or so going down some back roads leading off from the town common, I made it to Mast Road, and saw the other half of Bainbridge.

In most of the towns in this part of the state, there's always a Mast Road, and it's usually located in the hills. The first roads that came in here were built in the 1600s and 1700s, when the tall pines—property of the King—made wonderful masts for the Royal Navy. The roads that were hacked through the wilderness were named Mast Road, and from the bumps and jolts I received as I went to Craig Dummer's residence, it felt as if this road hadn't been repaired since the days of the Hanover kings.

This half of Bainbridge was not a bedroom community, and it definitely wasn't a place that would have been highlighted in any tourist brochure. Yet I didn't mind driving down this road, for it was a part of New Hampshire that was real, and would always be real, no matter which politicians were in the state, running for President, or how much money the tourists brought in each year to the ski areas and liquor stores. The homes were a mixture of small working farms and residences, of old colonials and single-story ranches, and trailers with rusting sides.

A few of the homes had two or three junked cars or washing machines in their front yards, and as I drove slowly, looking for No. 57, I could see that I was being watched: The old lady in baggy sweat pants at the trailer with the wood-frame addition hanging up her laundry. A farmer and his son working on a John Deere tractor. An older couple sitting on their front porch. They all looked at me as I drove by, and I knew that in a few minutes it would be known that a stranger had been passing through this part of town, driving a foreign vehicle. The neighborhood may have been rural, but they looked out for each other.

At a set of mailboxes that said "57–59 Mast Road," I made a right onto a dirt driveway that led into a wooded area for about a hundred feet and which dribbled off onto a front lawn that was packed earth—57–59 Mast Road was a two-story duplex, with separate entrances at each end, and with brown paint that was flaked and peeling. There were no cars around, but there were ruts in the ground near both ends of the house that showed where some vehicles had been parked. I got out of the Range Rover and headed to the right side of the house. A stairway of about a half dozen steps led up to a small deck and a door, and the arrangement was mirrored on the left side. Crickets chirruped in the tall grass and a crow was chattering at me as I went to the door. A nameplate under the doorbell said "Kotowski." Wrong end of the house. I rang the doorbell a couple of times and peered through the door anyway and it looked like no one was home. There was an open kitchen area and a living room in the distance which I could make out, but no television, no radio and no lights were on.

I got down from the deck and went over to the other side. The windows were open on the second floor of the duplex, letting in the slight breeze, and the afternoon seemed much hotter than the morning. At the left side of the house, the nameplate said "Dummer." Ah, another success story for the inquisitive and investigative reporter. But the doorbell went unanswered, and when I peeked through the window again, I saw a silent house. This one was dirtier than its partner. Dishes were piled high in the sink and there were a couple of cardboard pizza containers on the table. In the living room area there was a scattering of newspapers and magazines and a pile of clothes. Craig Dummer didn't seem to be doing that much with himself this time around.

For a moment I thought of leaving my business card in the doorway, but decided against it. I wanted to come upon him cold, and have him tell me in his own words about what happened that night five years ago, when he and his partner let millions of dollars' worth of art walk out the front door.

As I drove back out on Mast Road and into town, the air still not cooling me off, the early-warning system for this neighborhood was still in place, and at least a half dozen people took note of me as I went by.

I resisted the temptation to give them a cheery wave.

Four hours later that day I was back in Tyler Beach, having made an early dinner engagement with Diane Woods of the Tyler police department. I was hoping to take her to Grace's Beach House, which is on the south end of Tyler Beach. Grace's Beach House is owned by one Grace Grayson, a stocky and buxom woman in her late fifties who has short-cropped blond hair that's streaked with gray and black and who works in all parts of her restaurant, depending on her mood. Some nights she tends bar and on other nights she's the hostess, seating people at tables with views of Tyler Harbor and the strong lights of the distant Falconer nuclear power plant. But on all nights she's loud and demanding, sometimes telling the cowering tourists to "haul yer ass over to that corner table," and she loves to tell stories about her past—she has claimed on several occasions to have been a porno film star in the 1960s, a gymnastics instructor in California and a gunrunner for a rebel group in Haiti.

It's an odd place, and thank God it hasn't been written up yet in the *Globe*, but if you don't have reservations, forget about getting a table: the line to get in often spills out onto Atlantic Avenue.

But reservations or not, dinner for us this evening consisted of hot dogs and Coke, and this sumptuous meal was shared on the front seat of Diane Woods's unmarked police car, a dark blue Crown Victoria with blackwall tires and a whip antenna on the trunk. Unmarked though it might be, it was also instantly identifiable to those Tyler residents who dabbled in things illegal, though it was useful for grabbing those out-of-towners who thought a beach town was a license to raise hell.

We were about a block away from Grace's Beach House, and I looked at it longingly as we crawled north on Atlantic Avenue, stuck behind the usual late afternoon flow of traffic from points south such as Salisbury, Lawrence and Lowell. In this part of Tyler Beach, Atlantic Avenue is two lanes and both of them head north, and it looked like Boston's Southeast Expressway during high commuter time. I had the window down and Diane was nervously tapping the steering wheel as she drove, balancing a half-eaten hot dog in one hand while driving. Both of my hands were free, as I had finished my own dinner earlier, but I wasn't sure if that was much of a prize: the hot dog felt like a lump of cold seaweed, unmoving in my stomach.

I hadn't changed from my day's visit to Manchester and Bainbridge, and Diane was equally casual: white denim jeans and a short-sleeved red shirt that was flapping over the waistband, the better to hide her .357 Ruger, detective shield and handcuffs. Diane swore under her breath as brake lights up ahead from both lanes lit up, and she said, "Look, Lewis, I know you wanted to go to Grace's and have a half-decent meal, but I've been sitting on my butt all day and I was getting tired of it."

I looked over at her and said, "Your butt looks pretty good from here."

She said something that I'm sure the area third-graders would have been shocked to hear, coming from a police officer who loves to come in and talk to them. Diane said, "Some days you just get tired of sitting there, reading and rereading reports, making phone calls, trying to track down leads and taking phone calls from a whole host of shitmeisters, like the State Police and the AG's office and our lovely friends in the news media. So you need to get out and get some fresh air, and I'm sorry, Lewis, I couldn't spend another hour or so just sitting. I needed to get my blood revving again."

The low-slung police radio chattered the usual noises of a weekday summer evening at Tyler Beach, from a stolen car to a couple of drunks barricaded in their motel room, refusing to leave and tearing the place up. Around us was a mass of people, swarming three or four deep along both sidewalks. There was not a single parking space to be found. Cars that crawled past us had their radios going, and just by sitting still, you heard rap music going into metal and into hip-hop and rock. But no classical. I guess they had their own beaches to go to.

Through it all, Diane Woods steered the car, talking to me but looking at what was going on. Little things like burned-out taillights or open containers of beer didn't even cause her to tap her brake pedal: she was out for bigger prizes. She finished her hot dog and took a sip from a cup of Coke that been stored between her legs, and then was going to say something but just stayed quiet instead.

A woman skated by on rollerblades, eyes half closed, listening to a tiny tape player strapped to her tanned upper left arm. She had on a lime-green string bikini and her flesh was tanned and taut and seemed to spill over the tiny green fabric. There was a chorus of shouts and car horns as she skated south. I even saw Diane sneak a look in the rearview mirror.

"Not a bad view," I observed.

"You get them all the time around here," she said, braking again as the traffic ground its way north. "Jesus, I'm beat, Lewis. You know, I wouldn't mind a summer here, just listening to the music and skating around. Not a bad lifestyle, at least for a change. Get to sleep late, at least."

"What's new with the diver case?"

She looked over at me, a bit of mustard in one corner of her mouth, and said, "Officially and what I tell the news media, the case is proceeding along."

"Unofficially, the story's different, then."

"Yeah." She brought the cruiser to a stop again. "Damn traffic. Yeah, the case isn't going anywhere. First of all, no one's claimed the body. No missing person report has been filed, no landlord has gone into a cottage and found that his tenant was missing, and no empty boat's been washed up ashore. The wet suit had no rental tags on it, and none of the dive shops report any of their gear missing. Autopsy . . . Well, the diver certainly didn't drown, that's for sure. Not enough water in the lungs. So the case is going in the 'I'll get around to it when I can' file unless something breaks soon."

She eased off the brakes, and I said, "Well, obviously some people know, Diane. The guy or guys who took care of the diver, and the diver's friends or family. Which tells me that this wasn't a dispute over a title search. Something a bit heavier."

Diane flicked her tongue out and caught the bit of mustard, and I felt better for some strange reason. She said quietly, "Maybe I'll have a talk with your buddy Felix."

I said, "Not sure if buddy's the word. But feel free to try. How's the rest of the department working?"

By now the traffic in the left lane had come to a complete stop, and there was a blare of traffic horns from up ahead. Diane sighed and said, "We're not getting squat information about the chief and how his treatments are going, so everything's up in the air. Both of the deputy chiefs are busy setting bureaucratic land mines for each other, and I'm turning into one of their favorite weapons."

"For example?"

"For example, one deputy's supposed to be in charge of administration, and the other is supposed to be in charge of operations. With the chief around, I usually went straight to him and left those guys out of it. But now both are fighting for the detective bureau—i.e., me—and I'm getting conflicting orders—like how to file certain reports, when I should be working and when I should be talking to the state. Petty crap like that. And then I got the diver case, the usual summer nonsense, the felonies and stuff and phone calls like you wouldn't believe."

We moved up ahead some, but the left lane was stock-still. The sounds of the horns were getting louder. "Sounds like it's time for a vacation."

She had both hands on the steering wheel and I could tell that she was tensing up. Something was bothering her. She said,

"No, it sounds like I need something more permanent, Lewis. Like a change in direction, or maybe careers." She turned to me, her tanned face looking weary. "But being a cop's all I know. That's all I've ever done, and I've given practically everything I've got to this department and this town, and I haven't been winning much all summer."

"Has that Roger Krohn been helping much?"

Another blast of horns from up ahead, and Diane actually smiled. "He's a funny character, that one. One day he's the tough, cynical Massachusetts detective who's seen it all, and another time he's just amazed at how things are up here in New Hampshire. I tell you, he keeps on talking about how he wants to get out of Massachusetts and come here, maybe find a nice local job, and I get the idea he's scouting out the chief's position."

"Sounds morbid," I said. We moved forward a bit more, and then stopped. Nothing moved in the left lane.

"Maybe so," she admitted, "but you know how it is with cops. We have a secret network that lets us know who's hiring and who's firing. Who's in at what department and who's not. Roger's just taking advantage of what's here. I really think he's gunning for the chief's job." She paused, was going to speak, and then seemed to change her mind.

I said, "You were about to say?"

That same smile. "I was about to say that I believe he's gunning for something else besides."

"Oh," I said. I thought for a moment and said, "Think he's gunning for the Tyler detective bureau? In a truly nonprofessional way?"

She grinned this time. "Unh-hunh. That I do."

"So how is your love life, Diane?"

Before she could answer we found out why the left lane had been at a standstill while our lane had continued to move ahead. A late-model Chevrolet, bright red and with mag tires and increased suspension, was stopped in front of a dress shop while the driver talked to two young ladies, who were leaning over and talking back to him, and while in the process of doing so, were revealing a remarkable amount of cleavage from their skimpy bathing-suit tops. The driver didn't seem to mind the tie-up he was causing and seemed to ignore the blaring horns, and based on his view at the time, it seemed understandable. Not particularly bright, but understandable.

Diane muttered something and pulled up next to the Chevrolet and yelled out, "Hey, you! Move it!"

The driver kept on talking and Diane leaned on the horn and said, "I'm talking to you, mister. Move it!"

He turned and looked over at us. He had on a black baseball cap, worn backward, and his long brown hair fell to his shoulders, which were bare, and it seemed as if he had spent about two weeks growing his mustache. He was smoking a cigarette and he removed it with one hand, the better, I suppose, to speak to us. He flipped the butt toward Diane, saying, "Fuck you, lady. I'm busy."

Well.

Diane said something under her breath and slammed the Crown Vic in drive and pulled it ahead and over, blocking his way. She threw the Crown Vic back into park and the cup of Coke that was on the seat fell to the floorboards, but by then she was out of the car, pulling a nightstick from underneath the seat and carrying it one hand. I got out just in time to see her reach into the Chevrolet with the nightstick, and then pull the young man with the foul mouth out, using the nightstick under his chin. His two female friends, seeing what was going on, melted back into the crowd.

God, Diane moved fast. The driver swore and swung at her, just barely missing her face. I went around to the front of her cruiser, going to give her some help, but Diane had grabbed one arm and had tucked the young man's thumb under his hand, and was pulling the arm up against his back. He yelped and his legs gave way, and Diane slammed his chest down on the front of the Chevrolet. I winced. Diane had him in what she called a "thumb come-along," which was guaranteed to make prisoners do what cops wanted. As a joke once, she had tried it on me, and after a few seconds she had let go when I started yelling. The pain and stiffness in my arm had stayed for almost a week. Using the thumb come-along, Diane could have made me do anything she wanted, from tap dancing to signing over my bank account. It hurt like a son of a gun.

Diane told me once that one of the Tyler police's secret fears was drawing a crowd along Atlantic Avenue during the height of the beach season and ending up with a riot that would drive a stake into Tyler Beach's reputation as a family beach. With the amount of drinking going on, all it would take would be a couple of guys shouting "Off the pigs" and throwing a couple of bottles. Things could get nasty real quick.

So by virtue of that fear and Diane's natural speed, by the time I had gotten around to the left fender of the Crown Vic, ready and willing to offer any assistance that I could, she had handcuffs on the driver and was walking him to her cruiser. His hat had come off in the process, his head was down and he was moaning, probably wondering what the hell had happened to him. I opened the rear door of the Crown Vic and said to Diane, "Here you go, Detective. Always glad to help."

I swear, her smile had dimples by then. "Thanks," she said, tossing him into the backseat. He lay down, his arms handcuffed behind him. On his left shoulder blade, there was a tattoo of a bulldog.

"Do me a favor?" she asked, breathing fairly hard.

"Name it."

She nodded over to the Chevrolet. "Pull this nitwit's car over to the side, will you? Gotta open up the traffic."

I felt somewhat odd as I did what she asked, stepping into this stranger's car and driving it all of six feet so it was next to the sidewalk. Hardly any type of crowd had formed during the sixty seconds or so of this little incident, but those people who did glance at me gave me a look that said "cop." Since I've been called worse things, I didn't let it bother me.

After switching off the engine and locking the doors, I went back into the Crown Vic and handed the keys over. She threw them down next to her metal clipboard and we headed down one of the lettered side streets that connect Atlantic Avenue with Ashburn Avenue—both streets run parallel to the ocean—and from there it was just a short drive to the Tyler police station. As we drove, the guy in the backseat moaned a couple of times and said, "You broke my goddam hand, lady. You broke my goddam hand."

Diane said, "Save it for when we get to the station." She looked over at me and said, "You know, once I get this fool processed, I'm just gonna head home to my condo, shower in cold water and go to sleep."

"Sounds like a hell of a schedule."

The moaning resumed, and I spared him a glance and almost felt sorry for him. Here he was, young and probably considering himself good-looking, driving a car that he's proud of owning and being in Tyler Beach during a hot summer night. All he wants is some action, some good times to take back to his life in Massachusetts, and he almost gets there, talking it up to a couple of babes in good-looking bathing suits, and in the process of trying to impress them on how tough he is, he ends up in the rear seat of a police cruiser, being taken to the police station by one member of the Tyler police department that I guarantee does not have a bleeding heart. Diane would probably have let everything slide if it weren't for the language and the flying cigarette butt.

It'd be enough to make me vacation at home.

The Tyler police station is a one-story concrete structure that looks like it belongs at a nuclear testing site. It didn't take much of an architectural genius to design the building, and this lack of effort shows in a lot of ways: it's always too cold in the winter and too hot in the summer, and during a few spring and winter storms, when Ashburn Avenue floods out, the police dispatchers have to use two chairs: one to sit in and the other to rest their legs on, so as not to be ankle-deep in water for an entire shift.

It's adjacent to the beach fire station of the Tyler fire department, and Diane rolled her cruiser out back, where the door for the booking area leads to. As she brought the cruiser to a halt, I said, "Diane, you know, it would have been just as easy for me to bring this nut's car to the station, instead of leaving it on the street."

She was smiling again. "I know, Lewis. Haven't you figured it out?"

I reached for the door handle. "Sure. You're going to call to have it towed."

"Right," she said, getting out of the cruiser. "That way, this clown gets to pay a seventy-five-dollar tow-and-storage charge, in addition to his other fines."

I got out and she looked over at me from across the roof of the Crown Vic. "That'll give him a little lesson in the pocketbook on how not to talk back to ladies."

I said, "I'm not too sure if he's going to take it that way."

She laughed. "Ask me if I care." Diane went to the rear door with a smile and said, "You know, this just put me in a good mood. Driving along, bitching and moaning to you, and bang, the adrenaline rushes right through you and cleans out your whole system. I'd recommend it to anyone."

"Thanks, but I prefer something a bit quieter."

From inside the cruiser I could hear the driver moaning again and Diane said, "Thanks for dinner."

"You're welcome. But next time, let's do it someplace that doesn't involve driving."

With that, Diane got her prisoner out of her car and I headed over to my Range Rover, which was also parked in the police lot. Through the good graces of Diane Woods, I have a "Press Parking" pass which I can toss onto my dashboard and which lets me park for however long I need to at the Tyler police station. One of the many secret privileges of being a magazine writer, I suppose.

When I got to the Rover and unlocked the driver's door, someone called out "Lewis! Lewis Cole!" and I turned and saw Roger Krohn walking out of the booking-door entrance to the police station. He had on jeans and a pressed light pink polo shirt, and around his left wrist he was wearing a gold bracelet. His thick brown hair seemed as perfect as ever, and he was smiling at me as he strode across the parking lot.

I shook his outstretched hand and he said, "How are you doing, Lewis? Gotten over that crazy swim you had, pulling in that body?"

"Oh, I guess so."

"Yeah," he said, shaking his head. "I talked to a couple of my friends down at 1010 Commonwealth in Boston, and they couldn't believe what had happened up here. Man, what a case. Headless and handless diver. Something as crazy as that belongs in New Jersey, not New Hampshire."

"I'd have to agree with you there, Roger."

He glanced around the parking lot and said, "I was just getting free for the night, and wondered if you want to go get a beer and maybe something to eat. You've been here awhile, you probably know the places. That sound okay?"

At first I was going to say no and head home by myself, but his smile was so wide and his tone was so eager. I'm sure it must be lonely sometimes, being up here in a resort town by yourself.

"Yeah, I know a good place," I said. "It's within walking distance, but it can sometimes get noisy. You mind noise?"

"Hey," he said, holding his hands open. "I'm from Boston!"

"It'll help," I said, relocking the Rover's door. "But not by much."

CHAPTER

EIGHT

W e were on the outside deck of Grace's Beach House, so we couldn't make out too much of the screaming coming from the second-floor dining room, but I could tell that Grace Grayson was in her usual form. A couple of older men were standing at their table—which I could see through the sliding-glass doors leading inside—while Grace went at them. A waitress with long black hair slid open one of the doors and I heard Grace yell, "I told you, and I told you again, we don't take no American Express. Now you get me something else or some cash or I'm calling the cops on both of you."

The waitress, laboring under a tray that looked as if it was holding a squadron of boiled lobsters, merely shook her head as she went by, but some of the diners inside were cheering Grace on. The door slid shut and it got somewhat quiet. Roger Krohn, sitting on the other side of our dinner table, raised his Budweiser and said, "Hell of a way to run a restaurant. Thought the trick was to make the customer happy."

I lifted my glass of ice water in a return salute. A beer had sounded nice for dinner, but the memories of Felix's disapproving gaze a couple of days ago was still too fresh, and so I had decided to go with a cup of Tyler's best. There had been a line to get in but a little wheedling on my part and the fact that I had made an earlier reservation had helped. The furniture out on the deck was wooden chairs and tables, and most were stained with the remains of past dinners. There were no empty tables.

"Grace doesn't care about making her customers happy," I said. "She just cares about bringing customers in. Most of these people are transient, just tourists. They hear about Grace's Beach House from friends and decide to go see the show. They have a hell of a time and go home and tell their friends and family, and then *they* show up in a month or so. A nice little cycle."

Before us were the leftovers of a typical summer dinner: a few cold french fries and half-eaten rolls for Roger, who had taken care of a fried clam dish, and the empty shells of two one-pound lobsters for me.

Roger turned to take in the view. From the deck you look over tiny cottages that are rented on a weekly basis by tourists from places as nearby as Salisbury and as far away as Quebec City, and a few hundred yards from the mass of cottages and stores is the harbor that is shared by the fishermen and boaters of Tyler and Falconer. Beyond the harbor are the flat grasslands of the marsh, and the squat concrete-and-steel buildings of the Falconer nuclear power plant, still quietly humming away, generating electricity for a million New Englanders and producing radioactive wastes that squabbling politicians couldn't decide where to store.

Roger said, "You know, a guy could get used to this view. Could get used to living up here in a place like this."

That was something Roger had talked about through most

of the dinner, about how much he had enjoyed his brief time up here in Tyler and how he wasn't looking forward to returning to Boston. We had exchanged the usual small talk about our backgrounds, and once again I was surprised at not feeling any guilt about glossing over my years in government service. Instead of telling him the truth—which could have gone on for a half hour or more—I said, "So after a couple of years at DoD, I got tired of shuffling papers and lucked out in getting this magazine job."

A convenient lie, but one I've never had the guts to use with someone who knew anything about magazine work. They would have raised an eyebrow or two, then would have rushed back to their office and made some phone calls, and I would have gotten some very unnecessary and dangerous attention.

Then Roger had smiled and said, "Then for a while we were both working for the same group of guys?"

"Oh?" I said, hoping I was appearing terribly disinterested, when in fact I was anything but.

"Yeah, but I had to wear a uniform. Spent a few years in this man's Army, learning to kill people and blow up things. Went to jungles and deserts and came out with my skin intact, and what did I do? Decide to become a cop, so people could continue to shoot at me."

We had both laughed at that and now he shook his head and said again, "Yep, a nice view to get used to. Beats hell out of looking at three-deckers."

"It seems like there's something going around," I said, remembering the conversations I'd had with Paula Quinn of the *Chronicle* and Diane Woods about their careers and lives over the past week. "You're the third person in almost as many days who's told me that they don't like what they're doing."

He spun back in his chair and rubbed the neck of the bottle across his too large chin, and said, "No, don't get me wrong, Lewis. I do enjoy my work, always have. It's the place where I'm doing it that I don't like."

An original thought, I guess. Big-city blues. Paula Quinn and I once went to see a concert in Boston at the Berklee Performance Center. The concert was fine but after spending nearly fifteen dollars to park and another hour in the city traffic, dodging drivers who think a yellow light means go fast and a red light means go faster, Paula had said, "There's only one thing better than coming to Boston. And that's getting out of Boston."

I said, "Boston getting you down?"

He grimaced. "Look at the news, Lewis. It's not just Boston. It's most of the cities in this country. New York City is ungovernable. Los Angeles is no better—people are busy choking on the smog and fumes—and in Chicago, man, the color of your skin can get you killed if you go down the wrong block. I got a cousin, he's a cop in a Manhattan precinct, and he tells me some cops are setting up off-hours death squads. Can you believe that? Death squads. They go out at night and snatch guys they know are guilty, and bang-bang, it's taken care of. It's either that or keep on arresting and shoving them into court. And the way courts are, chances are someone's case will get plea-bargained down to shit, or charges will get dropped, or the case file will disappear and the guy will walk. This way, at least, the guy's off the street."

I chose my words carefully, because the look on his face didn't match the words he was saying. "Sounds like you don't approve, Roger."

He looked surprised. "What, you think I'm nuts? Last time I checked, this is supposed to be America, right? Constitution and all that. And death squads don't belong here—this isn't Central America or Brazil."

"You sound like someone who's up to making some changes."

"Bah." He eyed the waitress as she went by, looking at the short denim miniskirt she was wearing and her tight white T-shirt. The tray was now empty and she played with it in her hands as she went back inside the restaurant, rolling it among her slim fingers like a ship's wheel.

Roger said, "You know, I was like that once, full of vim and vigor, ready to change the world and make things better, and that was knocked out of me after about a month on the streets. It's just too big and complex, and there's too many groups, all fighting and screaming at each other. It's hard to help any of them, let alone make a difference. The young rich kids who think that you're under their hire and direction. Your Third World groups, who think we lie awake at night dreaming about better ways of oppressing them. Your working-class stiffs, who're just lookin' for a break, and your politicians, who love you when the bullets are flying and who can't be found when it's budget time."

I swirled the ice around in my glass. "Replace the name Boston with a hundred or so other city names, and I guess you're making a fair statement, Roger."

"Yeah," he grumbled, "but that doesn't mean I gotta be happy. Place like Tyler, though, a guy could make a stand, make a difference. Not many places like that left. The way I figure it, some bright boys after World War II managed to screw up the cities in their quest to make a perfect world, and that's fine. I guess that's what bright boys are used for. Me, I'm not that bright, and I can't figure out how to make things better. All I know is how to be a cop, and I know that whatever I do is being wasted down in Boston."

I eyed him and said, "Word is on the streets that you might be interested in staying in Tyler after the exchange program is completed. Anything to that little rumor, Detective?"

It seemed for a moment he was going to sit up in indignation and deny everything, but instead he smiled shyly and said quietly, "The thought's entered my mind. Nobody's talking much about the chief and his condition, and in my mind, that means the news isn't good. For me, I could do worse, Lewis, and this'd be a good chance to start over fresh. Besides, there's something else interesting that's got my attention here in Tyler. Know what it is?"

I said I didn't and in a brief second I prepared myself for whatever he was going to say. I'm glad I did, for he looked at both sides of the restaurant and leaned forward and said, "This is going to sound crazy, but I really think Diane Woods is one good-lookin' woman. What do you think, Lewis? Think she might be interested?"

Oh my. I'm glad I had prepared for something odd, and this one definitely set the unusual meter on its head. I said, "Interested in you, Roger?"

He shrugged, with a sheepish grin. "Maybe so. Is she dating, do you know?"

I was going to say something definite and decided not to, and after a few moments sorting through about a half dozen options, I said, "Roger, that really should come from her. I know Diane, but I feel uncomfortable talking about her personal life, and there are some things about her personal life that I don't know. So why don't you ask her?"

And in my mind, I offered a silent apology to Diane. Sorry, kid, sometimes thinking fast on my feet isn't my best skill.

With that, Roger finished off his beer and said, "Well, I just might ask her. Listen, I gotta go, Lewis. I got two more weeks in this exchange program, and I'm sure I'll be running into you later."

He left by going back through the sliding-glass doors, leaving me alone at the table. As I finished my ice water, I wondered if I had been looking at the next chief of police for Tyler, New Hampshire. It certainly seemed likely.

Then the waitress with the long black hair and denim miniskirt dropped off our check. I looked to see if Roger had left any money, and all I saw was his dirty plate, cold french fries, rolls and some napkins.

About then I smiled and thought he'd fit right in at the Tyler police department, and he'd know how to handle the town manager and the three selectmen who ran this town.

On my way back to my Rover I took a stroll along the Strip, just to work off some of the dinner and to see the sights. It was about 7 P.M., and the day was still well lit. Many of the people walking along the crowded sidewalk were still wearing their bathing suits, though some of the women had slipped on shorts for the sake of whatever modesty was alive in these times. At the center of the Strip is the Beach Palace, an old two-story wooden building that stretches over two blocks and contains the Palace Ballroom, which offers concerts and comedy shows during the summer, along with the annual Miss Tyler Beach beauty pageant. Around the Beach Palace are video arcades, jewelry stores, T-shirt emporiums, bars, restaurants and fried-dough and popcorn stands.

Most of the people walking along the Strip seemed to be families, and there were a lot of wide-eyed kids eating ice-cream cones and holding hands. Even with the trash in the gutters and the idiot electronic sounds coming from the arcades and the dusting of beach sand that got into everything, the people on Tyler Beach this night seemed to be at peace with each other. An illusion, I'm sure, but I was content.

I rounded a corner and headed for the police station, and one of those special moments just reared up and tickled at my mind. A group of laughing kids were walking up the sidewalk, talking about the night ahead. A Jaguar XJ-12 rumbled down the street, two young women in the front seats, with long black hair and wearing identical dark sunglasses. Out on the horizon, past the flat marshlands and the woods that hid Route 1, the sun was easing its way down, giving everything out there a pinkish glow. Birds rose and dove out on the marsh, and even the one-story police station looked magical.

And at that fleeting moment, it felt good to be alive, and I remembered, as I always do, my own debts, my own obligations. Before reaching my Range Rover, I went to an ATM machine on the street corner, withdrew two hundred dollars, and decided I had something to do before going home.

About an hour later, after spending most of the previous time at a Market Basket supermarket, I drove down a side street off Route 286 in Falconer, Tyler's poorer cousin to the south, and pulled into the small parking lot of a church. The building was white and had a little steeple, and it belonged to a small fundamentalist group that didn't have very many members in this part of the state. But in its basement it had something special for the people of Tyler, Falconer, Tyler Falls and the other towns in this part of Wentworth County, and that's where I was headed this summer evening.

It was still light, though fast approaching dusk, as I parked at the rear basement entrance to the church. I had planned on just leaving the boxes of groceries at the rear door, knowing that people started rolling in about that time, but a man was there to meet me as I got out, and I felt the faint flush of self-consciousness as he shook my hand.

"Henry Larson," he announced. "I'm the minister here, and we do appreciate your donation, ah, Mr. . . . ."

"Cole," I said, opening up the rear tailgate. "Lewis Cole, of Tyler."

The Reverend Larson was about my age but slimmer. He had on gray polyester pants, black dress shoes and a white short-sleeved shirt, and had two pens clipped in his shirt pocket. He was nearly fully bald and his black hair along the sides of his head was closely trimmed. He was quiet but smiling as we worked, and in his eyes you saw an utter belief and conviction about what he was doing and about the basic goodness that was out there. It was a feeling that I envied him for having.

He helped me carry the boxes of groceries to a kitchen area in the basement, which was already beginning to fill up. Long tables with light pink paper tablecloths were lined up on the floor of the basement hall, and about twenty or so people were standing in a line where the evening meal was being served, cafeteria style. The people were all of ages, weights and heights, and they said not one word as they waited to be served. The Chambers of Commerce in this part of the state may hate to admit it, but we do have our poor, our homeless and those people along the edges who just can't make it. Along the walls were homemade banners consisting of cloth and cutout letters that contained Bible verses, but it didn't seem as if the people in the line were interested in reading them just then. Maybe later, when a more direct hunger was taken care of.

After we had packed the boxes away, the good reverend again shook my hand and said, "We're going to have a service here in a while, if you'd like to join us."

I smiled and gave him the most polite shake of my head that I could, and said, "I have other commitments, but thanks for the offer."

"Well, if you can't do that, Mr. Cole, then I do insist you sign our Memory Gift book," he said, and from a desk in the kitchen area he took out a brown, leather-bound book. It had cream-colored pages and he opened it up for me and said, "We ask that people who give us donations at least sign this book, and maybe note in whose memory the donation was made."

I took the book and placed it on a stainless-steel counter. The pages were set in ledger style, and the reverend had opened up the book to a blank page. "What for?" I asked.

He smiled, ever confident, ever unshakable in his faith and belief. "Each service we hold up this book and give prayers for all of the names contained within it. Each and every service, Mr. Cole. Without you and these benefactors, we wouldn't be able to do our work."

Something about what he said made sense, so I took out a pen and under "Name and Address" wrote, "Lewis Cole, Tyler, N.H.," and in the "Remarks" section, I wrote, "In memory of Trent, Carl, Cissy, and the others."

No doubt I was breaking the law and a solemn agreement in writing down those three names, but so what. I was in a church. That was considered a sanctuary in most quarters and I would leave it at that, and would leave my fear in this building.

And I would also leave out the name of George Walker. He would have to seek salvation from somebody else.

When I got home I decided I had been cold turkey for long enough and so I uncapped a Molson Golden Ale while calling Felix Tinios. The phone rang twice and all I got was Felix's answering machine—which had a charming message: "At the tone leave a message"—and so I did. I took a sip from the beer and unlocked the sliding-glass doors, removed the broomstick from the runner and went outside to the deck. Night was coming along just nicely, and out on the waters of the Atlantic, I noted the lights of the fishing boats, returning hesitantly to these shores after the *Petro Star* had fouled the waters with its cargo of alien oil. The scientists and oceanographers had said that in a while the ocean in this part of the world would recover, but it made one wonder at how many hits a system like this could take before just rolling over and giving up.

The *Petro Star*. I took a long swallow of the Molson and almost winced at how cold it was, traveling down my throat. That was a project I had ignored for a while, and one that was going to have to be left alone for a few more days. Something else was tickling my fancy, and I wanted to play with it, even though it meant that the nameless one, the man who had sent the *Petro Star* out, would go on unheeded and unfrightened, content that he was far away from his handiwork.

Still, I had patience. Most of the time. He and I would meet somehow, of that I was sure.

Out on the far horizon, a dot of light went by, moving fast, and along with the sound of the helicopter engine made me want to rush inside, but instead I stayed there, waiting, not allowing the old ghosts to chase me away, and in a few minutes the sound was gone.

About ten minutes later I was in my deck chair, feet up on the railing and halfway through with my beer, remembering that I had a damn column to write, when the phone rang. I went back inside, picked up the receiver and Felix Tinios said, "You called?"

"That I did," I said, looking at the bottle of Molson's in the inside light. It was almost empty and I decided it would be my solitary beer for the evening. "I've been thinking a bit about our last chat, and the request you made, about seeking my help."

He breathed some and said, "That so?"

"Yeah. You still looking for my calming influence, and for that 10 percent figure you quoted?"

"That's still there, Lewis. If you want it."

"I think I do, Felix. I really do."

"Well," he said, and there was a pause and he said again, "Well, Lewis, and don't take any offense, but I want to make sure that you're taking my advice. I don't need you boozy and slow. I need you on target and sharp."

There was another light out on the horizon, but it was too far away for any sound, and I was glad. I said, "Your safe house contains three Winslow Homers that were stolen from the Scribner Museum five years ago, and it's in Maine," and I hung up the phone. Then I went back outside, to see which stars would appear first in the evening sky.

After another five minutes and a long phone ringing session had passed, I went back inside and answered the phone when it rang again, and Felix said calmly, "That was a hell of a demonstration, Lewis. I'm just glad that I'm calling you on a pay phone. And I take back everything I said about you not being sharp."

"Forgiven and forgotten, Felix."

Then his voice lowered. "How the hell did you figure the second part out?"

"Meet me tomorrow at ten. Then we'll talk. And, Felix, I want to see the paintings."

He laughed. "After what you just did to my heart rate, you deserve it."

"Fine."

We talked a bit more, and after I hung up, I washed out the beer bottle and put it in the green recycling bin. I then returned to the deck and sat there, just watching the waves roll in and crash against my cove, and every now and then catching the faint whiff of petroleum, reminding me of other commitments, other promises.

Still, it was good to be moving again.

CHAPTER
NINE

The next day was Thursday and I waited for Felix in the sole parking garage in Porter, the northernmost community in Wentworth County and New Hampshire's biggest port. The famous shipyard here—which once built a ship for John Paul Jones—is nearly two hundred years old, and the town's port has driven a lot of the state's prosperity. Porter's history has run the gamut from the luxurious mansions of its merchants to the whorehouses which once serviced the various naval vessels which docked there. It's still a working port, with salt piles and scrap metal and the occasional tanker, such as the *Petro Star*.

Porter is now a popular tourist attraction because of its history and the fine Federalist homes and brick buildings which are crowded on the narrow streets. Through the foresight and hard work of some of the residents in the early 1960s, a lot of Porter's history was preserved and many of the city's older homes were saved from being torn down for parking lots or for those hideous concrete office buildings that look like they belong in a Tomorrowland at a Disney World. These spirited residents were welcomed with open arms by their fellow townspeople and businessmen in Porter, and their work was praised to the skies in the local newspapers during those controversial years. Right?

Of course not. They were criticized, yelled at and sued by everyone who thought they were standing in the way of progress. Some of them actually had to move out of state to escape the hate mail, and it took years before their work was appreciated. To this day that part of Porter's history isn't much talked about.

Still, their victories lived on. The parking garage I was in, for example, was built on a lot that once held a supermarket that had an enormous plastic revolving milk bottle at its entrance. The garage wasn't much of an improvement but it would do. This day it was practically full, and the main reason was the convenience of being downtown and the ridiculous price: twenty-five cents per hour, which would get you a few minutes or a few seconds of parking in Boston or New York. A few minutes earlier a station wagon with Connecticut plates had pulled in and the overweight driver, with sunglasses perched above his shiny forehead, said to his blue-haired wife, "Did you see that? Did you see how much they're charging? Quick, you gotta get a picture of me in front of the rate sign. They'll never believe this back home."

A few minutes after they had left, Felix Tinios rolled up, and I got my first surprise of the day. Just a few days ago Felix's red Mercedes-Benz convertible was parked near my house, but on this day he was driving a blue Ford Taurus. I took a look at the rear bumper and saw a square inch or two of sticky adhesive centered on the bumper. I got in and he deftly paid the parking attendant a quarter for the privilege of coming in to pick me up, and in a minute or two, we were in traffic.

"I guess you know in your gut when something's serious, but when you see the proof, then it really becomes real," I said.

"What do you mean?" Felix asked. He had on madras shorts and a white polo shirt and wraparound Italian sunglasses. His thick forearms were dark and were covered with fine black hair, and he had a watch on one wrist and a gold bracelet on another. "The day you leave behind your Mercedes-Benz and take a rental car for a drive, then I know it's serious."

He glanced over at me and smiled as we sailed through a yellow light. "Maybe I borrowed it from one of my many friends."

I pushed the electric switch that lowered the window and felt the breeze wash over me, and I said, "First of all, it's too clean. But it's the rear bumper that says it all. You scraped off the rental sticker after you got the car. You been driving rentals for long?"

"Here and there, ever since the postcards and the phone calls started. I didn't want to make things too easy for them."

We left the downtown of Porter and got onto a traffic circle that was the junction of I-95, Route 4, Route 1 and Route 1A. We spent several minutes going around the circle, and I didn't insult Felix by asking him if he was sure we weren't being followed. I settled down in my seat, feeling a queasy sort of nervousness about what I was getting into, but also feeling a quiet triumph that at least I wasn't just getting into another six-pack of beer.

Then Felix made a violent turn and speeded up the Taurus as we shot off an exit and got onto Route 1, heading into Maine. We drove through a strip that had gasoline stations, restaurants for truckers, an auto parts store, and two adult bookstores—one on either side of the highway, how convenient—and then we passed a park that had a submarine out of water, the USS *Albacore*. It was an experimental submarine, built in the teardrop design, and on its black sail were painted its numbers in white: 569. The same yahoos who didn't like the renewal of Porter thirty years earlier were also against hauling a submarine up on land for a museum, and thankfully the yahoos were batting zero. It was a hell of a place, and I had gone through the submarine twice, amazed that men had actually worked in such tight quarters, hundreds of feet beneath the ocean.

We crossed over a drawbridge that spanned the Piscassic

River. I turned to the right and looked down at the brick buildings of Porter's waterfront, a scrap-metal pile near the state pier and the cranes and sleek black shapes that were on the other side of the harbor, at the famous Porter Naval Shipyard. It's the oldest naval shipyard in the country, and it's built vessels from wooden sailing ships to nuclear-powered submarines, and it also built the *Albacore*.

As the Taurus's wheels touched the soil of the Pine Tree State, Felix said, "All right, I can give you the fact that you learned about the Winslow Homers by just doing some basic research. Jesus, I practically spelled it out for you, Lewis, saying it was stolen five years ago and it made a big fuss at the time. But how in hell did you find out the safe house was in Maine?"

A blue-and-white sign said "WELCOME TO MAINE. THE WAY LIFE SHOULD BE," which seemed to me a fairly presumptuous slogan. We passed through Kittery and went past a series of discount malls and outlet shops selling everything from Brooks Brothers suits to Black & Decker tools.

I said, "I didn't find out."

"You didn't?"

"Nope. I guessed."

He looked over at me and I wished his sunglasses were off. I wanted to see the look on his face. He said, "You can go on, if you'd like."

I shrugged. "You said that the valuables were taken from this state five years ago. All right, that tells me they're now out of state. Then you said you went 'up there' to check on the safe house, and that you did that in an afternoon. That means you didn't travel to Quebec or New Brunswick. So you went to Maine. Where we are now, right?"

He shook his head. "So right."

The road was now two-lane, and at about seven or so miles from Porter, we entered the town of York. Like my home state, Maine has an odd relationship with the outside world. It's known for its fishermen and "Down East" lore and quiet, biting humor, but that's only the coastal part of the state, the part that makes the

TV shows, movies and Sunday newspaper travel supplements. Travel inland from the coast and you'll find great tracts of wooded wilderness, owned by paper mills and wood-pulp companies, and small towns struggling with their budget from month to month, and proud poor people who've never eaten a lobster in their life.

At the intersection for Route 1A, Felix made a right and we entered York, going past the Civil War monument in the center of town. The homes were small and set back, and there were a few shops for the tourist crowd. We drove past the library, the Old York Historical Society, a Congregational church and the town hall. Most of the homes were old colonials or Federalists, and most of those buildings were painted the same as the church and the town hall: white.

Felix said, "Didn't those early settlers ever hear of another color besides white?"

"Maybe they wanted to symbolize purity. You know anything about purity?"

He just laughed and then pulled into the empty parking lot of a Catholic church, St. Christopher by the Sea. It was angular-shaped, built to look like a ship. I looked over at Felix in disbelief and he said, "Who ever bothers cars parked at a church?"

The church was on a small road called Barrell Lane—I'm not sure why it has an extra "l" in its name—and our walk took only a few minutes, as we headed down to the harbor. We went through a small residential area on a hill near Barrell Lane that was clustered with a lot of pine and oak trees. Most of the homes were built away from the main road, off the small lane, which was called Landing Lane. Felix and I said not one word to each other and then he turned and went into a vacant lot, pushing through some brambles and thorns. They didn't seem to bother him, even though he was wearing shorts, and I followed him into the overgrowth. The land was dry and there was the whirring sound of crickets. I knew it would seem funny to anyone watching us, two grown men thrashing through the underbrush in a small Maine town. But Felix wasn't laughing and I didn't feel particularly amused either. We walked for a couple of minutes and then Felix hunched down and I joined him. The ground had cleared away some and we were near the base of a birch tree.

Before us was a dirt driveway that led up a slight incline and curved around before a two-story house. It was a large Cape, with dormered windows on the second floor and with black shingles. It had white vinyl siding and to the rear I could make out an addition, built out toward the harbor. The shades on the front windows were drawn and there was a tiny front yard, fenced in by split-wood railings. There was a paved area for a vehicle to the right but no garage. It was quiet. I could hear Felix breathing and I said, "So, this is it?"

He nodded, took off his sunglasses and squinted some. A trickle of sweat was running down a smooth cheek and he said, "I never want anyone seeing me enter the driveway and walk down, so this is why I go this way."

"And here I thought you were just trying to get back to nature."

Felix folded up his sunglasses and slipped them into his shorts as he stood up, smiling. "My idea of nature is an outdoor barbecue."

I followed him as he went onto the dirt driveway and then up the flagstone path to the front door. As we got nearer, I said, "Doesn't look like much of a safe house. Too much growth and trees around for people to hide. Would hate to defend a place like this."

Felix said, "Just blending in, my friend. Just blending in. This is a place to lie low and wait for the shooting or shouting to stop. Nothing fancy or loud. Just a place to keep clean and to wait."

"Ever been used?"

"Not for what it's been designed for," he said, unlocking the front door. "And as you've figured out, it's now being used as a storage center."

Inside the house there was a kitchen area to the left and a dining room set to the right. The air was musty and smelled of a harsh cleaner. The light seemed strange, as if it were coming in through some dirty gauze filter. Something seemed wrong to me, right away, and it took a moment to figure it out: the kitchen, the counters and the metal dining room set looked like something out of a 1969 Sears catalogue. There were bright pastel colors and funky little daisy flowers painted on the refrigerator, and there was a lot of stainless steel along the counters. There was a wainscoting along the walls that seemed to be made of fake knotty pine and the floor was yellow linoleum, the type that used to come in big rolls. The house felt like a time capsule, or a "model home" that had never been inhabited. It was clean and unscratched and perfectly preserved, and it seemed spooky, like we were walking into a crypt or a tomb.

Felix had moved ahead of me, and I went out to an open area that split off to the left and to the right, to closed doors and a side stairway, leading upstairs. "Bedrooms," Felix said. "Never used."

There was a railing before us and a short set of stairs that led down to a lower living room. Two brown vinyl couches flanked a glass-topped coffee table, and there were two easy chairs clustered around a Zenith television set in the far corner. It looked like a large black-and-white set, and there were a handful of magazines on top of it, next to an old rotary-dial telephone. The floor lamps looked like set decorations from a made-for-television science fiction movie from 1970. We went downstairs and the floor had wall-to-wall white carpeting that had faded to something that looked like yellowed ivory. I went to the television and looked at the magazines. The top one was a faded 1971 issue of *Cosmopolitan*, the chatty magazine that would collapse if italics were ever outlawed. The far wall was floor-to-ceiling sliding-glass doors whose view was hidden by a dark brown curtain, and the near wall had a large picture window that looked out to an overgrowth of brush. To my left was a door that led down to a cellar, and I closed the door after opening it. It seemed too dark to go down the stairs.

There were two closets near the television set and I opened one and smelled a lot of mothballs and counted three wire hangers clumped together in one corner. The other closet was a bit more cluttered, with a couple of rakes and a shovel, some crumpled-up paper bags and an open toolbox.

Felix said, "Done with your snooping?"

"It's called satisfying one's curiosity. Where are they, Felix?"

"Over here," he said, taking the key ring again in his hand. He undid a lock to the sliding-glass door and it moved slowly to the right. The odd feeling of being in a bad place tickled at me again, and I saw that the curtains were on the other side of the glass door, so that they were always blocking what was there. Felix grasped the curtains and tugged them open, and I felt my chest move and it surprised me, since for a few moments I had forgotten to breathe.

"There," he said, satisfied with himself, and I walked through the open door.

The paintings were on a wooden frame against the far wall, hanging crookedly but still bright and alive. In their position they partially covered two windows, but since the light blue curtains on those windows were closed, it didn't make any difference. This floor was hardwood and there were three lawn chairs, and part of me observed "sunroom" as I walked closer. There on the left was *Fog Warning*, with the solitary fisherman, hard at work in his dory, heading for the far-off sanctuary of his schooner. Then there was *Eight Bells*, the two sailors on deck, huddled together like sodden animals, having survived a terrible ordeal, their tools and instruments of civilization trembling in their cold hands. And then *The Gulf Stream*, the black sailor looking off in the distance, exhausted, either not seeing or not wanting to see the sharks beneath him, and it seemed as if the eyes of the broaching shark were looking straight at me.

"My God," I said. Felix started to say something and I held up my hand to shut him up. I took another step forward, looking more closely at the canvases and the heavy paint, trying to think through how odd it was that these paintings were created over a hundred years ago up the coast at Prout's Neck, and how they had traveled far and had been looked at by hundreds of thousands of people. Then they had been ripped away and hidden and here they were, for five years, gathering dust in this empty house, far away from home and the place they were created, only yards away from the ocean and yet a million miles away from anyplace their creator had hoped for. Winslow Homer. He had some imagination back then, painting alone at Prout's Neck, but I doubted that even he would have thought that his work would have ended up in York in the home of a criminal.

Felix stood next to me and, not turning, I said, "How did they get here, Felix?"

"I don't have answers, but I have guesses."

"Those'll do," and I thought, my God, after all these years, how sharp and clear those colors are, as if they had been touched upon the canvas just a week or so ago.

He said, "A lot of times, guys go out on their own. There's always a competition, always jockeying for position. Let's say that someone wants to make an impression on his superiors. So he plans and makes the hit, a big hit, one that gets in all the news. The paintings are stolen and they get stashed here, and then the word gets up to someone that somebody who works for him was involved in one of the biggest crimes of the decade. What do you think this superior's reaction's gonna be?"

I rubbed at my chin, still staring at the shark's eyes in *The Gulf Stream*. "Unless he's an art aficionado, he'll probably be horrified. Every State Police unit in New England, the FBI, Treasury and Customs are all running around the landscape, trying to find out who stole the paintings. And it's his guys. A lot of unexpected heat."

Felix nodded. "Horrified's a good word. A lot of unexpected heat that he doesn't need, especially if he's up to his ears in something else that's delicate. So—in any event, the end result is the same. Again, my guess. The higher-up can't believe that guys who worked for him actually pulled a stunt like this and they all go for rides. Maybe there's a foul-up. Someone doesn't say the right word and all of them disappear without any one of them saying where the paintings are. They end up here and peace breaks out and for five years they're forgotten."

"Until this summer," I said.

"Until this summer," he agreed. Felix crossed his arms and stepped forward, cocking his head, as if he were a graduate art student and was trying to make an interpretation or something of Homer's brushstrokes. "Somehow, somebody got the word that these paintings were in a safe house that belonged to Jimmy Corelli. Maybe only a couple of people besides myself know the location of this particular safe house."

Felix turned to me and there was not much warmth in his smile. "In this type of occupation, it's easy to lose track of people. So. Here I am, Lewis, with stolen artwork that's worth millions of dollars, and some bad guys want it back. Nameless wonders that leave messages on my answering machine and send me nasty notes."

I stepped closer to look at the paintings and for a moment I felt the sense of awe and peace that Justin Dix had talked about back at the Scribner Museum. It seemed amazing that so much could be expressed with just a piece of canvas and some oils, and that anyone could have such talent. So much beauty, terror and history, all speaking silently to whoever was standing before them. I murmured something and Felix said sharply, "What did you say?"

"I said you could give them back."

"Not a good joke."

"True, if I was joking, but I wasn't joking, Felix." I took another step and looked at the brushstrokes, trying to think of the steady nerves and eyes that could make such shapes. "We could leave here and make a phone call to the Maine State Police, and in a half hour, they'd be safe and out of this house. Your nameless wonders would—"

Felix raised his voice and said, "My nameless wonders would stop playing games with me. They would be plenty mad and would just wait for the right time to put a couple of copper-jacketed slugs into my skull. Not a good joke, not even a good comment."

"I thought you were confident in your skills?" I said.

"Confident, yes," he said, looking angry. "But not suicidal. Look, Lewis, I don't want to play the heavy here but we have an agreement. You're not thinking of—"

It was my turn to interrupt him. "No, I'm not going to call the cops when I get back to Tyler. It was just a thought, Felix. You made a good point. I'm still aboard."

That seemed to relax him and then I swallowed, thinking of what I had just done. Felix Tinios. His background, being raised in Boston's North End, and then ending up living in North Tyler as a "security consultant." One who had a dark and long history, and who was competent with almost every type of weapon. And in a few short words I had threatened something that he thought was his, something extraordinarily valuable.

Nice going, Cole.

It must have been those three paintings. Something about them had just reached in and seized me.

I said, "What now?"

Felix rubbed his hands and said, "I pass along a message to the people who are sending me hate mail. Tell them that I want a face-to-face. We'll begin the negotiations, and hopefully, in a week or two, this'll all be behind us, and the two of us will have significantly fatter bank accounts. Sound like an approach?"

"It does," I said, and I followed him as we went back to the living room, not bothering to say that I had my own approach, and that those three paintings had just decided that choice for me. I would not do anything to hurt or threaten Felix, and in doing so, I would follow his lead and leave the paintings be.

But those promises were for Felix only. They weren't for his correspondents.

Once they had the Winslow Homers, well, I'd see what I could do.

Outside it was still quite warm.

L
ater in the day we had lunch at the Weathervane Restaurant
on Route 1 in Kittery, which is directly across the street from
the Kittery Trading Post, a large sporting goods and outdoor
store that likes to pretend there's no such place as L. L. Bean. For
lunch I had a lobster roll and Felix had fried squid, and he offered
me a couple of chunks, which I politely refused. I make it a rule
never to eat any type of seafood that I don't feel comfortable in
picking up when it's alive. Felix had a beer and I joined him, since
he was driving and I was feeling fairly good about myself, about
taking part in something, about getting out of the house. Felix
was looking somewhat pensive as he held his beer bottle in one
hand. Around us were full tables of tourists, coming to this part
of Maine for the two miles' worth of outlet shops along Route 1.
It was loud and I'm sure no one could hear what we were saying.

I said, "What's the point, Felix?"

He turned. "Hunh? What did you say?"

"I said, what's the point? You're skimming along the edge of
something quite dangerous here. You know that. Do you really
believe that these people are going to happily give you large sums
of money for the safe house's location, and then leave you alone?
That's a hell of a risk, even for you."

Felix looked around and leaned over the polished wood of
the table. "What makes you think I have a choice?"

"You don't?"

He shook his head and said, "Look at what I do for a living,
Lewis, what brings in my income. A lot of that is based on fear
and respect. I roll over and play wedding-night virgin for these
guys, give up the safe house without a fuss, and the word gets
around, how long do you think I can still keep on working?"

"I get the point," I said. I scraped at the bottle's label with
my thumb. "Do you think these nameless wonders are connected
with your past? Are they from Boston?"

A waitress with short blond hair and a decade or so older
than me walked by, carrying a full tray of fried food and three
lobsters, and I heard her murmur, "Just another hour, Lord, let
my feet go for another hour."

Felix stared at his own bottle. "There's some sort of connection with my past, I'm sure. But again, it's not something I can poke around and ask questions about. Don't want to make waves, Lewis. I don't want any future employers to think I'm one to welcome trouble. They like things quiet and discreet. Dealing with famous stolen art doesn't exactly meet that requirement."

"So. Job security. That's what's driving you."

He smiled a bit, and I saw that his five o'clock shadow was a few hours early. "And other security, too."

"Oh?" I said, and then it came to me. "Sorry. Dumb move on my part. I suppose in your line of work there's not much of a pension plan."

"Or a health plan. Or much of anything else, Lewis. One of these days I might get unlucky. Well, that's part of what I do. But there's a variety of unlucky out there. One is the type that ends you up in a lonely grave somewhere, with no visitors on your birthday. Another is the one that concerns me the most—maybe ending up in a wheelchair, or trying to get by on a couple of shattered kneecaps, and with a bank account that's shrinking every month and Social Security thirty or so years away. So I'm investing in my future. No one else will."

At that moment I felt as though I knew more about Felix Tinios than at any other time. Usually he's all finely tailored clothes and correct wines in his kitchen at home and gruff seriousness about what he does for work, but sitting here in this seafood restaurant with paper plates and plastic forks and crumpled napkins before him, I thought I had caught a glimpse of what little voices were whispering inside of him.

I guess we had kept silent for too long and he was concerned about what I was thinking, for he put his empty beer bottle down and said, "Let's get back to Porter, so you can get your butt home. And I'll let you know the moment I hear anything from my nameless wonders."

"I'll be there," I said, and followed him outside into the warm afternoon.

Later that night I was on the back deck of my house, having safely made it home, but also feeling sour. Earlier in the afternoon I had spent a couple of hours in front of my Apple Macintosh Plus, trying to write my monthly column for *Shoreline*. Tomorrow was Friday and my deadline for the issue which was currently being put together—February—and all I had to show for my two hours of work was an empty file folder in my computer marked FEBCOLUMN. I had snuck into the PETROSTAR file folder a couple of times but had gotten depressed over the scanty information that was being stored there. There was probably a real column or even a magazine-length piece in that file, but not for some time. I had to find the man's name, the man who gave the orders. Yet that wasn't troubling me as much as it should. Something else was.

Tomorrow, for the first time ever, I was going to miss a deadline for my magazine. I suppose in the grand scheme of things it didn't mean that much, especially since I had an extremely generous work arrangement with the editor of *Shoreline*, one Seamus Anthony Holbrook, a retired admiral in the U.S. Navy. A couple of years ago, feeling light on my feet and with another scar healing on my side, I had visited him at his office in Boston, in an old brick building near the soiled waters of Boston Harbor. I had just terminated my employment with the Department of Defense, and they were fulfilling the terms of our agreement by getting me a job as a columnist for *Shoreline*. Holbrook—who had leathery skin and not much white hair and looked as if he had spent his Navy years aboard a clipper—got to the point: "You supply a column each month, subject of your choosing. If it's crap, we either don't run it or we rewrite it and run it under your name."

This time, I couldn't even supply them with crap. Holbrook probably wouldn't care that much that I missed my deadline. He was just following orders in allowing me to work for *Shoreline*, and I would never be fired. But I didn't like the idea of a column appearing with my name and someone else's words.

Yet short of having a lightning bolt of inspiration poke me in the nether regions and spending the night writing, there wasn't much I could do about it.

I picked up the glass of ice water and took a long swallow, hoping it would do something good to counteract all of the fat I had been eating that day. It was low tide and the waves were farther off, and I looked over at the grassy mounds and trees of what was once the Samson Point Coast Artillery Station. I was lucky to be here, for hardly any one ever came to this house to bother me. The south end of the artillery station—which was now part of a state wildlife reserve—had been closed off to tourists and walkers since the discovery of toxic waste in some of the old bunkers. New Hampshire's financial condition being what it always is—about five minutes away from bankruptcy—I was sure that toxic dump wouldn't be cleaned up in the near future. So my privacy was protected through someone else's pollution. What a deal.

I left the deck and went upstairs to my bedroom. There's another deck that leads off to the south wall of the house and which is much smaller than the first-floor deck. I undid the window and screen and walked outside, thinking maybe that I would take out my telescope, but there were clouds rolling in, and it didn't look good.

Instead I looked to the south, to Weymouth's Point and the beach where that mutilated diver had washed ashore only a few days ago. I still remembered the surprise on Diane Woods's face when I told her I had no interest in doing a column—which would never appear—about the type of people who could kill and mutilate a man like that poor diver. A job I had worked on at the beginning of the summer had led me down some dark paths and had come quite close to causing me serious harm, and I wasn't in the mood to go walking alone again anytime soon. There was the matter with Felix, but that was different. I wasn't by myself.

The diver, though. I should give Diane a call, to see if anything new had been learned, and to find out at least if the diver was now resting in a grave somewhere, a quiet place where he belonged.

Poor Diane. She was probably still fending off the advances of Roger Krohn, and was probably also wondering how she could work for him if he did become the new police chief of Tyler.

I turned and was going back into my bedroom when I caught a quick movement, one that made me think someone was there, and I was going to whisper "Paula?" until I saw that I had been fooled by the gathering dusk and my own reflection in a wall mirror. I leaned my back against the railing of the deck and thought of that evening, back in June, when Paula Quinn had been here and had spent the night.

It seemed so long ago. From the time I had met her Paula had given me messages in a variety of languages, telling me that she was interested, and I had given her my own: not now, I'm still working things through. But then there was June and there had been some blood spilled and I was feeling a terrible urge to prove something, and Paula had come here willingly and for a few brief and sweaty hours it had been wonderful indeed.

Until that moment early in the morning, when she was sleeping in my bed and I had stepped out onto this very deck and had discovered that damnable lump on my side. I had been angry and upset and some sharp words were given back and forth to Paula, when I wouldn't—or couldn't—tell her what was going on. And now I was here and she was in her apartment in Tyler. I wondered if she was thinking about me.

I stood there on the deck for a while, just looking into my empty bedroom, and then I decided on two things: one, brooding wasn't going to solve anything, so I was going downstairs and read two or three back issues of *Smithsonian*.

And second, I wasn't going to wait around, breathlessly anticipating Felix's phone call. I was going to do a little work on my own tomorrow.

I stepped back into the room, closed the screen door, and made my way through the evening twilight with no problem, heading for the lights downstairs.

CHAPTER

TEN

As I was sleeping Thursday night and into Friday morning, the clouds had thickened, for it was raining heavily by the time I got up. It was still fairly warm and so I enjoyed standing in front of my sliding-glass doors on the first floor, wearing nothing but a pair of shorts, looking out at the rain falling against the gray waves, a cup of tea in my hand. It made me feel comfortable, secure and also a bit slow. Something about rainy days dials down my energy level, and I hadn't done much since getting up an hour earlier. I had called Felix and had left a message on his machine, telling him I would be gone for the day, and I had also received a call from Diane Woods, who was looking for a quick lunch date. Felix wasn't home, and hadn't been home for quite a while, and I guessed that in addition to renting a car, he was also renting a room or apartment as he was working his way through the maze of dealing with his "nameless wonders."

Diane seemed glad to talk to me, and I sensed that something was bothering her. Not that she was scared or anything, but just that she wanted to talk and couldn't do it over the phone from a police station. So the date was made, and in the space of a few minutes I had completed two phone calls. It had been a slightly productive morning, even though in a few hours, Seamus Anthony Holbrook would realize that I hadn't completed my monthly column and he might have some nasty questions about how I defined "productivity." I had sent him E-mail through my computer and modem, asking for the first time ever for a deadline extension.

There was even still time to make another call, to see how Paula Quinn was doing.

I thought about that as I stood there, watching the pattern of the rain on the glass of the sliding doors, hearing the muted rush of the Atlantic Ocean coming my way.

Lunch with Diane was quick. It was at the Whale's Song, a restaurant in the Tyler Beach Palace complex, which was within quick walking distance from the Tyler police station. The rain was still coming down, and as we walked up D Street, heading for the Whale's Song, I noticed a lot of older men and women standing in the doors of the shops and restaurants, looking up at the clouds. Owners, I thought, business owners who were probably cursing the weather gods for making it rain on a Friday before a busy weekend. The profit margin for most businesses at the beach was always thin, and the *Petro Star* disaster had taken a razor blade to even that slim margin. Another rainy day or two could mean bankruptcy filings in the fall, or if the bitter taste of desperation was even stronger, perhaps a fire of "suspicious origin."

We sat in a rear booth that offered some privacy, and after a bowl of chowder and tall glasses of iced tea for both of us, Diane leaned back in the booth and said, "It's been one of those weeks." Today she had on a light blue rain jacket over a white polo shirt that said "Tyler Police Softball" in red script over her left breast. Obviously she wasn't on undercover duty this week. The hood was thrown back and some of the strands of her brown hair were wet and clinging together.

"Who's on your hit list for getting you down?" I asked.

"Aah," she said, "the usual. The diver case is going nowhere. Almost a week after he washed up, you'd think someone would have reported him missing. Or a rental shop would have noticed their gear had never come back. Or even the news coverage would have triggered someone's memory, somebody's thoughts. But it's been too quiet, Lewis."

"Makes you wonder how this guy fell through the cracks," I said.

"Oh, I've been wondering about that, too, along with the State Police and the Attorney General's office. You look at the fact that this guy has been missing at least a week, and when he shows up, missing the parts of his body that can help identify him, that tells you the type of people involved. So it also makes me think that this guy's hands were dirty."

"I'm sure there's a dreadful joke there about a guy's hands being both missing and dirty, but I'm not going to touch it."

She wrinkled her nose at me. "Thanks for small favors. You know, I'm of a mind to do one of two things. One is to really press hard on this case, maybe use some of Roger Krohn's contacts in the Mass. State Police. Or even talk to your pal Felix Tinios, for whatever amusement that may bring."

A teenage waitress with jangling bracelets and a look that said she couldn't care how much of a tip we left came by and dropped off the check. My hand was quicker than Diane's and to forestall her frown I said, "Expense account, Diane. Don't worry. So. Pressing hard is one of your options. What's the other?"

Her blue raincoat was big around the shoulders and she seemed to shrink into it a bit as she said, "It's been a long summer, and it certainly started off with a bang with that mess you were involved with in June."

"Don't remind me."

"As if you could forget. Or me. You know, in a few weeks it's going be Labor Day weekend and this summer is going to be over, and I'm taking a week off to go to Massachusetts. In those seven long, wonderful days, Lewis, I'm going forget I'm a cop, I'm going to forget what's on my desk, and I'm going to try to remember what it's like to share a bed with someone, both day and night."

"And while you're tussling with your companion and the sheets, you don't want to think about a diver with no head and hands."

"Exactly." She picked up her chowder spoon and tapped it a few times against the empty bowl. "That's even the feeling I'm getting from the state boys. It's obvious this guy was hit for a reason, and the fact that we're not getting any civilian calls tells us that he was connected. So we're not going to shed many tears for him."

"Wrapped up, then, in a week or two?"

Diane shrugged. "Unless something breaks. Which I doubt."

I left ten dollars on the bill and looked for our waitress. She was in the far corner, talking to a busboy whose long hair was up in a hairnet and who had an earring in his left ear. I motioned to him and he smiled and went back to talking with the young lady. I gave up and said, "What else is out there, Diane? Personal problems?"

She smiled and said, "Hardly. Here, look. Got some pictures back from our last break together. Actually got a weekend off, toward the end of June. And if I'm lucky, I might get another midweek break in a few more days."

Diane slid the photo envelope over and before opening it up I looked around. The nearest table was empty and the waitress was still chatting with the busboy who had novel grooming. I slid

out a few photographs. There were scenic shots of beaches and a
lighthouse, and there were a few of Diane and a couple more of
another young woman about Diane's age, strolling along a sidewalk near some shops. Both had summer dress on—bathing-suit
tops and shorts—and in one print, they were sitting at an outdoor
restaurant's round table, holding up drinks and laughing. Both
had sunglasses on, and Diane's companion—Kara Miles—had
her arm around her. In another print, they were still holding the
drinks and were kissing. Kara had short blond hair, with the sides
almost razored down, and she wore a multitude of earrings in
both ears.

"Kara's looking fine," I said. "You two were in Provincetown?"

Diane nodded. "The same. And that's where we'll be going
once Labor Day comes and goes and these tourists return to their
real lives."

I put the photos back into the envelope and slid them over to
her, and they disappeared into her raincoat. "It must be nice to
have a place like that to go to."

She shook her head. "Tell me about it. It's almost like a
refuge, a place where you can feel normal. You feel real light,
knowing that you don't have to carry around this pretense, this
goddam heavy mask."

"Not concerned about running into someone from your
hometown?"

Diane said, "Oh, just a bit, but what's the risk that someone
from a beach resort would travel three hours or so to go to another beach resort?" She looked around and leaned forward some
and said, "But I do have a problem, Lewis, on that same subject.
Personal matters. And I need your help."

"My help? On a personal matter?"

Her face seemed to flush and I couldn't remember the last
time I had seen Diane embarrassed. She cleared her throat and
said, "It's Roger Krohn. You know, the Mass. State Police detective?"

"Sure. The guy with the out-of-state grin who wants to become the next police chief of Tyler, if the current chief doesn't come back from his medical leave."

"Yeah, the same." She looked around again and said, her face screwed up in what looked to be a combination of dismay and resignation, "He asked me out."

Oh my. So the silly boy went ahead and did it. "He did what?"

Her face had some additional color in it. "He asked me out. Jesus, do you know how awful that was? I can't remember the last time a guy asked me out. We were going over some files and he asked me out on a date. Even said it was going to be a date, not a dinner between co-workers."

"So what did he say when you said no?"

The color in her face deepened. Something tickled at me and I wasn't sure if I should laugh or show some sympathy. "Diane, what did you tell him?"

Diane couldn't look at me and gazed down at the empty chowder bowl, as if she had discovered something fascinating there, and she said, "Well, I hemmed and hawed. I told him I couldn't, because I was seeing someone else."

"Oh. You don't mean you told him about Kara, do you?"

Even with her embarrassment, I sensed the beginnings of a smile about her face. "No, I didn't. I just didn't say anything. And then he asked me who I was seeing . . ."

"And?"

She looked around and then looked at me and shrugged. "I told him I was dating you, Lewis."

I didn't feel like laughing. "You told him what?"

"I told him we were dating, Lewis. Look, you don't know the type of lies and deceit that I have to go through on a weekly basis, and I didn't want to get him asking a lot of questions if I just stayed quiet. So I said that you and I were seeing each other."

"Marvelous," I said.

Then Diane said, "Wait. It gets better."

"It does?"

"Um," she said, and then giggled. "He was real apologetic. Said he felt bad about putting me on the spot like that, and he wanted to know if the two of us would go out on a double date with a friend of his who's coming up to the beach next week. So I said yes. Dinner for four at Roger's rental condo."

Oh my. "Diane . . ."

"Lewis, look. It'll be a hoot. One night, pretending to be my boy-toy. Just look at it as a favor. You know, I might be working for Roger Krohn in a couple of months, and this'll be a chance for me to get on his good side. And it'll also be a chance for you, knowing what kind of things you get involved with."

I was starting to feel a rush of the giggles and I was going to say something rude, but something else came up. "A favor?"

She nodded, biting her lower lip. "Yeah, a favor."

"All right." I looked over and saw that the waitress and the busboy were gone, and that we were practically alone in this part of the restaurant. It was getting late and I was resigned to leaving the ten-dollar bill on the check and walking out. A big tip for bad service, but not everything was perfect, even in beachfront restaurants.

I said with a smile, "For the pleasure of my company and a few public displays of affection in front of Roger Krohn and his friend, I'm going to need a favor or two from you. Some traces on a few people that are connected with a story I'm working on. I'll give you their names, DOBs and Social Security numbers, and you give me what's there in the computer files."

Diane stuck her tongue out. "Good thing I'm not asking you to sleep with me. God knows what you'd be demanding then."

I started to get out of the booth and Diane followed me, zippering up her raincoat. "We could always try it and see what happens."

She kicked at my shins and missed. "Losing your aim?" I said.

"I'll lose you," she said, and then—surprisingly—she slipped her arm through mine. "Here. Let's play pretend at least until we get back to the station."

I've always liked the touch of a woman, so I said sure. It was still raining fairly hard when we walked back to the station, but not once did her touch waver.

Two hours later on that rainy day Cassie Fuller of the Scribner Museum of Art was looking at me across from her desk, her chin resting on her folded hands, elbows on her clean desk. A fresh red rose was in the silver vase, right next to the miniature statue of Michelangelo's David. At her elbow her IBM clone hummed along, the screen blank. The rain was still coming down and it seemed las if the museum was doing a brisk business that afternoon. Justin Dix, the museum's security director, was out for the afternoon at a museum conference in Boston and Cassie gave me an inquiring gaze as I sat there, water beading down my green parka shell.

"What you're asking me to do is against office policy, against this museum's regulations," she said, one eyebrow raising up archly.

"I figured as much, before I asked you."

"Then why did you ask me?"

"Because you don't seem to be the type of woman who cares that much about policy and regulations."

She laughed, tossing back her thick mane of black hair with practiced ease. "That's so true. Justin's given up years ago trying to limit my lunch break to thirty minutes. We went round and round and he was full of threats and such, but he gave up."

"And why did he give up?"

She raised both of her eyebrows. "I wore him down, that's why. And I also run this office quite well."

"Were you working here when the Winslow Homers got stolen?"

"Mmm," she said, nodding her head, her chin still nestled in her red-fingernailed hands. "That I was, and only for a few months before the theft. There was another woman working here, an Ann Morse, and I was her assistant. I remember, after the paintings were stolen, having to answer the phone calls, day in and day out, from those idiots who call themselves reporters. Some of them actually asked me questions about art and the value of the paintings." She laughed at the memory.

"That was funny?"

She sat back some, waved at me with a hand. "Of course it was. I knew nothing about art or sculpture or paintings. I was fresh up from Massachusetts, and I saw this as an office job. Nothing else. It had phones and typewriters and a photocopier, and that's all I cared about. That and the paycheck."

"Did you know either of the two guards who were working that night?"

She shook her head. "No, not really. They worked at night, so I only saw them during museum events, like the Christmas party. In fact, the most I ever saw of them was when they were brought in for questioning a couple of times by Justin, the Manchester cops and the FBI."

"What was that like?"

"Oh, nothing much. Craig—the kid who was in college at the time—he looked so scared, like he couldn't believe this was happening to him. And Ben, well, Ben was a cop before he came here, and he looked awfully angry, like the paintings were stolen and he couldn't do anything about it."

"I imagine things calmed down after a while," I said.

"Yes, they did, and I began to like it here. Very quiet, very peaceful, and in a while I did begin to pick up on the art that was here. Even took a couple of night courses. Then, when Ann left a couple of years later, well, I moved up and saved the museum money because I did the job so well they didn't have to hire an assistant. I did it all myself."

"So you still like it here."

She shrugged. "I do, though now I find it can be boring sometimes. Especially around budget time. Which is why I like a little excitement here and there." She leaned forward and winked. "Like right now, for example."

Cassie got up from her desk and went over to the bank of black filing cabinets, unlocking one of them with a key. She was wearing a light green dress that fell below her knees but had a slit up both sides, and her stockings today were black. She rummaged around in the files for a few minutes, humming something, and as she searched, she lifted one foot up, and a gray high-heeled shoe dangled from her foot.

In a few minutes she relocked the filing cabinet, went over to a small copier, and after another five minutes or so, came back to her desk and handed me some papers, tucked in a tan folder.

"There you go, Mr. Cole," she said, eyes glittering with excitement at the naughty thing she was doing. "Information on the two guards who were working the night when the paintings were stolen, including their Social Security numbers and dates of birth. There are also some newspaper clippings, including the obituary of Ben Martin."

"Seems thorough," I said, taking the folder and slipping it under my shell parka.

"That's the only kind of job I do. What kind of job are you doing, Mr. Cole? Is this just a magazine article or an investigation?"

She was dancing too close to the truth for comfort, so I said, "Sometimes there's not much of a difference between the two."

"Hmmm," she said. "Did you really think that Justin Dix was going to give you this information?"

"Probably not, but maybe after a while."

"Why would he do that?"

I said, "Because of my charming personality."

That got another laugh out of her, and she said, "If that's true—and I have no reason to doubt it—then you're about ten steps ahead of the charming personality game from Justin Dix."

"What kind of boss is he?"

She thought about that for a moment, one hand gently tracing the stem of the rose at her desk, barely brushing across the thorns. "Oh, an all right man, but with some nasty things back there, behind his cool museum exterior. He's had some very bad problems, especially after the theft."

"Such as?"

"Such as I really don't want to get into that right now." She leaned forward again and a bit of black lace escaped through the cleavage of her light green dress. I did my best not to look too hard. "After all, I must keep some things secret."

I thought about that for a moment, and I rubbed the smooth cardboard of the folder. "Cassie, not that I want to put you at any risk or anything, or get some more secrets, but I was wondering, in addition to this information—"

"You also want Justin's date of birth and Social Security number?" she asked, her voice neutral.

I nodded, thinking that if she made a fuss, I could still be out of the building in a minute or two, with the information that I really wanted. Still, with what was going on in Justin's past . . .

Cassie wrote something down on a slip of paper and passed it over to me. "I do his payroll every week and his taxes once a year. Here you go, and good luck in whatever the hell you're doing. I don't think I want to know any more."

I thanked her and got up to go outside to the wet weather. She looked up at me, her gaze direct and forceful, and said, "You owe me a big one, Mr. Cole."

"That I do. What can I do for you?"

She winked. "You just go. I'll think of something along the line."

So I went, the cardboard folder and the papers safe under my parka shell, with a favor owed to one Cassie Fuller. It seemed to be something I could live with, and something that would be more fun than the favor that I was going to do for Diane Woods.

An hour later the rain had lightened up some, and I was standing before a headstone at the Manchester Memorial Cemetery. A slipped ten-dollar bill to the cemetery's caretaker brought me to Ben Martin's grave and the simple granite tombstone. Ben Martin and his wife, Melissa. Both born in the same year—high school sweethearts perhaps? She had preceded her husband by three years. He had died only two years after that night in the Scribner Museum.

In my folder was an obituary indicating how Ben had died. His Oldsmobile had been found one May morning in the parking lot of the Pine Tree Mall in Manchester, and Ben had been in the front seat. The two officers on patrol thought at first that he was sleeping, but after rapping on the windows with their nightsticks and looking further, they found that he was dead. Apparent cause of death was a heart attack.

"Apparent," the story said. No indication of whether an autopsy was conducted. The story also briefly mentioned his career with the Manchester police department and the citations he received, including one for rescuing a young boy on the ice on the Merrimack River one February, many years ago, but the bulk of the story had talked about that awful night at the Scribner Museum.

It was quiet in the cemetery, and it seemed as if the roads and the cars were very far away. Water was beading down the sides of the polished surface of the Martin headstone. Poor Ben Martin. Works all his life and feels comfortable and proud of what he's done, and in his obituary, his final notice to the world before ending up in this plot of ground, all that is mentioned is his role in the greatest art theft in New Hampshire's history. Not a good way of going out.

Besides the circumstances of his death and his funeral, the obituary also mentioned two sons. Dennis and Owen. One lived in Seattle and the other in Los Angeles. Both had gone far in their lives, and had flown back for the funeral of their father. It seemed odd that both had gone to the West Coast. To get as far away from Manchester and New Hampshire as possible? Or to get far away from their parents?

No autopsy. I twisted a bit of the sod and grass with my foot. That was sloppy work, considering his history. A possible suspect in the theft of the Winslow Homers, one who indicated that he recognized the two cops who came to the door of the museum that night in July five years ago, and when his dead body is found, he's taken to a funeral home and is put in the ground three days later. Cause of death is probable heart attack.

Sloppy. I could think offhand of a couple of ways to have murdered Ben Martin and made it look like a heart attack, and only a good autopsy would have turned up anything.

I looked around at the rows of stones that unfolded before me, standing there silent and still, but each one representing a family or friends who had been torn apart at the news of someone's death. People who had trudged here with sorrow in their hearts to put someone away in the ground. I'll always remember, they would have whispered. Always.

A couple of crows came by, calling to each other. It was a harsh and sharp noise. I wondered if anyone remembered the diver who came ashore near my home last week. His body was still at the county morgue, still unclaimed, and would probably end up in an unmarked grave at the county farm in Bretton.

Unmarked graves. I knew the feeling too well. Old friends of mine were dust somewhere in the Nevada desert, unmarked and unvisited. One of these days I would return and pay them homage, but not today, or tomorrow.

Instead I turned and headed back to the Range Rover. I had one more stop to make before the day was over.

Since I was in the area, back to Bainbridge I went, to the home of the other guard who was working that night. The rain had finally let up and I had switched off the windshield wipers as I drove into town. It was near dinnertime—or supper, if you prefer—and I wanted to wrap this piece of business up and then go get something to eat. Nothing against this part of the state, but there were dozens of fine restaurants within five miles of my home. Around here, I wasn't too sure if I'd be able to find even that fine little Scottish restaurant with the golden arches.

The center of Bainbridge looked as quiet as the last time I

went through. My overactive imagination was fascinated by the two classes that lived in the town: the wealthy ones who saw it as a place to sleep and play, and the not so wealthy ones who saw Bainbridge as a place to escape from. Did they ever talk to each other, or did they hide in their homes and trailers at night, fearful of what the others were plotting?

It was near 6 p.m. when I found myself back on Mast Road, past the small-town mix of small homes and dreary farms. I thought I saw the shades in some of the windows move a bit as I drove by, and it seemed as though my "watchers" were back at work, gathering intelligence, seeing who was invading their turf on this warm and muggy July night. At the 57–59 Mast Road set of mailboxes I made a right onto the dirt driveway and drove the bumpy hundred feet or so to the brown two-story duplex that was home to the Kotowski family and one Craig Dummer. Again, there were no cars parked out front, and it didn't seem las if there were any lights on at either end of the duplex.

I got out and walked across the muddy lawn to the Dummer side. Out in the fields beyond the house a soft curtain of mist hung low among the stalks of corn, and it was quiet enough for me to hear water dripping from the eaves of the duplex.

Up on the stairs in front of the Dummer residence, I rang the doorbell, and there was no answer. I rang it twice and it had that empty sound that tells you someone has moved on. I bent over to look into the window, and as I did, I faintly made out the sound of something tinkling.

I got up and turned, just as a man came up the stairs swinging a length of heavy chain.

CHAPTER

ELEVEN

It was the chain that saved me, of course. If he had come up behind me with a baseball bat, a knife or an ice pick, the first and perhaps only sound I would have caught would have been his feet upon the steps. Even then, it was a damn near thing.

I crouched down and ducked, as the chain chattered at me as it swung over my head and struck the side of the house. The man was heavyset, with a thick beard and thin black hair, and he had on a greasy set of dark gray mechanic's overalls and heavy worker's boots. He grunted with the exertion and he pulled back his arm again, saying, "Damn you, I warned your people this would happen!"

I had no idea what the hell was going on, but another part of me was thinking things through, and in the few seconds it took for him to draw back his arm I made it toward him in two quick steps and popped him one on the nose with a fast right. I think I hit him harder than the conscious part of me had planned, but running through my mind as my fist traveled those several inches was the hard knowledge that if I didn't stop this right now, it would get even nastier very quickly.

The bearded man yelped and dropped the chain, and I kicked it over the side and gave a sharp push with both of my hands into his chest, noting that he had an oval name patch that said "Drew." He had both hands up to his nose and slipped back on the stairs, and ended up on his back in the mud.

I leaped down after him, looking for the chain and thinking longingly of all my wonderful loaded weapons, all of them an hour's drive away at home. Then everything went quite strange as Drew started crying. I stopped, suddenly feeling like a school-yard bully who's just done something awful in front of a nun.

"Go ahead," he said, wiping away blood and snot with his greasy hands. "You can look everywhere you want, but you're not going to find it. That's what I told your people this afternoon when they told me you were coming."

My chest was beginning to hurt from breathing so hard and my right hand ached, so I sat down on the steps and said, "Drew, the name is Lewis Cole, and I have no idea what you're talking about."

By now he was sitting up, legs muddy and splayed out, holding a torn and dull gray handkerchief to his nose. He eyed me suspiciously, as if I had just told him he had won the lottery, and he said, "You're not from Interstate Recovery?"

"Who?"

"The repo men," he said. "The repo men who've been look-ing for my wife's car."

"No, I'm not a repo man."

He blew his nose, whispering, "Ouch, damn it," and said louder, "Then who are you working for?"

I said, "I work for a magazine. Called *Shoreline*."

Drew still looked suspicious. "Prove it."

From my wallet I pulled out my business card, which I designed and ordered on my own, and passed it over to him. The card is light blue and the magazine's logo is centered in the middle, the letters of *Shoreline* curling like a wave to a lighthouse. The ink is dark red and embossed, and my name is below the logo, along with the word "Columnist" in italics. There's my post office box number and home telephone number in Tyler just below my name. This little rectangle of cardboard and cheap ink was like a passport, opening up doors and people's memories, and it was rare that it failed me.

Today was no exception. "Jesus," he said, looking at the card while holding it in his thick fingers. "I thought you were someone else."

"Obviously."

He slipped the card inside an overall pocket. "Those bastards at Interstate, they told me someone would be coming by today to get the car, and I told 'em if anybody stepped foot on my property, I'd bash their head in. Then I saw you drive up in your fancy four-by-four, and something just snapped. I grabbed that chain and came out here after you."

He snuffled some more, looking almost amusing, like a black bear who was licking an ice-cream cone, and he added, "Well, shit, I hope you're not here trying to sell me a magazine subscription. I ain't got the money."

I smiled at him. "No, I'm here looking for your neighbor, Craig Dummer."

He patted his nose once more, and then carefully refolded his handkerchief. I noticed that he folded it so the worst of the stains were inside. He put the handkerchief away and said, "Craig. What a little shit. Look, I gotta put some cold water on my face. Come on in and we'll talk. The name's Drew Kotowski."

I held out my hand and he shook it firmly, not attempting any of that macho nonsense of squeezing until bones popped. "Nice to meet you, though I wasn't thinking that a couple of minutes ago."

Drew grinned, and there were a couple of back teeth missing. "That's all right. Neither was I, if you're counting."

I followed him over to his side of the duplex, and the chain that he was trying to use just a while ago to beat in my head was still on the ground. I decided it looked nice there, curled up in the mud and grass.

It took Drew about ten minutes to clean up and I refused his offer of a beer, though he did get a Budweiser for himself. I followed him out to the steps on his side of the duplex. He seemed embarrassed at what the inside of his house looked like, though it seemed clean enough. A few dirty dishes in the sink, toys scattered across the faded kitchen tile and a refrigerator that had notes and recipes plastered on its door.

He leaned against the side of the house and I sat on the railing and he said, "We're only two months behind on that car, a lousy two months, but the bank won't give us room to breathe. You see, my young 'un, Bridget, she's been in the hospital with this lung problem. No real health insurance and I've been payin' what I can, but I can't make that monthly car payment. Not yet anyways. I tried talkin' to them and it's like talking to a tree. They just don't listen. They just want their goddam money. So they sent the repo men after us, and let me tell you, it's been like playing hide-and-seek ever since then."

"Where do you work?" I asked.

He took a swig from his beer. "Car repair shop in Manchester. Money's okay but they got a lousy health plan, and forget about retirement or bennies like that. My wife, Joan, now, she's been helping at a day care in Bedford and that helps, but not enough."

Drew's nose was reddened and there were brown patches of dried blood underneath his nostrils. It seemed amazing that only a matter of minutes separated this cheery little conversation from when he was trying to wrap a heavy piece of chain around my head. My own right hand ached and the knuckles were scraped raw.

"Do you know Craig Dummer that well?"

He shrugged. "Well enough, I guess."

"Is he out working?"

"What do you mean?"

"I mean, is he coming back soon? I'd like to talk to him."

"That so? What about? You trying to sell him a magazine subscription?"

So another session of the Great Lie began again, and I said, "I'm writing a story about a place he used to work at, the Scribner Museum. He's got a couple of leads I want to check up on. I just need a couple of minutes to talk to him and that's all."

"Hah." He shook the brown bottle around, churning up the beer. "If you want to talk to him, I'm first in line. The little bastard skipped out, about two, three weeks ago. Moved everything out and left me hanging with two months' rent."

"You were his landlord?"

"Yeah." Drew stood up from against the wall and said, "This house used to belong to my parents. After they died, I worked nights and weekends, subdivided it up so me and my family could live in one side, and we could rent out the other end. Craig came in quiet enough and didn't cause much trouble, though he was late on the rent every now and then."

"No idea of where he went off too, I guess."

"Not a goddam clue. Even called the place where he worked as a security guard, and they didn't know squat."

"Did he leave anything behind? Mail or belongings?"

He scratched at his beard and said, "Tell you the truth, I cleaned some shit out of there a few days ago, but there's still some junk left. Let's go take a look."

I followed him off the steps and we trudged through the wet grass and mud to the other side of the duplex. We went up the steps to Craig Dummer's place and Drew pulled out some keys and unlocked the door and we went in.

We went into a kitchen, and right in that moment, in the sound that was caused by our steps and the smell of the air in the apartment, you could feel the emptiness, the quiet stillness. I felt a slight tang of disappointment. Ben Martin was dead, returning to the soil in a cemetery in Manchester. And Craig Dummer had packed up and was gone. Too much emptiness.

Drew said, "I cleaned up some, but there's still a mess here. Lot of trash, stuff people don't like to bring with them when they get on with things. But I got lot more cleaning up if I want to rent this place out."

The kitchen was cleaner than when I last saw it. The sink was empty and the pizza containers had been taken away. The floor was grimy, though, and my boots crunched on crumbs and other dirt as I went into the living room. I kept quiet as I looked around, and Drew followed me, beer in hand. I guess it showed how much things had changed in the last few minutes that I felt comfortable in turning my back to him.

The room had light green wall-to-wall carpeting, and there was a couch along one wall, covered by a red-and-black-checked blanket. Two chairs were by another wall, and there was an empty bookshelf, the bookshelf being handmade from two cinder blocks and two lengths of wood. There were a couple of paperbacks, with their covers torn off, tossed in a corner near the shelves, resting atop a hardcover book. I squatted down and picked them up, the pages feeling damp in my hands. The books were part of a men's adventure series, taking place after World War IV or something like that. Not my brand of reading, but still, they didn't deserve to have their covers torn off.

"You want to keep those books, you go right ahead," Drew said. "You working for a magazine and all that."

"Thanks," I said, not wanting to disappoint whatever fantasies he had about magazines and their writers. "I just might do that."

The hardcover book had been dumped in water once, the pages curled and sticking together, the covers cracked and bleeding ink. It felt heavy and I thumbed through it. *Art of the Medieval World*, it was called. An expensive book, with lots of color plates and black-and-white photos. Too damaged to travel?

I dropped the books, wiped my hands on my jeans, and went upstairs, to a bedroom. The plaster was light gray and cracked, and there were evenly spaced holes along the walls that showed that posters had been tacked up there once. The bed was in the middle of the room, but it was just a frame and bare mattresses. There's something depressing about looking at a naked bed, as if some awful thing had happened there and the evidence had been stripped away.

Under the bed I found some magazines. One *Playboy*. Some copies of *Guns & Ammo*, one *Soldier of Fortune* and one *ArtWorld*, which he subscribed to. Our Craig Dummer had some quirky tastes, not something that was easy to pigeonhole. Drew saw the *Playboy* and picked it up and kept it in his hands, saying with a grin, "Thanks for finding this. I'll get to read it 'fore the wife gets home."

The closets were empty, save for a sweaty smell and some wire hangers. I guess it's a rule that you always leave a place with more wire hangers than when you arrived.

I closed one closet door and said, "Where did you say Craig worked?"

"Some computer place out near Bedford. DiskJets or something like that. He worked as a security guard, afternoon shifts."

"And they don't know where he went off to?"

"Nope. Right around the time he skipped out on me, he also quit his job. Just phoned in one day and said he was leaving."

From the bedroom I went into another room that could have been a second bedroom, or a study, but from the square impressions on the light green carpeting, it looked like it had been used for storage. I stood in the empty room, looked out the windows down at my Range Rover.

"Relatives?" I asked. "Does Craig have any family in the area?"

Drew thought about that for a moment and said, "No, not that I know. He never talked family."

Off in the distance the clouds were breaking up, and it looked like I would have some sun with me on the drive back to Tyler. Some consolation.

"Did he ever tell you about a job he might have had, five years ago or so, at the Scribner Museum?"

Drew laughed. "Listen, the only time I ever talked to the little bastard was when it was rent time. That was it. Most of the time, he did his thing and I did my thing, and we left each other alone. That was fine, right up until he left. Tell you what, you do find him, I'll give you a finder's fee or something. That rent he owes could practically make up the two car payments I owe the bank."

"I'll see what I can do," I said, which was about one step up from a lie.

With that over, we went outside and I shook his hand and headed over to the Rover. Drew stayed with me and said, "So this is going to be in a story someday in a magazine?"

"Maybe so," I said. "Sometimes, though, you do the research and things just fall apart, and there's nothing there to write about."

"Hmmm. Writing. How many pages do you write a week for your job?"

I thought for a moment and said, "Six, maybe eight."

"Six or eight pages a week? And you get paid for it, enough to live on?"

"Yeah, that I do."

He shook his head in wonderment. "Man, you poor bastard. I couldn't imagine working like that. Jeez, what I do, Kenny—my supervisor—he says, change the oil. Or adjust the plugs. Or check the belts on that Chevy's engine. Something right there that you can touch and work on, and it's not going anywhere. It's right there in front of you. That's a job you can like, even though it don't pay much. But writing . . . Jesus, trying to think of things and give 'em the right words . . ."

It seemed as though Drew shuddered and I said, "Like to ask you one more thing, before I go."

"Sure."

I opened up the door of the Rover. "You knew I was coming. Not because of the phone calls from the repo company, but because your neighbors let you know that I was poking around. Am I right?"

Drew grinned and held up his beer bottle in a salute. "Hell, yes, you're right. We look out for each other in this part of town, keep an eye on the houses and everybody's kids." Then he looked bleak for a moment. "No one else will."

I got into the Rover, and as I went out the driveway I looked up in the rearview mirror, seeing him trudge back to his house with beer and *Playboy* in hand, and it felt good for a moment, knowing that he pitied me.

A s I headed east to the New Hampshire seacoast on this Friday evening, I stopped at a convenience store on Route 101 to get something to eat. The store was called Greg's Place and had a set of gas pumps up in front and two picture windows that were covered up by posters announcing yard sales, pancake breakfasts, a school play and a couple of lost cats. The store was typical New Hampshire rural, with cans of motor oil and brake fluid two aisles over from soups and canned meat, and there were fresh homemade pies and muffins in one corner.

At the rear of the store, by a deli-type counter, I ordered a steak and cheese sub to go, and a man about my age with a chest-high white apron began slicing up a roll. His hair was thin and blond, and it looked as if he made a big production of keeping each strand in place. As he worked, I wandered over to a cooler and picked out a bottle of lemonade. As I did I looked through an open door, and saw that I was looking into someone's living room. A young boy and girl were sprawled out on the floor, drawing on pieces of paper, while a small black-and-white television set showed some evening game show. A tired woman, her hair done up in curlers, rested in a chair, holding a sleeping baby in one hand and holding up her head with the other. She wore pale pink slippers that had scuffed bottoms, and she would not gaze in my direction. The two kids on the floor looked up at me with a blank stare and I backed away. While my steak and cheese was on the grill, I went outside and filled up my Range Rover with gas. Traffic went by, a car every three or four seconds, and I tried not to think about the future waiting for those children.

After paying for my meal and the gas, I drove east, eating with one hand, tossing some things around in my head. It seemed odd, didn't it, that at about the same time Felix was getting phone calls and messages from people about the location of that safe house, Craig Dummer would up and leave both his job and his home. And it also seemed odd that when I asked Justin Dix about Craig's home address, he said the museum always knew where Craig Dummer was living. Yet he had been gone for at least a couple of weeks when Justin gave me his Bainbridge address.

Then there was the matter of Ben Martin, retired Manchester police officer, who was the one who let the thieves into the museum, and who was found dead two years later in his car, and there's no autopsy, no records of anything being mentioned about his death having any connection with the theft of the paintings. Nothing. Body found and in three days Ben Martin is in the ground.

And then there's Cassie Fuller's information, about Justin Dix and his problems. What kinds of problems?

A lot of odd things, either pointing to sloppiness or pointing to a plan.

When I had finished with my evening meal, such as it was, I was about fifteen miles from Tyler, and the traffic on Route 101 was beginning to fill up, as it seemed everyone in the central part of the state wanted to get to Tyler Beach this evening. Traffic jams are rare in New Hampshire, but I was tired of dealing with this rarity, so I fooled everyone and got off at an exit in Exonia. By traveling through back roads that didn't have traffic lights and never experienced traffic jams, I was in Tyler Beach in almost no time at all.

At home I ate a couple of apples, to add to the nutritional balance of my on-the-road meal, and I watched a little television, one of those PBS programs that have journalists stationed in Washington trying to tell the rest of us what in hell was going on down there. As I watched the program, listening to the predictions and ruminations, I felt one of those odd tastes of nostalgia, sitting there in my quiet living room in my home in Tyler Beach. There had been a time when I was in that world of the Beltway and powerful men and women, of sharp decisions made and awful stories buried or hidden. There had been some quiet and also some frenzied times back then, when I worked for the DoD and learned so much in so little time. On some evenings with Cissy, we would watch one of these programs, sharing a bottle of wine after a wonderful meal, and for dessert we would giggle at how wrong all of those bright and self-important reporters were. Once Cissy was wearing nothing save a black silk robe and she had her head on my shoulder, saying, "Sweet Lord, Lewis, if those well-paid morons know so little about the stuff we work with, can you imagine how wrong they are about everything else?"

I told her I could imagine, and I could imagine other things as well . . .

With a sharp movement I shut off the TV and went out to the rear deck, breathing deeply of the salt air, not even being bothered that much by the pungent odor of the *Petro Star*'s gift to these shores. I was brooding, and brooding is hardly ever healthy.

I held on to the railings of the deck and looked out at the familiar lights of the Isles of Shoals, and something made me stop thinking, so I stopped.

I looked out again, to the Samson State Wildlife Preserve and its rolling hills and trees which mask the concrete bunkers and old foundations of the Coast Artillery Station. The park closed at dusk, and since it was already a good couple of hours past sunset, the park should have been empty.

Yet there was someone there, standing on one of the low hills, looking in my direction.

I shifted and tried to look again, without appearing obvious. Not that my night vision is that great, but there is usually a faint glow on the horizon in that direction from the city of Porter, and the person's shape was silhouetted against the evening sky.

Sure. Just a stargazer, or someone waiting for a girlfriend or boyfriend.

And then the person started moving, clambering down the small hill, heading south. Toward my beach. Toward my home.

I went inside and shut the sliding-glass door, making sure it was locked. From the living room I picked up my 7x50 binoculars, and I raced upstairs, trying to keep my breathing even. I slipped into my study, which has windows facing north. I brought the binoculars up to my eyes, and even through the screened window, I had a good view of the man as he clambered over rocks and boulders, heading even closer in my direction. My hands were shaking and the shape was darkened, since he had come down from the hill and was no longer being backlit through the good graces of the city of Porter. It seemed as if he might be carrying something in his hands.

From the study I went across the small hallway into my bedroom and knelt beside my bed, reaching down to a rectangular piece of foam rubber which was under the mattress and frame. I slid the piece of foam out, pulled off the cloth covering, and picked up my 12-gauge pump-action Remington shotgun with extended magazine. I didn't bother to see if it was loaded. All of my weapons are loaded, for it's a sure thing that with an unloaded weapon and a sudden threat coming into your house, the sudden threat will always win.

I don't like those kinds of sure things.

Taking a small flashlight off my nightstand, I went back downstairs, running checklists through my mind, wondering who the man could be, and not liking the situation one bit. Sure, he could be a night beach wanderer. Sure, he could be someone lost and scared, and seeing my house here, wanting to come over just to borrow the phone.

Sure.

I still didn't like it. He was trespassing. On my land. At my home.

It took me only a moment or two to decide to go outside. Being outside, I had areas to move to, places to hide behind. Inside the house, I was trapped. I decided to go with maneuverability against the security of my house. I slipped out the front door, ducking down as I went around the house, and then I felt the hot breath of shame against the back of my neck as the man came up my small backyard, whistling and switching on a flashlight in his hand.

"Felix," I called out, switching on my own flashlight. "You came about ten seconds away from having to answer some very stern questions."

As my light hit him, he gave me a rueful smile as he walked closer. The light from my small flashlight made his dark face look even more black, as if he had a two-week shadow of stubble on his face. He had on black high-top sneakers, gray sweat pants and a white tanktop.

He shook his head. "Wasn't trying to be a sneak, and I knew about fifty feet away that you were waiting for me. Helpful hint, next time you're scurrying around the upstairs getting your shotgun. Don't leave the bedroom lights on."

"Thanks," I said. "Why the roundabout walk?"

He shrugged. "It's just that I know some people are trying to keep tabs on me. I decided to walk over here the back way, keep things nice and quiet. Of course, I didn't expect you to nail me with a light and a shotgun."

"I didn't know it was you, and I didn't know it was a visitor. I like my privacy."

Felix tried to make a joke of it and I wouldn't let him. "Don't you know you're supposed to trust your fellow man?" he asked.

"I tried that once," I said. "Damn near killed me, and it brought me here, Felix, and it still might kill me in the end."

That comment seemed to make him think. He just nodded,

slowly. "I've always wondered, and you've never told me. They must have done something awful to you, Lewis. Something awful indeed."

I decided to drop it. "You want to come inside?"

He shook his head. "Nope. Want to keep moving if you don't mind. Wanted to let you know I've made contact with the people who have been sending me the notes and messages."

"You have?"

"Yep. The meet is on for tomorrow night, Saturday, at seven P.M. It's gonna take place at the Vault Restaurant in Porter. And it's with a guy I know from my past. One Tony Russo."

I switched off the flashlight, not wanting to light up things too much, and not wanting Felix to see what kinds of emotions were moving across my face. After a bit I said, "Do you still want me there?"

Felix's voice was brisk. "Yeah, I do, Lewis. Tony and I don't have that great a relationship, if you know what I mean. I used to work for him, years ago, about the time I was being bounced around and when I did some stuff for Jimmy Corelli. I had to do some things for Russo . . . Well, I'll tell you later, but what I had to do for Russo is the main reason I'm here and I'm freelance. But yeah, I'd like to have you there, Lewis."

"My calming influence, as you say?"

"Whatever you want to call it. I just don't want to be near Tony Russo and lose it if he starts in on me. I want you to help keep me focused and on the straight and narrow. I've already told him that you'd probably be there, and he didn't have any problem at all."

It seemed as though the sound of the waves grew louder. "All right, then."

Even in the darkness, standing there by my house near the ocean, I could sense Felix's smile. "Look, there's a bar a couple of blocks down from the Vault. The Frozen Chosin. Let's say you and me meet there at about six P.M., we'll go over a couple of things, and we'll walk over to the restaurant. We go in, do some discussions, and by Sunday we'll do the exchange and when it comes Monday morning we'll both be making healthy deposits in our bank accounts."

"That easy?" I asked.

"Oh, it's never that easy, but as much as Tony is . . . well, Tony still has a good head for business. If he wants the safe house's address and the paintings and he's willing to pay, it'll be a sweet deal for all of us."

There didn't seem to be that much to say. I went over and picked up my shotgun and said, "Well, Felix, I guess we're on for dinner tomorrow night." There came the sound of his laugh and there was a quiet movement, as if he was coming near to shake my hand or touch me on my shoulder, but the moment passed and he was back heading to the beach, walking to the dark hills of the wildlife preserve.

When I got back into my house, I smelled the sweat of fear upon me, and I wasn't sure if just a shower would take care of it.

Tomorrow night seemed very far away.

CHAPTER
TWELVE

The Frozen Chosin is a rarity among the scores of restaurants and bars in Porter, in that it wasn't designed to be a specific type of place for a specific type of customer. There is a lot of money to be made in Porter from tourists who don't like the sand and the noise of Tyler Beach, and there are many restaurant consultants who've convinced businessmen and businesswomen what type of place to open and what kind of food and drinks should be served.

But the Frozen Chosin is owned and operated by one Art Cloutier, a sixty-three-year-old ex-Navy Yard worker and ex-Marine who still limps on his right foot from the frostbite he suffered while taking part in that horrible retreat from the Chosin Reservoir in Korea in 1951, and who's told many a person that he doesn't give a good damn what anybody thinks about his place. He serves a handful of beer brands, some mixed drinks and free popcorn and he has a dinner menu that can be printed on a four-by-five postcard. Those customers who don't know their history and who come in looking for a frozen margarita or daiquiri usually leave with their faces red and their steps quick.

His place is in downtown Porter, near enough to the waterfront to see ships glide into the harbor. It's on two floors, with lots of brass, old wood and some plants, though no ferns. American and Marine Corps flags are on the walls, along with old photographs from Korea and pictures of some of the scores of submarines that were built at the Porter Naval Shipyard. On this Saturday evening the place was just beginning to get crowded, with sunburned tourists standing next to burly men in jeans and oily T-shirts who'd just finished a shift at the shipyard, along with a good mixture of the artist and writer crowd that Porter has always attracted.

Felix and I were at a small table in an alcove that had windows overlooking the downtown, and we saw the foot traffic of Porter, the people in shorts and casual clothes, many carrying shopping bags, thronging the sidewalks outside. The windows were open and rock music from a loft apartment down the way echoed softly in the early evening streets. Felix and I were dressed almost identically in tan chinos and short-sleeved shirts, although Felix looked almost naked, not wearing a jacket to cover a holster and pistol. Both of us were weaponless that night.

He picked up a glass and swirled some ice around, looking outside, his features set. "The thing is, I'm not too sure how Tony Russo is going to approach this. There's a couple of ways, you know. Start off sharp, try to get me fuzzed up, needle and poke. Or he just might try it soft, build up gradual and then just let it all hang out." The ice cubes rattled again as he moved his glass. "Then he might fool us and just lay it on the line. He accepts my demand, we arrange the meet, and we give up the address of the safe house and the paintings tomorrow. And tonight we leave good friends after coffee and dessert."

"From the way you're acting, I don't think he's going to fool us, Felix."

"Yeah, I know."

I took a sip from my own glass. We were both drinking ice water. This wasn't the kind of night to be drinking any type of alcohol. When I had ordered two glasses of ice water, Art Cloutier—wearing a black tanktop with an American flag that said "These Colors Don't Run"—glared at me and was going to say something nasty, until I slid a ten-dollar bill over the stained wood of the bar.

"Why Porter?" I asked. "You'd think he'd be wanting you to come to Boston. Having someone with his reputation . . . well, it seems odd that a guy connected with the Boston mob would be traveling an hour or so north to Porter."

"Yeah, I thought about that, too. My guess is that he knows the safe house is somewhere in Maine, and he's working out of a place around here. Thing is, too, the post office box I replied to is in Porter."

"Is that how it worked, when you made contact?"

Felix nodded. "I finally sent a card back, saying I was ready to talk, and I told them the final and absolute price for the address of the safe house. Within two days, Tony Russo called and left a message on my answering machine, and he set the time and place. The Vault Restaurant. Tonight."

"Does it make you nervous that he set the time and the place?"

Felix turned and smiled at me. "Why, are you worried about an ambush? What do you think this is, *The Godfather*? Think Tony Russo is going to get up to take a crap and when he comes back he's gonna blow us both away?"

I rattled some ice cubes of my own. "The thought's entered my mind a couple of times."

"Just a couple of times?"

"All right, a couple of times in the last thirty seconds."

He took another sip. "You writer types think and worry too much. Listen, Lewis, I've been in situations like this before, where the stakes were a hell of a lot higher, when you were negotiating between two groups who were fighting and had a history of dumping bodies in car trunks. You want to talk nervous, then nervous is when you're sitting across from someone whose brother's just been nailed by your pals. That's nervous. But talking's a good sign. It means the other side is serious, is looking for a settlement. And putting the meet in one of the most popular restaurants in Porter, well, that's another good sign. Look. I'd be a hell of a lot more nervous if he wanted to meet at a gravel pit in Tyler Falls at midnight. Then I'd be wearing a Kevlar vest and I'd have a guy or two as backup in the woods with a scoped AR-15. So, Lewis. Relax."

Felix turned away and I didn't bother telling him that I was already relaxed. Well, that wasn't the whole truth. It wasn't relaxation, and it wasn't fear. It was something else. It was like I was racing above it all, like an ice skater on an incredibly smooth lake surface, gliding away and moving with no effort or thoughts. I was with Felix and a Sousa march was playing on the speakers and even the ice water had a mysterious taste to it, a taste that hinted of something exciting and wonderful.

When Felix turned around again I said, "Tell me about Tony Russo, then. You said you would."

He looked at his wristwatch. "We don't have that much time."

"Maybe so, but I want to know."

He looked down at his glass, and for a moment I had to strain to hear his voice. Art Cloutier was yelling something about how Douglas MacArthur was an idiot in World War II but managed to learn something in Korea, and I leaned forward some more.

Felix said, "Like I said last night, one of the several good and heavy reasons that I'm up here, remote and away from the action, is because of Tony Russo."

"Oh."

"Yeah, oh. Back when I was in my twenties, Lewis . . . well, it's hard to explain. You're young, connected and invincible. You eat the best food, you go all over the country and you pull in some great bucks. You look at civilians and the way they have to earn a living, Jesus, doing nine-to-five shit that would drive anybody batty. I mean, humping and working for some company, so that after you work for fifteen years, you get four weeks' vacation out of fifty-two? That's living? And going week to week not knowing if the place you're working for, if it's still gonna be there a week from now?"

The words were something, but his eyes, his manner, were telling me something else. "So how come you're still not in Boston? Or New York?"

"Hmm," he said, finishing off his ice water. "Many a time I've been asked that question. And you're probably one of the few people I could give a good answer to. It just started after a while, seeing how nobody who was connected was much older than their forties or fifties. It's 'cause they die out. They get killed or they go to prison. So it started eating at me, wondering if that's what I really wanted. Making great money and pulling off incredible deals, and then ending up in a prison, taking showers with a dozen tattooed bikers, all 'cause I got ratted on by someone turning state's evidence. Or driving somewhere and getting a piece of piano wire wrapped around my neck 'cause I winked at someone's sister. Back then, when I started thinking like that, well, I wasn't fully in. I still had some room to maneuver. Then, one weekend, I was working for Tony Russo."

I said nothing, watching as Felix reached into his glass and yanked out an ice cube, which he popped into his mouth and crunched for a moment. He said quietly, "It was summer, sort of like the weather we're having now. Me and another guy—Ricky Grimes, he got killed doing a bank job in Connecticut later—we were told to pick up two people and deliver them to Tony's house. We had a nice Lincoln Continental, and we drove out to East Boston. Well. We picked up two kids. Brothers, maybe ten or eleven years old. And they were waiting on the porch, like they were expecting us. No mother or father there to say goodbye. Even today, I wonder where they were. I think they were in the house, hiding. Out of shame. We took 'em out to Boxford, up on the north shore, and they just sat in the backseat, not saying a word. Ever been to Boxford? If there's a house in that town that's worth less than a quarter million, then I'd eat my shorts."

"That's where Tony Russo was living?"

He poked at another ice cube with his fingers. "At the time, yeah. Nice place, with a long driveway and a house that could fit twenty people, with big windows. We drove up and a couple of Russo's people took the kids in. Ricky and I were told to wait."

"Then what?"

Felix shrugged. "The kids never came out. And I don't know if they ever did. One of Tony's boys came back an hour or so later and sent us home, and that was it. Oh, maybe I overreacted or something. I don't know. Maybe the kids were spending the night with Tony, maybe he was their godfather or something. Maybe. But I just remember seeing those two kids go up the walkway, and then they started holding hands, and they looked back at me, like I was going to come rescue them. I got a strange feeling that night, one I've never been able to shake, and right then I knew I wasn't gonna work for Tony Russo or Jimmy Corelli or anybody else ever again. They demand obedience, Lewis, utter and unquestioning obedience, and I wasn't going to give it to them, or anybody else. So I left, and I've never gone back."

He stayed quiet for a few moments, and another Sousa march played over the speakers. I looked outside and back at Felix and said, "We should get going."

"We should," he said, and in several seconds we were outside in the warm and troubled night, heading out to see Mr. Anthony Russo.

The Vault Restaurant is four blocks from the Frozen Chosin, located on the ground floor of an old five-story hotel whose upper floors have been turned into condominiums. The building is a lot of old brickwork and turrets, and granite steps flanked by two large lions, lead up to wooden double doors at the entrance to the restaurant. Felix held me back as I started walking up the steps, and I nodded in understanding when we fell behind two couples who were going in the same direction. Both men gave us quick smiles as they led their women up the steps. Safety in numbers.

As I followed the two couples, I almost started laughing at the utter absurdity of it all. The couples in front of us—two husbands and two wives in their early fifties—were going out for a quiet evening in Porter in their best summer clothing. I'm sure they had pleasant expectations of a nice meal, good companionship and interesting conversation, but I'm also sure that in their wildest imaginings they couldn't know that they were serving as human shields for the two well-dressed and polite men following them. I patted the head of one of the lions for good luck as I went in with Felix.

The hostess took care of the couples, and when she came back, standing behind a wooden lectern, Felix winked at me and said to the hostess, "We're here for Mr. Corelli." She made a check mark on a notepad and pulled up two menus, and we followed her into the dining area. The inside of the Vault is heavily carpeted, with deep mahogany wainscoting along the walls and carved panels in the ceilings. The lights were faux Tiffany lamps, and there were sets of tables with white tablecloths and secluded booths that were separated from each other by bookshelves filled with old leather-bound volumes.

She took us to a rear booth to the right that was about the most secluded, and a man was sitting by himself with a drink before him. He looked up and she said, "Well, the rest of your party has arrived," and he replied, "Isn't that nice."

Felix slid in first, saying, "Tony," in an oddly strained voice, and I sat next to him, conscious that I was smiling, and yet I was looking quite hard at Tony Russo. From the story Felix had told me, I was expecting a jowly old man with stained clothes and wet lips, with "Child Abuser" tattooed on his forehead, but the man sitting there could have been a model for whenever *Esquire* runs its fashion spreads for men in their late forties. He was wearing a dark blue suit and white shirt with a striped club tie, and his light brown hair was cut close and sculpted to his head, showing me a man who knew he was losing his hair and wasn't going to put up with the indignities of a toupee or a hair transplant. His skin was lightly tanned and I saw that he was squinting his eyes while looking across the table, like he was slightly disgusted at the two of us.

Tony nodded back and looked at me and said, "So. This is your adviser?"

"That's right. Lewis Cole. A magazine writer, lives down near Tyler Beach."

He looked at me and didn't offer his hand, and I returned the nongesture. With a motion of his eyes, Tony dismissed me instantly and said, "When you worked for me, Felix, you had a good future. You were an up-and-comer, worked sharp and didn't ask any questions and got the job done. Now you live in this rotten little state and make your money by hiring out to whoever's got the biggest checkbook, and for your counselor you get a guy who earns a living by stringing words together. Can't understand it."

I looked over at Felix, wondering how I was going to achieve my mission of keeping him calm, for while the words weren't that harsh, Felix's hands were tight against a water glass.

"Let's just say he's a bit more trustworthy than some of the people I used to run with back in Boston," Felix said, his voice flat. "Some of those people have forgotten a few things, about family and respect."

Tony stared right back. "So you say. You're late, you know. Is that respect?"

The hand was still tight against the glass. "It's whatever you make it."

I stepped in, saying, "Well, have you ordered yet?"

"No," he answered, still looking me over. "Just the drink. And to show you how late you are, I gotta take a men's room run. So. Stick right here until I get back."

"You can count on it," Felix said, and after Tony got up and left I said, "Felix, I knew this was going to be a strange favor to take care of for you, but you're making it difficult, right from the start. I thought you were ready to take off his head with a butter knife."

Felix stared straight ahead. "Yeah, well, I didn't think it was going to be so tough, seeing the bastard face to face. I started thinking about things Tony has done recently, and I started losing it."

"Started thinking about what?"

"About this." He reached down and pulled out his wallet, taking out two photographs. The first he handed over immediately. It showed Felix with a younger man who bore a bit of a family resemblance. They were on the deck of a boat, smiling toward the camera, both wearing loud bathing suits.

"Guy next to me is Sal Grillo, my cousin. You sort of met him last week."

"I did what?" I asked, and when he handed over the next photo, I almost dropped it on the fine tablecloth. It showed Sal again, on the shores of a rocky beach, wearing a wet suit. I handed both photographs back to Felix, aware that my face was getting quite warm.

"How long have you known, Felix?" I demanded. "And how come you didn't tell me right away?"

He carefully replaced the photos in his wallet. "I just found out this morning. Another message on my answering machine, telling me to negotiate tonight in good faith. That Sal was a signal, one I should take very seriously. I made a follow-up phone call, to a contact I have with the medical examiner's office, seeing if that diver's corpse had a tattoo of a rose on its wrist. It did."

"Jesus," I murmured.

"I wasn't going to keep it a secret, but I didn't want to get you spooked." Felix turned to me, his lips compressed, his face dark. "I was wrong, right from the start. I should have clued you in. And I'm doubly glad you're here. Try to keep things calm, will you?"

A lot of things were racing through my head, including an

urge to get the hell out of that restaurant, along with an urge to start yelling at Felix for keeping secrets from me, and then Tony came back. I swallowed hard and stared at him, trying to think of what creatures were living behind such calm eyes.

He sat down and Felix asked, "Anyone else joining us?"

Tony picked up the menu, a long brown folder with Vault embossed in gold letters. "No. This is an easy deal, Felix. One I can handle on my own. I don't need someone holding my hand."

I picked up my own menu and said, "Well, Felix and I don't usually hold hands. At least not in public," and Felix smiled just a bit as he started leafing through the pages of his own menu, and I felt like I had gained a bit of a success.

When our waitress came by, Tony looked up and said, "Hon, we're both late for something, so I think we'll only be ordering appetizers. Is that okay with you guys?"

With Felix's revelation about his dead cousin, I knew I didn't have the appetite for a full meal with Tony Russo sitting across from us. So I nodded and Felix said, "Sure," and when the waitress tried to hide her frown, Tony said, "Don't worry, we'll make up for it in the tip."

The waitress was in her early twenties and she smiled at Tony's comment. The funny thing about the Vault was that, for all of its Victorian splendor, the waiter and waitress uniform was blue jeans, white shirts and black bow ties, but right then nothing much seemed funny. The headless and handless diver. A relative of Felix's . . .

After she took our orders Tony folded his hands and said, "Let's get down to business, Felix. The number you mentioned on your postcard is not of this universe, do you understand that? There is no way anybody is going to pay you that amount of money."

Felix buttered a roll and said, "That's the number, Tony. It's not negotiable. You're going to have to live with it."

"Bah," Tony said. "Listen, we want that address, and we want what's in that house. All right? It's ours. Now. You know where the house is, and we appreciate that. So give us the address as a gift, and we'll toss some business your way. We'll both end up with something and there's no hard feelings. But this demand for money, for such an amount, is way out of line. You don't have the weight anymore. You're nothing, Felix. You're a loner and we could take care of you without getting permission."

Felix put down his butter knife and smiled. "That just shows how stupid you are, Tony, and why you're here, on my turf, talking business to me. You're doing this, all for a loner?"

"You are a loner. You've got nothing behind you, no friends, no influence."

Felix eyed him as he bit into his roll. "You may be surprised at how many friends I still have down in Boston."

Tony waved a hand in his direction. "You mean the Old One? Forget it. All he cares about is eating and sleeping. He's no longer in the middle of things, Felix. He's retired. Just an old dog."

"Maybe so. But do you want to find that out?"

Tony shook his head and reached into the basket of rolls, and I decided to try to keep things focused and said, "Why the interest?"

"Did you say something?" Tony asked, not looking at me as he unpeeled a pad of butter. I felt like kicking him under the table.

"Yeah, I said something. Why the interest? What's in the safe house isn't something that you can fence, or advertise that you own. It's stuff that's as hot as plutonium. So why the interest?"

Tony talked back to me, using his own knife as a pointer. "Because they're a symbol, a sign of respect. Something strong and out of the ordinary, something that can be given as a sign of honor, or held up as an example of what can be done under the right circumstances. Besides that, why we want that house or what's in it is none of your business or concern. Just the fact that we want it is enough."

"So Felix should just trust you, is that it?"

The waitress came back, carrying a tray and our orders. As she began to set down plates Tony talked back to me, even though he was looking intently at Felix. "Don't you worry about

Felix. He knows the way we do business, our approach, our means of getting attention."

By now a sly grin was on Tony's face, as he said, "Even with all of that, Felix, we were wondering when you were going to come around. You were quite difficult, not wanting to talk until we agreed to negotiations. Even when we sent that calling card to you last week, you demanded a sit-down. You know, we wanted it to wash up in your backyard, but we misjudged the tides and it ended up the next town over. For a family member and such, we wondered why you didn't get back to us sooner. Still, here we are, talking, so I guess that counts in your favor."

Even with Felix just telling me a few minutes ago, the words from Tony seemed to bore right into my chest. I wondered how Felix was doing. With my right hand, I reached under the table and patted him on the knee. An odd gesture, but it seemed to do something, and I sensed him unwind a bit. Tony started eating, still smiling

"I've talked before, in circumstances almost as trying, Tony," Felix said, his voice held calm, by fury, I guess. "Negotiations are always important, no matter the circumstances. So. What was the word that got you here? How did you pick up on me?"

"You want me to give up my trade secrets, that's it?" Tony asked.

Felix took a spoonful of soup. "These are negotiations, right? That means give-and-take, Tony. Play the game, why don't you. My guess is that someone from the Corelli family was involved, and you got the word. A good guess?"

Tony smiled and dabbled at his lips with a white napkin. "Good try, Felix. You remember Frank Corelli, Jimmy's older brother? Well, he's in a nursing home now and I still visit him once a month. He's an old-timer, Felix, a real gentleman, even though he's losing his mind and he gets fed by tubes. One day I was there and we were talking old times, and he told me—right out of the blue—that his brother had ordered those paintings stolen. Can you believe it? Jimmy Corelli, who'd only look at a painting if it showed a woman with bare tits, he ordered the hit on a museum. But then something got screwed up, big time, and they ended up in Maine. At one of Jimmy's safe houses."

I was beginning to feel a bit better, and started unpeeling and eating my order of jumbo shrimp. "But Frank didn't know where the house was."

Tony shook his head. "Nope. I tried to get that out of him and he just smiled up at me, drool running down his chin, and he told me how he missed going to Mass every week. So I poked around and I learned about you, Felix. You've been there. You know where that house is."

Felix rattled his spoon in his empty soup dish. "That I do, Tony. And it's going to cost you money."

Something seemed to crackle in the air of the restaurant, as Tony smiled back. "Oh, no, it's not, Felix. It's going to be a gift."

Before Felix could say anything I jumped in again and said, "Who's the buyer?"

Tony looked over at me. "What?"

"I said, who's the buyer? All that talk about signs of respect is so much nonsense, and you know it. What people respect is what you can do and what weight you carry. Those paintings don't do a thing for you or for your partners. The fact that you have three nineteenth-century pieces of art isn't going to impress Colombians or Jamaican posses. Not by a long shot. Besides, the cops and the FBI are still after them. So you're not doing this for symbols. You want money. So you have a buyer."

Tony opened his mouth as if to say something, stopped, cocked his head and then said, "Yeah, there's a buyer involved. And he's very interested in picking up something that was promised to him five years ago."

"The original buyer," I said.

Tony nodded. "A man who carries a lot of weight, Felix, and who's very interested in that address."

"Maybe I can do better talking to him on my own," Felix said.

Tony's face flushed. "An arrangement's been made, and there's no changes allowed. You work with me."

Felix seemed to consider that for a moment, and said, "All right. Maybe I knock my price down. Hell, maybe I even give them to you as a favor, for both you and your buyer. But I'd like to talk to him, see who he is and what's going on. I'm nervous about getting into consideration with someone I've never met."

Tony wiped his lips again with his napkin. "Is that possible, or are you just jerking me around?"

"You know what I've done in the past, Tony. Jerking around is not in my catalogue of moves."

He tapped his fingers on the tablecloth for a moment or two, and then pulled out a wallet, withdrew a fifty-dollar bill and tossed it on the table. "Let's go, then. He's outside, waiting in my car."

I got up with Tony, and Felix said, "Concerned about being seen in public?"

Tony said, "Concerned, yeah, that's a good word. But let's say he wants progress, wants progress so bad that he didn't want to wait for a phone call when I got out of here. So that's why he's in my car."

Outside we walked down a cobblestone alley that led to a parking area behind the restaurant. The night air was warm and the area was dark, with only a weak streetlight at one end. There was a wall of shrubbery and a six-foot wooden fence, with open spaces that led onto brick paths going into a small park. The lot was empty of people, with cars backed up to the wooden fence.

Tony was in front of us, car keys jangling in one hand, and he said to Felix, "You see, he'll tell you that I'm the man you've got to make deals with. Now, once we . . . hey."

He stopped before a Grand Marquis with Massachusetts license plates. Even in the dim light I could tell that the interior was empty. Tony bent over and looked in the driver's-side window and said in a puzzled tone, "He's gone."

I stood next to Felix, maybe a couple of feet away, when a man walked out of the shadows near the shrubbery and the fence. I don't think Tony saw him. Tony turned and was going to say something when the man came up to him and raised a hand, holding a silencer-equipped pistol, and shot him in the head.

CHAPTER

THIRTEEN

A lot of things happened at once, like an acid-induced slide show. Tony grunted and fell back against his car, a spray of blood fanning out behind him on the car's windows, and then he sat down hard, his legs splayed out. I think I might have said something. I don't know. Felix said, "Christ," in a low voice, and above the night sounds of Porter and traffic going by and chamber music from the restaurant, there had been the sound of the gun firing—like an ax handle striking a watermelon—and a rattling clink, as the spent shell was ejected from the pistol and fell against the hood of an adjacent car.

The man turned, a wisp of smoke rising up from the silencer's opening, the pistol now trained on us. The stories about a person's whole life racing through one's mind at a time like this were proven false, for what it's worth, for all I thought was, what a waste. What a waste to end it here, in a conflict I knew almost nothing about, with so much left undone, with so much to do after surviving that awful day in Nevada. I couldn't even look at the man's face, which was hidden by a black ski mask. I just saw the shiny blackness of the silencer, looking over at me. It seemed as big as a bus.

The man's hand moved, and the pistol dropped down. He looked over at Felix. He said quietly, "We'll be in touch."

Then he left, walking through an opening in the dark fence and into the park.

Tony was sitting before us, back against the car, head slumped forward. I wanted to look away but I couldn't help staring at the man who just a few moments ago was threatening Felix, was looking at me with disdain, was thinking and breathing and doing everything with forty or so years of memories. Now, one pull of a finger later, this man was turning gray and was slumping farther forward, and the spray of blood that had come from the back of his head now had little rivulets running down the glass of his car.

"Move," came Felix's voice. "We've got to get out of here," and I did just that. I looked down at the asphalt of the parking lot and shut everything out and walked and strolled and breathed deeply until I was on a main street, in the damp air, hearing footsteps behind me and thinking it was Felix, and not really caring. All I wanted to do was move and put that restaurant and that dead man as far away from me as possible. The streetlights didn't seem to be working, for the night was quite dark.

Somehow we ended up down by the harbor, at Walker's Park, a place famous in Porter for its flowers, landscaping and theater shows during the summer, and this evening was no exception. Families and lovers and friends were on blankets among the trees of the park, watching some Broadway show on a stage in the middle of the grass lawn. I spared it a quick glance as we walked by, and then Felix and I were on a wooden pier extending out to the waters of Porter Harbor. Before us were the lights of the Porter Naval Shipyard. Off to our left was the Memorial Bridge, a drawbridge going into Kittery, Maine, and the smell of the water and the fuel oil and the sharp memories proved too much. I knelt down by the pier and threw up into the harbor.

I got up after long minutes, rubbing my face with my handkerchief, feeling salt tears run down my cheeks. Off in the distance the sirens had finally started.

Felix said, "Did you see anybody you knew at the restaurant?"

"What?"

His voice was insistent. "Did you see anybody there who recognized you, who knows Lewis Cole of Tyler?"

"No, nobody at all—"

"Good. By the time the cops get there, our dishes will be in the kitchen and probably will be washed. No prints. The reservations were in a fake name, and the hostess doesn't know you or me at all."

"Felix—"

He said, "We can't go to the cops, Lewis. I want to get that out first and straight. There's no way you and I want to be connected with what happened back there."

I was clenching my fists and twisting the handkerchief. "Considering this little meet went off with the good humor and grace of a lynching, I can see why you're not proud, Felix."

Felix leaned on a pier railing, grabbing it with both hands, shaking his head. "Christ, what went wrong, what went wrong. . . ?"

"A lot of things went wrong," I said sharply, balling up my handkerchief and shoving it back into my pants. "Where should I begin? Like you saying this was going to be quiet and diplomatic? Well, sometimes you know shit, Felix, and thanks a lot for taking me along for the lesson."

He kept shaking his head. "Tony Russo. Someone just whacked out Tony Russo. Man, that takes so much balls—"

"Stop it!" I nearly yelled, conscious that we were near a family park that had a lot of cops working in it tonight. "Will you for once in your life start speaking in English, and leave that damn slang back in Boston?"

Felix turned, glaring. "English? You want English, Lewis? Okay, here it is. Straight English. Someone just murdered Tony Russo tonight, murdered him in a public way, in a goddam restaurant parking lot. You and me were his guests. Word will be getting back to Boston pretty quick that Felix Tinios was with Tony Russo when he got killed. You think his friends in Boston aren't going to believe that I was involved, that I knew the shooter, that I set the whole thing up? And how long before his friends start coming up here, looking for me and looking for you for good measure?"

There was some laughter coming from the people in the park, people sitting in lawn chairs and on blankets, sipping wine or cola, eating from picnic dinners. It seemed too peaceful to be true.

"No danger, you said," I pointed out to him. "Remember that day, the day they found the diver and you tried to get me to help you out? You said no danger. You were going to be the lightning rod, I was just going to be an adviser. No problem. Just lies, right, Felix? Jesus, you couldn't even tell me something straight about your cousin."

His voice was dull. "What do you want to know?"

"Why in hell he got picked as a message would be a good start."

He shook his head and said in a sharp tone, "My cousin Sal is from Boston. He was up for a week, wanted to get away from the big city. Slept on my couch. Did some drinking and screwing and he was into diving, so he did that, too. Then one day he was gone. I didn't think much about it. Sal wasn't one for making big departure scenes. Even when the body came ashore, I didn't put it together, until his mother started calling me, saying he never came back home, and I got that call this morning."

More laughter came from the park. It seemed like a foreign

sound. "Felix. Your own cousin? You knew that the diver—God, the diver I hauled in to shore—was your own cousin, and you still came here tonight? All that stuff about family and honor— I'd think the first thing on your agenda would involve firearms, not the paintings. Why didn't you give up the paintings after your cousin was killed?"

His hands still gripped the wooden railing of the pier. "There's a time and place for everything. Those paintings are one matter, and my cousin Sal is another. Tony and his friends probably thought that by taking care of Sal they would impress me and scare me into giving everything up without a price. It didn't work. I just agreed to talk, that's all. Sal is personal, and one of these days I'll take care of it. But the paintings are business."

I was walking in a tight circle on the pier, trying to work off the nervous energy, the artificial high that had come from all of the chemicals being dumped into my bloodstream at the sights and sounds of Tony Russo being shot. "Oh, that sounds so nice and logical, Felix. So continue with your logic. What in hell just happened here tonight? We were meeting with Tony Russo, trying to work out a deal to get the safe house to him, and someone else jumps into the picture with a pistol and silencer. Who the hell was that? Competition? Or the buyer trying to cut Tony out of the deal?"

He bent his head for a moment, as if he was checking on the condition of his shoes. "Probably the buyer. Tony's job was to get me on board, and now that Tony's job was done, he was killed. No percentage for him. Now it's just me and the buyer."

Felix stood up, rubbing his face with both hands. "Or maybe it was someone trying to move in on Tony, who found out about the paintings and wanted to take the matter away from him."

I took another deep breath, trying to control the trembling in my chest. "Don't be so fancy, Felix. The man was set up by the buyer. Tony came with the buyer and when we got out to the car, the buyer was gone and the shooter was waiting for him."

Felix looked over at me. "Remember the old story about the farmer and the mule? Before he went to work, the farmer got the mule's attention by hitting him over the head with a two-by-four.

BLACK TIDE • 173

The same has just happened to me. Remember, the shooter said he'd be in touch. This isn't over, Lewis. There's still work to be done."

Another siren wailed away in Porter, and I felt sorry for the cops and detectives and reporters whose Saturday night had just been ruined. "Maybe so, but you're going to be doing it alone for a while, Felix."

He turned and looked at me sharply. "What do you mean by that?"

I held up a hand and started walking off the pier. "I mean this has gotten too weird and too complex. I'm taking a break."

Felix said, his voice straining with disbelief, "What do you mean, you're taking a break?"

I turned. "Just what I said. Some time off, Felix. You're dealing with familiar territory. I'm not. And I need to catch my breath."

So I walked off the pier, half expecting Felix to come after me, or to stand there and yell Italian curses my way, but it didn't happen. I gave him one more glance and I saw him standing at the end of the pier, hunched over as in concentration or despair, looking out into the rolling waters of the Piscassic River and Porter Harbor. There was a twinge of sorrow there, and maybe a bit of regret. Felix looked quite alone, with some very bad things out there for him. I almost walked back.

But I thought again of Tony Russo, slumped against his car, the spray of blood like a red-brown peacock's tail on the car's windows, and I thought of how dark and big the silencer looked as it stared at my skull, and I kept on walking.

Just a break. Honest.

I got home about a half hour later and got a bad case of the shakes once the locked door closed behind me. I took a long shower, letting the hot water race across the sweat and stench of fear on my body, and it took a great effort of will to leave that glass-and-tile cocoon. When I got dressed I went back downstairs and disconnected the phone, and then made a quick survey of my weapons. Not that I expected anything untoward to happen within the next several hours, but it was comforting, even for a small moment, to have the weapons within easy reach, and I was taking any moment I could get.

After unlocking the sliding-glass door to the deck I went outside and breathed deeply of the night air. I looked up at the stars. In less than two weeks the mighty Perseids would start, three or four nights of great meteor showers, with meteorite trails racing almost halfway across the sky. It was something I had never seen before, because of the weather or the lack of a great night sky where I lived before, back in Virginia. But it would be different in two weeks' time.

On this night, before me was the great constellation of Pegasus, the winged horse, rising up into the dark sky. Within Pegasus are four stars that form a rectangle, and as I gazed up at them I named them in sequence with a whisper, "Alpheratz, Scheat, Algenib, Markab." Four stars, named by Arab astronomers centuries ago, during the Dark Ages of Europe, when Arabs were known for their culture and their learning, and before they were defamed as being nothing more than ignorant car bombers and oil drillers.

Usually the stars give me a sense of peace, of belonging, but in looking up at those lights on this evening, so soon after seeing Tony Russo snuffed out, the stars weren't working. I felt no peace.

I went back inside and reconnected the phone and dialed a number from memory, and when she answered, I said, "I need to see you tomorrow."

There was a pause, and then she said yes.

On a late Sunday afternoon the sun was beginning to sink beyond the marshes and low buildings of Tyler Beach, and I leaned back against the gunwale as Diane Woods maneuvered her sailboat, the *Miranda*, to catch the breeze. The boom snapped back and the wind filled out the mainsail, and we were off, heading to the west, back to the safety of Tyler Harbor. It had been a long and good day, leaving Tyler Harbor soon after a stand-up breakfast at Diane's condo and getting the *Miranda* underway for a run out to Cape Ann in Massachusetts. We both wore T-shirts and shorts and slathered a lot of sunscreen on each other, and even with the slippery goop on my skin, I felt the familiar tightening and coolness on my skin that signified a sunburn on its way. Lunch had been sandwiches and lemonade, balanced in our laps, and Diane was promising me a steak dinner when we got back to the harbor. The only foul part of the day was a stretch when we ran through a mini-slick of oil, and though it was possible that it wasn't left over from the *Petro Star*, the reminder of that past disaster didn't help matters.

"Damn mess," she had cursed. "And you know what's going to happen. Whoever did it will just pay a fine or do a couple of weeks in the can—if that—and next summer the dumping will still be going on."

I just nodded, not wanting to talk about the *Petro Star*. In fact, we hadn't talked much during the day, just worked in unison in keeping the *Miranda* underway and on a good tack. I'm not up on the nomenclature of what types of sails do what, but I can take orders and know when to draw in a line or just to sit down and shut up. Diane, however, could probably sail the *Miranda* to Dover, England, and back, and she delighted in heeling the *Miranda* over so far that the water was kissing the gunwales, which made me clamber up on the other side and gently inquire about what to do if she were to roll over.

As we settled in a steady run, I sat next to Diane and she looked me up and down and said, "You've got things bothering you today, Lewis."

I know better than to try to be the strong, silent and steady type around Diane. She knows me too well.

"A lot of things, I guess. You're a good one, Diane."

She stuck out her tongue for a moment. "That's my job. Being a cop and being nosy. What's the bother?"

The bother? A variety of items. Tony Russo, slumped against his car. Paula Quinn, bitter about me and what I can't do. And dead Sal Grillo, in the morgue at the county hospital in Bretton, and me not wanting to tell Diane a single word about it, though she would be happy to have progress on that case.

"Secrets," I finally said. "Secrets that are running things, I guess."

She nodded and made an adjustment to the tiller. "Something about you and that reporter, Paula Quinn?"

I was surprised. "You know?"

She smiled. "I guessed. You just confirmed. A couple of times, down at the station, when she's been doing a story about something, Paula would stop and just look at me and say, 'How's Lewis?' Or 'What do you know about Lewis?' Very casual, but in a self-conscious way. So. What happened?"

"Stuff happened," I said. The boat heeled over and some spray slapped up on the deck, hitting my bare legs with the water. "The night I learned I was sick, back in June, she was with me. I was upset and she was concerned and I couldn't tell her anything, Diane. Couldn't tell her a single thing. She was mad. Who could blame her? Since then, it just hasn't been that right between us, and I'm not sure if I want it to be right. I think I want it back before, before it went that far."

"That night, was it the first time?"

"Yeah. And you'll remember what was going on here last June. It was tense, quite tense, and when I got through with that mess, I guess I needed some reaffirmation. Paula and I spent the night and things were fine until I found that damn lump on my side. Ever since then, well, I wonder if I had spent that time with Paula, not because it was her, but because it was something I had to do to prove I was still breathing."

"You think too much."

"Curse of being a writer."

"Hah." Diane made another motion with the tiller and said

quietly, the wind blowing her hair about, "I know what you're talking about. Secrets. Both in my work and in my home, Lewis, sometimes I keep too many secrets and they're like a chain of rocks hanging around my neck. There are a couple of investigations going on right now in town that people would love to know more about, especially your friend Paula, but I'm keeping shut. And then there's my personal life. You know, it would be great, just once, if I could bring in Kara and show her where I work, show her my friends at the station and be proud of our relationship, instead of skulking around all the time."

"How does she feel about that?"

"Hah." Diane took off her sunglasses for a moment, rubbed her eyes. "She works for Digital in Massachusetts, and they're a bit more open there. Her friends at work know she's gay and it's no big deal. Sometimes Kara doesn't quite understand the politics of a small town. If I came out, Jesus, could you imagine the fuss? The fool selectmen would probably demand that I be fired and I would, and it would take years and tons of lawyer money to win a suit. No, not this year. Not worth it. Some secrets you have to keep, no matter how distasteful the process."

Distasteful. Good word for secrets. I knew the circumstances of Tony Russo's death and I knew the identity of the headless and handless diver, yet I could not say one thing. It would cause too much trouble and publicity, and those were two things I could easily live without. We stayed silent for a few minutes as we got closer to Tyler Harbor. There were a few seagulls out on the ocean air, most of them following the fishing charter boats, looking for a free meal. As the Felch Memorial Bridge—which spans Tyler Harbor—got nearer, Diane said, "Get ready to take down the sails."

"Aye, aye, Cap."

She stretched out a bare foot and gently touched my shin, and I was startled. Diane was not one for random touches. "Yes?"

"How are you feeling, otherwise? Your incision healing all right?"

"It's doing fine," I said, which was true. The fresh red of a couple of weeks ago was continuing to fade away to a dull pink.

Diane nodded. "Something bad happened to you years ago. Isn't that true?"

I thought of all the fancy dance steps I had used in the past to avoid this subject, and this time, all I said was "Yes."

She look satisfied, yet troubled. "Few years back, when we first met, I was intrigued by you, Lewis. A magazine writer who happens to move into a prime piece of real estate, one formerly owned by the Department of the Interior. That made my cop bones tingle. I thought you were someone in the Witness Protection Program, or some drug dealer who was trying to lead a new life in my town. Didn't particularly like those thoughts, of someone with a nasty past moving into Tyler without me knowing about it."

Good God. "What did you do then?"

"Did the normal tracing, and came back with crap. I got your early life, all right, but then the only thing after you got out of college was you entering employment with the Department of Defense and then leaving some years later. Period. I was going to do some more but then the chief called me into his office and in polite terms told me to cut the shit and get back to work. I guess some people from D.C. rattled his cage, and that was that. So. I know that and I know something bad happened to you, and let me tell you, I wouldn't trade my secrets for yours for the best sailboat on this side of the Atlantic."

I looked up ahead, at the white sands of the beaches and the tiny dots that each meant a person, a human life, enjoying his or her day in the sun. For a moment I wished I was there, lost in that great anonymous crowd, blending in and not being bothered, just content to be warm and safe. Not much of a fantasy, but there it was.

"Have you done any more traces on me since then?" I asked.

"Nope. Satisfied my curiosity. To a point."

"Good. Diane, please don't do that again."

She nodded. "You can count on that. But speaking of tracing, well, you remember our agreement?"

"What agreement?"

"Well, Roger Krohn has set up Wednesday night for a double date, with a friend of his from Massachusetts. Remember that? And you said you'd do it if I'd do some traces for you. It's a deal, right?"

Again, that awful scene, of Tony Russo slumped against his car. I hadn't bothered with the local Sunday papers today because I did not want to be reminded of it, not for a second. I folded my arms and said, "No, it's not a deal."

"Lewis! Cut it out, you promised!"

I turned away and sighed and said, "Look, I didn't mean it that way. I'll still go out with you and pretend you're my true love so that Roger Krohn stops sniffing around you at work, but I don't need that trace anymore."

"Hmmph." She kicked me with her bare foot. "A deal's a deal, Lewis Cole. I don't want you thinking that I owe you anything from this Wednesday night. We made an agreement, a promise, and I take those kinds of things seriously, as you should, too. Give me those names and we'll be even, all right?"

I didn't feel like arguing, so I said, "All right."

She smiled sweetly at me and said, "Now haul ass up forward and start bringing in the jib, or I'll keelhaul you, sailor."

"Promises, promises," I muttered as I went forward, and though I felt I was being stampeded into something, it was still nice to hear her laugh.

Later that evening I was back home, comfortably full after a dinner of barbecued steak and rice at Diane's. I had an ice water in my hands and I was sitting on my deck, just thinking. A few minutes earlier I had gotten off the phone with Diane, having passed along the birth dates and Social Security numbers of Justin Dix, Craig Dummer and Ben Martin. Diane said she would have the trace completed in a couple of days. Always keep your promises, Diane had said, and well, I had promised to do that. Maybe Felix could do something with that information. I didn't particularly care that much at this moment. He hadn't called and I was glad. The answering machine light glowed a steady green. That also meant no phone calls from Paula Quinn, and I decided that she and I would have to talk soon. Not tomorrow or the next day, but soon.

The breeze was soft against my sunburned skin and with the quiet winds came something else, a reminder of an earlier promise: the scent of oil, still powerful and ruling after many weeks since the *Petro Star* disaster. I tried to ignore the smell, tried to look at the stars and at the running lights of the ships out there on the lonely Atlantic, but the hydrocarbons would not let me go.

I leaned back, rubbed the cold glass against my face. It felt good against the sunburn. "Promises," I said. "Secrets."

Then I went inside and upstairs and began to pack.

CHAPTER

FOURTEEN

It was early afternoon on Monday, the day after my sail with Diane Woods, and I was nervous, with the back of my neck tense and my hands sore from having gripped the steering wheel of my Range Rover for long hours. I had gotten up with the sun, and after packing away some items, I had driven all that morning, and I felt as if I had traveled into another universe. Early this morning I had been on my lonely beach in Tyler, New Hampshire. This afternoon I was in Manhattan, and I was not enjoying myself. The drive through Massachusetts and Connecticut had been a long one, and the last half hour in this concrete-and-steel wasteland had been the worst.

I had found a parking garage near my target area, and that made me feel just a bit better. Leaving a Range Rover with New Hampshire plates out on the open streets of New York City was probably like leaving an engraved invitation for theft or mayhem, but I hoped that the garage would give me at least a couple of hours. I didn't intend to spend more than that in this city.

The air was hazy and hot, and as I looked up past the sky-scrapers, the sky was a bright yellow, with not a hint of blue. The air smelled of trash and diesel exhaust, and the loud bedlam—horns, sirens, construction noises—seemed to make my ears shudder. I was in a section of the city where there were shops selling videos and books about sex in all of its shapes and forms. The men who ducked into those tiny places seemed to walk in their own world, staring at their feet, their shoulders hunched over, fists in their pockets. The people about me on the wide sidewalks all seemed to be in a hurry, rushing to who knows where. In the space of three city blocks, I was asked for money by four different people, and I came across two three-card monte games, and a man with bare feet, sleeping against a stoop with a puddle of urine about his buttocks.

It seemed hard to believe, but this part of Manhattan made me yearn for the reason and sanity of the Strip back at Tyler Beach.

Within a few minutes, at my quick-paced walk—it only took me a few seconds to acquire the walking stance of the native New Yorker, which is two parts speed and one part intimidating look—I made it to the Port Authority Building on West Forty-second Street. Buses were grumbling in and out of the side streets of the terminal, and yellow taxi cabs sped about in long lines, hunting for fares and passengers.

Inside the Port Authority I passed a gauntlet of young men, both black and white, who seemed to be sizing up the people streaming in and out of the first floor. I followed the motto of the out-of-towner in Manhattan—keep moving and don't act as though you're lost—and I went to a deli counter and bought a cup of Coke and ice for two dollars. I leaned against a brick wall and watched the movement of people rushing in and out of the building. I wished for a moment that I had a telepathic ability to tap into each person's mind as he or she walked by. The black businessman in the expensive suit, wearing earphones. The young Asian woman carrying two large suitcases and wearing a wide-brimmed white hat. Two bearded men in suits and white shirts with no ties, arguing with each other in a language I couldn't understand.

After a bit I watched the activity around the banks of telephones, where I got the attention of two young white men, wearing jeans and leather vests and with long hair, who talked and joked with each other, but whose eyes seemed to belong to an early-warning surveillance system. Every couple of minutes they would talk in hushed tones with a businessman at the phones, and once I was sure I saw money being passed along.

I finished my Coke, tossed the cup into an overflowing trash bin, and strolled over to the phones. I caught the eye of the taller man. He made a motion and his friend was looking at me.

I nodded and said, "I need what you're selling."

The shorter of the two laughed. He had a silver nose plug in his left nostril. "Man, what makes you think we got anything you need?"

"I got eyes, and I need two long-distance numbers. What's the charge?"

The taller one shook his head and said, "Cop," and the other said, "Wait a sec, Jack. Look at his face, all sunburned like that. How many cops you know out in the sun all day? Where'd you get that burn, m'man?"

"On a sailboat."

They both laughed at that and the shorter one said, "Man, that's a story no cop could come up with. Why you need two?"

I smiled. "None of your business, right? How about a deal or I go elsewhere."

The taller one wasn't smiling. "Twenty a pop. Right now."

"You'll get your first twenty for the two numbers," I said. "Then I want to test them both, right here, and you get your other twenty."

"Deal," the shorter one said, and he passed over two slips of paper. I gave him a twenty-dollar bill and went to the closest phone, making sure my back wasn't turned to these two young entrepreneurs. Using the long-distance codes, I dialed two numbers from memory, numbers I had not had cause to remember for years. For the first one, a brisk female voice said, "White House," and I hung up. Then I dialed again, got an equally brisk voice saying, "Pentagon," and I was rude for the second time that afternoon.

I slipped another twenty-dollar bill to one of the Phone Thief Brothers, and then got the hell out of the Port Authority and made a quick walk back to the parking garage where my Rover was parked. My time in Manhattan was over.

Three hours later I was in the upstate New York town of Greenville, at a place called the Carriage Stall Motel near Route 32. It was a typical L-shaped motel with a swimming pool in place of a courtyard. I parked at the farthest point in the parking lot, and walked to the motel's office. A bell chimed as I stepped on the door pad and an older man came out, wearing a white T-shirt and sagging green work pants. He hadn't shaved that day and gray hair grew in tufts from his ears. I paid for two nights' stay with cash, and with an extra twenty slipped his way, I asked for a room that had no neighbors.

"I'm a light sleeper," I explained, and that didn't even make him shrug. On the registration card, I said my name was Norm Lincoln, that I lived on 1326 Oak Street in Decatur, Illinois, and under occupation I listed "financial adviser." I also said I was driving a Saturn and made up a license plate number. The manager must have been having a busy day, for he didn't ask me for an ID, which was nice. That meant I could stay. If challenged, I was going to leave and try my luck at a motel in another town.

Luckily I was on the first floor, in Room 120, which was the last unit on the end of the building. Moving in my luggage and gear was tiring, and I was glad for no neighbors, for I'm sure they would wonder why I had so many boxes, and by this time I was too tired to lie to anyone face to face.

But not too tired to lie over the phone.

When I was moved in, I checked the time and forced myself to calm down. It was 4:05 P.M. I had twenty minutes to get ready. The room had dark green carpeting that seemed as if it had been cut from the same bolt of Astroturf that had just redone the Giant's stadium in New Jersey. There were two single beds that shared the same style of dark brown patterned bedspread. The beds were separated by a nightstand that had a lamp and a digital clock.

After locking and bolting the door, I began unpacking the boxes I had brought in. They contained my Apple Macintosh Plus (now obsolete in home computer terms but still very capable of fulfilling my needs), the 160-megabyte hard disk, printer, modem, and length of telephone cable. It took me only a few minutes to connect the equipment on one of the single beds—all the while thanking profusely the Apple engineers who had designed the gear that allowed me to do everything without a single tool—and then I was ready. I powered up the Apple and inserted a backup floppy disk, and then called up a stored file that contained several months' worth of columns for *Shoreline*. I told the printer to start printing, and in a minute the little room was filled with the sound of the printer churning out old columns. Then I really got to work.

I think my hands were shaking as I dialed the phone number, using the stolen access code I had used earlier that day, and the phone was answered instantly.

"Pentagon, Office of Administration and Management," came the brisk female voice.

"Extension four-one-one-two," I said.

As I waited the long seconds for the phone call to be transferred, I thought about the victim I had chosen. It had been years since I had last walked the long and warrenlike corridors of the Pentagon, but I still remembered many of the names and several of the phone numbers of people who had worked in other sections of the Department of Defense. I had also written them down to be extra sure I would always have that information in case my memory ever got fuzzy. My particular section was now dead—both literally and bureaucratically—but I was sure some faces were still going to be there.

"Personnel, Grier," came the answer after one ring.

I tried to put some cheerfulness in my tone. "Hi, Peg. This is Walt Davis, down in System Security. How's it going?"

"Fine, I guess. What's this all about?"

I had just won the First Gamble. She had just accepted me as being a member of the Pentagon's security outfit that controlled their computer systems, and I'm sure my happy little Apple, busily printing away on a motel bed in upstate New York, was helping matters along by providing the necessary sound effects.

Trying not to sound relieved, I said, "Peg, we're having some system problems this afternoon with DefNet. Has the system been slow today?"

I knew the answer to that already. Everyone thinks their computer system is too slow, and Peg was no exception. I had just won the Second Gamble.

"Yes, and it seems to be getting worse," she said, breathing into the phone. "Listen, I really need to get going here—it's almost four-thirty. What's up?"

"Peg, it'll only take a minute to explain." Remembering Peg from my tour at the Pentagon, I knew she was a bit intimidated by the phone system, and was only introduced to the Department of Defense Network—DefNet—through some not so subtle threats.

I said, "The system has been crashing at odd intervals, and only affecting certain nodes. Some sections have lost months of work."

"Oh my."

"Yeah. So we're trying to stem the tide, so to speak, and we find that so far the crashing is affecting those old users that the system is identifying. When was the last time you changed your password?"

I could tell that there was concern in her tone. "Oh, maybe five or six months ago. Listen, are my files threatened?"

"Yes, they are—"

"Well, you've got to do something," she said, her voice getting a bit higher. "There's an audit I've been getting ready for months now, and I can't lose that work!"

Trying to keep my voice cheerful was beginning to be a chore. "Tell me, are you logged on to DefNet right now?"

"Yes, but I was going to log off and catch the bus home"

"Peg, there are two ways of taking care of the problem. One takes me about a half hour to talk you through—"

Her voice was getting panicky. "I can't miss my bus!"

"—and the other involves just changing your password. We've found that new users—people whose passwords are less than a week old—are immune to the system problem. If you change your password now, you'll be all set and you can catch your bus."

There was a sigh, and I heard over the phone some desk drawers being opened. "I swear it was easier back when I started. Typewriters and filing cabinets. Everything you can hold in your hand. You know, when I first started working on these damn things, I lost a whole day's work because of a thunderstorm? Sweet Mary. Hold on, here's the manual . . . Okay, I've got the section on changing passwords. It says, 'Press Control P.'"

"Okay," I said, dimly remembering what the screen probably looked like to her. "What do you get?"

"It says, 'Password Options' and underneath it says, 'To change current password, press 1.' Is that the one?"

I started typing on my own Mac, just typing gibberish, so she would hear the keyboard sound over the phone. "Fine. Peg, I'm monitoring you through my own terminal, and now the system is telling you to type in your old password, and then type in your new one. Do you see that?"

"Hmm," she said. "That's right. Okay, here goes. Old password . . ." From the phone I heard her own keyboard clicking away, and then she said, "Here's the new one. Okay, it tells me to retype the new password to verify it and it's accepted."

"Damn," I said, trying to put some conviction in my voice. Her voice, concerned again. "What's wrong?"

"Oh, I've got a glare problem with the phosphor system on my monitor," I said, making up this verbal gibberish to go along with the typing gibberish that I was performing on the keyboard. "To ensure that the system's fine and your files are protected, I need to verify your new password. All I can tell is that it looks like it begins with the letter 'P.' Am I right, Peg?"

"No, Walt. It should be an 'R.'"

Please, God, I said. Please.

"An 'R,'" she added, "for my favorite hockey team. The Rangers."

I typed in some more keystrokes and said, "Peg, you've saved your files. Good going. Look, you go get your bus, and the next time I see you in the Pik Quick Cafeteria, I'll buy you lunch."

"That's a deal, Walt," and she hung up, and I hung up. I got up from the bed, breathing hard, and then went into the bathroom to splash water on my face and my hands, which were still trembling. I felt triumphant, but I knew my real work was ahead. All it would take would be one phone call from Peg to the real people in System Security, or a check with her own personnel files, to learn that there was no such person as Walt Davis.

I went back to the room.

In another minute I had disconnected the motel room's phone and had connected the phone line from my modem to the wall jack. Using a special software program in my hard disk, I programmed the computer to call a certain number in Virginia, using the second of the two long-distance numbers that I had bought earlier that day. I knew that by using these long-distance phone numbers I was trafficking in stolen property, but I figured it was going to a good cause. Not a very good excuse, I admit, but I was too busy to come up with a better one.

I got the sound of the dial tone, and then I watched the software program as it dialed the number in Virginia. There was a sound of clicks and beeps, and then a high-pitched whine as a computer in the basement of the Pentagon answered. My computer modem seemed to whine back, and then there was a high-pitched beep, and my Apple's screen went blank.

Then a single sentence scrolled across:

Who goes there?

Someone in programming had a sense of humor. I typed in:

Rangers

and the screen, instead of displaying the letters, showed this:

*******.

Then the screen went blank again. I chewed on a fingernail, and from outside, a man in the parking lot was yelling at his wife for drinking too much, and more words scrolled across:

Welcome to DefNet
Enter data or programming request, or hit "M" for
Main Menu

I could have shouted, yelled or tap-danced. I was in. Instead, I typed:

Go archives

and being a big old dumb computer, that's exactly where it sent me.

There are computer systems and then there are computer systems. The people who put DefNet together were under a challenge: to create a secure system that authorized users could use both in and out of the office and yet was so user-friendly that almost anyone could operate it after a half-day training session. Generals and admirals usually aren't very patient when it comes to working on computers. DefNet tied in big chunks of information from other systems used at the Department of Defense, everything from budgetary to personnel to historical information, and DefNet also had connections to other federal agencies. The Department of Defense being who they are, it was a one-way street. Someone from DefNet could poke into the OMB, but not vice versa. National Security, y'know. But the DefNet system allowed someone—authorized users, of course—to roam around at will, looking for whatever data they needed. It reminded me of being in an enormous library with a passkey that let you go into back rooms and hidden stacks of books.

The designers of DefNet were under enormous burdens in creating this system, operating it, and making it as perfect an example of being user-friendly as ever was. But these groups of unnamed programmers and designers had one big advantage: they were under contract to the Department of Defense.

Need I say more?

I had spent some years at the DoD, and was quite familiar with the horror stories of $200 screwdrivers and $650 toilet seats. In fact, I was quite familiar with my own horror story, which beat out those stories for sheer terror by a mile. Which meant that the clowns who had almost killed me and who had sent this country's budget mess into very strange places, also got me the information I was looking for within fifteen minutes.

It was like following a long string, and while I unrolled the information, my Apple's hard disk sucked it all in and stored the data I was receiving.

When I got into **Archives**, I asked for **Shipping Registry**. Once in that system, I typed in a search request for *Petro Star*, and it came up with a two-page listing of its construction, crew make-up, ports of call and cargoes carried. It also confirmed that the ship was owned by Petro Associates, registered and incorporated in the ship's supposed homeport of Monrovia, Liberia, and owned by a corporation consisting of a group of Thai businessmen in Burma.

I tapped the keyboard for a moment without typing, and then typed in Go corporations. The screen flickered for a moment, and then this appeared:

Corporations
1. **Domestic**
2. **Foreign**

I slapped down a numeral 2, and then the screen showed:

Foreign Corporations
1. **North America**
2. **South America**
3. **Europe**
4. **Asia**
5. **Africa**
6. **Oceania**
7. **Other**

Once in the Asian section, it took me another two minutes to get to Burma. Another search program—thank you very much—for Petro Associates, and by God, there it was:

Petro Associates
1. **Ownership**
2. **History**
3. **Current Factors**

I didn't think my finger trembled when I punched in 1, but I did know that I took in a deep breath when this showed up:

```
Petro Associates Ownership:
Majority owner: Cameron Briggs, New York, NY
More information available (Y/N)?
```

"Got you, you son of a bitch," I whispered.

In the next five minutes I bounced around the system, getting more information about Cameron Briggs, and my heart pounded so hard that I thought the sound would crack my computer screen. After having spent weeks working on this search and having come up with only a few lines of information, it was intoxicating to have pages and pages of data being sucked into my softly humming computer. Seeing all of this information unroll before me was like drinking a bottle of wine in five minutes on an empty stomach.

The name was familiar and it was easy to see why. He was a big-time businessman in the Northeast, active in politics and one who got his name in a lot of newspapers and business magazines. DefNet was a dream—I got the listing of businesses that Cameron Briggs owned (he was a majority owner in twelve, with most of them being computer companies), his credit rating (impeccable) and personal life (forty-two years old, divorced, no children). I had enough information on Cameron Briggs to hang him out on a very long rope and see him twist for some time in a cold breeze.

Then I saw something that stopped me with my hands over the keyboard. Right after his personal information, there was this notation:

```
Cameron Briggs (Personal):
Criminal Investigations (Y/N)?
```

I might have damaged the "Y" key, I pressed so hard, and this is what I got:

Cameron Briggs (Criminal Investigations)
See Op Harpoon
JD Files
J. Carney/Contact JD
File Number: OC-NE-423

"'Curiouser and curiouser,' said Alice," I quoted, and as I was poised to go on, the screen froze, and then went black. Then this appeared:

DefNet Password Verification
Please Enter Confirming Password:

The room's air conditioner seemed to have kicked in, for I felt a cold breeze on the back of my neck. "Whoops," I said, trying to keep my voice light. "Big Brother is on duty tonight."

I typed in "rangers" (or ******* if you prefer) and got this in return:

DefNet Password Verification
Invalid Response
Please Enter Confirming Password:

"Damn it, Peg, why didn't you tell me about the confirming password?" I said to the blinking screen. I waited, looked at the computer and thought for a moment. This was a way for the system to poke up while someone was on-line, to verify that he was really an authorized user, and thereby prevent easy access by people who might steal their co-workers' passwords, or who might be involved in a piece of phone scamming. Having a second password that kicked in after five or ten minutes of use would be an easy way to keep the system safe. Such a system hadn't been in place when I was at the DoD, and I guess I should have been proud of the system improvements, but I wasn't.

I was thirsty for some reason, knowing that at this moment someone from the real System Security at DefNet was responding to an alarm, that there was a problem with this particular user, and no doubt a phone trace was being conducted—

In one quick motion I reached over and pulled the phone line free, closed down my file, shut down my Macintosh, and the computer hummed to a halt. I got up and began unsnapping connections and pulling the cardboard boxes together, throwing the computer gear in without even bothering to make sure that they fit snugly in the foam protectors in the box. As I worked, I ran through a variety of scenarios, knowing that a trace was probably underway even at this moment. Would the local police respond? Perhaps. Maybe a well-placed phone call and a sheriff is at the manager's door, checking on this particular phone. Or would they send a military response? Where was the nearest base from here? West Point? Or Plattsburgh Air Force Base?

Minutes to respond to the call from System Security, more minutes to get to this motel, long minutes, and I was working with seconds.

I had no clothes in the room, just my computer gear, and I forced myself to be calm as I walked to the Rover and back, and it took only three trips. I left the room key on the counter and got in and started up the Rover, and as I drove out of the parking lot, I looked up to the rearview mirror. I thought I saw a dark blue Ford LTD or Crown Victoria with black sidewall tires pull in front of the manager's office. If so, that was one hell of a response.

But I wasn't sure, and I didn't want to find out, so I kept driving. Yet I was sure of one thing as I entered traffic on Route 32.

Cameron Briggs and I were going to get to know each other. For in his computer file were three addresses where one could find Cameron Briggs: one was in New York City, another was on Long Island and the third was a summer address at Wallis, New Hampshire, sometimes called the Gold Coast of New Hampshire, and all of five miles from my home.

It was hard to keep my speed under the limit all the way back.

CHAPTER

FIFTEEN

It was Wednesday night in Tyler, two days after my road trip to the city, county and state of New York, and I was still tired. That and the two beers I had with dinner made it hard to keep awake, but I was trying, for the evening was almost over, and favors were about to be exchanged. Diane Woods and I were at a condo unit that Roger Krohn was renting for the month he was staying at Tyler Beach, and we were sitting on an outside balcony, three stories up from the condo's parking lot, overlooking the beach and the sands and the crowded streets of Atlantic Avenue.

Joining us on the balcony was one Rhonda Dwyer, Roger's date for the evening. It was hard to keep my eyes off of her—not because she was any great beauty, but because she dominated any space she inhabited. She had on black stretch pants and a white pullover that had a lion's face silk-screened on the front, which was appropriate, in view of her mane of blond hair. During the evening and through dinner Diane had attempted on several occasions to enter into a meaningful discussion with her, and Diane had kicked me under the table a couple of times at my not so innocent smile when her attempts had failed. Rhonda worked at the Suffolk County courthouse in Boston, which is where she had met Roger, and during the night she hadn't said much. She had just laughed a lot whenever Roger said something witty or amusing, and it seemed to me that she was either well trained or well paid.

"Fireworks should be starting soon," Roger said, leaning a hip against the balcony's railing, a bottle of Budweiser in his hand. "That's one thing I'll miss when I move back home—the fireworks every Wednesday night. The first night they lit off, they sure as hell surprised me. I thought I was back in the Army, back in the desert. Real loud, but real pretty. You know what they say. There's not a problem in the world that can't be solved by explosives. Still, it gives this place some charm. I like it here."

"Hah," Rhonda said, tossing back her hair. "You can keep this place, Rog. It's too damn quiet for me. And the sand—Jesus, it gets into everything." She sipped at a cocktail glass, working on her third or fourth gin and tonic. Diane was sitting next to me, looking out at the night sky and the dark swath of the ocean. I could sense tonight was a strained event for her, pretending to be something she was not, in exchange for the future good graces of someone she expected someday to be her boss. I think her pride was taking a few hits tonight, as she masqueraded as my date.

Between us was a round, glass-topped table which held the dirty dishes and remains of our meal. Dinner had been steaks from the outdoor grill, baked potatoes from the microwave and chilled salad from the refrigerator, and during one moment in the kitchen when we were alone, Roger had nudged me with his elbow and said, "No wonder you were so antsy back when we had dinner and I was asking you about who was going out with

Diane. You could have told me, Lewis. I would have understood."

Actually, I thought of saying that no, Roger, you wouldn't
have, but I just smiled and said, "I usually let Diane speak for herself. She's that kind of woman. Um, Rhonda seems to be a nice
person."

Roger dismissed her with a wave of his hand, which was
holding a fork to test the baked potatoes. "Ah, she's just an old
family friend. I mean, we see each other now and then, but it's
nothing serious. Just whenever both of us are in the mood to get
together. But when she found out I was here for the month, she's
been up visiting a couple of times. Sunning herself on the beach
and shopping at the malls up in Porter and Lewington. No sales
tax here, and she loves that, along with everybody else, it seems."

"I guess a quarter of a million tourists can't be wrong."

Out on the sands I made out the flickering flames where the
fireworks were to be sent up. They usually go up at 9 P.M.—give
or take a few minutes—and it was getting near that time. I like
fireworks. I've never been able to say just why. Maybe because I
liked the larger rockets that they represented. Or maybe it was
just the child in me, enjoying the bright lights and loud noises. In
that case, I suppose I should like Boston's Southeast Expressway
at night, but that was never the case. Roger looked over the railing and said, "Christ, traffic's backed up all the way to the lights."

"Guess Wednesday night is still popular," I said.

"I guess. Look, Lewis, you want to give me a hand with the
dishes before the fireworks start up?"

I said sure and we both took a handful of dishes as we went
through a sliding-glass door into the condo's interior. The living
room had little furniture and the kitchen was equally empty
of the photos and clutter that people usually acquire when
they live in one place for a long time. The summer had been
fair—not the best one in years but definitely not the worst—and
Roger had told me that he had gotten a good deal for his month's
rent. The condo unit made me feel uncomfortable, as if I was
in a bad place that was hiding behind a mask, pretending to

be a home, waiting for the next hopeful man or woman or family to move in. I would have a hard time going to sleep in a place like this. Not enough memories, not enough thoughts. Everything was just smooth concrete and plastic surface.

As we wiped the dishes down and started filling up the dishwasher, Roger looked thoughtful and said, "You know, I almost put another month's deposit on this place."

"You did? Why's that?"

He looked past me and at the two women on the balcony, and he lowered his voice. "I had lunch today with Bruce Gerrity and Gage Duffy, the town manager and the chairman of the board of selectmen. Between you and me, things don't look good for the chief, and they're very interested in me. Very interested. There's two deputy chiefs who both want the guy's job, and they're afraid if they give it to one of them, the other'll make a stink and ruin the department's morale. So they're looking for an outsider."

"You said they're interested in you," I said. "Is the interest two-way? Are you ready to give up the big-city life and come up here to New Hampshire? I warn you, it'll be different. People up here, if their mailbox gets vandalized, they expect you to do a real investigation, not just write and file a report. You think you're ready for that?"

"Yeah, I think I am," Roger said, closing the door to the dishwasher. "You know what I've said before, about the craziness down in Boston. Just a matter of time before things get so wild that I pull the pin. But I'm worried about a couple of things. Biggest thing, I guess, is how I'll be treated in the town of Tyler if I do take the chief's job. There's always that tension between the out-of-towner and the townies in small towns, Lewis, and it's even worse when it comes to police departments, and it's triple worse if it's someone from Massachusetts taking a New Hampshire job."

I washed my hands in the sink. "First time I've ever heard that expression. Triple worse."

Roger smiled and put away some barbecue sauce and ketchup in the refrigerator. "Oh, it's just something I picked up.

You know, I was wondering if I could count on you, Lewis, if I do get the police chief's job."

My ears seemed to tingle at that last sentence. "What was that, Roger? Count on me? I'm afraid I'm not much of an accountant. I just push words for a living and rely on a monthly magazine to keep me afloat."

He twisted a couple of knobs on the dishwasher and the sound of flowing water kicked in. "You may say that but you're fairly well known in this town. I've talked to some of the people living and working here, and you're known up and down this coast."

"My mistake, I guess."

"No, I don't think so. I think you've got some influence here—especially with Diane—and I know writers need sources of information. I'm sure we could find out a way where we could help each other out. Maybe you could give me some advice."

At that moment I felt uneasy at having this conversation with Roger and with being in the clean and almost sterile condominium, which was probably identical in shape, color and maybe even smells to thirty or so other units in this building. I decided to make the best of it and gave him a grin.

"Advice?" I asked. "Here's some advice. Always return a selectman's phone call, no matter how late or how drunk they might be. Treat the head of the Chamber of Commerce with respect, since the other business people see him as a moneymaker for the beach. If you're ever in a dispute with a townie or a tourist, always be on the side of the townie. The tourist won't be here at town meeting time. And don't be afraid of arresting prominent citizens. Just make sure your case is airtight and your résumé is up to date. Got it?"

He smiled. "Maybe I should have taken notes."

I wiped my hands dry on a piece of paper towel and smiled back. "Give me a 'get out of jail free' card, and I'll type something up."

"Deal," he said, tossing a dish towel at my head. It missed and struck a cabinet door, and I laughed along with him as we left the kitchen. If Tyler was to get a new police chief, it could do worse.

Out on the balcony I touched the back of Diane's neck just as I watched a flickering orange trail of sparks shoot up from the beach sands. She reached up for a moment and patted my hand. There was a sudden and quick blossom of light, of green and blue and orange. For a brief moment the parking lot and the buildings and the empty sands of the beach were lit up like day, and you could note the upturned heads of the crowds out on the sidewalk and the sands. Diane said, "Look at that," and Rhonda just said, "Ooooh," and then there came the teeth-rattling boom. The sound of the first rocket echoed across the beach, and by the condo buildings, and from far off on the sands, there were the faint cheers of the hundreds of people, pressed in together, watching an ancient Chinese weapon of war at work. Something to cheer for. Not bad, for an hour or so.

After about a half hour Diane and I left, and we held hands as we went back in from the balcony. Rhonda was blushing as she hesitantly said good-bye, while Roger was still smiling, probably over our last conversation and my advice. We both made the promises that are lies—about wanting to do this again real soon—and Diane followed me as we went down three flights of concrete stairs and out to the parking lot. We got into my Rover without a word. The air was muggy and warm, and the traffic on Atlantic Avenue had lightened up some by the time I joined in.

"Well," I said, "that was certainly an evening I won't forget anytime soon."

"Me, too," Diane said, with resignation in her voice. "Listen, when we get back to my place, remind me. I have the background information you requested on those three people. And, Lewis," she said, her face serious in the glow from the passing streetlights, "I've got a couple of questions about that for you."

"I'm sure you do," I said. "And I've got a question for you,

Detective. Tell me, did Roger's date do anything for you? Any chance the two of you will get together soon?"

She seemed to glare at me, and then giggled and punched me on the shoulder. "Sorry, hon. I like my women with something between their ears, and not necessarily on their chest."

"Oh, really?"

"Really," she said, seeming to sink lower into the seat. "Now, why don't you just shut up and drive. Playing games is tiring and I'm beat."

I did what she asked. We drove south along Atlantic Avenue and were slowed down a bit in the traffic around the Strip and the outlying motels and hotels. We passed Baker Street and at a hotel called the St. Lawrence Seaway, a plastic banner outside fluttered in the breeze. The banner said "Under New Management." I looked away, troubled by memories that weren't so old. In a minute or two we went by the fire station and the police station, and then I took a right as we hugged the small harbor that belongs to Tyler and is shared by the town of Falconer. The nuclear power plant's lights were bright orange and white. The trees near Diane's condominium eventually obscured them. The condo complex Diane calls home is Tyler Harbor Meadows, on the northern end of Tyler Harbor, where it narrows to meet the tidal flow of the Wonalancet River. It's made up of about a dozen town houses built near the water's edge in a horseshoe formation, and I pulled into an empty spot in front of No. 12, Diane's place.

As we got out, I said to Diane, "Mind living so close to a nuke plant?"

"Hell, no," she said. "Beats living next to a chemical factory. Least this way you know there's only one thing out there—radiation. Chemical factory, you never know what they're dumping out. But I do miss the protests."

"Why's that?"

She made a funny face. "Town of Falconer always needs help with the protesters, and it's a good chance for me to put on a real uniform and make some overtime. Sometimes civil disobedience just means money for the civil service."

I followed her in and we went up a set of carpeted stairs. The stairs made a sharp turn and there was a kitchen to the left, overlooking the parking lot and the harbor, and to the right was a small living room, with a low wooden counter holding up a television and stereo system, and a tan couch with matching chairs. Another set of stairs started in the kitchen and led upstairs, to a bedroom and a study.

The kitchen had a white tiled floor, a glass-topped table and white tubular chairs. There was a floral arrangement in the center of the table. "I'll be right back," she said as she went upstairs. I went to the refrigerator and poured myself a glass of orange juice. Pasted on the front of the refrigerator were two pictures of Diane's lover, Kara Miles. The pictures seemed to have been taken out on the *Miranda*.

Diane came back from her upstairs study, yawning a bit, holding a file folder in her hand. She had changed from her jeans and polo shirt to a white bathrobe, and her feet were bare. A joke quickly came to mind, of her being in a kitchen and being barefoot, but she looked tired and I decided to let it pass. She passed the folder over to me and I glanced inside. Three sheets of paper, covered with Diane's neat handwriting. Unlike many cops I know, Diane can write in simple, declarative sentences, and she can write without using such words and phrases as "perpetrator" and "dead corpse." At the top of each page was a single name: Justin Dix. Ben Martin. Craig Dummer.

She sat back, hands in her lap. "There you go, Lewis, and along with this info come some questions."

"Fair enough," I said, taking a sip of orange juice.

I felt uncomfortable at getting these three sheets of paper, considering what nastiness I had encountered last Saturday night, when one Tony Russo was shot to death in front of me and Felix Tinios, and all over the matter of those three paintings. I tried to ignore that vivid and bloody memory of Tony Russo gurgling to the ground after being shot. I wasn't that successful. Right then I could have given the three sheets of paper and the folder back to Diane without a single feeling or regret, save a pang of guilt for having made her do some work that I no longer desired.

She motioned to the folder I was holding. "Those three men were all working at a museum in Manchester called the Scribner Museum. Five years ago they were there when it was robbed of three very rare and valuable paintings. But I guess you already know that, right?"

"That's true."

"You're doing a story or a column about this museum theft, right?"

"I was," I said. "But now I'm thinking of letting this one slide by, Diane. It's too crazy and too complex."

She nodded. "That's good, Lewis. Very good. I'd prefer you just let this one drop. You know, doing background searches like this, sometimes you trip off alarms. The other police agencies and their computers want to know why you're suddenly interested in their cases, in their suspects. Especially with a screamer case like one. Even though it's five years old, a case that big doesn't get forgotten that easy. When I started sniffing around on those people, I got questions tossed my way. All right, that's part of the business. Which usually means you share with other cops what you're doing, and you've got a cooperative arrangement going on. But that didn't happen this time around, Lewis."

The orange juice was cold and crisp, but there was another taste there, one I didn't like. "No, I imagine it didn't. You had to lie to them, didn't you?"

She was rubbing her hands together. "I did, and I didn't like it. I had to tell them this was just a practice drill, that I wanted to see how fast I could get some background info from a number of different agencies about a big case, and this one seemed to be a case that would work well. Not a great lie but it worked."

"I'm sorry I made you lie, Diane," I said.

Diane motioned with her fingers. "What's another lie among many? It doesn't bother me that much and I'll sleep well tonight, but it's got to stop, just for a while. No more background checks or info checks, unless you clue me in as to what you're doing. I can't go out stirring up people I work with without a better excuse in my back pocket."

Damn. My half hour traipsing through the records of DefNet the other day, searching out information about Cameron Briggs. I didn't want that effort to go to waste, not when I was so damn close.

"Not even one more?"

"Lewis . . ."

"Just one more. All I need to know is something about a criminal investigation, something called Op Harpoon, or Operation Harpoon. It has—"

"Lewis!" she said, interrupting me. "Have you heard one word I've been saying?"

"I have, but—"

"Look. You and I, we've developed a professional relationship here. Sometimes I've let you cross over some lines that other cops wouldn't. Fine. I can live with that. Most of the time it has worked out for the better, and I've grown comfortable with it. But on these three names, we had an agreement. Information on these people for you in exchange for your company this evening with Roger Krohn. As far as I can see, the exchange has just occurred, and it's over. We've both settled our deals, and it's done for now, and for a while longer. No more."

I guess I couldn't give up that easily. "Diane, I'm in the middle of something, something that I need just a little help on."

Her voice was sharp. "Why don't you do some work yourself, Lewis?" she said, rubbing at the side of her head before slapping her hands down on the table. "And while you're at it, why don't you just leave?"

The white scar on her chin was pale, which was a warning sign as visible as the fireworks we had just seen over Tyler Beach. I would have gladly traded those three sheets of paper about the museum theft for one paragraph about Operation Harpoon, but when I looked again at Diane, I would have traded all of that just to clear up that angry look on her face. It was late. I was tired. I couldn't think of anything good to say.

I touched her hand. "Okay. I'm leaving."

She looked away and said, "Sorry, I'm just tired. Try me again later or something, will you?"

I squeezed her hand. "I'm sorry too, about pushing you."

A squeeze back. "Fine. Now leave, before my woman comes here and finds me trying to seduce you."

That gave us both a smile to hold things onto, and I left, with the flimsy cardboard folder in my hand, and I walked down the stairs and out onto the condo parking lot. I thought about the woman back up there in the condo. Diane Woods, my oldest friend here in Tyler Beach, who never once had seriously pressed me about who I was or what I did in my past. Not once. Now, not only was I hiding from her the identity of a homicide victim in her town, I had just spent the past ten minutes or so making her increasingly angry with me. What an accomplishment.

I guess I wasn't made for easy. I got into my Rover and drove away.

It was getting late and close to midnight, but the spat with Diane Woods had woken me up some. I stayed on Atlantic Avenue, heading north, past Roger Krohn's place. I had that confirming feeling that he and I would be spending some time together, when he came back here as the new police chief of Tyler.

Traffic was even lighter than when I had first driven past here with Diane, and the night air was still quite warm. I had the window rolled down and the stereo tuned to a classical music station from somewhere south as I rolled up the short coast. I drove by the Victorian splendor of the Lafayette House and the parking lot that led to my home, and I felt that little tug of unease you always get when you drive by your home and don't stop. You wonder what's going on in the empty and darkened rooms, and your imagination can race ahead of you, thinking of what might be occurring there while you're away.

After a few hundred feet, I crossed over the invisible line between Tyler and North Tyler, and I continued north, hesitating a moment as I passed Rosemount Lane, where Felix Tinios lived, in a ranch house that was near the ocean and which was remote enough so that no one could ever easily sneak up on him. I wondered where he was spending his hours this evening, for he had told me he was relying on a motel or hotel room in the area, and was staying far from his nest. There was that damn folder on the seat next to me, and I almost stopped and slid it under his door, but that would not be right. I would have to do something, but not tonight. No, not tonight. I had another destination ahead of me.

There are a couple of small beaches in North Tyler, none of which match the magnitude of Tyler Beach, and in a matter of minutes I crossed yet another invisible line and entered the town of Wallis. With the new town, the scenery and the homes that inhabit this part of the seacoast began to change. Most of the coastline turned from sandy beaches to a rugged collection of rocks, boulders and fissures, and most of the homes were transformed from rental cottages and condominiums to estates that would be right at home in Newport, Rhode Island, or on the Gold Coast of Long Island. Summer homes, of course, though many of them had been sold to successful businessmen and businesswomen and converted to year-round living. There are about a dozen of them and each summer tourists in cars with out-of-state license plates pulled over and helped the stock of the Kodak and Fuji companies by taking picture after picture of their elegance.

Most of the homes are set back away from Atlantic Avenue and have wide green lawns and gravel driveways behind fences or gates. Even at this hour of the night, every home I saw was well lit indoors with soft lights and outside with bright spotlights, and the cars parked before the great doors were all foreign.

It only took a couple of minutes and then I found the place I was looking for—No. 4. It was easy enough, since the numeral 4 was inscribed in brass on the brick wall adjacent to the wrought-iron gate. Another success story for the investigative reporter. I pulled over to the side of the road and switched off the engine and got out, my feet crunching on the dirt and gravel. A pickup truck zoomed by, and was followed by two bulky men on Harley-Davidsons. The full-bore throttle of those engines made the hair on the back of my arms rise up.

I leaned against the Rover's fender. At my back was a sea-wall—or berm—made of rock and dirt, hiding the tumbled mass of rocks that at this point made up the shore of New Hampshire's seacoast. Beyond the mound of dirt and the rocks was the sound of the ocean's waves, roaring in and then roaring out, no doubt disappointed that they couldn't touch the expensive mansion across the way. The house was huge, with two large wings on either side that were made up of fluted columns and floor-to-ceiling windows. The gate was closed and the driveway was made of crushed stone, going up to a circle at the front of the home. The lawn looked like a green carpet and seemed to be one of those expanses of grasses that have not once ever felt the foul touch of a weed. There was an Audi parked out front. There was no movement in the yard or from the windows of the home. It seemed quiet and peaceful, yet the man in that lovely and elegant home had done something horrible to this seacoast. Whenever the wind shifted, I still caught a whiff of the foreign oil which had been dumped here.

Cameron Briggs. It was fairly ironic that he had a summer home on a part of the coast which was polluted by a tanker that he owned, but it was probably just a matter of time. There were many creaky tankers in the Petro Associates fleet, and it was probably just fate or kismet that one of those tankers would fulfill its destiny right on his doorstep. Another example, I suppose, of God showing that He had a sense of humor.

A Nissan slid by on Atlantic Avenue, its radio blaring some trumpet march, and the sound made me jump. Then a little voice began to whisper urges at me, encouraging little messages that said I should walk across the street and clamber over the brick wall and stroll up to that quiet and rich home and start pounding on the door, demanding entrance, demanding Cameron Briggs, demanding answers.

Sure. Then I would spend the night in the Wallis police lock-up. I thought that right about now Diane Woods would be content to let me rest there. Felix couldn't bail me out, and Paula Quinn, well, I guess it was time to see Paula again. I hadn't talked to her since that uncomfortable hour or so in the park so many days ago. It would be good to see her again.

For professional reasons, of course.

Before getting back into the Rover, I again caught the scent of petroleum, and I couldn't guess if the spill had caused Cameron Briggs any discomfort.

But I was going to find out.

SIXTEEN

Before having lunch with Paula Quinn on Thursday I spent an hour or so at the Gilliam Memorial Library, which is near the center of town and about three miles away from Tyler Beach. Among its cool stacks of books, quiet reading areas and softly whirring fans, it was hard to believe that one of the Northeast's largest beach resorts was only about ten minutes away, and that sweating people in bathing suits supported the operation of this quiet library. A true story, but it was a miniature tale of how New Hampshire has supported itself for many a year: not from a sales tax or an income tax, but from an unrelenting reliance on the dollar of the tourist.

Which was fine, so long as you didn't mind paying high property taxes, and so long as a recession or an oil embargo didn't keep the tourists away. A gamble, but one that our governor and citizen legislature take with determination every two years.

During my time there, I found some additional information about Cameron Briggs through the usual references, such as *Who's Who*. He was about three years older than me, was born in New York City, and went to a private school called Collingwood, and then spent four years at Phillips Exonia, just down the street. From there he did the standard routine at Harvard, getting his MBA and then instantly working his way through a number of business and real estate companies. Names like Park Avenue Associates and the Briggs Management Company, as well as a couple of companies that seemed to be computer firms. Conquest Software. Brass Cannon Systems. Married to the former Joanne Ward Maynard and divorced, no children. Residences in New York City, on Long Island and in Wallis, New Hampshire. Active in a few charities in New York City: the Metropolitan Opera, the Central Park Trust and the Harbor Preservation Society.

But in this semi-official listing, nothing about Petro Associates. Nothing at all.

Why the big secret?

I spent ten cents and made a quick copy of Briggs's entry, and then put the red-leather volume back on the reference shelf. I had the basics, but nothing I could touch, nothing I could hold in my hands. I needed some more information before I went traipsing up that gravel driveway, and this little entry from *Who's Who* wasn't going to do it. I glanced up at the wall clock. I had another half hour before my lunch date, and I went back to work.

In those thirty minutes I searched through the indexes of the Boston *Globe*, the New York *Times* and a couple of years' worth of *Reader's Guide to Periodical Literature*, and I found not one reference to Operation Harpoon.

Secrets, and this library wasn't going to help, as good as it was.

After lunch at the southern end of the beach, Paula and I walked for a while, each of us sipping on a cold drink, and we sat on a park bench near the harbor, looking at some of the moored boats and the gulls flying overhead. Most of the moorings were empty, with trawlers and lobster boats out doing a hard day's work on the lonely ocean.

Paula wore knee-length white shorts and a short-sleeved red blouse, and through the meal she'd had on her dark sunglasses, but for some reason that didn't bother me. She laughed a lot as we ate and I felt good about it. I enjoyed seeing her eyebrows arch above her sunglasses. I tried to guess in my own mind what her eyes looked like. I guessed that they were shiny and slightly mischievous, and I was happy with my fantasy.

She sipped on a large 7-Up and ice and allowed herself a small smile. "Every April or so I get anxious, waiting for summer to begin. Just waiting for those warm days, getting your shorts out, and not worrying about keeping your oil tank filled anymore. I know it sounds crazy, but sometimes the happiest day of the month is taking down the storm windows and putting up the screens. It means summer's here. No more cold mornings. No more heating bills. No more frost to scrape off the windshields."

"Right," I said. "And then you start digging out the insect repellent, you start paying higher electric bills because of air conditioning, and your clothes start to fall apart because you're sweating all the time."

She laughed and said, "Well, I tell you, in April I'm waiting for summer to roll in, but right now is when I start waiting for it to roll right out. I start thinking about cool nights, foliage, pumpkins and empty roads. In October, it takes me all of ten minutes to get to the police station from the *Chronicle*. A day like today, well, how does forty minutes sound? Forty minutes, to get from the center of town to the beach. I'm getting tired of it, and I'm getting tired of writing beach stories. Today's the first of August. Labor Day's only four weeks away, and I can hardly wait."

"You working on anything fun?" I asked. "And are you still looking to get out?"

She played with the straw in her cup for a moment. "No to the first one, Lewis. I'm just biding my time, until Labor Day passes, and then I'm taking a week off. That means a yes to the second question. I'm still job hunting, and I'm going to make some calls during that week. Maybe make an appointment or two. I tell you, right about now, I'm not too sure if I can spend another summer writing stories at the beach. It's the same stuff year in and year out. Accidents, arrests, beach business results, number of tourists passing through every weekend. Just change the names every year, and some years you don't even have to do that. How about you, Lewis? How goes *Shoreline?*"

A lot of things had been going on with my life recently, none really connected to *Shoreline*, but I decided then to try something, and I said, "I'm thinking of doing a follow-up on the *Petro Star* spill, sort of talk to some leading residents who live on the seacoast, ask them how the spill might have affected them. Everybody does a story about the fisherman or the guy who owns a motel at the beach. I want to try somebody different."

"You got anybody in mind?"

"That I do," I said, wondering if this really constituted lying. "A guy named Cameron Briggs. Lives up in Wallis. You ever hear of him?"

Then Paula surprised me by giggling so hard that her sunglasses slipped down her nose. She pushed them up and said, "Lewis, my poor boy. You really don't read the *Chronicle* that much, do you?"

My skin seemed to warm up, and I was sure it wasn't from the sun moving in any closer. "Whenever I see anything interesting on the front page, I do pick it up. A couple of times a week, honest. Paula, it takes me more than an hour a day just to read the New York *Times* and the Boston *Globe* and"

"Look," she interrupted. "The *Chronicle's* just a small-town paper, but you should read it more often. Not because I work there—though that's a good reason—but because there are times when we report on some interesting stories in spite of ourselves."

I knew I was being set up but I didn't care. "Such as?"

"Such as the front-page story last month about the annual Wallis Fashion Show to benefit the Exonia Hospital. You see, on the front page there was a photo and story—both done by the paper's best reporter, yours truly—and in the photo was a model, the head of the trustees for the Exonia Hospital and one Cameron Briggs. For the last three years the fashion show has been held in Wallis, on the grounds of Mr. Briggs's summer home. So to answer your question, Lewis, yes, I have heard of Cameron Briggs."

There are times when I have been tempted to tell Paula every detail of my past life, and what I used to do for the Department of Defense, but this was not one of those times. For one thing, I doubt she would believe me, and for another thing, after this I was too embarrassed to even bring up my former job.

Reading the local newspaper. Not a hard thing to do. It can even prove helpful once in a while. Think you can remember that?

I tried not to look too stupid and I said, "What kind of guy is he?"

By then she had stopped laughing. "Oh, typical idle rich, up to the rural sticks of New Hampshire every summer, away from the hustle and bustle of Manhattan. The guy who tries to fit in by hosting the year's biggest fashion show every summer and then showing up in tan pants and Dock-Siders with no socks. So rich he can be comfortable anywhere. The society women around here just adore him. Without the fashion show, about the only highlight is the occasional golf tournament or sailing party. I've interviewed him a couple of times about the fashion show. If you do get a chance to talk to him, good luck."

"Why's that?"

She shrugged. "Hard to explain. He's the perfect gentleman, the perfect host. I've talked to him when he had these old society girls hanging off his shoulders, cooing and giving him air kisses. He was smiling and telling me how he enjoyed being up here, giving something back to the community, but there was something wrong with his eyes, Lewis. They weren't looking at me, they weren't looking at the society women, they weren't looking at the models." For just a second Paula's voice turned solemn. "I don't know where his eyes were looking, but it wasn't nice. It was like he wished everybody there was dead and gone, so he could stop with the act of being the nice rich boy, up here to do good. I think there's something very hard inside there, Lewis, and I wouldn't ever want to be alone with him."

Remembering how I had left Diane Woods the other night, I decided not to press things and I asked her about the latest gossip regarding a selectman in North Tyler and his habit of going to an adult bookstore in Porter. After a few minutes of talking and another bout of laughter, Paula said it was time to go. As she got up and slung her black leather purse over her shoulder, she said, "Next time we get together, I'll bring that clipping about the fashion show. If anything, you'll like the model in the picture. She had a nice bod."

I winked at her. "Oh, I'm doing just fine now, thank you."

She kissed me on the cheek, not sisterly at all. "Put your eyes away, you brute. And I'll see you later."

"I'd like that."

Another smile. "Me too."

She walked over to her Escort and I headed to the center of Tyler in my Rover, and though I was stuck in traffic on Route 51 for about fifteen minutes, I couldn't stop smiling.

After my lunch with Paula, I stopped at the big Shop 'N Save grocery store on Route 1 in the center of Tyler. I do most of my eating in restaurants but I do have to get the essentials every now and then—such as paper towels, trash bags and the odd food item—and this day seemed to be as good as any.

I took my time, strolling the clean aisles and enjoying watching the young women with children who seemed driven to load up those wheeled grocery carts with as much food as possible. Me, I don't think I've ever used a wheeled cart in my life. With only a couple of items left to get for the day, I was in the frozen-food section picking up six containers of Minute Maid lemonade, when he came up next to me.

"Been a while, Lewis," the voice said.

I recognized the voice right away and finished putting the containers of lemonade away in my grocery basket, covering up a copy of the day's *Chronicle* in the process. I looked over at Felix Tinios, who had a bag of grapes in one hand. He had on dark khaki shorts with big pockets that looked as if they came from a British soldier on the North African front in 1942 and a yellow T-shirt that had some Italian phrase on it I couldn't translate.

"Which has meant some peace and quiet for me," I said. "How about you?"

He had a big smile on his face and said, "You're getting sloppy. I've been following you since you had lunch with that reporter chick of yours, all the way up to the store. If I had been somebody else, you might have been in a load of trouble."

"Somebody else, like certain nameless wonders?" I asked, remembering Felix's own phrases. "Nameless and gutless wonders who've been sending you postcards?"

He nodded. "Maybe so. Look, let's talk, just for a moment."

I followed him to a wide area of the store, which had rows and rows of videotapes for rent. The way these large grocery stores have expanded has always amazed me. From developing your film to having a pharmacy indoors and now a landscaping section and movie section, well, it made me think about what they would offer next. A car dealership next to the produce section? Oral surgery next to the juice aisle?

By the ranks of the videotapes there were a couple of park benches for the older set, and while I'm sure Felix wouldn't like to be lumped into that category, I was also sure the young cashiers and bag boys wouldn't have any objection at all. I rested my light load of groceries on my lap and said, "What's going on, Felix?"

He handed over a postcard to me. "This is the latest contact."

The postcard was an aerial shot of Tyler Beach, showing

Weymouth's Point and just catching the southern end of the Samson State Wildlife Preserve. With a magnifying glass I would have been able to make out my house. I flipped the card over. Felix's address—a post office box in North Tyler—was typed, along with yesterday's date and the message. It said in capital letters:

YOUR COUSIN AND RUSSO WERE MESSAGES. DON'T IGNORE THIS ONE. THE MAINE HOUSE IN ONE WEEK OR WE VISIT 1201 CENTENNIAL.

"What's at 1201 Centennial?" I asked.

Felix hunched forward as he took the card back from me. His voice was firm. "That's where my father lives, Lewis. In Brockton."

I thought for a moment, just looking at the tensed-up figure of Felix. Around us people were shopping and the cashiers were busy bleeping groceries through the scanners, and it struck me how loud a grocery store is. Couldn't someone just come in and shop in peace?

"This is going places you didn't expect, Felix."

He rubbed at his forehead. "I guess that's about the smartest thing I've heard in weeks. Yeah, this one has gone to some very strange places." He looked over at me, his face grim. "It's been a very long time since I've been concerned about anything I've been involved with. I've always thought that I was slick enough so that I could never be caught, never be bothered, never be hurt. This one's changing that, and I don't like it."

"Who do you think they are, Felix?" I asked. "People from Boston with a grudge against Russo? Someone back there that you angered, somebody with a long memory?"

He shook his head. "I wish I knew. I've been asking some discreet questions and I've heard nothing, nothing at all. That's surprising. And what surprises me more is the fallout from the hit on Tony Russo last week."

"The surprise being?"

"The surprise being that no one's asked me anything about it, nothing at all. Which makes me think that Tony was doing a little freelance work and wasn't talking much to anyone. Which makes me think it was someone working with Tony who killed him off, all for my benefit. Either the buyer or someone connected to the buyer."

I handed the postcard back to Felix. "So what's your next step? Suggest another meet? Continue negotiating?"

He took the card and rubbed at its slick surface for a moment, as though he was trying to sense the identity of the person or persons who had sent it to him, and then he crushed the postcard in his hands. "Lewis, I'll always deny saying this, but I'm getting the hell out of this one. I don't care about the money anymore. These guys . . . well, they're just too loony. They have no sense of business. Something more than business is going on and I don't want to find out what it is. I think I'm going to give everything up, but I need one favor, just one. And before you say no, remember Christy. Last time I saw her with you, you were smiling."

I wondered if I looked flushed at the memory and said, "Are you still looking for help?"

Felix nodded. "Still looking for information. I know you had started looking into some things about that museum theft. If you could just finish and pass it along, well, I'll appreciate it. And tell you what, I'll give you a finder's fee. About half of what I offered earlier on. Then it's over and you and I can go down to Boston and see a Red Sox game and I'll take you to an Italian restaurant you could only dream about."

I moved my hands against the smooth plastic of the grocery basket. "Information, then. No more face-to-face negotiations with me there holding your hand."

He shook his head. "Just info gathering. That's it. Then it's over."

Shoppers milled about us on the shiny tile flooring. Hundreds of food and grocery items were freshly wrapped in their protective and sanitary packaging and the baggers and cashiers moved every one along, and a man from the North End of Boston was sitting patiently at my side, waiting for my answer in his quest to save himself and his father.

"You got it," I said. "But then it's over."

He nodded. "Agreed. Then it's over. Thanks, Lewis."

As he got up to leave, I asked, "If you intend to give the paintings up, Felix, then why the info gathering? What's the point?"

While for a brief moment earlier his face had looked troubled, now it looked determined. "When I know who they are and when they get their paintings, then I intend to hunt them down. Nobody threatens my father, Lewis. Nobody."

After leaving Felix at the grocery store, I drove through a number of side streets and one shopping-center parking lot, and by doing so I managed to avoid most of the traffic on my way home. The parking lot of the Lafayette House was full, but I slid through with no fuss and went down the bumpy and ill-maintained-for-a-purpose driveway and before I parked my Rover in the sagging shed that serves as my garage, I saw a surprise waiting for me. A woman in a two-piece black bathing suit was sunbathing on my front lawn, lying on her back on a folding lounge chair.

I stopped and the woman sat up, shielding her eyes with her hand. She waved at me and I half-waved back, and then I parked the Rover in the garage. After grabbing the plastic bag of groceries, I walked outside. The grass on the lawn was sparse as always but the sight was overwhelmed by the lawn furniture and the woman sitting there. One Cassie Fuller.

"Hi there," she said, smiling widely. Her bathing suit looked as if it was made out of some thin wet-suit material, and her tanned and full skin was slick with either baby oil or suntan lotion. The bathing suit didn't leave much to my imagination, and her legs were quite long and flawless. I was suddenly aware that the sun was very hot and that I was growing thirstier with each passing minute.

"Hi yourself," I said, feeling self-conscious with the grocery bag swinging from my hand. "How the hell did you find out where I lived?"

The smile barely faltered. "Some welcome, Lewis Cole. I thought you might enjoy a surprise, of having me show up at your doorstep on a day off. All it took was a few phone calls to your magazine and the Chamber of Commerce people here at the beach. You're fairly well known around here. You should be flattered."

I tried to smile back. "Actually, I'm not. And I'm sorry for the initial rudeness. I don't often get uninvited guests."

She was sitting up and leaning forward, showing me some more square centimeters of tanned skin, and she said, "Well, this looks like your lucky day."

Jesus. "Maybe so. Feel like a drink?"

"Absolutely," she said, and she spun off the chair in what looked like a well-practiced move. She picked up a small white towel and wiped her hands and dropped it on the lounge chair, and she followed me up the steps as I unlocked the front door.

Inside I threw open the sliding-glass doors to the deck and the sounds of the waves were louder as I put away my meager groceries. Cassie looked around the rooms and made approving noises, and she joined me out on the deck with a glass of lemonade and ice. I had been quiet as I moved around the house, putting things away and making the drinks. Cassie was the first woman other than Paula Quinn or Diane Woods that had been in my house this summer. She was a bit overwhelming, from the exotic scent of her body oil to her skimpy bathing suit and her bright eyes, which seemed to be equal parts laughing and mocking.

Outside she leaned against a railing and said, "Hell of a view, Lewis. At my house, all I have is a tiny backyard and a couple of squirrels that raise hell, and an old man next door who says he's a birdwatcher, but his binoculars always seem to be pointing at me. I'm jealous of what you've got here."

"Thanks," I said. "I've lived here a couple of years and I've still never gotten used to it."

"Hmmm," she said, sipping from her drink. A bead of ice

water came off the glass and rolled down her wrist, and a quick snapshot of an image came to me, of touching the bead of water and wiping it away with my fingers. I looked away and out to the ocean.

"How goes the magazine article about the museum?" she said, and I paused for a moment before replying. In all the times I've worked on "articles" that never appeared, I had uttered the Great Lie without qualms or guilt, but this time there was something about her look that made me stop for a moment.

And then I said, "It's going," and I wondered if she sensed my lie. I tried to cover it up by asking, "How are things at the Scribner?"

She shrugged her bare shoulders. "Nothing much going on. Papers come to my desk and leave my desk. Typing and dictation get done. It can get extremely dull in Manchester."

"How's Justin doing?"

"Justin?" she asked. "He's busy being Justin. A dreary security man who works every day to try to make up for something bad that happened years ago, and who probably doesn't know that most people don't give a shit. It's done. It's over. Finished. He's not much fun to be around."

"In what way?"

Again, that cool shrug. "All work and no play will make anyone a dull boy. All he talks about is the job and the museum, and nothing else. Politics, society, gossip, and I've tried it all."

"And why won't he talk?"

Cassie finished her glass of lemonade and carefully placed it on the railing. She turned to me, reached up and gently grabbed my ears, leaned forward and gave me a quick kiss on the lips. She tasted salty, and then she moved back and shook her head.

"Lewis, one of my many faults is that I'm a quick study, and at this moment I think I like you," she said, her voice a bit rueful. "And I know that if I stay here longer and get to know you more, I'm going to start disliking you. I came here for a friendly visit and to rattle your cage a bit, and to see what might happen with the two of us, and all you've done since I've been here is to interrogate me. You've not once asked a question that's not related to my job or Justin Dix. You've not once asked a question about me. And if you're going to do that for the first ten minutes of my visit to your home, then there's not much to look forward to and I'm going to leave now and keep on liking you."

A number of arguments came to me, sentences that would try to convince her to stay. I gave up. Sometimes being truthful is the best course.

"You're a sharp one, and I won't disagree with anything you said, Cassie," I said. "I think I like you, too. It's just that—"

"Hush," she said, holding up a hand and moving away from the railing. "We'll just leave it at that. I'll see my own way out, and maybe, if you stop doing whatever you're doing, you might come back to the museum for a visit."

"I might do that," I said, but by then, she was already through the sliding-glass door, and I fought the urge to follow her out and to see her walk back up my driveway.

Instead I stayed out on the deck for a while, until I was sure that she was gone, and I finished my own drink and picked up her glass and smelled her scent for the last time. I went inside and did much of nothing for the rest of the afternoon. Seeing yourself perfectly in a mirror, warts and faults and all, tends to take the energy out of one's day.

CHAPTER

SEVENTEEN

On Friday morning I had a quick breakfast of tea and toast, then drove into town to pick up the morning Boston Globe and my mail at the Tyler post office. I tossed the mail on the seat, threw the Globe on top, and drove back home. I got a glass of orange juice, grabbed the sheaf of mail and went outside. I sat on a fake-redwood chair and propped up my feet on the wooden railing. The morning was sunny and it looked like a good beach day. I felt sure that within a mile radius of my home, there were probably a couple of thousand people who were in a better mood than me.

I flipped through the mail quickly. A postcard from Dr. Ludlow, reminding me of a follow-up appointment, scheduled for this Sunday afternoon. A flyer from Sears and one from J. C.

Penney, a bill from the local cable company, a request for money from the Nature Conservancy that I saved for later and an ivory-colored envelope that almost froze me to the chair, it surprised me so. My name and post office box in Tyler were neatly typed in the center of the envelope. In the upper left-hand corner, there was the embossed logo for *Shoreline* magazine, and between the magazine's name and its address in Boston was this line: Admiral Seamus A. Holbrook (Ret.), Editor.

The admiral. Writing to me. I've worked as the New Hampshire columnist for *Shoreline* magazine for a couple of years now, and I've only met the admiral once, when I visited the editorial offices and he hired me. Since then my contacts with *Shoreline* have been brief and infrequent. Every two weeks a rather substantial paycheck is deposited electronically from *Shoreline* into my account at the First Porter National Bank. I never go to their offices, I never get any phone calls from anybody in the editorial department and I never go to their annual Christmas party— which I understand from the society pages of the Boston *Herald* and the Boston *Globe* is quite magnificent, since it's held in their brick office building overlooking the slowly improving Boston Harbor.

In exchange for this wonderful arrangement, all I have to do is file a column each month through my modem. The arrangement I had with the admiral is that my column would appear, sometimes edited, sometimes not, and if they considered it crap, another column would be inserted under my name. When I was going into the hospital earlier this summer, in one three-day space of time I had written two columns ahead of schedule. But only once have I ever missed a deadline, and that had occurred last week.

I tapped the heavy envelope against my teeth as I thought about that. Miss a column and get a letter from the editor. Makes sense. But maybe something else was going on. There was a new administration in Washington, and maybe past embarrassments were quietly being disposed of. Perhaps my little electronic sleuthing in DefNet last week had been detected. Then this letter could be something else, a dismissal. Promises had been made, of course, that I would be set for life in exchange for what the Department of Defense had done to me and my friends in Nevada. The promise included this job at *Shoreline*, but this wouldn't be the first time that promises had been broken. Just ask the South Vietnamese, the Kurds or the Bosnians.

With one motion I tore open the envelope and a thick piece of stationery came out, embossed with the same seal and words as the upper left-hand corner of the envelope. It was a simply written message:

> Cole—
> Have you forgotten what a deadline means?
> You've got another two weeks.
> —Holbrook

Well, there had been that arrangement back then. I had been promised total freedom to write anything I wanted and to submit a blank sheet of paper if I felt like it, but something had changed. He still wanted a column, no matter what the arrangement had been. It looked like the admiral's blood was slowly becoming the fluid of an editor.

I put the letter and envelope down in my lap and looked out over the ocean. The air was hot and still and I remembered what Paula had said yesterday. She was getting tired of summer and wanted it over, and I could see her point. It was hard to do your work with so many people around you, vacationing and having a good time. Their sense of relaxation and play was intoxicating, and it was hard to keep focused, something like being a janitor in an opium den. In a few weeks Labor Day and the traditional end of summer would be upon us, and the tourists and their intoxication would leave.

But I had so much to do in that time. The *Petro Star*. My column. And my promise to Felix, and in remembering that promise, I thought with another smile of Christy, and decided Felix would be the first I would attend to, later today.

In the meantime, the waves were something to look at.

Back in June and about three days after my surgery I was curled on one side, watching a soap opera on television and wondering what had happened to all those wonderful game shows I had watched as a kid growing up in Indiana. At least those shows pretended they were passing on some sort of knowledge, ranging from history to art to Hollywood. I'm not too sure what kind of knowledge the soap opera writers were trying to provide, though it seemed to revolve around whose bed got warmed. The door to my hospital room then opened and Felix came in, with a woman I hadn't met before, which wasn't surprising, considering Felix's sweaty track record. Felix had on a soft black suit with a white shirt and no necktie, and if I had been feeling better, I'm sure I would have said the woman was beautiful, so beautiful that she could have easily made some fashion photographers in New York City swoon. She had long dark hair and lightly tanned skin, and wore a light blue two-piece woman's suit with ruffled white blouse that was both executive-looking and something that should be worn with a teddy underneath. She smiled and nodded and sat down in one of the room's chairs, crossing her legs.

Felix said, "How's it going, Lewis?" and I whispered back, "Doing better," as he bustled about my room. He had another bouquet of flowers, which he put on the windowsill, and another bag of books. I remembered once telling him that as a high school student I had loved the novels of John D. MacDonald, and with each visit he had brought a couple more paperbacks with him. The books remained on the windowsill, out of reach. I was still not all together since the surgery. The body rebels against being put to sleep and cut open, and mine was no different. I was easing in and out of sleep, I was sloggy with constipation, and I felt greasy, since all the nurses could do for me was a sponge bath. You try sponge baths for a couple of days in June and see how good you smell.

Felix sat on the arm of the second chair and said, "This is a good friend of mine, Lewis. Christy Gunn. We were going to do some shopping at Faneuil Hall today and thought we'd stop by."

She smiled at me and said, "Nice to meet you, Lewis."

I nodded back, too tired to say much, and then Felix smacked his palm against his head and said, "Damn it, hon, did you put money in the meter?"

"No, I thought you did."

Felix laughed and said, "Any more tickets, it's the Denver boot for my car. Hon, you stay here with Lewis. I'll be right back." He left, and I think I was even too tired to feel shy at being alone in a hospital room with such a beautiful woman. Yet if Christy felt equally uncomfortable, she hid it well. She smiled at me and deftly took off her jacket and slung it over the back of the other chair. Even with the ruffles in the blouse, it was easy to tell that she was quite well proportioned.

Christy said, "The both of you seem very interesting."

"Really?"

"Really," she said. "Felix told me a lot about you on the drive over here. About how the two of you met, the places you've both gone to and the things you've done. He called you a holdout, one of the last ones left with any sense of duty and responsibility."

That was getting a bit too deep for me, and I tried to change the subject by saying, "How long have you known Felix?"

She smiled again, wider. "Oh, we've been friends for a while. Occasionally business associates. In fact, he asked me to come over today and visit with you."

"He did?"

"Unh-hunh." She got up from her chair and sauntered over, and then touched my cheek for a moment, and I closed my eyes, enjoying the touch. Christy said, "He asked me to do something special for you. Felix has arranged everything, and we have an hour together. We won't be disturbed."

I closed my eyes, conscious of the throbbing pain in my side that the codeine pills couldn't quite mask, and of the smell of my skin and the sheets and that cloying perfume that Christy was wearing; my mouth was still dry. I opened my eyes. She was still there, breathing and smiling. Oh, to be whole again.

"I would like a drink of water," I finally said.

She nodded, went to the tiny bathroom, filled up a cup and came out again. While the sight of her was something that I'm sure would have stirred me at any other time, on this day the taste of the cool water upon my dry tongue was all that I lusted after. She held the cup, and while I drank, she touched my cheek with her free hand.

When I was done, she put the cup down on a counter and then washed my face with a wet towel, and I looked up at her and said, "And what exactly has Felix arranged?"

She smiled again. "What do you think?"

"I'm not sure."

She laughed and touched my cheek again. "Oh, stop looking so stunned." She went over to the windowsill and began rummaging around the book bags. "Felix knows you love these books, and he also knows they haven't been touched since he's delivered them. So. I'm here to read to you, if you'd like."

I shifted, grimaced some as the pain blossomed a bit on my side. "I would like that very much."

She pulled out a couple of books. "The ones here are all by the same author. Is there a special one you'd like?"

"The one that has the color blue in the title," I said. "That's the first one in a very good series."

She took out the right paperback from the bag and pulled the chair close to my bed, and she opened up the book and started reading. She read with one hand and held my hand with another, and for the next fifty or so minutes, I was intoxicated with so many things: the sight and smell of her, sitting so very close to me, the warm caress of her hand upon mine, her quiet and strong voice, and the words themselves, written so many years ago by a craftsman who knew the power of phrases, sentences and paragraphs. Not once did she pause or stop for a rest or a drink. She kept on reading, and I wondered how much longer she could keep on going.

Then came the knock upon the door. She looked up, disturbed. Then she looked over at me with another smile and leaned forward and kissed me on the lips.

"Felix is fond of you, Lewis," she said, and then she got up and put her jacket back on. There was another knock and Felix came in, an innocent look upon his face, and said, "Well, I got caught up in something. I hope you don't mind."

"Nope," I said.

He looked at his watch. "Well, it's getting late. Tell you what, Lewis, I'll come back in a couple of days for another visit." He winked. "Alone."

"That would be fine," I said.

As they left, Felix turned to Christy and said, "I hope everything went all right."

She touched my cheek as she left. "He was a perfect gentleman," and Felix said, grinning, "Of course he was."

Christy had left the book on my bed. I picked it up and resumed reading where she had left off. The book had her scent upon it for the rest of my stay there.

It was late on Friday afternoon after a wonderful lunch and I had a headache. I had spent a lot of last night's hours reading and rereading the files that Diane Woods had provided me with, and on this day I had gotten to work. Earlier this morning, when it was finally a reasonable hour on the West Coast, I had talked to Dennis and Owen Martin, the sons of Ben Martin, the former Manchester police officer who had been on guard duty that night at the Scribner Museum. Dennis lived in Seattle and maybe that city's rainy weather had something to do with his mood, for when I started talking to him, he had just two words in reply before hanging up on me and those words weren't "Merry Christmas."

His brother Owen—living in Los Angeles—was only marginally better. He had listened somewhat patiently to my lying spiel: I was doing a follow-up story on the theft for *Shoreline* magazine, and I was wondering what could he tell me about his father and his museum job. Owen had said, "I really can't answer that question, Mr. Cole."

I was in my upstairs study, phone to my ear, pen and pad of paper in hand, bare feet up on my desk. "Excuse me?"

"You see," he said, his voice clear over the thousands of miles, "I was already living out here before he retired from the police department. All I knew about his job at the museum was what he told me in his letters. It was just a job, something to help out with his pension plan, and it kept him busy. He worked a lot of years as a cop, and that was all he knew. He was scared of staying home during the day—I think he would have worked just as happily at McDonald's, serving burgers and fries, so long as he made a buck and felt like a wage earner. He was not one to take it easy and loaf. With Mom being dead, I think being alone in that house would have driven him crazy."

"What happened after the theft, then? Do you remember that?"

Even three time zones away, I could make out the sigh of despair in Owen Martin's voice. "A lot of strange things can happen to you because of the little choices you make, Mr. Cole. I found out in school that I had a knack for engineering and so I'm out here working for Lockheed. My brother Dennis can make things with his hands, beautiful pieces of pottery, and so he's up in the Pacific Northwest. My dad, he needed a job after retirement and was happy as a museum guard, and that choice killed him."

His voice was stronger. "You see, my dad kept clean in his years on the force. Even piddly shit like taking free lunches or Cokes during the day, he wouldn't do it. He was always proud of the uniform and the badge, even if some of the guys he worked with weren't. So imagine what it was like, after retirement as a cop, to be a suspect in the biggest art theft in New England's history. To be interviewed by detectives you knew, who you worked with. To be grilled and followed by the FBI. It broke his heart, and it killed him."

I doodled a bit on the pad. "The news reports said that your father thought he recognized one of the fake cops over the video monitor and that's why he let them in."

"Why they let them in," he corrected me. "There was another guard on duty that night, and maybe my dad recognized someone and maybe he didn't. He was getting to be an old man, and his eyes might have played tricks on him."

"Do you think he did recognize someone? And then later changed his mind?"

"I don't know. He never said much about this whole crappy thing afterward."

"Did your dad have any interest in art at all?"

"No, not at all."

"Did anything unusual happen after the theft, like visitors, odd phone calls?"

"Jesus Christ," he said, exasperated, "you mean shit-ass phone calls like this?" and then he hung up on me, which was probably a reasonably good idea out in California.

Later that morning, I had started work on tracking down Craig Dummer, Ben Martin's partner that night, who hadn't left much of a trail since he had moved out of that duplex in Bainbridge. The police records that Diane had pulled for me still listed Bainbridge as his address, and still gave DiskJets as his place of business. I called DiskJets, pretending to be the New England Savings Bank, wanting to verify his place of employment for a car loan. A bored clerk at the other end said he had left on his own nearly four weeks ago, and there was no record of a new job. No relatives listed in his job application. No other information of any use. Previous place of employment? At that question the bored clerk seemed to perk up a bit, and she said, "Um, can you hold for a second?" and when she did that, I hung up, not wanting to have to explain myself to her nosy supervisor.

Calls to the Bainbridge town hall were of equal use, as well as a call to the Bainbridge post office. No change of address had been filed. Nothing else was available at the State of New Hampshire's Department of Motor Vehicles in Concord. You can do a lot with phone work, but this Friday wasn't one of those days.

Craig Dummer was on the move. I rubbed at the base of my aching head. I didn't like the coincidence of Felix Tinios receiving those postcards at about the same time Craig was leaving his home in Bainbridge.

I also didn't like Justin Dix, the museum security head, not having a better handle on Craig Dummer's location. When I had met him and had gone over the painting theft, he implied that he and other police officials always knew Craig's whereabouts. But he had been wrong, either through oversight or on purpose. Then there was Cassie, and her odd reactions. The tiff yesterday, was that real or manufactured? And earlier, she had said that Justin had problems and secrets of his own, and in looking through the information Diane had gotten for me about Justin Dix—including his credit history—I thought I had something.

The security director of the Scribner Museum had trouble paying his bills, and the year he suffered the worst was the year the Winslow Homer paintings had been stolen. I fired up my Apple computer and in another hour or two of info-surfing— including a couple of not very legal entries into the data banks of some credit bureaus—I found that among his overdue bills, Justin had also suffered a car repossession, along with a partial garnisheeing of his salary at the Scribner Museum, the same year the thefts had occurred.

"Who will guard the guardians, eh, Justin?" I whispered, while looking again at Diane's handwritten report. And for the benefit of any Roman ghosts haunting this particular stretch of the New Hampshire seacoast, I repeated myself in Latin: *"Quis custodiet ipsos custodes?"*

For lunch I had a lobster roll, french fries and a salad, which I ordered from the kitchen at the Lafayette House, my hidden neighbor across the street. To get to my home means traversing the parking lot of the Lafayette House, but I reached a mutual agreement with the management of Tyler Beach's most famous hotel when I first moved here. They've left me alone, and I've kept an occasional eye on the parked cars of their guests during my comings and goings. Though I've never eaten or stayed at the Lafayette House, I have reached a slightly illegal agreement with the head chef. In exchange for ordering meals right out of the kitchen, I pay the menu price in cash, right to the chef's pocket, plus 10 percent. Both of us think we're getting the better deal— he gets extra cash in his pocket that goes unrecorded, and I get great meals that I don't have to cook and clean up after.

But lunch and an hour or so of relaxed reading didn't make me feel any better. I went upstairs to the bathroom, took three aspirins and tried to convince myself to improve.

When I came out of the bathroom, I went into my study, past the ceiling-high bookshelves and to my desk, where the Apple Macintosh computer was still on, humming quietly away, its electrons doing a tremendous dance that made so much work and information gathering so easy. I sat down, letting the faint squeak-squeak of the chair work its way into the knot of my brain. I was still trembling a bit with energy from all that I'd done this day, and I felt a stirring of success. I had done well. I had learned a lot. I was on a roll, and I knew I shouldn't walk away yet. I knew from my past work at the DoD that there were days—we called them Gold Star days—when everything went right, when all the codes were broken, all the information fell together, all your calls and inquiries were answered. On Gold Star days, you worked until your eyes rebelled and your fingers trembled with exhaustion, because you were never sure when another bout of luck like that would happen again.

From the files on my desk I picked up the one marked *Petro Star*, searching until I found the printout of Cameron Briggs's business interests, and got the number I wanted, for his main office in New York City. I looked at the time. It was just past two in the afternoon.

I dialed the long-distance number and it was answered on the first ring. "Briggs Associates."

Answered on the first ring. Not bad. Maybe there was hope

for American business yet. I cleared my throat. "Public relations, please."

"One moment." I was put on hold, and instead of the mind-numbing monotony of hold music, I was given an audio feed of CNN Headline News. Nice touch.

A click, and then a woman's voice, "Public affairs, Mr. Rossum's office."

"Is Mr. Rossum in, please?"

"Hold on."

As I listened to a CNN report on fighting in South Africa, I rehearsed the patter I was going to try. For the first time this day, I would identify myself as Lewis Cole, writer for *Shoreline* magazine out of Boston, Massachusetts, who was looking to schedule an interview with Cameron Briggs.

Another click, and a man's voice. "This is Gus Rossum."

I opened my mouth to say something and then I stopped.

And I hung up on him.

A few hours after that I walked out of my house and locked the door. I then got into my Range Rover and drove up the trail to the Lafayette House parking lot. I had changed from my shorts and T-shirt of earlier that day and was wearing my working clothes, which included a navy-blue blazer and necktie. My reporter's notebook was on the passenger's side of the Rover. I was prepping myself for a little work. My headache was gone.

As I drove north on Atlantic Avenue, heading for Wallis, I thought of Mr. Gus Rossum of the public relations department of Briggs Associates, and decided he was probably used to getting hung up on all the time. Probably number-two item in his job description. But unlike a lot of other callers he probably received, I had no malice in disconnecting my call to him. It wasn't personal. It was strictly business. In those few seconds of waiting for him to come to the phone, I had decided that a truly Gold Star day would not depend on dancing the formal game of schedules, questions and return phone calls that PR people are so adept at performing.

So this evening, I was going to pass up that game and try another.

Traffic was steady but not too heavy, and it only took a few more minutes than usual to pass over into Wallis, and there it was. The number 4 in brass on the brick wall, and I was doing quite nicely, thank you, for the wrought-iron gate was open. I turned left and went up the crushed-stone driveway. Little lamps set into the side of the driveway lit my way up to the house. There was a light gray Audi parked there, the same one I had seen the other day. The house and its two large wings were as big as I remembered them, and lights were on behind every floor-to-ceiling window.

I went up the brick steps to the wide front door as if I belonged there, carrying the reporter's notebook in my hand. Before I rang the bell I pulled my press identification card out of my wallet and slipped it into my shirt pocket. The bell made no sound that I could hear from outside, but the door opened up in less than a minute and a man answered, wearing lime-green shorts and a white hip-length polo shirt. He carried a golf club in his hands.

"Yes?" he asked, and from his tone and manner and from what Paula Quinn had told me, I knew I was standing before Cameron Briggs.

My Gold Star day wasn't over yet.

EIGHTEEN

In working where I did, in the unofficial Marginal Issues Section of our little group, our workday was sometimes interrupted by the occasional visitor. It always followed the same pattern. We were told by E-mail or memo from our section leader, George Walker, that a visitor would be by during a certain time. Our desks would have to be cleared of anything that could not be allowed to be seen by the uncleared or the uninitiated, which meant—at least for our section—that our desktops for the most part would be thoroughly empty.

Then the visitor would come by, herded by some higher-ups. They'd go into George Walker's office—the only one with a door—and engage in about ten minutes of idle chitchat before coming out for the tour of our work area. That usually took about another ten minutes, since our section was so small. However, I recall once when a retired senator who was serving on some intelligence board, and who had a propensity for liquid lunches, stopped at our information center and railed on for long minutes about our subscribing to the Tass news service, back when there was a Soviet Union to be scared of. The ex-senator slurred a lot of his words, but basically, his point was that we shouldn't allow such Communist propaganda into the Pentagon.

From the pained look on his escorts' faces, I didn't envy them their job that day, or any other day, for that matter.

On one particular visit, the gentleman coming by was a new Assistant SecDef for some office or whose main talent was being from the home state of the current President and a hefty campaign contributor. He had also been a big executive in one of those food conglomerates.

On most days, we called these visits sheep shows when George wasn't around, but on this day, cattle show seemed more appropriate. The man was large and bulky, with a bright red face and a grin that seemed stitched in with wires. George did his best, which wasn't much. I caught the eye of Cissy Manning, and she winked in my direction while going past the information center. My next-door neighbor, Carl Socha, had disappeared, though on some occasions he'd stay and on rarer occasions he'd actually Play the Game and be fawning and friendly and the best DoD black budget employee ever.

One day at lunch in the center courtyard of the five-sided palace—known affectionately as Ground Zero—I'd asked him why, and in a quite reasonable and serious tone, he'd said, "Lewis, I'm very good at what I do, but I'm also working against three hundred years of history in this country and about fifty years of history in this building, when my father and my uncles were only good in this department for being mess stewards or working in construction battalions. I'm doing everything I can to clamber up that hill, and if it means kissing butt on occasion, so be it. One of those nitwits we meet might one day get kicked upstairs to become SecDef and he might need a bright guy for his staff, and in the fine tradition of affirmative action programs everywhere, he just might pick me, and I might be in a position to help my brethren. So that's why I do what I do."

I'd said that was a hell of an idea, and asked him to pass the ketchup.

Then on this occasion George Walker brought the new Assistant SecDef around to the different cubicles. He hemmed and hawed a bit when he came to mine, mainly because I was sitting in my chair, feet up on my desk, trying my damnedest to do the previous Sunday's New York *Times* crossword puzzle.

"Um," George said, not even daring to cross over the threshold into my office space, as if he was afraid I was going to contaminate him with some Bohemian virus. "This is, um, Lewis Cole. One of the more unique members of our section."

I nodded and went back to the crossword puzzle. I don't do the puzzle to impress anyone—in fact, I do it in pencil, and I've never succeeded in even getting close to finishing one off. I do the Sunday puzzle for two reasons, though: to stretch my mind and to bring myself back to earth anytime I feel like I'm getting too cocky for my own good.

The new guy, with his escorts and hangers-on grouped around him, poked his head in and said, "How's it going, young man?"

I was stuck on a five-letter word for a mountain range in North Africa, and I looked up and gave him my best government employee smile and said, "Not bad, but I sure could use a Coke and an order of large fries."

Well. Some faces dropped and others turned red, but the new guy gave a satisfied nod and went on with the tour, as though nothing had happened, and I wrote in the word "Atlas." About five minutes later Trent Baker came by and said in his patrician New York voice, "I'm sure that you're quite aware that Mr. Walker is upset with you."

"Quite," I said, trying to remember the name of the French premier during the Vichy regime. Trent smiled and walked away, looking like he moonlighted as a model for GQ. Coming from one of the richest families on Long Island, he had decided to dedicate his work to his nation instead of the family business. A rare bird. I don't know if he realized that his sense of devotion and loyalty to his country were now considered an anachronism by Those in the Know. Then I shrugged and wrote in "Laval."

About ten minutes later George Walker called me into his office and shut the door and said, "Cole, you're one of our best, which is why I'm directed to give you wide latitude, but why do you insist on making my job difficult? Why do you insult the visitors who come here and make the whole section look bad?"

At the time George Walker was going bald toward the front of his head, and when he was upset, the whole front dome of his skull glowed a dull red, like a heated doorknob.

I shrugged. "I don't know, George. I guess I have an attitude problem toward rich yahoos who come in here because they're connected. They make a mess of things for a year or so before getting bored and moving on, leaving the rest of us here to clean up after them."

George shook his head. "That's not an attitude that's going to get you anywhere, Cole. Not at all."

I winked at him, which I think disturbed him almost as much as my Coke and fries crack. "George, let's take a page from our work and look what's before us. You and I and everybody else here didn't quite fit in, and we've been classified as oddballs. That's why we're here, in the Marginal Issues Section."

"That's not its title," he snapped. "We're the Room 112 Subgroup."

"George, you're not following procedures. You're letting your emotions cloud your analysis. This is the Marginal Issues Section, and that's who we are and what we do. The only career path for me is your office, and I certainly don't want your job."

Well, that comment didn't sit well, and George started moving papers left and right on his desk, and he spoke low to me and said, "Cole, I'm doing everything possible to get out of this section, and if you want to stay here, fine. But I'm not."

I left and looked back through the glass of the door. His head was bowed over his work and the color was quite red. Poor

George. He had a plan to move on up, and part of that plan, I later learned, was treatments to restore hair to his bald spot.

He had gone through one treatment before he and the rest of the section were killed.

That memory came back to me as I sat on a stone bench in the rear yard of Cameron Briggs's house and watched him at play on his putting green, knocking little golf balls into a series of holes in a lawn that was so perfect and smooth it made the grass out front look like it belonged to a wild Nebraskan prairie. This was the first time I had ever been up close to a putting green, and it was true, the balls did make a little rattling echo each time they went into the hole. As I watched Briggs at work, I was reminded of that Assistant SecDef, for Briggs was a lot like him. Not in physique or dress—Cameron was about my height (six feet) and ten years older, with short salt-and-pepper hair, but was in better shape than me and had a slim muscularity that spoke of determined hours in a health club. No, it wasn't the shape that reminded me of that ex-hamburger maven turned DoD official. It was the attitude of being above it all so much in terms of class and money that nothing mattered. I guessed it was the self-confidence that came to somebody when they had money, enough money to buy anything: handsome looks, an oceanfront home worth millions of dollars or a fancy job in the Pentagon.

I got a taste of that self-confidence not more than fifteen minutes ago, when he had answered the door and, after listening to my lying spiel, invited me in for a drink and conversation. While making my drink in a room that had a bar that would not look out of place at the Lafayette House, he had said, "You'll note that there's nobody here tonight. Just a week ago I got sick of them just hanging around, and I gave them all—the cook, gardener and maid—two weeks off. Gad. Sometimes you just want to be alone, away from people, especially people that you support, that just keep on looking for more money."

By now my jacket was off and I was drinking a weak gin and tonic. I was bowing a bit to the surroundings, for I had decided my usual Molson Golden Ale wouldn't quite fit in with the fine Mr. Cameron Briggs and his summer cottage. My reporter's notebook was in my lap and Briggs kept up a running commentary as he stroked each golf ball into a hole in the putting green.

"Hmm," he said, his voice firm and low, like that of a former radio announcer. "*Shoreline* is doing a story about the residents of the seacoast and their reaction to the *Petro Star* spill. Hmmm."

The ball popped away from his putter and in a second or two made that satisfying clatter into the hole. He nodded and moved. The putting green was next to a stone patio that butted up against the house, which had high, elegant-looking glass doors leading inside. There were other stone benches and a lot of shrubbery, and more indirect lighting from small lampposts set into the ground. There were no insects buzzing around, no flies, sand fleas or mosquitoes. I guess it is true, the rich are different from you and me, and the reason this night was that they could afford superb insect eradication.

Briggs popped another ball in. He looked up at me. "Suppose there is no reaction, Mr. Cole? Does that pose a problem for your story?"

I sipped at my drink and said, "No, it doesn't pose a problem for the story, but it does pose a question. Why the lack of reaction?"

"Hmmm," he said, looking down at the ball with a firm look of attention. "That's a fair question, deserving of a fair answer."

Another ball went down under the rapid fire of Cameron Briggs, and he was finished. He made a grasping motion with the club that suggested some taste of triumph, then sat down across from me on another bench and held his putter with both hands, twirling it back and forth, almost like a baton.

He said, "My answer, I guess, is that I didn't speak quite clearly. It wasn't a lack of reaction, but a lack of the expected reaction. I'm sure you came here looking for the standard comment to plug into your standard story, about the standard outrage and how upset we all are about this tragic environmental disaster on these pristine shores. Bah. I may sound cold and heartless. I really don't care about that. The oil on those shores is the price we have to pay."

Briggs held the golf club still and moved forward, leaning into the club and almost using it as something to prop him up. "We live in an advanced, technological and extremely complex society, Mr. Cole, and if there's more than a few thousand people out there who realize how complex it really is, I'd be surprised. You know, I made some very bitter enemies out there, back in the eighties, when the Cold War seemed to be getting warmer. Some collection of do-gooders came by, wanting to get my name on a resolution for a nuclear freeze or some numb-nut petition, and I told them it was a waste of time. I told them that there would never be a nuclear war. Never. They couldn't believe me when I said that, and they demanded proof. Do you know what my answer was?"

I looked into my drink for a moment. "Nuclear war would never come because it would unnecessarily deplete the customer base?"

He smiled at that one. "No, though that's amusing. No, I said there would never be a nuclear war because it wouldn't make sense. It was too expensive, too bulky and too blunt an instrument. I told them that if and when a war came, it would be simple and direct. In fact, I told them I could shatter this country in a week and all it would take would be less than ten million dollars and a hundred or so well-trained men. You know how I would do that, Mr. Cole?"

I decided he was looking for a more serious answer than my previous one, and I said, "Vulnerabilities. Choke points. Utility switching yards. Computer rooms. Some refineries, maybe a bridge or two."

Briggs nodded vigorously as I responded. "Exactly. My God, people don't realize how easy it would be." He swiveled and made a gesture to the north. "Up about an hour or so from here is an electrical substation in a remote part of the New Hampshire woodlands. At a party last summer, a Public Service of New Hampshire exec told me all it would take would be one man with a high-powered rifle and in twenty minutes this entire state would be in a blackout. That's just one man with a rifle. One man with an explosive charge in a computer room in New York City could take out the air traffic control system for the whole Northeast. Hell, you read about it all the time, Mr. Cole, how a computer chip burns out somewhere and the entire long-distance network for AT&T collapses. It wouldn't take much."

I doodled something in my notebook. "So do you have your hundred-man army ready, Mr. Briggs?"

He smiled again. "Hardly. But that's the point I make. More than 99 percent of the human populace stumble through their lives, not knowing—and probably not caring—about the elaborate juggling act that takes place every day to keep them alive. The gasoline trucks that slide into the neighborhood service station. The tractor-trailers that roll in and out of giant food stores. The pharmaceutical companies that make the necessary drugs and treatments. Such a juggling act the world has never known before, and it wouldn't take much to bring it all to a screeching halt. Can you imagine New York City if all the grocery trucks were to stop going in for a week? A month? Those fools told me that they prayed for no nuclear war, and I told them they should pray for no national truckers' strike. And while you're imagining no trucks moving across this country, imagine the impact of a national computer programmers' union, and what would happen if they sat home and didn't go to work."

Briggs got up and motioned to me to follow him, and since I was working, I did. We walked across the patio and through tall double glass doors and into the kitchen area, where I deposited my now empty glass. The kitchen had two enormous gas-fired stoves, side by side, and there was a walk-in cooler and freezer against a wall. Pots and pans of every possible size and shape hung from wooden beams overhead. If there is such a thing as kitchen envy, maybe I was feeling it about that moment.

From the kitchen we passed a formal dining room—tall

chairs grouped around a polished table that looked like it would cover a bowling alley—and through other rooms that I soon gave up trying to give names to. There were paintings on the walls—some nineteenth-century and some modern art—along with a collection of statuary and several wood-and-glass display cases with cut crystal and china. Somehow we ended up in the white-tiled front hall, and I followed Briggs as he pranced up a curving staircase, his leg muscles quite defined as he took the stairs two steps at a time. Through it all, he carried his golf club, and I was beginning to wonder if he slept with it.

On the second floor we went past closed doors that probably led to marble bathrooms or master bedrooms or a gymnasium, for all I knew, and then we were outside again, passing through another set of double glass doors, and we stood on a balcony that overlooked the wide front lawn. Iron grillwork served as railings and there were chairs and a round glass-topped table in one corner. From up here the view to the Atlantic was magnificent. I could see the lights of Porter off to the north and the warm glow of Tyler Beach and its adult and child playgrounds to the south.

"Look here, Mr. Cole." He finally gave the golf club a rest and leaned it against a railing as he stood there, arms folded. "The ocean. Some people see it as a playground, others see it as a fishery. And me? I see it as a highway, a liquid highway that needs no tolls or maintenance. A highway that brings commerce to and from this country, and makes it a world superpower. Look at Russia. Hundreds of years old and the poor bastards are still looking for a warm-water port."

"And last month there was an accident out there, and you still say that the smell and the mess didn't bother you."

A motioned hand, as though an errant mosquito had dared cross over into these protected grounds. "A nuisance. Nothing more."

I decided it was time for a hand grenade to be tossed his way. "What do you think should happen to the owners of the *Petro Star*?"

If there was a reaction, I missed it. Briggs pursed his lips a bit and said, "I'm sorry, but I was under the impression that the owners weren't on the vessel that night, and that it was the crew's fault the ship ran aground. If anyone deserves punishment, they do."

"But the owners were the ones that delayed repairs, hired a crew of inexperienced sailors and sent it up this coast with inadequate instrumentation."

"Something for the courts to decide, I suppose. Besides, it's been months. I'm sure that the beaches are returning to normal, and rather quickly."

"Did the smell hurt the fashion show?"

He turned and said, "Off the record, Mr. Cole, when those lovely old ladies are at my home, the only thing they can smell is money, either old or new, doesn't make much difference. I could have an open sewer pit in my backyard and they wouldn't care."

That was a sentence I'd remember for a while, and I said, "Some people would say that spill made a difference, though. Birds and fish killed. Tourist industry damaged. Fishermen losing a month or two of work."

"Insurance companies, Mr. Cole. That's why they exist, and they do quite well."

"Some people would say there aren't any insurance policies for wildlife."

Briggs turned to me and his look wasn't quite as friendly as before. "Mr. Cole, I do believe that your questioning betrays a lack of objectivity. Perhaps you've been exposed to too much environmentalist propaganda?"

"Perhaps there's some value on wild things that isn't insurable."

He nodded at that and said, "Do you miss the passenger pigeon, Mr. Cole? Or how about the snail darter, or the dodo? Or how about the dinosaurs? All extinct or near-extinct species, and if you're truthful with me, you'll agree that their condition doesn't keep you awake at night, seized with worry."

"Maybe not all night," I said, not wanting to blow this interview quite yet, "but I believe they deserve to be protected."

Briggs grasped the iron railing and said, "Two points, Mr. Cole, and then I think we're done. I saw a psychological study once, comparing two almost identical ads that ran in a national magazine which were placed as part of the study. Both ads were created by the same agency, and had the same look and a similar message. The only difference was that one ad was seeking donations for starving children and the other was seeking donations for starving elephants. Care to guess which ad drew the most responses?"

"The elephant, and that was an easy guess."

"I suppose it was. The response was nearly three to one, Mr. Cole. Three times as many people were willing to help starving animals than starving people. There's your environmentalism, Mr. Cole. Caring more about plants and animals than about people. I'm the type of person, as unpopular as it sounds, who cares more about people. The *Petro Star*—regrettable, but it's just a cost of doing business, of keeping that juggling game going and keeping nearly two hundred and fifty million people in this country alive each day. If anything's going to keep this country going, it's going to be business. It's not going to be the likes of those who care more about fish than a kid in New York City who can't afford to put gas in his car to get to work."

"You think everything's that black and white?"

A faint smile. "It's worked for me so far."

I decided to keep on as best as I could. "You said you had a second point?"

"That I did." He picked up the golf club and pointed at the ocean. "About ten thousand miles from here is an island nation that's busily stripping this country to shiny white bones, Mr. Cole. The Land of the Rising Sun. And do you know what they think of environmentalism? I'll tell you. I read a story last year that was so fantastic I had my secretary clip it out and file it. It said that Japan had over ten thousand rivers, and not one of them was wild. Not a single one. Each one was dammed and controlled and canalled. There was not a single wild river left in the entire country, a country with low crime, no illiteracy and practically no homelessness. They care about their people and they couldn't give a shit about plants and animals, and that's why they're going to take on and beat this country, Russia, Germany and the rest of Europe."

"That's some point of view," I said, wondering if my disgust was showing through my own words.

"I'm sure it is," he said. "And it's not a very popular one. There are many people out there who would like to skewer me for my beliefs."

Time for one last hand grenade. "There are a few people around here—mostly fishermen—who'd do the same to you if they heard you. Except they'd probably use a harpoon."

The owner of the *Petro Star* looked at me quite calmly. "I have no idea what you're talking about, Mr. Cole."

It was late when I got home and I was in a grumpy mood, which wasn't helped by the fact that someone had called me three times and had hung up without leaving a message. I knew that looking at the kitchen clock to see what time it was would probably depress me, so I pulled out a Molson and went to the rear deck to look up at the stars and listen to the ocean and try to let the thoughts and pronouncements of Cameron Briggs leave my soul.

Another cold swallow of the beer and I looked up and thought I saw a satellite moving by, but then the bright dot of light blinked out. Who knows. Maybe a hallucination. I was trying to work up a healthy rage against Cameron Briggs but it wasn't working. He had scored some good points, had made good arguments that I couldn't disagree with. It was true, what he said about how we lived, and I was as guilty as anyone else. The bottle in my hand was made by an industrial process I didn't understand, and was transported to the store and to my house through the use of internal-combustion engines. Even this old and wonderful house I lived in by the beach was heated in the winter by fuel oil, oil that was ripped from the earth in some faraway and polluted land and brought here. To be alive in this world today meant you were a consumer, one of the hordes who were scouring the planet of life and resources, and trying to be a green consumer just meant you were slowing down the process, that's all.

Cameron Briggs. He was the guilty party, the one that sent the *Petro Star* up here and who helped it in its disaster, but I don't think he could ever be brought to trial, for the number of his codefendants would number in the millions, and I and everyone else I knew would be standing right next to him.

I finished off my beer rather quickly, and knew I would have a headache tomorrow—hell, probably later todaywhen I got up. That man was a slick one, even when I tossed a couple of live ones toward him, and he had made no response when I talked about the *Petro Star* owners and the Operation Harpoon investigation. Slick. He had gone far, would even go farther, and I would probably end up dying in this house.

The ocean looked peaceful tonight, but I wasn't one to be fooled by the grandeur. Months ago the waters had been fouled with oil, every day boats out there dumped their trash, and a couple of weeks ago a damn body had been floating out there, Sal Grillo, the cousin of Felix Tinios. I closed my eyes and rubbed at my forehead. Sal Grillo and Felix and Tony Russo, in the parking lot of the Vault Restaurant in Porter, falling to the ground, a bullet in his head.

Too busy. Things were too busy. I opened my eyes and looked up at the stars. The Perseid meteor showers were returning soon, and I wanted to be out on my deck enjoying the sight of the long streaks of light cutting through the night sky. But I wouldn't enjoy them if I didn't have things taken care of, and taken care of quickly. The Perseids come but once a year.

I sat in the chair for a while. Then I moved back into the house, I guess, for when I opened my eyes, I found myself in bed and it was dark and I went back to sleep.

CHAPTER
NINETEEN

The bottle of ale and the late hour in going to bed made the sound of the phone even louder, and at first I tried to cover my head with a pillow. When the ringing went on and on, I stumbled out of bed and went downstairs. I looked at the clock this time. It was eight o'clock on a Saturday morning. I was sure I growled something as I answered the phone in my living room, my head aching and my eyes crusty, standing there naked before the morning sun.

"Is this Lewis Cole?" said the man's voice.

I muttered something in reply and the voice said, "Mr. Cole, this is Drew Kotowski calling, from Bainbridge? You know, Craig Dummer's landlord."

By then I was more awake and I sat down on the floor. "Oh.

Sorry I was incoherent back there. I'm usually not up this early on Saturday mornings."

He laughed. "Well, I'm going in to work a half day, make a little extra money, and I thought I'd give you a call here." He lowered his voice. "You still looking for this Craig Dummer fellow?"

"I am."

"Well, I know where he lives. He came back last night, looking to pick up some more of his stuff, and he even paid me his back rent. You want to know his new address?"

For some reason, I wished I wasn't naked. This seemed too important to discuss while being unclothed. "I would love to know his new address, Drew."

"Well." He breathed some into the phone. "Here's how it goes. A few days ago, I got a phone call from my bank, about my car payments. You know, I'm thinking that they're going to give me crap again, about being overdue, but you know what?"

I rubbed at the crusty deposits in my eyes and said, "What's that?"

"They told me that I was paid up, that they got a money order that took care of my back payments and even a couple of more down the road. I asked them who sent it, and they said they didn't know. No name. All that was on the envelope was the postmark. From Tyler. Where you happen to live, Mr. Cole. Right?"

"Along with a few thousand other people."

He laughed for a bit. "Well, maybe so, but I think there's only one person in Tyler who wants to know Craig Dummer's address, and here it is, Mr. Cole—he's living at 611 Southern Estates, in Exonia. That's down your neck of the woods, I believe."

After scribbling down the address, I said, "You said he came back and paid off his back rent. Weren't you surprised at that?"

"Yep, that I was. All he said was that he wanted to pick up the rest of his stuff and make the rent right by me. Funny thing is, you remember how that place looked when you were up here? It was pretty much picked over, and all he did was grab a couple of those books and magazines and then leave. But he gave me that rent, in cash, which was great, and with that money order the bank got, well, I think we'll have our heads above water for the first time in months."

"Good for you," I said.

"I don't think good had anything to do with it," he said, "but thanks again. And you be careful. Ol' Craig looked a bit wired this morning."

"Thanks for the call, and thanks for the warning," and after I hung up, I went back upstairs to lie down, and to think, and to let the headache run its course.

That afternoon I was in Exonia, the county seat for Wentworth County and home to the famous Phillips Exonia Academy. Besides the brick buildings of the school, Exonia has a tiny downtown built around a bandstand. There are restaurants, two bookstores, a card shop and an old movie theater that charges a couple of bucks less than the mall multiplexes in Porter or Lewington. It's the type of brick-and-granite downtown that looks good on a postcard, but my destination was out in the borderlands of Exonia, where it butts up against its poorer neighbor of Bretton, and where the homes and vacant lots don't appear on postcards.

Southern Estates is a trailer park on the Exonia River, and while some trailer parks in Wentworth County are neat and clean with well-ordered grass lots, Southern Estates didn't quite make it. The roads were potholed and rutted, and many of the homes seemed damaged, with plywood and duct tape used for repairs. Dogs ran along the muddy side of the road and tussled in the brown grass of the lawns, and the streets were laid out in a gridwork, almost like Tyler Beach, starting with the letter "A" and ending with the letter "X." One could tell that a lot of imagination and care went into the design and upkeep of the park.

Number 611 looked identical to its neighbors, except that it was on a dead-end street and the trailer across the way seemed empty, and it was next to a wooded lot. A rusting yellow Dodge

Omni was in the dirt driveway, and a man wearing jeans and no shirt watched me as I pulled in behind it. I got out and walked across the wet lawn. The man was in a brown folding chair, on a tiny porch that led into the trailer. He had a can of Budweiser in his hand, and his soft white gut was spilling over his jeans like a loaf of rising bread ready to go into the oven. His hair was shoulder length and light brown, and he had on round, wire-rimmed glasses. His feet were bare and dirty, and he raised the can of beer in a salute as I got closer.

"Craig Dummer?" I asked, and he nodded, and a tingling of anticipation and nervousness ran up my arms. This was him, this was one of the two men who was on duty the night the Winslow Homers were stolen from the Scribner Museum. Except for the thieves, the only other man who had been in that quiet and desperate building was now dead. But he didn't seem to be a man who was keeping some deep, terrible secrets. He looked pathetic.

"The same," he said, his words slightly slurred. "If you're from the Visa card people, the check went in the mail yesterday. If you're from the sheriff's office, I paid off that sleaze landlord yesterday. In fact, if you're damn near anybody, I paid you all off yesterday."

"Good for you," I said, passing over my business card, which he read with some interest and then dropped in his lap. I noticed a half-consumed six-pack of beer was being kept under his chair.

"A magazine writer, hunh? What are you looking for? A subscription?"

I leaned against the fender of the Omni. "Nope. Information. I'm doing a story on the theft of the Winslow Homer paintings from the Scribner Museum five years ago. I'd like to talk to you for a couple of minutes."

I expected a lot of reactions—from violent explosion to a sullen denial—but I guess I was surprised when he started laughing. "You know, I thought you guys would be coming to see me pretty soon. I'm just amazed that it took you so long."

"Why's that?"

He smiled, and I saw that his teeth needed brushing. "Easy, my man. I can count. It's been five years. Anniversary time. About a year after that shit happened, all you guys called me up again and asked me a ton of questions, since it was the year anniversary. When two years went by, nothing happened, and I figured I was free. This year, though, I thought, well, it's been five years, you'll probably get some hotshot reporter or writer stopping by, try to squeeze you for info, and here you are."

I shifted some, trying to look relaxed and not as nervous as I was. "So you must have about five more years of memories to share with me."

Then Craig showed me he was a quick-change drunk. There are happy drunks, who get more and more joyous with each drink and swallow, and then there are the mean drunks, who look for vaguer and vaguer excuses to punch somebody's lights out with every sip that passes through their lips. Craig was the third category, the quick-change drunk, who can bounce from either one of the previous categories with liquid ease.

"Hah," he said, and he wasn't smiling anymore. "Five years. You want to know what it was like, those five years? I'll tell you what—it was five more years of cleaning up after people, working late shifts and trying to keep awake while guarding a million-dollar piece of machinery that's not going anyplace. That's what those five years have been like"—he picked up my business card and squinted at it—"Mr. Lewis Cole, columnist for *Shoreline*. Five years of unrelenting shit, all because my nitwit partner let two guys into the museum after we were closed, after I told him it was against regulations."

"Reports I heard said he thought he recognized them."

Craig took a long swallow of his beer. "Yah, that's what the old geezer said. We were on duty that night and it was dull and boring like every other night, 'cept, of course, I got to look at all those paintings and pieces of sculpture for free. Can you believe that? For free."

"Really?" I asked.

His bleary eyes focused on me. "Yeah, I know what you're thinking. Blue-collar kid from a small town, going to school to get his criminal justice degree, maybe become a cop. What does he know about art? Well, I knew what was there. I remember once as a kid being taken into a museum in Boston on a class trip, and I almost missed the bus back to New Hampshire 'cause I didn't want to leave. I wanted to stay and look at all that wonderful stuff. It made my eyes tear up, that's how wonderful it was."

He looked down at the beer can in his hand. "In fact, I couldn't believe how I lucked out in getting the job at the Scribner. I got paid to be in that museum and keep an eye on things. I thought I had the greatest job. Walk through that big museum at night, nobody there 'cept for Ben Martin, just walk on those wide floors, all by myself. It was like those paintings were more alive after hours, without all the visitors poking around and walking and asking dumb questions. Lots of times, on my breaks, I'd go out and sit there in the dark, looking up at the paintings, and the streetlights, they'd make them look fresh, like they had just been painted. Man, I had a plan, you know that? Work there after school, make some money, get some experience, and then get my degree in criminal justice and get a real cop job and study art in those adult ed classes, go to Europe for a month or two, visit some of the museums, it was a hell of a plan. . . ."

His voice dribbled away and he stared down into his open can of beer, as if he was fighting back some tears, and said, more slowly, "That night, old Martin thought he recognized one of the cops at the door. Hell, he was such a big-shot veteran, he thought he knew everybody in the Manchester PD, and he said we should let 'em in. Give 'em a break, he said. They're just doing their jobs. What could I say? So we did, and just like that, everything bad that could possibly happen, happened, and there was no way I was ever going to work as a cop, Mr. Cole. Not ever."

Craig looked up, his eyes red-rimmed, face set with fury. "So they came in and guns were poked in our ears, and we were taped up and blindfolded and dumped in a corner, and I was so scared I pissed and shit in my pants, and the next couple of months all I heard from the Manchester PD and the FBI was 'Why did you do it? Who were you working with?' Can you believe that?"

I nodded in his direction. "You've got to admit, it's a logical place to look. Inside job maybe, with the two guards helping out."

"Hah." He swallowed off the rest of the beer and then bent over, his gut hanging out, hands scrabbling around for another can of Budweiser, from which he pulled off the plastic ring. "Logical, but think this one through. When the cops undid me, I stank so bad and I was so scared I was shaking and crying, but they thought I was such a good actor that I could soil myself like that. They even laughed at me, you know? They laughed at me, 'cause I shit in my pants. Jesus. Me and Ben Martin. They jumped all over us like we were instant suspects, like we were the only two guys who worked at the museum."

"You think they should have picked on somebody else?"

He popped open his beer. "Sure. There were other candidates, other guys who worked there. It could have been anybody."

"Like who?" He just eyed me as he tipped the can up to his mouth. I said, "How about Justin Dix?"

The Budweiser can came back down fast, as if he had tasted something foul in the beer. "Justin Dix? What do you know about Justin Dix?"

"I know he had money problems. You know any more than that?"

He slowly smiled and held up his can in a salute and said, "I think I'll use a phrase I read about once in a magazine article. No comment. Is that right?"

I thought that over for a bit and said, "Seems like you and Justin had a couple of things in common. Like money problems, Craig. You just told me you paid everybody off yesterday, including your landlord. Get lucky lately in Tri-State Megabucks, or are you trying to clean up your trail? Where'd the money come from, Craig? And why did you move here? Someone helping you out?"

Then his manner changed a bit, as if he had reached another plateau of intoxication, and he said, "Man, if it weren't for that, I wouldn't have had a job all these years . . . You think having something like the museum screwup on your record helps you get job interviews, you're wrong . . . Guarding computers ain't much . . . Jeez, why should I even bother telling you shit."

I stood up from the car and repeated myself somewhat. "Where'd the money come from, Craig? Who's been helping you out? Justin? Has he been watching out for you?"

He shook his head, finished off the beer. "Mister, screw you, and get off my property. I'm tired of talkin' to you, and if you ain't gone, I'm calling the cops. Let's see how your magazine likes shit like that."

I knew all of the cops in Tyler and most in North Tyler and Falconer, but I only knew the name of the chief in Exonia. I didn't think that little fact would help me if Craig came through on his promise. I tried to think of something snappy to say as I went back to the Rover, and I was still thinking about it when I drove back to Tyler.

On my drive home I succumbed to an urge to visit Tyler Beach on this hot Saturday afternoon. I parked the Rover at the Tyler police station, having thrown my "Press Parking" sign on the dashboard, and I walked up to the Strip, not feeling very good about myself. The lot had been empty of Diane Woods's Volkswagen Rabbit, and I had a feeling of relief that I wouldn't feel compelled to go into the station to see if she was there. There was still that strong memory of our last get-together, and how sourly it had ended, so I went out of the station's lot without looking back. I had that cold queasy feeling you get when your mother sends you to the nursing home to visit Grandma and you go to the mall to play video games instead.

Out on the Strip the summer games were continuing, and the sidewalks were pressed so full of people that they were even strolling out on the road. Tyler cops wearing orange safety vests were walking down the center of the slow-moving traffic, trying to keep it moving, and I saw how their eyes kept glancing down at the cars as they passed by. The casual observer might have thought that they were checking out the youth and sex of each car's passengers, while the not-so-casual observer would know that they were checking for open containers of alcohol or joints or mirrors or plastic Baggies full of green leafy matter.

At the Tyler Beach Palace the arcades seemed louder than usual, and there was an unyielding crowd around the ticket booth for the Palace Ballroom. Some rock group was playing there tonight, and there were to be a lot of black T-shirts and jeans around. I crossed the street and went over to the sidewalk bordering the wide white sands of Tyler Beach. I sat down on a park bench and watched the people for a while. There were young couples holding hands, whispering to each other as they went by, and older couples who strolled with a sense of contentment that something stronger than hand holding was bonding them together. A lot of kids, out by themselves, and even younger kids were scampering around under the watchful eyes of their parents or older siblings. There are bad days on the beach, when there are too many young people, whirling in and out of gangs and fights and accusations and thrown bottles, but this wasn't one of those days. And out on the sands there were still a lot of sun worshippers, all exposing their skin to the great sun god and cancer-giver Ra.

Beyond the sand were the shapes of the Isles of Shoals, and there was a freighter out on the gray waters, heading up north and to Porter, and I thought again of my visit to Cameron Briggs. I hadn't disturbed him, and I was thinking that maybe it was time to give what I knew to Paula Quinn, and let the Fourth Estate train their big guns on him. Then I'd do that damn column for *Shoreline* about something, talk to Felix some more about the Scribner Museum theft and do nothing else except get ready for the Perseid meteor showers next week.

In the meantime, I crossed my arms and waited for nothing in particular, just enjoying the show, and especially enjoying the bathing suits the women were wearing this summer. There was a combination of factors that I liked in seeing the women going by, ranging from the skimpiness of the suits to the amount of flesh exposed to the self-confidence and self-assurance in how they walked.

Tyler Beach wasn't a perfect place, for sure, but it would suffice for now.

After pretending to be a philosopher for a while, I got up and walked around for another half hour or so, and at every expired parking meter that I saw, I pumped in a quarter. Then I went home.

Dinner was takeout from the Lafayette House again. This night it was a sautéed mixture of sirloin tips and lobster meat, which I ate outside on the back deck of my home, with a glass of wine and my own self to keep me company. It took about five minutes to clean up after the meal, which is a cleaning average that I like, and then I went back outside with another glass of wine, carrying the phone with me. I called Felix's house and left a message on his answering machine, and sat back and thought some about Craig Dummer. Disappears for a few weeks, even though Justin Dix had implied that he was under constant surveillance. Then he reappears and this time he has some money. Pays off bills, even his old landlord, which took some effort. So. Is he paying off bills because it's the right thing to do, or because he wants to eliminate anybody out there looking for him?

And where did he get the money? It couldn't have been that much of a windfall, based on his current living arrangements. So why the move?

The wine felt good easing through my mouth and then through the rest of my body. A lot of coincidences in a short time span. I didn't like it. The whole issue of Winslow Homer paintings comes alive after five years, Felix starts getting postcards, his cousin gets dumped in the ocean, one Tony Russo gets killed in front of us and Craig Dummer pays off all of his bills, quits his job and moves to Exonia.

I could talk to the Manchester police, but I got the feeling from Diane Woods that they weren't particularly enthusiastic about people asking questions regarding the museum theft, and with Diane and me currently on the outs, there wasn't much I could do in the law enforcement area.

Still, there was the FBI. They were in on the theft right from the beginning, and were probably still actively involved, up to a point. Right. I took another swallow from the wine. That's a bright one. Go up to a federal police agency, give them your name and address and start asking questions, and who knows what roads they'll go down, trying to find out stuff about one Lewis Cole, stuff that should never be made known.

Maybe it was time to see if Justin Dix's financial situation had also suddenly improved.

I sat out there for a while, thinking things through, as the sky darkened and the first stars started coming out into the early evening sky. Only a few running lights were out on the dark waters, and it seemed as if even the boaters knew that summer was drawing to a close, and that it was time to put away the toys for the fall and winter. Only a few weeks to Labor Day. The nights were coming sooner and the evenings were getting cooler. There's a difference between a cool evening in June and one in August. In June, the coolness is just the last gasp of spring and winter; you know that the hot and pleasurable nights of summer are approaching. But a cool night in August tells of a summer drawing to an end, with the cold fingers of September and October waiting to touch you.

The phone rang and it was Felix returning my call. "How's it going?" he asked.

"I was about to ask you the same thing," I said. "Progress?"

"Some, though nothing I want to talk about over the phone."

"Want to get together tomorrow?"

"Sure."

"Then name the place," I said. "And time. But don't make it too late. I've got an appointment down in Massachusetts."

"One o'clock," Felix said. "At the place we've been to before, the one with the crazy ice-cream sundaes."

I knew the place well, and I knew the games that Felix was playing. Very safe, very conservative and very circumspect. That's what kept him alive in a career where sharp elbows didn't mean a thing, but sharp knives did.

"I'll be there," I said, "with some progress of my own."

"Glad to hear it. And, Lewis?"

"Yes?"

He seemed to take a deep breath. "Thanks for coming back with me on this one. Ah, I usually like to work alone on a lot of things like this, but I appreciate all you've done."

With those two sentences, I felt as if Felix had exhausted his sensitive-male quotient for the month. I said, "Not to worry. You owe me a meal. And not at the restaurant we were at last. I think it'll be a long time before you and me can eat there without getting arrested."

That got a small laugh, and he said, "Tomorrow, Lewis," and he hung up. I put the phone down on the deck and finished my wine, and sat back, looking up at the stars. I waited, hoping to see a taste of what was going to happen next week, when the great Perseid showers were to take place, and for once I wasn't disappointed. Two shooting stars flared across the night sky, quicker to see than to describe, and in their dying moments, they gave me a sense of tranquillity and beauty.

I thanked them for their gift, then I went to bed.

CHAPTER

TWENTY

On Sunday afternoon I met Felix at the Conquerin' Cone, an ice-cream store on Atlantic Avenue, just over the line from North Tyler and into Wallis. About five minutes from the Conquerin' Cone was Cameron Briggs's summer home, but I felt confident the man had never been here in his life. The place is across the street from a rocky strip of beach that is usually frequented by the locals, and it has picnic tables in a dirt lot with faded blue golf umbrellas overhead. The building is one story with peeling white paint and those yellow lightbulbs outside that supposedly drive away summer insects but instead just give the customers an unhealthy glow about their faces. Not the type of place a guy like Cameron Briggs would visit.

It's relatively well known for its elaborate sundaes—some of which take a family of four to consume—but Felix loves the place because it stocks some obscure brand of Italian ice that he enjoys. In the times I've been with him, he's not been shy about ordering two or three at a time and then eating them all at once. "It saves walking back and forth," he once explained.

I had a small dish of fudge swirl ice cream. Felix sat across from me, two empty cardboard dishes at his elbow, working steadily on a third one that contained a lemon type of ice. We both had free cups of ice water, for the owners of the Conquerin' Cone realize that odd fact of nature: eating ice cream makes you thirsty. Felix had on a white tank top and faded blue shorts; the tank top was loose around the shorts, hiding from everyone except me the fact that he was carrying a weapon.

"Well, it seems like things are coming to a bit of a head," Felix said, scooping another little pile of yellow slush into his mouth. "I exchanged postcards last week and the meet seems to be on for sometime this week. Maybe Wednesday or Thursday. Exchange of the paintings for some money—a hell of a lot less than what I was asking for—and then that phase of the business is over with."

The ice cream had real chocolate fudge in its swirl, which made for a fiercely loyal group of customers for the Conquerin' Cone. I said, "And what happens with the second phase? Does hunting season open up?"

Felix nodded, scraping a bit more ice. "That's true, my friend. Hunting season opens up. Damn thing is, though, I don't have names. Just postcards and that shooter with a mask that took care of Tony Russo. Besides that, I have nothing. It's going to take some work trying to catch the tracks of this one. No names, no faces."

I waved at him with my spoon. "I've got two names, and two faces. I can't guarantee that they mean anything, or that they're connected with what's going on with you, but they are making things curious for me."

"Go on," Felix said.

"Head of security for the museum is a guy named Justin

Dix," I said. "Seemed to be a straight shooter, until I did some research. Turns out he's a man who's run up a number of debts. Even had his car repossessed once. Perfect in for someone who wanted to steal three paintings and get away with it. Money in exchange for assistance."

"And the second guy?"

"Craig Dummer. One of two guards on duty that night. His partner, one Ben Martin, a former Manchester cop, conveniently died a few years back. Craig wanted to be a cop, but the museum theft took care of that. That's not the kind of thing police hiring boards are thrilled to learn about. I talked to him yesterday, after he skipped out from his place up in Bainbridge. He used to have the same debt problems that Justin had. Now he claims he's paid everybody off and he made a reference to someone looking out for him, maybe a sugar daddy or something. He's living in Exonia, and he won't say why."

Felix nodded, finishing up his Italian ice. He looked slightly amusing, hunched over the stained picnic table, studiously eating his treat with a tiny wooden spoon, but I wasn't about to laugh and I don't think anybody within eyeshot would either.

"Connection between the two?"

"Justin was Craig's boss. And there was something odd, back when I started poking around this, Felix. Justin implied that Craig was still under suspicion, that his address and whereabouts were always known, but he gave me a bum address for Craig in Bainbridge. When I went there, Craig had moved out a couple of weeks earlier. So either Justin was sloppy in his record keeping—which didn't seem apparent at the time—or he was helping out Craig."

"Anybody else?"

I paused, and said, "There's Justin Dix's secretary. A Cassie Fuller. But I don't think she had anything to do with the theft. She had only been at the job for a few months before the paintings were stolen. I don't think that's enough time to check out how the security system was working."

Felix seemed to consider all of this as he reached out and

crushed the three empty cardboard containers with his right hand. "Nice information, Lewis, but I've got a problem with what you're saying. Care to guess what it is?"

I finished off my own treat. "It's apparent. It's too obvious."

"Exactly." He wiped his hands clean with a napkin and looked over at the people at the Conquerin' Cone's windows. Seemingly satisfied that there were no assassins in line, he looked back at me and said, "It's too damn obvious, Lewis, that a security guard or his boss or anybody there would be involved in the theft."

"Then again, maybe that was their perfect cover. No one would suspect them simply because it was so obvious."

He shrugged. "That sounds too much like philosophy, and when someone mentions philosophy, I usually reach for my semiautomatic."

"I think someone famous said that once, but I'll let you keep that quote. Felix, I know it's obvious, but it's something. Look. Everything started happening the minute you got those post-cards. Your cousin gets killed. Tony Russo gets killed. Justin Dix loses track of Craig Dummer, and Craig Dummer suddenly ends up in Exonia, with a full bank account. That's too much weird-ness, even for something like this."

Felix tossed the containers into a trash barrel, and I heard him whisper, "Three points," and then he said, "This whole thing has a taste of the weird. I don't like it, not at all. Too many shadows and hidden messages. I like things direct, out in the open. This ain't doing it, and I'm not going to be happy until it's all there, laid out before me."

"Might have a long wait."

"I'm patient."

"Except when you're hungry," I pointed out.

"Yeah, well, everybody has their faults." His expression changed slightly, as if he was looking at me differently. He said quietly, "I don't know why I'm going to ask you this, but I am. It just makes sense, as odd as that sounds. Closing the circle. When the exchange happens, do you want to be there?"

"Still looking for my calming influence?"

Felix shrugged. "Maybe I am. You do have something there. Maybe it's your calming influence, or the way you're looking at things. All I know is, I'd feel better if you're there."

"No more meets at restaurants?"

"Nope. Restaurants are for eating."

And I don't know why I said it, except it did make sense. "All right. I'll be there."

Felix looked pleased. "Good. Look, why don't we go up to Porter, to the Diamondback Lounge. We can catch the afternoon Red Sox game, get a couple of beers, see if there are any nubile fans who need to learn about the infield fly rule . . ."

"Sorry," I said, getting up from the picnic table. "I have a doctor's appointment."

"A doctor's appointment? On a Sunday afternoon in August?"

As I walked away I said, "He's a special kind of doctor."

For a special kind of case.

An hour later I was in the Cambridge office of Dr. Jay Ludlow. I sat naked on his examining table as he poked and probed the scars on my knee, back and left side. He asked me the usual questions, from weight gain or loss to sleeping habits, and he looked intently at a file folder I guessed belonged to me. He wore tan slacks and an open-necked shirt, and he ran his hands through his thinning curly hair on a few occasions as he did his job.

Then he nodded and said, "You can get dressed," and so I did.

I joined him in his office, which had a big wooden desk and the standard medical school certificates, and he opened my file and said, "I'll tell you two things, Lewis. One is that you're doing well in your recovery. The incision is healing nicely, and I couldn't find any signs of a recurrence of your tumors. Which leads me to my second point."

"Which is that you can't predict if and when another tumor might appear."

"That's very true," he said, leaning back in his big swivel leather chair, rubbing at his eyes, looking tired. "One good piece of luck is that none of your growths so far has proven to be malignant. But that doesn't mean your luck is going to hold. It also doesn't mean that the next one won't be malignant. Hell, even another benign tumor like the one I pulled out of you could hurt you. All it would take would be a tumor growing in a space that can cause some serious damage. Like your spinal column. Or your stomach. Or your brain. What it does mean is that you should be concerned about your health, about your future."

"Doc, I'm concerned every damn day."

He had a wry smile. "Sorry for the lecture. It's just frustrating, working this case, Lewis. And I won't go into explaining that again."

At that moment I felt sorry for him, a doctor who had gone to a fine school and had probably hoped for a fulfilling and satisfying career, and instead, because of something he had done once, had ended up in the debt of some men in Washington who had long memories and even longer résumés. This debt, like all debts, had to be paid off, which is why he was in his office on a perfectly lovely August Sunday afternoon, dealing with a man with a spook past who couldn't answer any questions that would help in his work.

I cleared my throat. "One of the last times I saw you at the hospital, Doc, I told you what happened to me was a hell of a story. Like to hear part of it?"

He sat straight up, as if he had discovered he had been sitting on a tack. "It's not necessary, but if you'd like . . ."

"Agreed," I said. "A story, probably one that won't help your questions, but might help you in understanding me. It's a story about a black section of the Department of Defense. This section analyzes issues and concerns that are too hot or too weird for other groups, other subdivisions. It's a fairly close-knit group, and one particular man counts a woman he loves very much and his best friend among his co-workers. One day they're sent out to a government range in Nevada, on its yearly field qualification tests, to prove that the group could operate in adverse conditions if it had to. But it wasn't much of a test. It was just day after day of monotony, climbing up and down piles of rocks and sand. Through the incompetence of its leader, this group then discovers it's lost. It finds itself in a restricted part of the range. It finds itself near a pen holding sheep. And before anything can happen, before hardly anything is said, two Huey helicopters roar overhead."

I stopped for a moment, conscious that I was breathing faster and that the room seemed to be getting warmer. "Am I keeping your attention, Doc?"

He slowly nodded, as if he didn't want to disturb my concentration. "Go on, Lewis. It's an interesting story."

I found with disgust that my voice was beginning to waver. "The helicopters are modified with outriggers, like crop dusters. They begin spraying the ground, they begin spraying the sheep, and they begin spraying the Department of Defense section that wasn't supposed to be there. And you can guess that the spray isn't a new form of insecticide. These Hueys weren't on loan to the Department of Agriculture. Nope, these Hueys are black— just like the section, how ironic—and they were testing a new biowarfare agent. The test proves to be quite successful, except for one point. All of the sheep and all of the men and women in that section die, save for one man."

Dr. Ludlow whispered something I couldn't hear, and I felt my cheeks getting wet. "This man survives and is hospitalized and almost immediately a soft-tissue tumor starts growing on his kidney. The tumor is removed. Then for no apparent reason, the survivor becomes slightly paranoid. He's in an underground Department of Defense installation. He's not allowed any visitors, any mail or any phone calls. He's seen his woman and his best friend die. He's not sure what the future holds for him, and he begins to think that if certain people had their way, he would suddenly die of heart failure. So he bullies and scams his way out, and in exchange for absolute silence, he will be supported for the rest of his life."

I took out a handkerchief and rubbed at my eyes, and said, "That's the story, Doc. And remember, it's just a story."

The doc turned in his chair, looked up at his certificates, and in a steady voice said, "I've always been amazed at how we cattle pay our taxes each year to support the likes of people who can kill you or harm you without a blink of an eye, without a moment of lost sleep, without hesitation." He turned to me. "I just hope nobody's been listening in to this little exchange, Lewis. It could cause some problems for both of us."

"Don't worry," I said. "I still have a few bites left if I depart unexpectedly."

He smiled. "Good move. So have I. Pre-addressed envelopes stored in safe locations, to be sent to various people and agencies in the event of my untimely death. All totally unnecessary and the result of my paranoid tendencies, you realize."

"Of course. I seem to share your paranoid tendencies, and I'm sure there are other people out there just like you and me, Doc."

The doc's grin was wider. "Hell of a thing. Maybe we should form an organization, start up a newsletter."

I got up and shook his hand. "Don't push your luck."

His hand squeezed mine back. "Pushing luck is all that you and I do, every day."

"As someone once said, that is a true fact." When I got to the door, I turned and said, "Don't take this wrong, Doc, but I hope it's a long, long time before you and me see each other professionally."

He began writing in my folder. "By the time you're on I-95 and heading north, I'll forget that you were even here this afternoon."

"If you don't mind, I'll return the favor," I said, and I left.

When I got home I checked my answering machine, as always, and the steady glowing green light of the machine meant that at least for these past few hours no one had been looking for me. That was a pleasant thought. I poured myself an ice water, went out to my rear deck, and sat and sipped and wondered about dinner. Up north there was a dark band of clouds moving majestically to the east, like a squadron of black battleships gliding out to battle. I sipped at my water, raised up a pair of binoculars, and watched two sailboats fleeing the onset of the clouds. There was a shiver of anticipation and fear along my back as I saw the fragile craft try to escape the winds and the lightning. In the dark mass came that sudden flash of lightning that is always a surprise, and it looked like a giant flashbulb had gone off from inside the clouds of black vapors. The heavy rumbling came just a few moments later, and I remembered an earlier storm, one I had come through a couple of weeks ago, after finding the mutilated body of Felix Tinios's cousin down on the wet sands of North Beach.

Just a few days more, Felix had predicted. Just a couple of more days, and the matter of the paintings would be taken care of. The exchange would occur and I would be a part of it (for reasons I still wasn't sure about). Then Felix would go on his private mission. I would come back home and work on that overdue *Shoreline* column, and ponder when I was going to blow Cameron Briggs out of the water by releasing his Department of Defense file to the Boston *Globe* and the Tyler *Chronicle*. Finally, I would think with joy and anticipation about the upcoming Perseids.

Another flash of light, another rumble. The wind picked up speed and it was a strange breeze, sometimes warm and sometimes cool, and it was oddly refreshing, tossing about my skin. I raised up the binoculars again. The sailboats were still there, probably heading for Tyler Harbor. I lifted my water glass in salute, and thought for a while. I was enjoying my stay here on the deck, knowing that I could leave at any moment and be sheltered in my hundred-and-fifty-year-old house, yet I still had a feeling of envy. Part of me wanted to be out there, on the heaving and slick fiberglass deck of the boat, wearing foul-weather gear and looking back at the advancing storm, nervous and scared and exhilarated all at once, knowing I was on my own, and that the nearest Coast Guard station was many miles away.

A paradox, those feelings, but it was a paradox I faced each day, and one I would meet again when I went with Felix the day or night the Winslow Homer paintings were turned over. But it wouldn't be the end of it, not yet, and I wondered how I would keep an earlier promise, that I would try to return those three masterpieces to the Scribner Museum. Deck and sailboat. Home and with Felix. Safety and danger.

More rumbling, and the clouds sailed on. I sat for a while longer, waiting for the storm to pass by, and I wasn't sure how long the wait would be. All I knew was that I was ready.

TWENTY-ONE

Well, I was having a friendly and comfortable Monday morning until the phone rang. Earlier I had eaten a quick breakfast with Paula Quinn at the Common Grill & Grill, and we didn't discuss much of anything, except for the usual small-town gossip of who's sleeping with whom, which selectman from which town had the mental capacity of a turnip, and when did we think the Goddam Tourists Would Get Up and Finally Leave. Though the conversation wasn't that significant, it was a definite improvement over how we had gone through most of the summer. I mentioned in passing that I had just completed another doctor's appointment, and Paula asked me how it had gone, and I said fine.

She then reached across the table and touched my hand, just

for a moment, and said, "Whatever does happen to the two of us, I do owe you one thing, Lewis, and that is my regrets. No matter what happened back then in June, I shouldn't have reacted like I did. I should have just been there when you were in the hospital, no matter what kind of friendship or relationship we have. Instead I got angry and sulked and stayed away, and that wasn't right."

That was the most Paula had said to me in a while, so I told her what she said sounded pretty good to me and she laughed and tossed a roll at me. We gave each other a brief kiss before I headed to the post office and home.

My mail this Monday was also fairly good, with a bank account statement that showed my monthly check from DoD via *Shoreline* was still being deposited on time, and I also got the latest issue of *Astronomy* magazine. I then spent a lovely hour on the back deck, reading, drinking lemonade and wondering what the poor working population was doing on this fine Monday morning in August, and that was when the phone rang.

And that was when everything went down the gutter.

"Cole? Lewis Cole?" came a male voice, one that tickled at my memory for a moment.

"You've got him."

"Well, I've got more than that, I guess. This is Justin Dix calling, from the Scribner Museum."

"Oh. Morning."

"Hah. There's not much good about it and that's what I want to talk to you about. I need to see you today."

"Can't be discussed over the phone, Justin?"

Again, a sharp noise. "Not a question of can't, Lewis. It's a question of won't. I won't discuss it over the phone."

"All right, I guess I can make it up to Manchester in time for lunch—"

"Forget lunch," he said, and in his voice was a sense of one who was in charge, who was used to having his orders filled and who didn't seem much like the man I had talked to over a week ago.

"No lunch?" I asked, looking down at the *Astronomy* magazine in my hands. Guess I wouldn't finish it on this Monday morning.

"Nope. Don't feel much like eating with you, Lewis."

Well. I suppose I could have tried to pump him for information, wheedle and whine a bit, and try to find out why he was treating me like a museum visitor with dirty fingers, but something about his tone irked me. I didn't like the sense he had, that he possessed some power over me, that he had some sort of control. He was mad about something, but I wasn't going to give him the satisfaction of word-dueling with me some more.

"But you want a meeting, is that it?" I asked.

"That's exactly what I want."

"You got it," I said, and left it mostly at that.

Within the hour I met Justin Dix at a McDonald's restaurant in Rayburn, a small town just off Route 101 which had the advantage of being halfway between Manchester and Tyler. When I walked in, my stomach grumbled at the smells, and I tried to tell my stomach to shut up. I'm sure that deeply buried in the hidden archives of McDonald's corporate headquarters is a secret study on how to make the smells of its food go right to the pleasure and hunger centers in one's brain. But on this morning, my mind wrestled free from the scent of temptation and I avoided the midmorning lines that offered guilty pleasures for under five bucks.

Justin was sitting in a rear booth. I didn't even bother with the pretense of buying something before I walked over and sat down. He had on a dark blue suit and white shirt with light red tie, and his double chin seemed to have developed a bit more since I had last seen him. His thick brown-and-gray hair looked a little mussed, as if he had driven here with his car windows open, and behind his black-rimmed eyeglasses there was no cheer in his eyes.

Justin had his hands around a cardboard coffee cup and got

right to the point. "I want to know who the hell you think you are, and what you're up to."

I got comfortable in the plastic booth and said, "You know who I am. I write for *Shoreline*. You also know what I'm up to. I'm doing an article about the Winslow Homer thefts. For this we had to meet at a McDonald's in Rayburn?"

His beefy hands seemed to caress the coffee cup and I thought he probably preferred them around my throat. "I talked earlier today to a Gus Straccia. You know the name?"

"Can't say that I do."

He smiled, and I was mortified at what he said next. "Well, that's pretty unusual, Lewis, considering he's the assignments editor for *Shoreline*. I called him and asked him about you and your article about the museum theft, and he had no idea what I was talking about. Said all you write for that magazine is columns, and you've never done a feature-length piece for them since you started working there."

I made a note to call down to Seamus Anthony Holbrook and to tell the admiral to keep a lid on his staff and whatever they discussed about me and my employment, and then I promptly erased the note in my mind. It wouldn't work. I was late on my column and Admiral Holbrook wouldn't have much sympathy with me. It was my own damn fault that I didn't keep track of the magazine's masthead, but I had dealt with Admiral Holbrook on everything else, so keeping up on who was on the editorial staff was something that slipped my mind. So much for my DoD training.

Instead of acting as embarrassed as I felt, I said, "Just because the assignments editor doesn't know about the article doesn't mean I'm not working on it. I am. I just haven't told them, that's all."

"You seem to be a man who likes secrets."

That was inching in too much to my former job, and I said, "I do what it takes."

"Oh?" he said, putting on a fake tone of query. "Is that so? Then tell me what you can about three odd happenings that have popped up in my life recently. The first is that Cassie Fuller came to me the other day and warned me off about you. Said that you were a coldhearted bastard who only cared about getting things from other people, and she didn't trust you. And that's all she'd say. Second is some gossip that came my way through some banking friends of mine. Seems someone's been showing some interest in my credit history lately."

He looked at me as if he expected an answer or an explanation, but I said, "You mentioned three odd happenings. You have a third?"

Justin nodded sharply. "That I do. I'm not too sure who the hell you think you're dealing with here. You think I'm a fool? A loser? Well, I still have friends and contacts with the Manchester police department, and that's where the third happening came up. Seems a few days ago, somebody made inquiries at the Manchester police department into my background, and that of Craig Dummer and Ben Martin. I'm sure you remember those gentlemen. A friend of mine at the department found out and passed that little gem along, and the interesting thing, Lewis, is this. That inquiry came from the Tyler police department, from a woman detective who's known to be a friend of yours. Is that your normal mode of operation? Asking your lover to do your dirty work?"

He was right about my mode of operations and was wrong about my relationship with Diane, but I didn't feel like correcting him. "Without admitting to anything, Justin, you've got to agree that a man with your credit history raises a number of questions about your possible involvement with the theft. You seem to always have money problems, and that could have been some temptation. A reporter who's doing his or her job looks at all the information, all the possibilities."

Justin raised up his coffee cup, as if he was about to throw it at me, and instead he did something that was even more disquieting. He began at the top of the cardboard cup and started gently shredding the container into tiny strips, using only his fingernails. They must have been sharp.

"Leaving aside your insults regarding my professionalism and my personal life, I've got something to tell you."

"Then tell me."

As he worked on stripping the coffee cup, his voice lowered and took on a narrative quality, as if he was telling a story he had told many times before. "I must imagine you are single, Mr. Cole, for I'm not sure if you will understand what I say here and now. But give it a try. It will make a difference in everything else."

I looked around the plastic booths and chairs of the McDonald's, and out of all the people there, eating and drinking and smoking—the kids, the housewives and the truckers—not a person was smiling. Not a single one. Maybe they were all secretly concerned about the fat they were pouring into their veins and arteries. None of those fantasy McDonald's commercials would be filmed in this restaurant anytime soon, and it was probably a good thing, because what was going on between Justin and me would probably soil this place for some time to come.

"Elaine and I have been married for nearly twelve years," he continued, "and one thing that they never mention in the women's magazine articles or in the marriage books is the hard fact that marriage is a series of battlefields. There are contests to be fought and won over jobs, chores, sex, relatives and damn near everything else. In good marriages, the fights are just words. No violence, no furniture or dishes thrown. Just words. And you learn about yourself, and your partner. You learn about what battles are worth fighting, and which ones should be given up after a few minutes. Pretty soon you know which territory belongs to which partner, and which territories can change hands over time."

"You make it all sound very attractive, Justin," I said. "Ever think of becoming a marriage counselor?"

He looked up from his work with the coffee cup, ignoring my comment. "The weak ones are those who give up after a couple of battles, who can't stand the battle of words. The strong ones keep on going with the fight, and sometimes, well, sometimes they come across a battle that's just damn near impossible."

"Like finances," I said.

Justin nodded. "Finances. Money. That's the territory, the Alsace-Lorraine, the Danzig Corridor, the favorite place for all battles. Money. Who earns it, who controls it and who spends it."

"Were you the only wage earner?"

"Hah." He looked around at the midmorning crowd and said, "There was a time in this fat and wonderful country when one man could support a family and a house on one weekly paycheck. That time's dead, my friend, and won't ever come back, even if they do put tail fins back on cars. No, Cole, she worked. As a mid-level manager over at the Manchester Mall. Whatever money she made would come in and would go right out the door, Mr. Cole. Right out the door. Clothing. CD player and disks. Redecorating the house. At first I didn't mind, because I was doing well at the museum, but things started getting tighter and tighter. Bill collectors started calling, at home and then at work. You see, my name was also on the charge cards. Then I had trouble making my own payments, and one day I had my car repossessed. Ever have a car repossessed, Cole?"

Justin held a piece of cardboard in his hands, and instead of tearing it in half, bent it back and forth, over and over again. "In this state, they don't even require the repo men to come see you. They can take your car anytime after the bank warns you that a repossession is possible. So one day at work, I go out at lunch, and my car's gone. First instinct is that it was stolen. You don't want to believe that it got repoed. So I called the cops, the Manchester cops I deal with regularly, and I have to go through the humiliation of having them tell me that my car was picked up by repo men. Then I have to go over to their grungy office—by begging for a ride—so I can pick up all of my belongings from the car in a paper bag. That was it, that was the one thing that put me over the edge, and Elaine and I have been in counseling, and still go every now and then, because there's something in that marriage I want to save."

He looked up at me, his eyes still bleak behind his glasses. "So I have a credit report that looks like it belongs to someone who's spent time in the county jail, and each time I check the mailbox, I look for those dunning letters and the envelopes with pink slips in them. But Elaine and I have stuck together, and it's been worth it. I grew up alone most of the time, Cole, being a single child and all. I hate being alone. So I did what I could to stick with my wife. Last time I checked, that's no crime."

"That's some story," I finally managed to say.

"No," he said. "That's some truth. And here's another truth, Mr. Lewis Cole, columnist for *Shoreline* magazine. You put a stop to whatever you're up to, or by God, if I see a magazine article with my name in it, you'll regret the day that you walked into the Scribner Museum."

"You seem to know your art history, but I don't think you're doing well on your constitutional history, Justin," I said. "You ever hear of something called the First Amendment?"

He managed a smile. "You ever hear of something called the FBI?"

That I had. "Go on."

"I still have contacts with the FBI over the Winslow Homer thefts, Cole, guys I became friends with," he said, now smiling confidently. "All I need to do is to say a few words about you harassing me, and then bad things will start happening to you. Like a tax audit, perhaps. Everybody else may think that the FBI became a Boy Scout troop after Hoover died, but I know better, and so should you. There. Do you get the point now, Cole?"

"I do," I said, feeling fairly vanquished but wanting to know one more thing before skulking away. "I just have a single question, and then I'm gone."

"One question, then."

I tried not to look at the tiny scraps of cardboard littering the plastic tabletop. "It's about Craig Dummer. Last time you and I talked, you said that you were keeping close tabs on Craig Dummer. You told me he lived in Bainbridge, but when I got there, he had left, weeks ago. Disappeared and it took me the longest time to find him, but you thought he still lived in Bainbridge. Why was that? Were you protecting him?"

He dismissed my question with a wave of his hand. "Please,

Cole. Look, first of all, that's two questions. Second, I was just trying to show you that things were in control. Truth is, Craig Dummer was never a suspect."

"He wasn't?"

Justin shook his head. "Nope. We and the FBI and the Manchester cops looked at both Craig Dummer and Ben Martin pretty closely, and it just wasn't there for Craig. He was just a kid, still in college. No record, no nasty relatives, nothing driving him at all. And Ben had retired and was finding things rough out on his own, and we knew that he was trying to buy some land up at a north lake, for a retirement home, but the financing fell through. Plus the fact of the two cops coming in and Ben saying he recognized them . . . well, Ben was number one on the suspect list from that first day."

"His sons dispute that little history lesson. One told me their father had nothing to do with the theft, that Craig Dummer let in the fake cops."

He looked smug, as if he had just won a free Big Mac for lunch. "What do you expect him to say? That they thought dear old Dad did it, and they wish he had been arrested before he died?"

"Speaking of which, he did die rather strangely, don't you think?"

Justin looked a bit surprised. "Oh, come on. He was a retired ex-cop with heart problems. He was found dead in his car. Heart attack."

"But no autopsy was done."

"None needed. Look, Cole, it's done with. Someone hired Ben Martin to look the other way when the hit went down, and for all we know, the paintings are in a basement in São Paulo or Tokyo. So forget about your conspiracy theories, leave everything else to the FBI and the cops, and forget about me. Got it?"

With that and without waiting for an answer from me, he got up and left me there in the booth, with the mess of cardboard scraps before me. I thought for a moment and then swept them up in my palm, and tossed them in a bin on my way out.

It was the least I could do, since I hadn't spent a penny there.

I left the McDonald's in Rayburn feeling as if I had spent the previous half hour hovering over their deep-fry vats, being wreathed in a noxious cloud of steam and grease. I had backed down before Justin Dix and had turned over on my back and opened up my stomach and throat to his sharp claws of an argument, and all without a whimper, because he had uttered those three magic letters. FBI. Guys and gals I definitely did not want to get interested in me, in a man who knew some dark secrets that could raise holy hell in a lot of newspapers and magazines.

And which would end my current noncareer and take me away from my home at the beach, my den and nest of safety.

So I drove back on Route 51, heading east to the ocean and Tyler, feeling foul and grumpy, and for no good reason at all, I took an early exit, which led me into Exonia.

I guess I wanted to spread my bad mood around.

I found Craig Dummer sitting in a lawn chair at the side of his trailer, but instead of raggedy jeans, this time he was dressed in gray sweat pants and a stained tank top, and he was only working on one beer.

"Are you on a liquid diet?" I asked when I stepped out of my Range Rover.

Craig eyed me for a moment and then held up his Budweiser can. "Can do worse than this, I suppose. Least this has calories and carbohydrates in it. What do you want?"

I stood in front of the Rover. "Information, as always."

"Didn't you get enough the last time you was here?" His light brown hair was still shoulder length but looked like it had been freshly washed, and his eyes seemed brighter behind his round, wire-rimmed glasses.

"A writer's work gets done here and there, but never gets done on the first try," I said. "I'm interested in you and Justin Dix."

"You are, are you? And why's that?"

"Because you two have some things in common," I said.

"You both worked at the museum when the Winslow Homers got stolen. You both had financial problems. And it seems you both spend a lot of time dancing around the truth."

"Mmm," he murmured, taking a swallow from his beer. "You've been spending some time talking with Justin, then?"

"I have."

"What do you think?"

I shrugged. "Except for one glaring example, he seems fairly competent."

"Competent," Craig said, repeating the word, almost as if he was savoring the syllables. "Competent. Yeah, that's not a bad word. I'd have picked reserved, or centered, but competent will do. You want to know something interesting about Justin?"

A stupid question, but I let it pass. "I'm sure you know the answer to that, so why don't you go ahead."

He rested the Budweiser can on his soft gut, and I made another resolution never to let myself sag that much. "If in the year I worked at the Scribner, if Justin had more than one sentence to tell me at one time that wasn't work-related, then I must've slept through that day's worth of work. He was always quiet and aboveboard, and he sent me and Ben and the other guards out on our training sessions, and he did some of his own training, but that was it. No talk about baseball, football or our families. Strictly business."

Craig nodded, as if he was remembering a touch, a scent, a lost memory. "The only time I ever saw him lose it was the day after the paintings were stolen, when Ben and I were being interviewed by the Manchester cops and the FBI. He was shaking and crying and trembling, like he wanted to grab us both by the ears and start chewing on our throats. I think he impressed the cops and the FBI agents, but he didn't impress me. And later, Ben told me that he didn't impress him either."

I thought for a moment and said, "You think it was an act?"

He winked at me and lifted the beer again. "I think it served its purpose."

"What purpose?"

He held his arms out. "Think about it, man. There he was, responsible for the most important museum in this state, responsible for its security and to make sure everything was covered, that he didn't have crazies working as guards, and in one night, it's over. It's over. He looks around at the cops and the FBI and he has to play the act, has to act like he's loony, though he was always one for having a real cramped way of looking at things." He swallowed again from his can of beer. "You know, Ben and I had a few minutes together after that, and he said what went through Justin must've been like what happens to a woman who gets raped. You're not the same person. Nothing's the same anymore. Look. You've talked to Justin, right?"

"That I have."

He leaned forward a bit in the lawn chair. "Don't you think it's strange that he's still at the museum five years later?"

"You think he's being protected?"

Craig shrugged. "Maybe, maybe not. But I think it's strange that he'd go back there, to the scene of his biggest screwup ever. Every day, going to the same place and going into that room, knowing that's where the three paintings used to be. Man, that's a level of pain and hurting yourself I don't think I understand. It'd be like getting in a car accident that kills your wife, and then driving the same car after wiping her blood off the upholstery. That's morbid, don't you think?"

Something came to me and I said, "When did you leave the museum, Craig? Was it right after the theft?"

I had struck at something, for his whole body stance changed. Before, he had been in the lawn chair like a lump of white dough, soft and yielding and relaxed, even in my presence. But with this one question, he had drawn into himself, as if his muscles had tightened and expanded.

Craig said, "About a month or so later."

"Did you leave on your own or were you fired?"

He allowed himself a small smile. "Fired. One day I came to work five minutes late and he shit-canned my ass that morning. But it was all a game. I just knew that he was waiting for the first excuse, the first reason to get me out of there. Ben Martin didn't even bother waiting for that kind of decision. He just upped and quit." Craig shrugged. "Can't really blame Justin Dix for doing that."

I thought of something else and said, "What I don't understand is why you seem sympathetic to Justin, Craig. You told me he wasn't the friendliest boss, that he blamed you and Ben for the thefts, and then he fired you a couple of months later for something as minor as being a little bit late for work. But you don't talk poorly about him, Craig. Why?"

Then he said something with a smile that surprised me. "Haven't you ever heard of worker loyalty?"

"What? What kind of loyalty? You haven't been at the museum for five years."

Then he tossed the empty beer can behind him on the trampled lawn and looked at me a bit blearily, and I knew he must have been drinking some more beforehand. This last can must have reached some sort of limit within him. "You know, they really shouldn't have laughed at me that night, after I got freed . . . It could have been different . . ."

"Who shouldn't have laughed at you?"

Another change of expression. "Who the hell are you anyway?"

"What do you mean by that?"

He shook his head. "I've talked to other reporters and magazine writers, you know. But none of them were like you. For one thing, you're too old. Most of 'em were just out of college, working their way up and out. Go away. I'm tired of talking to you."

"Craig, I—"

"Go away," he said, his voice louder. "Before I call my lawyer."

And for the second time that day, I retreated.

When I got home I had that annoyed feeling that comes when you realize that you haven't been following the little guidelines and paths that you've set up for yourself. I've convinced myself that, except for my health—which I had no control over—I was reasonably independent. Oh, the arrangement I had with *Shoreline* was great and I was making a good salary, but with my other interests and some judicious saving and investing, I could do fairly well if *Shoreline* went bankrupt or Admiral Holbrook retired and was replaced by someone who had a lesser interest in national security and promises made to me and the Defense Department.

Part of that independence in lifestyle was connected to my independence in action, and I've also convinced myself that no one could ever make me do something unless I wanted to do it, that I would never be pushed away from something that I wanted, by any means or threat.

Some thoughts. Twice this day, I had backpedaled from confrontation—once when Justin Dix had threatened me with a phone call to the FBI and once when Craig Dummer had threatened me with his lawyer.

It was like the legal establishment—the FBI and private lawyers—were suddenly ganging up on me. It didn't make me happy, but at the moment, there was nothing I could do about it.

Later that night I was up in my study going through some papers and such, and I came across the file folder with the information I had gathered about the *Petro Star*. I remembered my breakfast meeting earlier that morning with Paula Quinn and I decided that later in the week I would anonymously mail her some of the information I had learned about Cameron Briggs, and then let her and her fellow brothers and sisters in journalism turn their sharp pencils and words upon Mr. Briggs and his unique environmental opinions. It would be fun to watch the media herd gang up on Cameron Briggs and strip him down to his designer shorts. I hoped that it would be successful enough so that he would at least get fined, maybe even do some jail time.

Though at this point I would be happy if all that ever happened was that the Exonia Hospital would move their fashion show somewhere else.

But something tickled at me, something that had to with the FBI. And when I started browsing through the printout that I had stolen days ago from the Puzzle Palace while I was in the state of New York, it came to me, on the very last page of Cameron Briggs's printout.

It made me smile. Tomorrow I would get my revenge against the legal world at the expense of a phone call or two, and that seemed to be a hell of an achievement.

CHAPTER

TWENTY-TWO

It had taken me about an hour and a half to get here on this Tuesday morning, to Maine's largest city—Portland—and I expected my time here wouldn't last as long as the trip back. Once there I parked on the restored waterfront—Portland wisely having followed the path of its older but smaller sister Porter to the south—and walked past a number of restaurants and brick buildings that contained lawyers' offices and consulting groups. There was a ferry landing if I wanted to take the ocean route to Nova Scotia later that afternoon, but on this muggy day, I had other work to do.

At a phone booth near a marina, I took out a roll of quarters and a folded sheet of paper, and I started dialing. The piece of paper was the last printout in Cameron Briggs's Department of Defense file, and this is what it said:

```
Cameron Briggs (Criminal Investigations)
See Op Harpoon
JD Files
J. Carney/Contact JD
File Number: OC-NE-423
```

In the times I had looked over Cameron Briggs's file, I had skipped across this jumble of words and letters, not knowing what they meant, until I had thought yesterday about the FBI, and their titular boss, the Attorney General, who headed up the Department of Justice. Or the Justice Department, depending on how you said it. JD, then.

I spent a couple of minutes on the phone with Information and other folks and after I pumped in a number of quarters, the phone rang and a quick, professional man's voice said, "Justice Department, Criminal Division."

"Mr. Carney's office," I said.

"One moment."

There was a clicking and a distant ringing, and a woman's voice answered. "Mr. Carney's office."

"Morning," I said. "This is Ron Allan calling, Protocol Office at the State Department. I have Mr. Carney's name here on an invitation list for a reception in September. Could you verify the spelling of his last name, please?"

"Certainly," the woman said, and she did.

"And his first name? I'm sorry, but this list is handwritten, and all I can make out is the first letter. A 'J.' You know how it is."

The woman laughed for a moment and said, "I certainly do. Mr. Carney's first name is John, but everyone who knows him well calls him Jack."

"And his title?"

"Deputy Assistant Attorney General, Office of Special Investigations."

"Jeez, sounds like he's been there for a while."

"Oh, he has. About four or five years."

"Thanks a lot," I said, and she said it was no problem, no doubt thinking she was assisting another secret ally in the bureaucratic world of D.C. And who was I to shatter her illusions?

Though it was past the noon hour, I didn't have much appetite for lunch, and I just wandered around the port area for a while. I walked down one pier and sat on the old wood, looking at a large, rusting oil tanker at a pier on the other side of the harbor, shadowed by cranes and other pieces of equipment. On the stern were the letters PETRO STAR and below that, in smaller white letters, was MONROVIA. I just sat there, breathing and thinking, looking for the first time at the ship that had brought me here and to New York City and other places.

Before I got depressed, I left the dock and spent a marvelous half hour in an antiques store that had old navigational maps, matted and framed, and polished brasswork with little placards that claimed the gear had been pulled up by divers from wrecks in the Gulf of Maine. There was an old compass that I thought would look great in the living room, but I had to pass it up. Money was no problem, but in paying for this old antique, I would have to use a credit card and that was not possible. I didn't want any records of my being in Portland on this Tuesday.

When it was about a half hour past noon, I went back to the same phone booth—having been lucky the first time around, I thought it wouldn't hurt to try again—and I dialed the same number, and again spoke the magic words: "Mr. Carney's office."

This time, I got a different woman answering the phone. Her voice sounded younger and bit unsure, which I had been counting on. It being lunchtime, Jack Carney's regular secretary would be gone, replaced by someone who was a temporary or someone in a secretarial pool who wasn't experienced and who might be easily flustered.

Which I hoped.

"Yeah," I said, deepening and hurrying my voice. "Could you put Jack on the line? This is Greg Samson, from the House Subcommittee on Crime."

"Um, could I have your name again?"

I muttered something like I couldn't believe the incompetence of certain hired help, and repeated my name, louder. "And could you hurry it up? I'm already late for a meeting with the congressman."

She murmured something back, and in a moment a man's voice came on the line. "This is Carney."

"Hi, Jack, this is Greg Samson," I said. "I don't know if you remember me, but we met a couple of months ago, at that AG's party in Bethesda." Given the current Attorney General's fondness for parties—as reported in the papers—I was gambling that Jack Carney would have been there. I was right, since Carney said, "Unh-hunh."

And I continued with, "I'm a staff assistant on the House Subcommittee on Crime, and I need to have a quick question answered, and then I'll leave you alone."

Carney sounded slightly cautious. "Well, Greg, this is generally not the way things are done. Why don't you write up the request and put it through channels?"

"You're absolutely right, Jack, but I thought this would save us both some time. I got an inquiry from Congressman Hughes, the subcommittee chairman, about an investigation that he heard something about, and he just wanted to know what it entailed. He wants something quick, and I thought if you could give me a brief rundown, it would save me time, it would save you and your staff time, and that would be the end of it."

"What's the investigation?"

"Something called Operation Harpoon. It's a few years old, and he thinks it took place in the New England area. I guess some constituent's got some questions about it."

"Mmm," came his voice. "That sounds familiar. Let me get to the files here. Hold on." He put the phone down on his desk and I grasped the phone receiver tighter, feeling the slick plastic get slippery in my hand. Long minutes stretched by, and my breathing seemed to slow. Then came that clattering noise when someone picks up a phone, and I thought to myself, Lewis, you are one very bad boy. And very bright.

"Operation Harpoon," Carney said. "An eighteen-month investigation, centered in eastern Massachusetts. Coding here says it was a corruption case. Investigation ended about six, seven years ago. No resolution, no arrests, no convictions. Case closed out."

"What kind of corruption was it looking into?"

"Let's see," came the voice of Jack Carney, and in the next three seconds I learned that while I might have been a bad boy, I certainly wasn't very bright.

A couple of tourists near me were walking across Commercial Street, and an oil tanker nearly clipped them, and in doing so, the driver of the truck slammed on his brakes and leaned on his air horn. The screech of brakes and the bellow of the horn seemed to blast right through my head, and Carney's voice changed.

"Uh, Greg?" Carney said. "Could I put you on hold for a moment?"

"Sure, Jack," I replied, and I hung up on him. I took out a handkerchief, wiped down the phone, and walked two blocks to my Range Rover. I thought about what might be going through Jack Carney's head right about now. All he knew was that someone from a pay phone had been scamming him, looking for information about Operation Harpoon, and then had hung up on him, not bothering to wait around for a phone trace. It made me wonder what kind of guy Jack Carney was. If he was embarrassed about the scam, he might keep it a secret and get on with his life. But if he was angry—or worse, curious—then he might do some digging.

I drove back to New Hampshire on back roads, avoiding the main highways wherever I could. As I headed south, I wondered if I was just being paranoid, on the road to insanity, but in remembering other places I had been, my actions seemed fairly sane and quite logical.

Before working in what we called the Marginal Issues Section of the DoD, I had bounced around other departments and sections for a number of months, gaining experience and building up a little knowledge of what I had gotten into. The year I joined up, the DoD did this for some of us new folks to give us what they called "depth and breadth" of knowledge. You were usually assigned to some senior official for a week or two, and then moved on. They called it the Mentor Program, and God knows if it's still being used. I rather doubted it, since my exposure—in a few instances—had been incredibly dull (most bureaucrats being the same everywhere), but in one memorable instance, exquisitely terrifying.

The man's name had been Grayson. He wouldn't tell me his first name, saying, "Young fella, by the time you get high enough up the ladder to have earned the respect to know my first name, I'll either be dead or getting a sunburn in Puerto Rico, working on my retirement." He smoked unfiltered Camels, wore government-issue eyeglasses, and had an undying hatred and fear of all sorts of enemies, both foreign and domestic. In the first few days I was with him, he had said, "Don't take offense, sonny, but I think this Mentor Program is an absolute waste of time. Sounds like something that a damn fool Democratic congresswoman from Colorado thought up. So you just stay out of my way."

Staying out of his way meant sitting in his outer office, reading newspapers and feeling out of place for the first day, until he tossed me a book and said, "Here, read this." It was E. B. Sledge's horrifying account of being a Marine in two of the worst Pacific battles in World War II—*With the Old Breed*—and when Grayson saw that I had finished that in a day, he gave me a couple more books to read. William Manchester's *Goodbye, Darkness*. Philip Caputo's *A Rumor of War*. And a work of fiction by James Webb,

Fields of Fire. After my fourth day with him, Grayson took me for a cup of coffee at one of the half dozen or so snack bars in the five-sided palace and said, "Whatever you end up doing here, young fella, remember this bottom line. It all comes down to two things: killing somebody else and protecting your own. Everything else is fluff. You can work in public affairs or research or with those corrupt contractors or whatever, but it all comes down to this. You're working to kill people you've never met, and you're also working equally hard to protect people you've never met, but who also happen to be your neighbors. Nothing else matters. Read those books again in a few months. They tell the real story, of guys—and now women, God help us—who are sent far away to do our bidding. Sometimes orders get fouled up. Sometimes they get nitwits for bosses. And sometimes their gear doesn't work, because some business guy's only interested in screwing the government."

He finished his coffee. "Remember that," and I always have.

I also remembered one more thing with Grayson. One day he told me to be at work early and then we went for a drive, using a stripped Chrysler that belonged to the DoD motor pool. He just said one thing as we headed to our destination, and that was this: "I have it on good authority that you're going into some type of research and analysis work. You may find this interesting."

After some long minutes of driving, we ended up in Maryland, in a suburban community. We drove up an unmarked driveway and we showed our identification cards to a gatehouse guard who wore a simple blue uniform that said "Security" on its shoulder patches. The uniform looked as if it belonged to a retired cop or a college student, but the guard looked like an ex-Marine who wished he were back in the service. The building we went to was a featureless concrete-and-metal cube, and after some more negotiations with guards and two elevator rides, I think we ended up in a basement. As we processed through, Grayson smiled at a man about his age and said, "Thanks for the favor, Tom."

"No problem, Colonel," the man said, and I felt a bit uneasy.

I had come to the conclusion earlier that Grayson was a bit of a nut, heading off to retirement with some strange thoughts about books and government service, but the respect he was being shown in this building changed my mind. We were given badges that said "Visitor" to wear around our necks on tin chains, but Grayson's was light blue while mine was red. We were both visitors, but as George Orwell might have said, some visitors are more equal than others.

In the basement we went into a small viewing gallery that overlooked a row of consoles and some large screens on a near wall. There were plush chairs in the gallery and a coffee setup in the rear, and we sat down, coffee cups in hand. The gallery was open, so we could hear the murmur of voices and sounds from below. The largest screen in the center of the room was blank, but then it flickered into focus, and it became an aerial picture of a highway along an ocean coast. The highway was nearly empty, but the waves were moving in to the rocky shore, so it wasn't a static shot. Grayson leaned over to me and said, "In case you're wondering, this is live time."

"Where is it?"

Grayson chuckled. "Well, of course, that's classified. But I'll tell you. It's the coastal highway near a town called Barranquilla, on the road to Cartagena, Colombia. On the road is a certain drug lord, hurrying to Cartagena to see his mistress. This gentleman has unusual tastes, which his mistress is all too glad to satisfy. For a price, of course. This gentleman's mistress has been in Europe on a shopping expedition for two weeks, and has just returned. So he's driving back to get, well, he's driving back to get reacquainted."

The murmur of voices from the workers below us grew a bit louder, and the view of the highway and ocean rotated a bit and tightened in on a stretch of road. There were four dark-colored vehicles there, moving in a single line. They all looked like Ford Broncos.

"Where's the picture coming from?" I asked. "Satellite?"

"On some days you'd be right, but not today," Grayson said.

"This is one of our new surveillance platforms." He paused and smiled again. "Everyone's heard of the Stealth fighter and the Stealth bomber. But why does everybody think we've stopped there? Don't you think there'd be times when we'd want to take good live-time pictures without being noticed? Look now."

The road curved a bit, near an outcropping of some rocks which were awash with water and foam from the waves. A flash of light winked from the rocks and the lead Bronco disappeared in a bigger flash of light and a ballooning cloud of smoke. The other three Broncos swerved and braked, but in a matter of seconds, there were four burning hulks on this bright morning on this coastal highway in Colombia. Armed men in camouflage gear came out from the rocks, moving swiftly and surely. Some of the survivors from the Broncos tried to fight. Others tried to run away, and a couple were crawling. It didn't make much of a difference one way or another. I turned away a few times, not wanting to see what was going on. My mouth was dry, and it came to me, in a way that almost made me laugh with disgust, that I was in a room thousands of miles away, yet I had a comfortable and safe ringside view of at least a couple of dozen people being killed.

I finally said, "No prisoners?"

Grayson replied, "That wasn't the point. I don't think the public or news media have gotten wind of this, but here are our new marching orders. We've gone beyond sanctions, extradition treaties and burning crops, Lewis. It's something a lot dirtier and tougher. This isn't a matter of taking prisoners away for a trial somewhere so they can end up in a plush prison cell with color TV. This is a lot more final."

On the screen the armed men had gone to the side of the road. Two of them exchanged high-five salutes. The four Broncos continued to burn, and there were little lumps of clothing along the asphalt and roadside that used to be people. Then two helicopters came into view—black and unmarked—and in seconds they had landed and taken on the group of armed men. In another few seconds the helicopters were gone, leaving behind the rubble of an early morning drive. The screen flickered and then went out. A couple of people below me clapped. I felt like throwing up. Later this would change, as I read and learned more about my new line of work, but at that moment I was afraid that my coffee would end up on Grayson's shoes.

"Was this a lesson?" I said, my voice demanding, looking squarely at Grayson. "A lesson on how dirty I can expect my job to be?"

Grayson looked surprised. "Oh, it was a lesson, all right, Lewis, but not the one you're thinking of. I left one thing out when I was telling you about the drug lord and his mistress. Up to now this particular gentleman was using encrypted telephone gear, some of the latest stuff from his friends in Cuba. So we never knew where he was going or what he was doing, through the telephone at least."

Grayson rubbed the coffee cup for a moment. "Today, he made one mistake. He let his libido overtake his good sense, and he made one phone call in the clear. Uncoded. And we snapped that right up." He turned to me, his white skin even more pale in the artificial light. "Do you understand what I'm saying, Lewis? One phone call and we were there. We've got this little globe of ours wired, my young fellow, and don't you ever forget it. We've got satellites and listening ships and mobile vans and remote sensing units all over this planet. This time, some nut spoke in the clear and we were on him in an hour. One phone call, in the clear. Don't you forget that."

I didn't, and I haven't. A day or so later, after searching through the Washington *Post*, the Washington *Times* and the New York *Times*, I found two little stories of interest. One was that some U.S. Navy units were just concluding an exercise in the Caribbean Sea near the Colombian coast. And the other was a piece about a prominent Colombian senator who had died in an auto accident on the coast near Cartagena.

From that day forward, I stopped trusting anything I read in the newspapers, and I gained a very healthy respect for the power of a single phone call.

A single phone call. I thought about that as I waited at a traffic light in Kennebunk, on my way home to New Hampshire. One phone call. I had been busy these past weeks, working hard on the telephone, and I knew I had better stop it. Things were getting too crazy, and I didn't want to set off an invisible electronic trip wire with one phone call too many.

Though I never saw Grayson again, I always remembered what he had said. One phone call could mean a lot, especially if the listeners were out there. Waiting at the traffic light, I thought over the scenario of how it could happen. There could be a caller ID trace on any incoming calls to the Justice Department's switchboard. I had talked only briefly with Jack Carney, but with the latest upswings in technology, well, it wouldn't take much. There was a good chance that when I hung up on him at lunchtime today, some security section could have told Jack Carney that the strange phone call had originated from a pay phone on Commercial Street in Portland.

The light changed and I advanced, following two burly men on Harley-Davidsons, the mufflers on the motorcycles rumbling loudly in the afternoon weather. Then what? Then a flash call to the FBI office in Portland, and in a matter of minutes that place would have been flooded. The pay phone would be isolated and sniffed over, and agents would start canvassing the neighborhood. Who had been there? Who had been using that phone? Do you know what kind of vehicle he had been driving?

Some grunt work and a little luck. That's all it would take, and I would have polite men in suits and correct haircuts knocking at my door within the week, asking me why I had been harassing a Deputy Assistant Attorney General.

One phone call.

When I reached Ogunquit I left the main road and parked in a large lot near the beach and the main town area. Unlike Tyler Beach, there's no distinct strip in Ogunquit, just a real downtown with buildings and a lot of restaurants and craft shops, and a beautiful beach, as always.

There was a fair-sized crowd of mostly families. As I walked around, I noticed there wasn't the edge, the sharpness that I always felt when I was at Tyler Beach, and it only took me a few minutes to figure it out. Ogunquit is far enough up the coast from Massachusetts so that the young men and women from the urban sprawl in that state who enjoy raising hell would never think of coming up here. Too far to drive, and too many tolls to pay.

It made me think, only for a moment, about someday pulling up stakes in Tyler Beach if that urban colonization from Massachusetts ever got too far north.

After being there for only a few minutes, I had an early dinner, which consisted of two lobster rolls and two ears of corn, sold by a sidewalk vendor. I ate my dinner and drank an iced tea while sitting on a bench, looking at the ocean battering itself against the breakwater. This town was used as a setting once in a bestselling novel by Stephen King, about a killer flu virus that slaughtered nearly everyone in the world. I had read the book before encountering my own special virus. One of the main characters had come from this town, and thinking about her and the book and the survivors—who lived only to fight another evil—made me stop eating for a while. In King's book, the virus had come from a secret government installation out West, and that was striking a bit too close to home.

I then decided I didn't want to eat any more, and I threw out an ear of corn and a half-eaten lobster roll, and I kept on walking.

At a place in the downtown there was a store that made saltwater taffy, and there were wide windows in the building where people stopped on the sidewalk to see how it was made. Diane Woods had told me about this place, and she said it made the best saltwater taffy in the world.

From what I saw, it involved old machinery that looked as if it was installed around the turn of the century, with lots of cranks and gears and flywheels. The workers had on white smocks and paper hats, and through either boredom or long practice, they ignored the crowd that had stopped by the window. A phrase came to me "feeding time at the zoo" and in looking around, it wasn't clear who was on the outside looking in.

A man near me spoke to his companion. "Hank, I couldn't work there. I'd eat up all the profits."

His friend said, "Hah, that's what everybody thinks. They don't mind if you eat while you're working, Gil. In fact, they encourage it. You know why? Because in a few days, they'll get sick of it, and then they'll stop. Simple psychology. Don't make it forbidden and it loses its attraction."

I looked over. Both were dressed comfortably in designer jeans and bright-colored polo shirts, and each had a shoulder bag over his arm. The man called Hank leaned over and whispered something in Gil's ear, and they both laughed and then walked off. I watched for a moment as they patted each other on the back, and for a minute they held hands as they walked up the street.

It gave me an odd feeling, a sense of loss, and I knew why. This place and those men reminded me of Diane Woods, of who she was and what she hid and the great lengths she went to to try to be true to her own self. Earlier, in driving down to Ogunquit, I had thought of going to her and asking for her help in tracking down Operation Harpoon. With the news from Jack Carney of the extent of the operation, I'm sure Diane would be able to find something out for me. But seeing that PDA—public display of affection—brought something to me, and I knew I couldn't ask Diane for a favor. If anything, I owed her a lot, and after a moment or two of indecision, I went in and bought her two boxes of saltwater taffy.

Later that day, I was almost back home in New Hampshire. I started to slow down when I entered the town of York, home to a lot of Maine history, and also home to a secret safe house that belonged to a long-dead mafioso, which now was storing three Winslow Homer paintings worth millions of dollars.

I'm not too sure what prompted me—it certainly wasn't common sense—but I drove into the neighborhood of Landing

Lane and stopped near the driveway of the safe house. If Felix Tinios was here, I'm sure he'd be furious at my breach of security, but I was confident that no one had followed me down.

I parked the Rover, letting the engine run, knowing I wouldn't stay here long. Through the trees and brush, I could just make out the large white-vinyl-sided Cape with dormer windows on the second floor. Somewhere in this state was a secret agreement with a law firm, probably, that paid another business that paid another business which ended up paying the taxes and utilities for this quiet and empty house. It didn't seem possible that this house could be kept secret for years, but it could happen. This was a small Maine town, and neighbors usually minded their own business. Oh, there were probably rumors about what went on here—maybe a secret hideaway for a rich eccentric, or a hidden bomb shelter in case the nukes ever came back—but I'm sure those rumors never reached the ears of anyone who would care that much. That's not how small towns worked.

All that, for this address and this empty house.

Nothing seemed to be going on. It was quiet. The house was fulfilling its purpose, its role. It was being successful.

While the house was showing off its success, I wasn't too sure about myself. I got into the Rover, and in sixteen minutes I was back in the Granite State, home and with a lot ahead of me.

CHAPTER
TWENTY-THREE

Though it was early evening I didn't go straight home. I decided that the saltwater taffy in my Rover wouldn't wait. In Porter I got on Route 1A—Atlantic Avenue, the ocean route—and I followed the twists and turns of the coastline as I headed south. Out toward the east the long gray march of the Atlantic's waves came to the coast, and I spent a few minutes thinking of how many waves went by in a second, and I tried to figure how many would strike the coast in a day, a week or a month, and by then I was up to one hell of a number.

The radio was on WEVO-FM out of Concord, the state's capital, and I was listening to a classical music selection. The lights of the Isles of Shoals glowed steadily at me as I went farther south, through North Tyler and then across the town line into Tyler. I kept on moving, slowing down some as the traffic began to build up heading into Tyler Beach. With the sound of the music and the smell of the salt air and the feel of the cool evening wind in my face, I wished I could drive forever, and only stop when I reached the terminus of Route 1 in Key West, so many hundreds of miles away.

That was my wish, but reality was pressing me that evening, and I stopped only after another ten minutes or so of driving, going to a condominium built near the waters of Tyler Harbor.

The gift of saltwater taffy was a perfect one, one that was readily accepted. Then Diane Woods and I went out to the boat dock of her condominium. Diane brought along two lawn chairs, and I carried two wine coolers that she had pulled from her refrigerator. Most wine coolers taste like sugary fruit juice gone bad, but on this evening, to be with Diane, I would have drunk almost anything she had set before me.

We sat at the end of the dock, looking out to the twilight glow of the harbor's lights, and the brighter lights of the Falconer nuclear power plant, out near the marshes by the southwest end of the harbor. There were fishing boats and charter craft out there, swaying gently at their moorings. Diane's sailboat, the *Miranda*, was also there, sails furled and put away. Diane drank most of her wine cooler in a couple of swallows, and I sat and smiled and daintily sipped at mine.

"So what brings you here tonight, Lewis?" she asked, sitting back in her lawn chair. Her feet were bare and she had on khaki shorts and a T-shirt from the New Hampshire Police Academy, and her brown hair was getting too long. She spent a lot of time pulling it away from her eyes.

"Oh, something else I have for you, Diane," I said, looking out at the harbor. "Many's the time that you've had something for me, and tonight I just wanted to repay the favor."

"What are you giving me, then?"

"An apology, for pushing you when I didn't have a right to."

She nodded, looking at her hands. "I know. I felt bad about how we left things the last time you were here. I don't like fighting with you, Lewis."

"Me neither. And I also feel bad about what you went through at Roger's, playing that pretend game. I got the feeling toward the end you weren't enjoying yourself."

There was some silence after that, and I watched some seagulls dive around a fishing boat grumbling in from the harbor entrance after a hard day out on the ocean. Diane sighed and said, "You've not told me much about what you did before you came here, Lewis, but I know it was something quiet and unusual. Then every now and then you do something that makes me think you were a goddam spy, or a goddam mind reader, and I'm not too sure which is worse."

"They both seem about equal," I said.

"Yeah, they do at that." She drank from her cooler and said, her voice strained, "It's all part of the Great Act, of trying to pretend you're something that you're not, of knowing that if you want to keep your job, keep your position in this town, you have to lie every day about who you are and who you love. Maybe I'm a coward. Maybe I should just come out and take the heat, and get my ass fired and get my name in the papers while I sue the morons who run this town. And then try to get my job back, and move from my condo because of death threats and all that shit. Maybe I'll do that, one of these days, but not this week."

She sighed and sank deeper into the chair, crossing her bare legs. "No, not this week. I'm too damn busy, and I'm too damn tired."

"You're also too damn hard on yourself."

Diane smiled a bit. "Maybe so. Ever hear of a quaint expression called outing?"

"It's when a man or woman has his or her homosexuality made known, usually without their knowledge or consent. Sometimes by a vocal minority in their community who say outing is a political act, an act of self-defense. A way of publicizing influential and powerful gays who don't use their power for their brothers and sisters."

She shifted some and said, "Yeah, well, I'm sure those senators who were busily sticking knives into Julius Caesar would have called that a political act, too, Lewis, but you still end up with blood on the floor. No, outing's a scary thing, and that's something that troubles me. That one of these days, some crumb I've arrested will learn who I am. All it would take would be someone seeing me in Ogunquit or Provincetown one certain day, and then a few anonymous phone calls to the town manager and the selectmen. Maybe even letters with photographs. Then, as they say, the fun would begin."

She looked up at me. "Hell of a thing, isn't it? You get depressed and angry when you keep a secret, and you get depressed and angry when you wonder if that secret will ever be made public by someone with a grudge against you."

"Then somebody like Roger Krohn comes along and asks you out, and you get put on the spot. Especially if it looks like he might end up being your boss."

Diane shook her head, tossing her too long hair to one side. "Yep, put on the spot. And most times I can laugh it off, but not that night. Too much going on."

"It's been a hell of a summer for you."

Diane held up her bottle in a salute and I clinked my own against hers. "For both of us. Friends?"

"Always," I said. Then I pretended to take another sip and the two of us just talked for a while, as the sky became darker. When I thought Diane wasn't looking I held the bottle in my left hand and let its contents dribble into the salt water beneath me. Diane talked some about Kara and how the two of them were going to play hooky later this week, maybe take a day off and just go driving south, and I said that sounded like fun. Then a few mosquitoes started buzzing around our heads and Diane suggested that we call it a night, which I agreed to do. I said I had one last remark to make before going.

"Which is what?"

I shrugged. "Nothing major. I want to talk to Roger Krohn, and I need to know when he's going to be in tomorrow. I'm thinking of taking him out to lunch or something."

"Really? Well, I suppose I could leave him a message." She hesitated for a moment, and then said, "You're up to something, aren't you?"

At any other time, I might have tossed off that remark with a joke or a quip, but not on this night. Diane and I had just reaffirmed something dear to me, and I didn't want to jeopardize that.

"Yes," I said simply. "I am up to something."

I listened to her breathe for a moment or two. Diane has always been mostly realistic about what I do sometimes as part of who I am. I often go into her territory, and as long as I'm polite and don't do anything exceptionally illegal, she has allowed me some maneuvering room. On a few occasions I've helped her put away some particularly nasty people, people who belong away from the rest of us, no matter the opinion of some columnists for the Boston *Globe* or the New York *Times*. On other occasions, she has come forth with some necessary information that has cleared up a puzzle or two.

Tonight she said, "What does it involve? Anything I need to know about?"

I mulled that over for a second or two, thinking about Felix Tinios and his poor dead cousin, mutilated and dumped into the ocean like a bad piece of fish. Diane deserved to know about that at least, but for now, Sal was still dead and there wasn't much more that Diane could do.

"There's a thing or two I'll talk to you about, Diane, in a couple of days. As to what it involves, well, I guess you could say I'm helping a friend."

"Somebody I know."

"Yes," I agreed. "Somebody you know."

"Then I'd guess it might be Felix Tinios."

"And then you would have guessed right."

Diane stood up, but from the manner of her standing I could tell she wasn't upset. It was just a casual motion, a comfortable one, and I thought I could sense her smile.

"Then you be careful, very careful," Diane said. "Seeing you and Felix being buddies reminds me of the story about the lamb who lies down with the lion, but always keep in mind the real truth behind that story: the lamb is always the one who's in danger. Felix can hurt you badly, Lewis, and don't be offended, but I don't think he's that particularly frightened of you."

I put a hurt tone in my voice as I got up and followed her back to her condominium, carrying a lawn chair in my hand. "You mean, the pen really isn't mightier than the sword?"

She laughed. "Maybe so, but I doubt the pen is mightier than a nine-millimeter bullet to the forehead."

At the doorway to her condo, she took the lawn chair I had been carrying and said, "I'll tell Roger that you'll be buying him lunch tomorrow. Is that all right?"

"Perfect," I said. "And, Diane—"

"I know, I know," she interrupted. "You owe me one. Get out of here and go home, will you?"

"I'm always one to take the orders of cops seriously," and with that, I leaned over and kissed her on the cheek. "Thanks for the truce."

"Fool," she said, kissing me back on the lips. "You still don't know how to kiss a woman right." I shot back with, "So I should learn from the expert?" and we both laughed and she went into her condo.

I got back to the Rover and drove home, and the light feeling around my shoulders, where a heavy weight once rested, was wonderful.

At home the green light on my answering machine was blinking at me, indicating a call had come in: "Lewis Cole, this is Craig Dummer. What do you mean by coming around and harassing me? I tell you, you're in deep shit, man. I've got friends out there, friends who owe me favors, friends who'll take care of you hard."

The machine clicked and beeped, and there was another: "Cole, this is Dummer again. I think I've figured out who you really work for, and if you and your buddies don't cut the crap, I'm giving it all up. You got that? Listen, I've done some heavy shit before, back when it counts, and it don't scare me. So back off. You got that?"

Then the answering machine beeped its silence, and I said, "Yeah, Craig, I got that. But what the hell did I just get?"

And a final message: "Man, they shouldn't have laughed at me . . ."

I played the tape back twice. It didn't quite make sense. I had visited him twice, the last time being yesterday. Could that be called harassment? And then there was the comment about "you and your buddies." Who did Craig think my buddies were? The staff at *Shoreline*? I looked over at the digital clock on my TV's VCR. It was past eleven. I was tired and I wanted to go to bed. I knew that if I returned Craig Dummer's call, I'd probably wake him up and he'd be in no mood to talk. At this time of the night, I was beginning to share that mood, and I decided to talk to him tomorrow, on Wednesday. With that, I went upstairs and took a shower and examined my skin carefully, and noticed with a sense of pride that the scar on my side was healing quite nicely, thank you, and was working its way to a wonderful pale pink.

There were also no lumps on my skin either. For that small boon, I didn't feel any pride at all. Just gratitude.

About four hours later I was awake again, in my darkened kitchen, naked and trembling a bit, with sweat racing down my ribs, drinking ice water straight from a jug in the refrigerator. It was nearly four in the morning, and about ten minutes ago, I had been in the throes of one hell of a dream. It played at first like a snippet from a videocassette. The high Nevada desert. Bodies of my friends on the sand. Except this time they weren't quite dead. They'd get up again, weaving and stumbling, and flesh was falling from their bones, like the meat off a well-cooked chicken in a simmering pot, and they were coming to me, demanding and pointing and asking why I had lived . . .

Before they got to me is when I woke up.

The water tasted wonderful and I didn't drink too much, not wanting to cramp up my stomach or get sick. The light from the open refrigerator door was a tiny oasis in the kitchen, and when I put the jug of water back and shut the door, the sudden darkness poked at me and I went back upstairs.

I changed the moist sheets and opened a window wider, then I lay down on the bed, my breathing beginning to ease. I stared up at the dark ceiling and the noise began. A far-off whirring sound that I was sure was a helicopter, a helicopter coming here to my house, but before I panicked I switched on the light and listened closer, and recognized the sound as a mosquito in my bedroom, teasing me with its whine. I picked up a copy of *Astronomy* magazine from the nightstand and rolled it up, and in a minute I killed the mosquito and went back to bed and shut off the light. I usually get a dream like that about every month or so. With my quota filled, I easily went back to sleep.

In the morning I made three phone calls to Craig Dummer's house and got no answer. Then I went to have lunch with Roger Krohn in the center of town, and afterward we sat on a park bench and watched the traffic crawl by on Route 1, also known as Lafayette Road. It was a hot day, and even the shade from the oak trees didn't do much with the heat. Roger looked a bit tired, with that weariness around the eyes that's hard to hide in the daylight. I said something about that and he said, "Up late last night, doing a ride along with a couple of uniforms."

"Anything interesting?"

He shrugged. "A couple of things, though it's amazing what sets off the guys here in Tyler Beach. I mean, back in Boston, a couple of guys on a street corner drinking a couple of beers, that's no big deal, but here, hell, they make a federal case out of it. Open-container ordinance. You got a beer bottle or can in your hand and it's open and pow, you're in jail for the weekend and you have to come up with a couple of hundred bucks for fines and court costs. No thanks."

"No thanks for the aggravation, or no thanks for the law?"

"Either or," he said, folding his thick arms across his chest. "It'll just take some getting used to, an easier pace like that." And he turned and grinned, saying, "But I think I can make the adjustment just fine."

"You're beginning to sound more confident," I said. "Does it really look that clear?"

Roger looked around, as if he was concerned about who might be overhearing us, but all about us were people scurrying along the sidewalks, mostly tourists who looked as though they were wondering where in hell the beach was. Roger said, "The chief and his family are keeping things very close to the vest, but I don't think it's going to be that long. And I've already been told by the town manager and selectmen chairman that even though they're going to open up the chief's position to the usual advertisements and search committees, I have an inside shot. Maybe the only shot."

"That's pretty interesting," I said, not wanting to tell Roger what was really on my mind. Continuing this little deception, I added, "I've been thinking some about what you said before, the night Diane and I came over to your apartment."

"Really?" he said, and I could tell that though he was acting casual, what I was saying had gotten him interested.

"Really," I said. "About cooperation and working together, helping each other out. I've been considering what you said and I now think it sounds pretty intriguing."

He looked over at me. "Intriguing? In what way?"

I tried to act as if I was being a bit coy. "In a way that might prove profitable for both of us. You were right, back there, when you said I had a lot of contacts up and down the coast. I do have sources. A lot of contacts that even Diane Woods might not know about. With you coming aboard, well, I think you and I might have an arrangement that we could work out."

Roger rubbed at his chin. "What changed your mind? When I brought this up back at my place, Lewis, you acted like a society matron who was just propositioned."

I shrugged. "Thought it over, and I decided cooperation would be the best approach. Plus, well, I'm working on something and—"

"And you need my help? Right?" He had a giggly look of triumph on his face, a look that almost made me smile. He looked like a high school quarterback after scoring the winning touchdown.

"That's right."

"And what do I get in return? Besides your undying gratitude, of course."

"Of course. What you get is a piece of information that I've been holding on to for a while. About a major crime in this state that took place some years ago. I've got a couple of leads that could blow the case wide open."

He eyed me oddly, as if the words weren't making sense. "Why didn't you bring this to Diane Woods?"

Because of timing, I thought. If and when I find out about the paintings, after the exchange, then I'll toss a name or two your way. That's my information, and my gift to you for becoming the new police chief of this nutty and lovely town. And that might also be a way for me to get those paintings back to their rightful owners.

I said, "She has nothing to offer me right now."

"And I do?"

"Yep," I said, leaning back on the park bench. "Something your Massachusetts contacts would probably know, about an old investigation that took place in the state some years back. I need the information for a story I'm working on, but I want to get some deep background stuff that I wouldn't be able to get any-where else. You help me with this, Roger, and the information pans out, then you'll get the info on the crime."

"What kind of crime? Murder? Kidnapping? Robbery?"

I shook my head. "Nope. Look, this is a trial run for both of us, all right? So why don't we take it just one step at a time."

Roger seemed to mull that over for a few moments and then he reached into his back pocket and pulled out a tiny notepad.

"Go ahead," he said, uncapping a pen. "What do you need?"

So I told him.

I was at home that afternoon, trying once again to get a start on a column for *Shoreline* before I got another nasty note from Seamus Anthony Holbrook, when Felix called and invited me out to dinner for the following night. From the sounds of voices and music in the background it sounded as if he was calling from a restaurant or bar. When I asked him, he said, "Of course, Lewis. I still don't know who's out there, getting ready to receive those paintings."

"Haven't been home for a while, have you?"

"Nope. The nest is where they always look, and I don't plan to be back there for a while."

"Do you miss it?"

He laughed for a moment. "Lewis, it's just a place to keep the rain off of my head, nothing else. Home is wherever you decide to store your socks, underwear and ammunition. If a hurricane blew away my house tomorrow, I'd just collect the insurance check and go on to somewhere else."

I looked around at my own home, here in this spot for al-most a hundred and fifty years as a lifeboat station and officers' quarters, and now fulfilling the equally important mission of be-ing my shelter. I could not imagine not living here. I didn't want to tell that to Felix, so instead I changed the subject.

"Have you set the exchange?"

"Day after tomorrow," he said, his voice sounding relaxed, as though it was all finally coming together. "Meet is on for Friday night."

"Got a place?"

"Nope. I'll get a call into my answering machine a couple of hours ahead of time, setting up the place. And then we go on from there."

"Something tells me that when the exchange is over, you're not exactly going on vacation, Felix."

"Nope. I'm going hunting. And that's a fact."

Comfortable as I was in my home, there were promises to be kept, so I said, "Well, just tell me where to be for the exchange, but you're on your own for your hunting expedition. I've had enough thrills and chills these past couple of weeks."

He laughed. "Haven't we both, then? Well, we'll see about Friday night. It just might be some fun at that."

"Agreed."

After I hung up the phone, I went back upstairs to my study and actually got an hour's worth of work done.

After a barbecue dinner I sat out on the rear deck, glass of wine in my hand. Dinner was small and satisfying. There's something about eating near the ocean and the salt air that makes everything taste better. The solitude also helped, for a handful of miles south of me were thousands of tourists and day-trippers, jumbled tight into the sand with their warm drinks, soggy food, sand-encrusted towels and loud music. But before me was my tiny cove and the waves crashing into the rocks, and out beyond the horizon, the fine sight of the Isles of Shoals. Luck was also with me this day: there was no stench from Cameron Briggs's mistake, the *Petro Star*.

When I was through, I sat for a few minutes in quiet and peace, my legs up on the deck railing, watching the tilting and flying of a group of gulls. I finished my wine and sat for a while longer, not thinking any great thoughts in particular, just those random thoughts that give you the illusion that everything's fine and under control. When I went inside and started washing the dishes, I remembered that I had not heard again that day from Craig Dummer.

I hurried through the dishes, collected a couple of items and then left the house and got into my Range Rover.

Within an hour I was among some trees near the trailer park where Craig Dummer lived, looking carefully at his house. His car was parked in the yard, but there had been no sound, no movement, nothing for the thirty minutes or so I had kept the place under watch. A telephone call from a pay phone in Exonia to his home went unanswered, and I was not thinking good thoughts, not at all. I had parked the Range Rover off the side of an adjacent road and had bushwhacked through the woods to get to this point. Little voices inside of me were shouting about bad things and danger. It didn't seem to be a good idea to drive right up to the front of his house and become a memory for some witnesses.

I went across the yard, trying to look as if I belonged and as if I was just visiting, and I went up the wooden steps and knocked on the door. No answer. A few flies were buzzing around.

I knocked again, louder.

"Craig? Craig Dummer? It's Lewis Cole."

I looked around at the other trailers. Some kids were playing in the yards, some wheeling about in plastic tricycles of bright colors. Some little shouts of glee and joy, and they seemed happy, content. I was glad they didn't know what was going on inside my mind at this very moment.

Another knock. Another call. "Craig? Anybody home?"

No answer. I tried the door. It was unlocked. I went in.

The living room was a mess. Clothes were strewn about on the carpeted floor, along with newspapers and magazines. I gingerly stepped in. "Hello? Craig?" But the only sounds were a few flies trapped in the trailer. There was a TV set and a bookshelf and a brown upholstered couch, and a window that looked out to the woods. The bookshelf had a mix of paperbacks, criminal law textbooks and art history books. To the right of the living room was the kitchen, lined with dirty gray tile that looked the color of day-old dishwater. The refrigerator and the shelves were almost empty, save for the bags of chips and other snacks and the cans of Budweiser and some frozen pizzas. Dishes were piled in the sink and the water was greasy and scummy.

I went back through the living room and down a short hallway carpeted in a light tan color that seemed to show every scuff or stain that it had ever suffered. For a trailer, the building was wide and roomy. I could see why mobile homes like this one were popular. For not much money, you had the illusion of living in a real home, and for some families, this illusion would be the best that they could ever do. But I wouldn't want to ride out a tornado or hurricane in one.

The first door to the right led to the bathroom, and unlike the rest of the trailer, it seemed reasonably clean, as if it had just been washed. There was the usual stuff you find in a bathroom, and I left after a minute or so. Beyond the bathroom were two more rooms. One was being used as a bedroom, with a box spring and mattress on the floor, and more piles of clothes and magazines. The magazines were similar to the ones I had found in his old apartment in Bainbridge: art magazines and men's magazines. Quite a combination. I looked through the closets for a moment—some security guard uniforms and other clothing, boxes on the floor—and then I left. The room smelled of sweat and mildew, and I was glad to get out.

There was just one room left.

I took a breath, tried to ease the trembling in my hands and opened the door.

Nothing. Just piles of boxes, clothes and some pieces of furniture salvaged from the apartment. I looked underneath a desk. Nobody. Craig Dummer was not home.

So where in hell was he? And what did he mean by those messages he left on my answering machine?

Feeling a bit light-headed and almost relaxed, I went back to the living room and dumped a pile of newspapers and magazines on the floor so I could sit down on the couch. The couch gave a little belch of dust when I sat down, and my stomach twinged at what the papers had uncovered: a half-eaten cheeseburger resting on a greasy paper napkin. What a dump. I couldn't understand how anyone could live like this. Except for the bathroom, the whole mobile home was a health threat, was eligible to be condemned, was—

Except for the bathroom.

I was back in the bathroom, on my hands and knees. The white tile had been freshly washed, but in the center of the floor there was a rusty stain in the grouting that made me uneasy, and I didn't feel any better looking in the bathtub. It had also been scrubbed, but the washing couldn't hide gouges in the tub's side. I touched the gouges. They were sharp and raw. I sniffed the air, smelling nothing save the strong odor of cleanser. This room had been cleaned, and had been cleaned well, and not so long ago.

I got back on my hands and knees, looked some more, and behind the toilet I found evidence that the cleaners had missed something.

A human tooth, still bloody at the root.

CHAPTER
TWENTY-FOUR

In another minute of searching I found something else that almost made me use the toilet for something it wasn't primarily designed for—a piece of bone, with brain tissue still attached, about the size of a quarter. I dropped it and left the bathroom quickly. In the kitchen I ran the water and scrubbed and scrubbed at my hands, then I sat down on the dirty linoleum floor with my back against the refrigerator and tried to think. All of my alarms were jangling and voices were telling me to get the hell out. For a change I tried to ignore the voices. I went back to the storage room and the bedroom, and I started tossing the place, being careful where my hands ended up.

In the storage room I found a file folder that contained some of Craig Dummer's financial background. There were check stubs dating back almost five years, and something about the companies he worked for sounded familiar. In his bedroom I found some more men's magazines and a couple of videotapes of movies that never made it to Oscar night. The room made me feel awful, but I stayed, and it was in the closet that I found something that made me clench my teeth with both the anger and the joy of discovery.

Hidden way back in the closet, behind shoes and bags full of socks, was a shoe box. In the box was a black ski mask and a .380 Smith & Wesson automatic pistol, with silencer attached. I removed the magazine and counted out the cartridges. One was missing, and I was certain when it had been fired, over a week ago.

I was also certain where it had been fired. Into the side of Tony Russo's head, in front of me and Felix Tinios.

I spent the next fifteen minutes in that mobile home wiping down everything I had touched, and then I got the hell out.

At home I didn't do anything except sit on the back deck with my knees up to my chest, watching the stars rise in the east. It was a cool night for a change, another warning of the cold winter that was approaching. In the span of four short weeks the local population would plummet, as the motels and hotels closed up, as the owners of the cottages drained the water systems, shut off the electricity and nailed sheets of plywood over doors and windows. Four short weeks. I wondered where I would be, what I would be doing and what I would be thinking at that time.

The stars seemed very bright indeed. Upstairs in my study was the folder I had stolen from Craig Dummer's silent and haunted home, but that would wait. I needed to turn down the volume in my head, needed to make everything seem less edgy. I went back inside and from the cellar I pulled out my summer sleeping bag and a rolled-up mattress pad, and then I grabbed a pillow from the couch. In a quick movement upstairs and back, I retrieved my 9 mm Beretta, then I went out to the rear deck, carrying three Molson Golden Ales with me. I was sure that Felix wouldn't begrudge me this one indulgence.

I unrolled the mattress pad on the hard wood of the deck, spread out the sleeping bag and crawled inside. I sat up against a wall and sipped at the first of the Molson Golden Ales, letting the little movies, the dark fantasies and thoughts race through my mind as I looked out into the limitless black miles of the ocean. Craig Dummer, alone in the mobile home, being threatened. Taken into the bathroom, trembling and stinking with fear, sweat running down his face, urine leaking down his leg. Forced into the bathtub, a couple of gunshots to the head. Silencer, of course, though even with a silencer great chunks of bone and flesh are torn away. Then the body is taken out and the cleanup begins, but ends abruptly, leaving behind a couple of pieces of . . . well, of evidence. And then the pistol and the face mask, hidden, but not so well hidden. Left behind in the closet. Why? And why bother taking the body and doing the cleanup?

I was surprised at how quickly I had finished the first Molson, and I started working on the second. Out on the ocean a light moved, a light representing a boat, a man or woman, and a family, staying busy and trying to make a living out on the unforgiving ocean. Busy. The person or persons in that trailer had been busy, quite busy, with the corpse of Craig Dummer in the bathroom of that trailer. Somehow, the decision is made to take the body out and to hide the fact that Craig is dead. Keep it covered up, no publicity, no newspaper headlines, nothing to distract anyone from what is going on.

And what's going on?

Nothing.

Except for Friday. Day after tomorrow. The exchange of the safe house's location and the paintings for the money that was promised Felix Tinios.

Was Craig going to blow something on the exchange?

I thought about that some more, and somewhere between the second and third Molsons, I fell asleep.

Morning after the night out on the deck seemed to come early, but I managed to roll over and pull part of the sleeping bag over my head to get some more sleep. The less said about breakfast and what I felt like, the better. Suffice it to say that by ten o'clock I was in my study, nibbling on buttered toast and drinking an iced tea, looking through Craig Dummer's file, which was one of those accordion cardboard folders that open up. For all the mess and dumped clothes and dirty dishes and crumpled newspapers that I had found in his apartment in Bainbridge and his trailer in Exonia, the man had kept pretty good records. Year-by-year collections of pay stubs, W-2 forms and photocopies of job application sheets. In the five years since the theft at the Scribner Museum, Craig had worked at seven companies in the Manchester-Bedford-Concord area as a security guard, never lasting longer than a year at any job.

Not much of a career path. Then I got my first surprise. His salary. I'm no expert on many things, including the pay practices for security guards, but something seemed wrong about Craig Dummer getting paid about four times the minimum hourly wage. It was a hefty salary, one that didn't make any sense, and it was a wage that started out big with his first job and then grew by a few percentage points with each new job. Something seemed screwy indeed.

Then there were other surprises. Stuck in the folders of the file were torn-off sheets from a Gary Larson desk calendar. I smiled as I read each cartoon and then I looked on the reverse. Notes had been written on the back. I checked the dates; the oldest cartoon was nearly five years old. I looked again at the writing, which was crabbed and small and hard to read. The oldest cartoon had a note that said something like "The wait begins." Another said, "A whole year. Hard to believe." A couple were indecipherable, but one said, "Europe seems so far away," and another said, "What is to be done?"

A diary, or a journal. Or a record of something not going right, for many years in a row.

There were a few cartoons that made reference to someone called "The Man."

"Someone had a big mouth that night. I think I got The Man's name." The date was a week after the theft. A month later: "Confirmed! It was The Man." And a few months after that: "The Man is a sissy. Quickly offers a deal for my closed mouth." The most recent cartoon was just over a week old. On the reverse: "Such awful work. But it had to be done, hard as it was. Europe and the payoff awaits."

I checked the date again. The same day that Tony Russo was killed.

I went downstairs and made myself another iced tea, and when I got back to my book-lined study, I returned to the paycheck stubs. Seven different companies. DiskJets. Grayson Enterprises. Data Lock Systems. Blue Horizon Software. Uplink Corp. Ravine Data Service. Mycroft Computer Development. All seemed high-tech or computer-based, but something about their names nagged me. I took a couple of swallows of iced tea and put the sweating glass down on my desk, next to my computer. One of the paycheck stubs—for Mycroft Computer Development—said "A Division of Brass Cannon Systems" in tiny print at the bottom.

Brass Cannon Systems.

"I'll be damned," I whispered. I reached across the desk and pulled out the *Petro Star* file, and in the listing I stole from DefNet, there it was. Brass Cannon Systems.

Owned by one Cameron Briggs.

I quickly got on the phone and went to work, pretending to be one Sam Matheson, reporter for *BusinessWeek* magazine. A half hour later, I put down the phone and started rubbing my face. All seven companies were connected to Cameron Briggs, who owned some of them outright and held a major portion of the stock of the rest.

Craig Dummer and Cameron Briggs. Craig and The Man.

I leaned back in my chair, staring up at the ceiling. I wanted to pick up the phone and make a call, and ask Cameron if he had been in Exonia last night scrubbing down a bathroom, but instead I waited.

I'm glad I did.

In the afternoon I was out on the deck when the phone rang. I took it outside, trailing the long cord. It was Roger Krohn, and he didn't waste time.

"I have the information you wanted," Krohn said. "You ready?"

"Hold on, will you?"

I went upstairs and retrieved a pad of paper and a pen, and when I came back to the deck I held the phone to one ear as Roger talked to me.

"Operation Harpoon," he began. "Joint Suffolk County–FBI investigation into corruption and organized crime influences in and around Boston Harbor. Looking at all aspects of harbor business: who controlled the longshoremen's union, who had influence over the container traffic and who passed along what funds to what companies. Case was opened about seven years ago and was then closed out a little less than two years later, with no arrests, no recommendations, no future investigations."

"Who were they investigating?"

"The usual suspects. Local mob, government and business leaders. People who had influence on the piers, on what went in and out of the harbor. File indicates some preliminary investigative work had been done but then a budget crunch came and with nothing solid to move on, the case was closed out."

"Do you have the file right in front of you?"

A slight pause. "Yeah, I do. Why?"

"Got a couple of questions. On the organized crime side, were they looking at Jimmy Corelli?"

Roger laughed. "Hell, I don't have to look at the file to confirm that. Look, Lewis, anything serious going down in Boston or eastern Massachusetts back then, the feds and the Suffolk County

DA would be looking at Jimmy Corelli without question. It's a given, an automatic. They were looking at him right up to the day he croaked in Leavenworth."

"But is his name on the list?" I insisted.

I made out the sound of shuffling papers. "Yep, he's right here."

"Okay," I said, doodling aimlessly on the pad of paper. "One more question. On the business side of the ledger. You see anything there on a Cameron Briggs, a guy from New York City?"

A longer pause, and then Roger said quietly, "You're working on something that's not going to get my ass fried, right?"

"Absolutely," I said, and the doodles on the pad became darker as I pressed down on my black pen. In the afternoon light the ocean swells seemed gentler. I could make out the bobbing colors of the lobster buoys, waiting to be retrieved. I thought I could feel my breathing and my heart rate slow down as I waited for Roger Krohn's answer.

"One Cameron Briggs," he said simply. "He's there, Lewis."

"Thank you," I managed to say. "What do they have on him?"

"Just a scoping document. Somebody in the Suffolk County DA's office thought Corelli and Cameron Briggs had a secret business relationship. Some favors done back and forth, but like I said, no arrests. No recommendations."

No arrests, but a piece of paper that opened up a lot of doors, a lot of possibilities. "I owe you one, Roger."

"That you do," he said, "and we'll talk about that later. I'll be interested in what you've got, but in the meantime, I've got to get going. Want to get together this afternoon for a beer?"

"No, I'm afraid I'm meeting someone about then."

"Well, okay, then," he said. "We'll see about tomorrow."

"That's fine."

After I hung up the phone I held the pad of paper tight in my hands and brought it against my chest, and thought of dinner tonight with Felix Tinios, and how much I was going to enjoy that, for it had been a long time since I had impressed Felix with anything.

Jimmy Corelli, a Boston organized crime leader. Cameron Briggs, wealthy New England businessman. Craig Dummer, security cop and art lover.

Three men. Three Winslow Homer paintings. All together, in one package, and now, with just one survivor.

"Oh, Felix," I whispered, and I waited for the afternoon to drift by.

I met Felix at 6 P.M. sharp at a tiny restaurant called Rick's Place, which is in a small business complex on Route 108 in Exonia, a couple of miles away from downtown. The interior was tables and booths against one wall, with an L-shaped bar in one corner. It was quiet, small and out-of-the-way, and I guess it was perfect for Felix's needs. We both ate quickly and without much conversation, and I was almost trembling with excitement, knowing what tales I would tell Felix.

We ignored the dessert menu, and when the check came Felix looked at me and said, "You've got something, don't you?"

"What?"

"The way you've been sitting, the way you bolted through your cheeseburger and everything else, Lewis. You've got something."

My mood was such that I didn't mind being made by Felix. "That I do. A lot."

"Something about the paintings?"

I leaned forward. "Everything about the paintings, Felix."

He slowly nodded and said, "Go on."

So I told him. Told him that Craig Dummer was dead, blown away and dragged out of his mobile home in Exonia, but in his death he had left behind some important evidence. The silencer-equipped pistol and face mask, and the paychecks linking Craig to Cameron Briggs. And then there was Cameron Briggs, investigated a few years ago for having contacts with Jimmy Corelli. After that incident, three paintings were stolen from the

Scribner Museum and then ended up at a safe house owned by Jimmy Corelli, and after he was fired, Craig Dummer gets what amounts to a lifelong job with companies owned or controlled by Cameron Briggs.

Throughout the conversation, Felix listened carefully, his head cocked slightly, like a hunting dog hearing the sounds of something rasping about in the brush. Not once did he look away, and not once did he ask any questions. He just listened, comparing what I was telling him with what he knew.

When I was finished, I said, "It looks pretty clipped together, Felix. Five years ago Jimmy Corelli had those paintings stolen for Cameron Briggs, using the aid and assistance of Craig Dummer, guard at the museum. Then there's a screwup and the paintings end up at Corelli's safe house. Along the way Craig Dummer somehow finds out that Cameron Briggs was the customer, was The Man, and Cameron gave him lifelong employment to keep him quiet."

Felix shifted in his seat, looking uncomfortable. "But why keep him working? Wouldn't it have been just as easy to give him the money without going through the hassle of finding him a job every year or so?"

"Remember what Justin Dix told me earlier," I said. "Right after the theft, Craig and the other guard were under suspicion and were probably under surveillance for quite some time. Having Craig sit around and support himself with no job would have raised a lot of questions. But having him survive on dead-end security guard jobs, well, that makes sense. Nothing out of the ordinary."

Felix began playing with the salt and pepper shakers, moving them about in his big hand. They made tiny clicking noises. It sounded las if he was getting ready to roll bones. "So there's a screwup and the paintings sit still for five years," he said, speaking in a thoughtful tone. "Cameron Briggs wonders where his paintings are, and Craig Dummer wonders if he's ever going to do more than just guard pieces of computers. Maybe Craig was promised a big bonus when the paintings were delivered safely, and he was still waiting for that."

I nodded back and said, "Then Tony Russo finds out five years later that the paintings are at a safe house owned by Jimmy Corelli, a house that's in Maine. After a bit of checking, he finds out that Felix Tinios of North Tyler, New Hampshire, is the only one who knows that particular address. After some dark work he meets with you and me at a restaurant in Porter, and after some negotiations and some talking back and forth, he ends up dead in the parking lot. Killed by Craig Dummer."

Felix looked at me sharply. "Why do you say that? What makes you think the shooter was Craig Dummer?"

I told him about the calendar note, and Felix shrugged. "A note that could mean almost anything. You got better than that?"

"Yeah, because the pistol and the face mask were in his— Oh. Just because they were there doesn't mean he used them. Whoever killed Craig Dummer could have planted the mask and the gun."

Felix nodded. "Exactly. So then try this one for size. What was one of the last things that Tony Russo said as we were going to the parking lot?"

"He said we were going to meet with the buyer. He said the buyer was waiting in the car, and wanted to meet you, Felix."

"That's right. So maybe Tony—God rest his miserable soul—maybe he was telling the truth. Maybe the buyer was waiting outside, and that was your Cameron Briggs. Except that somewhere between the first drink and the check, he got out and loaded up and waited for Tony near the fence and bushes, waiting to eliminate a guy who could prove to be trouble later on. Sound reasonable?"

"Could be."

"This Cameron Briggs of yours. Does he have it, Lewis? Does he have what it takes to put down a guy like Tony Russo?"

I remembered what Paula Quinn had said earlier about Cameron Briggs, how there was no life in that man's eyes. "It's quite possible, Felix."

Then Felix's look darkened and he said, "You know something about this guy?"

"Yeah, I do. I found out he's the nitwit who owns the *Petro Star*, the tanker that had the oil spill in June."

"Jesus. I had to move out of my house for a month because of the stench when that happened. I'm beginning to like him just fine, Lewis. Where does he live?"

"On Atlantic Avenue in Wallis."

By now Felix's skin was flushed, and I was wondering about his heartbeat. "Makes sense, my friend. He lives a couple of miles up the road from my house."

I sipped at the rest of my ice water, for my throat was quite dry. "You think that's where your cousin Sal ended up?"

"Why not? You got a better place?"

I thought of Cameron Briggs's home, on a fairly quiet stretch of Atlantic Avenue. Lots of property with hedges and trees. You could bring someone in and come out with a corpse in the early morning hours, and there was a very good chance that nothing that went on would be witnessed. A very easy trip over the berm and into the ocean.

"No," I finally said. "I don't."

By then the restaurant's single waitress had come by to pick up the check. As the waitress stood at the cash register and started talking to the bartender, I said, "Cameron Briggs, Jimmy Corelli and Craig Dummer. But there's a couple of names missing."

"Oh? Really?"

"Yeah. The two fake Manchester cops. Had to be someone extra—I don't think Cameron Briggs would have been out there skulking around."

Felix looked over his shoulder and sighed at the sight of the waitress still jawing with the bartender. "Simple answer. From Corelli's organization."

"Guys disguised as cops?"

Felix grunted. "Hah. Lewis, a crew like Corelli's, it was probably real cops. He had them on the payroll. Probably took two of 'em from his crowd and sent them up to Manchester to do the job."

The waitress finally came back with a handful of change, which neither Felix nor I touched. Felix wiped his hands with a napkin. The back of my neck suddenly hurt and I held on to my water glass and said, "Felix?"

"Yeah?"

"Any names come to mind?"

"What?"

I swirled the glass for a moment. "You used to work with Corelli. You got contacts down there. Any names come to mind of cops who used to be on the payroll? Who might know their way around Manchester?"

Felix swore something in Italian and scooped up the change that represented the waitress's forlorn tip, and he said, "I'm heading for a pay phone. You hold on."

Which is what I did. The waitress looked over at me and gave me a weak smile, and from my wallet I pulled out three singles and shoved them under the plate that held my half-eaten cheeseburger. Felix came back and slapped me on the side of the shoulder and said, "You feel like going for a ride?"

I smiled up at him. "Why the hell not?"

In just an hour a lot of things can happen, and on this particular night, sixty minutes took me from a small town in southeastern New Hampshire to the famous North End of Boston, thanks to the ghost of President Eisenhower and the Highway Civil Defense Act of 1956. A true fact, one that is still not well known: the nation's interstate highway system wasn't built for commerce or travel or for anything having to do with peace. It was built in the 1950s for war, to speed up the transportation of troops and heavy supplies across the nation, against a forgotten foe once called the Soviet Union. Ask most students today about the Soviet Union and the Highway Civil Defense Act and you get a blank look, which is all right, according to the education experts. We're not supposed to be filling those young minds with rote facts. As to what we're filling them with instead, I'm not sure.

As for the North End, luckily the Highway Civil Defense Act had nothing to do with its traditional neighborhoods. The streets were narrow and winding, and most of the buildings were brick with granite stoops. Old men and women—some leaning on canes—sat outside on the narrow sidewalks in chairs and looked up at us as we drove by.

Felix laughed when he saw that I had noticed them.

"Nice-looking old folks, right?" he asked. "Look peaceful and quiet, just nodding off the years and collecting Social Security. Right?"

"Why do I get the feeling that you're putting me on?"

He laughed again. "Because I am. This is one of the last neighborhoods in this city—hell, maybe in this state—that have old folks like that. They're this neighborhood's intelligence service, Lewis, and they're working tonight as early-warning radar. In a matter of a couple of minutes, a few good men in some of these brick buildings are going to know we're here tonight. But then again, I don't have to lecture you on intelligence agencies, right?"

"Absolutely."

"One of these days, I'll get you to talk, you old spook."

"Maybe so," I agreed. "But this isn't one of those days."

That gained me a wide grin, and he found a parking spot and we stepped out and Felix locked the doors to his rental car, which was a light gray Lumina this warm evening. We began walking and I noticed Felix's odd gait. He had on black wrestling sneakers, designer jeans and a billowy summer shirt that hung over his waist, and I said, "Carrying, right?"

"You got it."

"I thought this was your home base, your own turf."

"That it is, but that doesn't mean there might not be trouble afoot. Some old guys around here probably don't have fond memories of me, and those who do have fond memories of me might be hard to get a hold of in time to intervene if something gets started. So I carry, just to be on the safe side."

"But here?" I said, a slight tinge of humor seasoning my voice. "I've always heard that this is the safest neighborhood in the city, a place that's home."

"And home is always the most dangerous place to be, Lewis. Look it up. That's where most murders take place. In the home."

I couldn't argue with that, and I followed him as he led me through the alleyways and crooked streets of the North End. It was a slightly comforting feeling, being in a strange and alien place and having a friendly guide along to show you where to go. I've not traveled much in my life, and I've always thought how pleasurable it would be to go to the most remote mountains of the old Soviet Asia, to the wide deserts of Australia and the hot jungles of equatorial Africa, but on all of these trips I would like to have a reputable friend and guide along. Not a guide-for-hire; just an old friend who knows the ropes and who'll watch your back and make sure that your corpse doesn't end up being a burden on the local embassy.

As of now, I have no such friends, except for Felix. I was content to let him take me into this foreign place, where the streets were quiet but filled with simmering tension, oaths broken and crimes planned and families loved. I was also content knowing that if my guide abandoned me this night, at least I could make it home to New Hampshire. I don't think that would happen quite the same way in Kazakhstan.

At a nondescript building like so many others, with brick walls and painted blank doors, Felix stopped before two men sitting near the stoop playing cards on a folding table. A window on the first floor was open and a woman was leaning out on a tasseled pillow, her fat arms looking like rolls of sausage, warm in the night air. The men wore straw hats and had glasses of wine before them, and Felix talked to them in Italian and they replied in the same language. I stood still, with that uncomfortable half-smile of the man who only knows his native tongue.

There was some laughter, and Felix bowed a bit—in respect, I thought—and then we went up the two stone steps into the building. The lights were set far up on the wall and seemed old, and a wooden stairway was before us. There were old and fresh smells mixed in together, of spices and hot sauce. From behind one of the apartment doors came the sound of some classical music. We went upstairs to the first-floor landing and then continued going up. At about the third floor I said, "One thing I've always been curious about, Felix."

"Yeah, what's that?" he asked, his head swiveling, eyes looking around at the polished wooden doors. None of them had numbers. I suppose if you had to ask, you didn't belong.

"You and your last name," I said. "You come from this area, you speak Italian, and you've worked with . . . well, you've worked for some interesting organizations. But you have a Greek last name, Felix. I don't understand."

"Not much to understand, Lewis," he said, looking at me finally, his face expressionless. "My father was Greek, my mother was Sicilian. An odd match, one that some members of my family never got over, and one that some business associates of mine never forgot. Some groups here, well, they can be as racist as the KKK. If you're not pure-blood, there's only so far that you'll go."

We stopped before a door and Felix knocked. "That's another reason why I got out when I did."

I said nothing and Felix knocked again, louder, calling something in Italian. A muffled voice answered, and we went in.

"Not locked?" I asked.

"Doesn't have to be," Felix said.

The apartment was small, with plaster walls and a dark oval rug covering a cracked linoleum floor. There was a thin couch on one side and a couple of chairs, and beyond the tiny living room was a kitchen. Old photos with ornate frames hung on the walls, and there was elaborate plaster scrollwork at the top, near the ceiling. An old man was sitting at a metal table in the kitchen, looking out the window. He was smiling at Felix. He had on a sleeveless white T-shirt and baggy gray pants, and black slippers on his feet. The kitchen had green tin cabinets and a small refrigerator and a two-burner hot plate. There was a photo of the Madonna on the wall—and I don't mean the singer—and more photos in elaborate frames.

Felix walked ahead of me and I followed, again feeling uncomfortable, as if I were in high school and accompanying a teenage friend while he was visiting a dying grandparent in a nursing home. The old man looked to be in his late seventies. He had wispy white hair and age spots on his wrinkled face and hands and clumps of white hair along his upper arms. Felix murmured something and held both of the man's hands in his and kissed them. Felix pointed to me and the man smiled and waved. Felix sat in the only empty chair in the kitchen, while I folded my arms and tried to look inconspicuous.

From his chair Felix looked up at me and winked, and said, "Old Gerry here wishes you good health, and he says he's pleased that you have come here with me."

"Tell him it's a pleasure to meet him," I said.

"Don't have to," Felix said. "I already told him that."

And then I was lost, for the two of them leaned into each other and talked for at least a half hour. At first it was all smiles and little giggles, as they talked like old friends who had not seen each other for years. Then it became a bit more serious, with little pauses and then tiny outbursts of statements or questions. Through it all, though, no voices were raised, and there was no yelling. In a way, it was like Felix was seducing the old man, trying to draw out knowledge or information. There was a fluidity in their language and hand movements that made me wish I had taken some anthropology classes in college. I felt as if I was witnessing some ancient ceremony, some rite of a young man seeking guidance from an elder of the tribe. It also made me ponder why tiny island states—Sicily, Ireland, England and Japan— have always managed to break out from their shores and go out to raise hell in the world.

In their talk a few times I caught the name of Jimmy Corelli, but that was all. Once I was embarrassed when the two of them

quickly looked at me and the old man whispered something and
Felix whispered back and then they both laughed. I ignored
them and looked out the window. Below the window was the
narrow strip of the street, and across the street was a building almost identical to the one we were sitting in. I could see shapes sitting by the windows, looking outside. So many quiet lives in
these buildings. On the cracked windowsill was an old black
pair of binoculars, with a frayed leather strap. It wasn't hard to
imagine the old man spending his long hours up here, gazing at
the tiny world which was before him. Out in the brightness of the
night sky I made out the landing lights of a jet going into Logan,
and it seemed as though I was a hundred years away.

Then it was over. Felix stood up and said, *"Molte grazie,"* and
pressed an envelope into the old man's hands, and kissed them
again. I nodded and smiled and the man waved at us and we went
out of the apartment and then downstairs. Felix was smiling and
I knew enough not to say anything until we were near his car, and
then I said, "Who was that?"

"Gerry DelCorso. Everybody down here knows him as
Uncle Gerry."

"Was he with the Corelli organization?"

Felix unlocked the car for both of us. "Nope, not at all." We
got in and he started the Lumina and said, "Gerry was . . . well,
it's hard to describe. He was a neighborhood guy, ran a couple of
stores. Dabbled in politics, worked in the church and was everybody's favorite uncle, you know? Helped with baptisms, funer-
als, let some of the families buy stuff on credit. After a while he
became a peacemaker, a guy that other groups would call on
when things were going to the shits and they needed an outside
negotiator to bring some sense to things. He became well re-
spected, and now, well, he's almost the unofficial historian of
what's gone on in these streets."

We pulled out into traffic and the way was slow, with lots of
stopping and going. I said, "It seemed to take a while. Was there
a problem?"

He drove for a moment, fiddling with the radio station and

then sitting back and saying, "Lewis, it's been a while since I've seen Uncle Gerry, so I had to get some necessary preliminaries out of the way. How he's feeling. How his family is doing. How I was doing. And then there was a problem, yes. One of the reasons Gerry has been trusted all these years is that he's always kept his mouth shut, and he's kept it shut through some pretty tense times, times that have never made the newspapers. So you can see he might not have been that eager to spill all about Jimmy Corelli."

We stopped at another traffic light, and again I was glad that Felix was behind the wheel, for he was extremely self-assured in handling the madness that is Boston driving.

"You were smiling when we left, Felix," I said. "So how did you get Gerry to talk?"

"Two things, really," he said, deftly pulling the Lumina in between a double-parked car and a delivery truck that seemed lost. Behind us a number of horns were blaring. "One is that since Jimmy Corelli's dead, his group is now busy yelling and shooting at each other and not doing a hell of a lot, and I don't think Gerry has much allegiance to whoever's running the show now. Second is that I was looking for the names of cops, and I wasn't looking for anything about anybody down here. Just cops, and that was all right. For a nice old man, Gerry's got a low opinion of cops."

"So, opinions and ancient history aside, what did you get?"

Felix looked over and smiled. "I got the names of two cops, Lewis. Does that sound all right?"

"Sounds just fine."

"Then let's keep on going."

"Won't argue with that."

At a 7-Eleven store Felix pulled into the parking lot and got out. I went with him to a pay phone and he said, "I told Gerry what I was looking for, and he came up with two names. Two cops that Jimmy Corelli had in his coat pocket, bought and paid for, and who Jimmy could trust to do a big-time, out-of-state job like this art theft. That makes a difference. You wouldn't send just anybody on a job like this museum caper. A cop who's in your pocket for fixing tickets, this would be too dangerous. So Gerry thought for a bit and came up with two candidates. Cal Maloney and Paul Demers."

"Still Boston cops?" I asked, thinking that if Felix didn't know, maybe I could call in another favor tomorrow from Roger Krohn, but as he does a lot, Felix impressed me.

"That's what I'm going to find out. You just hold on."

Felix dialed a local number and let it ring for a moment, and when it was answered, he said, "Sergeant Macklin, please."

I think Felix was amused by my expression, and he whispered, "What? You think Boston cops moonlight as altar boys?"

In response I just shook my head, and a voice came on and Felix said, "You recognize this voice? Good. Okay."

Some chatter from the phone that I couldn't make out, and then Felix said, "Need current info and bio on two of your guys. One Cal Maloney and one Peter Demers. Last I knew, they were active four, five years ago. Got that?"

I looked around the lot. Concrete barriers and puddles of liquid broke up the parking lot. Felix's rented Lumina looked to be the best vehicle in the area, and traffic roared by on a four-lane city street whose name I didn't know. Buildings of all varieties were around us, and I saw not a single tree. I bent back my head and looked up into the orangy night sky and didn't see a single star.

Felix's voice got a bit louder. "Well, I don't care."

A pause. Felix again. "You should have thought about that before you had that lovely weekend rendezvous with your babysitter, Kenny. Or do I have to remind you?"

The next pause was shorter and Felix said, "I'll be here. Ten minutes? You got it," and then he read off the phone number of the pay phone and hung up.

"Success?" I asked.

"Of course," Felix said, leaning against the side of the booth.

"We should know in less than ten minutes. My contact is very thorough."

"I should think so, considering what I think you have against him."

Felix smiled, and it wasn't a very pleasant sight. "We're always in a battle with what some columnists call the forces of good, Lewis, and we take our advantages and victories where we can. Old Sergeant Macklin has an unhealthy interest in teenage girls. One weekend in a Saugus motel and a full set of photos and videotapes later, Sergeant Macklin took on a part-time job. Working for us."

"Thought you were freelance."

"An extra set of prints didn't hurt."

We waited in the parking lot and I sat on the Lumina's hood while Felix kept his stance at the pay phone. Twice people came over to use the phone—a young couple and a guy in jeans and T-shirt who looked like he just got off a construction site—and Felix stayed there and smiled with his thick arms folded and the people veered off. I don't know what it is, but when Felix is in his working mode, he puts up something—a field, an aura, whatever—that makes people veer away. Even standing near him, I felt jumpy, which is probably why I stood up quickly when the phone rang.

Felix let it ring only once. A pad and pen appeared in his hand, and with his head cocked over, he started taking notes, saying, "Yeah, yeah, yeah," over and over again in a monotone, and then he said, as one word, "Thanks-okay-bye," and hung up.

"Well?" I asked.

Felix looked at me, his face troubled. "Gerry was right. Both cops, detectives, working for Boston five years ago." Then he stopped.

"And?" I demanded.

"And they're both dead, Lewis."

Everything seemed to smell worse right about then, and the light seemed to dim about me, and I said, "Dead? What else? Do you have how and when?"

Felix said, "Sure do." He looked down at his pad and said, "Peter Demers. Retired four years ago, moved to Florida and died of a heart attack two years later. Buried down there with his wife, according to the good sergeant."

"Great," I said. "And what about the other guy, Cal . . ."

"Cal Maloney," Felix said. "Also deceased. Died in a car accident five years ago."

"Where?"

"Newburyport, Massachusetts. Just over the border from New Hampshire. In the early morning hours of July 7."

July 7. The date sounded familiar. Very familiar. I said in a low tone, "Felix . . ."

Then his grin threatened to explode, it was so huge. "Exactly, Lewis. He died in a car accident, night of the painting theft. Paintings were stolen little bit after 11 P.M. on July 6, and he croaks in a car accident about 2 A.M. on July 7. Blood alcohol content at least point two. And you want to know something interesting?"

"Love to."

Felix stepped away from the pay phone and lowered his voice and said, "Among other things, Sergeant Macklin told me that the son of a bitch had a cocktail napkin in his pocket from a bar in Maine called the Whistling Buoy. In York, Maine."

"Any idea of what he was doing there, besides getting drunk?"

After folding the pad shut and putting it into his pants pocket, Felix said, "According to Macklin, story is that he got to the Whistling Buoy about a half hour before closing time and knocked back a few, and he tipped the bartender big, saying things were going great for him, couldn't be better. And about forty minutes later, heading home, he leaves the interstate just after crossing the border into Massachusetts and wraps his car around a tree."

"So he was the man, Felix."

"Yep. He was the man. Which tells me that his partner wasn't in on the storage."

Felix started back to the Lumina and I stayed with him, asking, "Does that make sense?"

"Perfect military doctrine," he said, opening his door. "Need to know. Both guys are in on the theft, but only one guy needs to know where it's going for storage. The safe house in York. But if he gets drunk and kills himself, then the address dies with him."

I got into the car the same time as Felix. "And Corelli would know, but he was busy doing time in Leavenworth."

"Right," Felix said, taking out his keys. "There he is, in prison, with bugs and stools all around him, and if you think he was going to breathe a word that he was involved in the biggest art theft of the decade, you're nuts. He waited and kept his mouth shut and died quiet."

After Felix pulled out into traffic, he added, "It floors me, though, that Tony Russo ends up knowing that the paintings were at the safe house in York. All he knew was that Corelli had them stolen. Would love to know how that happened."

I leaned back in my seat, suddenly feeling tired. Though Tyler Beach was only an hour away, it seemed like weeks. "Simple intelligence work, Felix."

"Oh? Are you going to reveal something here, Lewis, or just spin theories?"

I didn't rise to the bait. "Just spinning theories. Corelli couldn't have known everything by himself. A couple of other guys must have known pieces of the scheme. So Tony also keeps quiet, and one year he learns from Corelli's older brother that yep, Jimmy Corelli was behind the thefts. Another year, somebody else lets him know that Corelli stole them for Cameron Briggs. More time goes by, and he finds out that Cal Maloney was in on the theft, and he delivered the paintings to a safe house in Maine, but the dumb cop gets killed in an accident."

Felix sped up as we got on Route 1, heading north out of the city, and we passed large buildings and exit and entrance ramps and concrete-and-steel bridges.

"Yeah, makes sense," Felix said. "Then Russo starts poking around, asking questions here and there, tries to find out who knows where the safe house is located."

"You got it," I said. "Then your name comes up, you start getting postcards, and Tony goes to Cameron Briggs and says hey, the deal's still on, five years later. Then maybe part of Cameron is excited about finally getting the paintings, but another part panics about all of this coming out right now, and Cameron starts tidying up. Beginning with Tony Russo. And then Craig Dummer. Giving him money to pay off his debts and moving him out of his old place, and then taking care of him one bloody night."

"Not a bad yarn, not a bad yarn at all," Felix said, and we stayed quiet as we went through the mass of cities clustered around Boston, through the strip malls and neon lights of Danvers and Saugus and Medford. Then the bright neon and concrete were left behind us. I could even make out a few stars.

When we approached the exit for Groveland, I turned and looked at Felix, and in the dashboard lights his afternoon shadow looked blue-black and he had a thoughtful look on his face.

"Felix?"

"Hmmm?"

"The swap is on for tomorrow, right?"

"Well, in less than an hour it's going to be today. But yeah, tomorrow. Why?"

"Just remember one thing when we're there, Felix."

He thought for a moment, as another mile passed underneath the Lumina's wheels. "What's that?"

"Cameron Briggs. He seems to be in the mood for tidying up. Keep that in mind."

Felix looked over at me, with a gaze that made me glad he was not my enemy.

"It's never left my mind, Lewis."

I left it at that, and I think I dozed off soon after.

At about 3 A.M. I woke up at home with a dream, another damnable flashback about where I had worked before, but it was one I had a hard time remembering. The dream had something to do with a file on my desk, and there was a voice speaking aloud in my old office at the five-sided palace. It was a familiar one, whispering to me. "Something's wrong," the voice had said, urgent yet quiet. "Something's wrong."

I lay awake for a while, staring at the ceiling in the darkness. The sound of the ocean was there as always but it wasn't particularly comforting. There are times when I wake up from bad dreams, and the sound of the ocean and the air temperature and any imperfections in my bed's mattress conspire together to keep me awake. After about an hour or so I knew that this was one of those times. I swore softly and got up and dressed and went outside on the deck adjoining my bedroom. The stars were as bright as ever but I didn't feel like looking at them. Instead I sat down on the deck floor and remembered.

Something's wrong.

I sat there for a while and it came back to me, in dribs and drabs. I had been working for the Department of Defense for a few years before I got transferred—or, depending on your definition, shunted away to—the group that became known as the Marginal Issues Section. It took some time to get used to the working atmosphere in Marginal Issues. In other groups and sections in the DoD, even if it was all-civilian, there was a tight military structure to everything, from the style of coffee cup you could keep at your desk to the number of pencils you could requisition every month. But in Marginal Issues there was a loosey-goosey atmosphere that even George Walker couldn't quite stamp out. There was no dress code and lunches were long, and there'd be afternoons off if the weather was nice. Oh, George threatened us here and there, but there were two graces that saved us: first, where it counted, the Marginal Issues Section produced, and second, the members of the section all had some sort of cognitive talent that some higher-ups wanted to keep, even to the point of screwing up time sheets every month.

After a while in Marginal Issues, I learned that there were peaks and valleys, where you'd be working sixty to seventy-hour weeks, responding to a crisis at some flash point in the world, and other times when your desk would be clear and a two-hour lunch didn't make much of a difference. During those downtimes we were encouraged to root around and do research on stuff that interested us.

Something's wrong. I remembered the first time I heard that phrase.

It was during a month when I was doing my own project for the first time. It had to do with the Soviet space program, back when there really was a Soviet Union and people could call it an Evil Empire without laughing. Even with people on the ground (HUMINT) and satellites in the sky (SIGINT) and SR-71s and U-2s and surveillance vessels and listening posts in China and India and everywhere else, there was a lot we didn't know about that colossus of the East. We didn't know everything they were producing or doing, and the depth of our ignorance was shown that giddy year when all the walls came down. Before that year, there were a lot of mysteries in that dark empire, and one day, I started looking into one of them: the mystery of the second *Buran*.

The Soviet Union once had an aggressive space program, another fact that is conveniently forgotten in the history and science books. Well, remember this fact: if it wasn't for a special class of booster rockets that blew up too often in the 1960s, they would have beaten us to the moon by almost a year, and Neil Armstrong, Buzz Aldrin and Michael Collins would have been second-placers. But even with those booster failures, they had a number of successes, including the *Salyut* and *Mir* space stations, and it was well known that they were developing their own reusable space shuttle. This shuttle was called the *Buran* (Russian for snowflake, and I'll be damned if I know the significance of that). There were a lot of snickers in our aerospace community when it was learned what it looked like: it was almost a mirror of our own space shuttle, right down to the white paint and the black heat-shield tiles. No doubt the KGB boys had been busy stealing blueprints and such from our aerospace boys out in California.

The first test flight of the shuttle, unmanned, took place on November 15, 1988. After a couple of orbits, the shuttle landed safely at the Baykonur Cosmodrome. While the *Buran* never had a manned test flight while I was at the DoD, there was something else about that Soviet shuttle program that perked up our interest. A mystery, actually, about the discrepancy between their public announcements and the private information that we were picking up: they claimed they had built and tested only one operational *Buran*, whereas our satellites had shown two of the winged spacecraft on the ground at the same time: one at the space complex in Baykonur and the other on top of an AN-225 aircraft at a military airfield near Alma-Alta. There were a couple of test models and one *Buran* under construction at the time, but these had all been accounted for when the satellite photo was taken. This was the cause of a few late meetings and some memo barrages at the Pentagon. What was the purpose of the second operational *Buran*, and why were the Soviets keeping it under wraps?

And if that wasn't enough of a mystery, none of our satellites and none of our other snooping devices ever found that second *Buran* again. It had vanished.

Well, a few months after the second *Buran* disappeared, other crises popped up and resources got diverted, and the special task force looking into this puzzle got deactivated. Time and money were at a premium, and the *Buran* folder got dumped into that giant filing cabinet marked inactive—until one rainy March day when I stumbled across it and started getting to work. I spent long hours at my desk, plugged into the DefNet system, conducting a wide-range search, also known as an Electrolux Special—vacuuming up every piece of information that had anything and everything to do with the Soviet space program. I found some intriguing things here and there—like a classified radio transcript of a cosmonaut stranded in Earth orbit, who, knowing he was going to die, spent his last hours cursing Lenin, the Communist Party and mission control—and it was difficult to keep focused with such a wealth of knowledge before me.

Then I found a few bits of information that tickled my brain. For example, a few weeks after the picture of the second *Buran* appeared, some Canadian scientists near the Arctic Circle had measured an unexplained burst of energy from a *Salyut* space station. I recorded the date and did another Electrolux Special, and something else popped up that caught my fancy: on that same date, a spectacular meteor shower was seen by an Army Special Forces team in Outer Mongolia (what an Army Special Forces team was doing in Outer Mongolia was something I didn't have the Need to

Know). After some other research I found a study conducted by our cousins over at the National Security Agency (also known as None Such Agency) which determined through the monitoring of certain classified information traffic that one of the *Salyuts* was not a space station, but was believed to be an experimental laser battle station for the Soviets' own version of Star Wars.

Through some cross-checking over at NASA, I found out that the *Salyut* with the unexpected energy emission was also the one that the NSA thought was a laser battle station. Then there were two more tiny bits of information that seemed to make it all come into focus: two days before that *Salyut* energy burst and the meteorite shower, there had been a launch of what was called a weather satellite from Baykonur. But later that month the Soviets announced that the weather satellite had failed in orbit. Fortunately for them, none of our satellites had caught this particular launch. Then, a week after that meteorite shower witnessed by Army troops in Outer Mongolia (and me still intrigued about what they were doing there), a radio intercept from *Glavkosmos*, the Soviet space agency, talked about the "successful *Buran* excursion." Yet there had been no official—or unofficial—*Buran* launch at the time.

With all of this behind me, and a lot of thinking later, I came to work one weekend and wrote a detailed, informative memo that said it was apparent that (a) the Soviets had a working laser station in orbit; (b) the second *Buran* was in fact a large-scale target model that was destroyed in orbit by the *Salyut* and was designed to simulate one of our own shuttles; and (c) the Soviets had demonstrated the capability of destroying our space shuttles and satellites in orbit, and were a few years away from being the dominant space power.

I made a recommendation: that the *Buran* task force be reactivated and expanded, with extensive liaisons with NASA, the Pentagon's SDI office and the aerospace industry, and that the executive and legislative branches be notified immediately.

When I left work that Sunday evening, having locked my memo in my office safe, I felt tired and a little smug. But when I came back, about ten hours later, I was nervous with energy and a lack of sleep. And before submitting the memo to our section leader, I decided to engage in a little unofficial peer review, and I asked Cissy Manning to read it.

I had been with Marginal Issues a little over a month and was immediately attracted to Cissy, but I was too busy adjusting to a new office and a new boss and co-workers to do more than just look. She was polite to me and I was polite to her, and I got the feeling, on seeing the way she worked, that in some ways she almost ran the section, leaving George Walker to his budgets and bureaucratic infighting. This day she came into my office wearing a subtle perfume that got my attention, took one of my guest chairs, stretched out her long and wonderfully slim legs and started reading. I was admiring her ivory blouse and the way I could make out the lace of her bra through the almost sheer fabric when she looked up at me, her green eyes crinkling with concern, shaking her head.

"Something's wrong," she said.

It felt like my office safe was now resting on my midsection. "What's wrong?"

"This whole report," Cissy said, waving the pages in her hand as if it had a bad smell to it. "You've got some interesting things here, Lewis, but you're trying to take some scraps of driftwood and re-create the *Queen Mary*. You've interpreted information in a manner that only supports your theory, when in fact it could do the exact opposite. You make some real stretches, like changing a meteor shower into the reentry of space debris. And you didn't go deep enough."

"I didn't?" I said, snappish from the work I had done all weekend, and some previous weekends before that. "Like where?"

"Like the members of the *Buran* task team. You ever talk to any of them before you started writing this fantasy about a Death Star in orbit, zapping space shuttles?"

"Uh, no," I said.

"Well, if you had, you would have learned that just before

the panel deactivated, they decided the second *Buran* was just a ducky. Just an informal decision, one that wasn't put on paper, but it was one that calmed everybody down. A ducky. Nothing to worry about."

"A what?"

Cissy sighed and put my report down on my desk and picked up two pencils. She held them up. "Listen, young one, and learn something. Some of our spy satellites are wonderful indeed, and can read license plates from orbit and even newspaper headlines. But some are just lookers. They just reproduce what they see. You can take a picture of these two pencils, and your picture wouldn't tell you which pencil was real and which one was a miniature bomb."

The pencils clattered to my desk. "Now. Duckies. Back in World War II, we set up a fake army in southern England, commanded by General George Patton. The tanks were made out of rubber, but the Germans thought they were real, and they thought this army would invade at the Pas de Calais. I'm sure you can remember what really happened at a place called Normandy, with a real army. Closer to home, a few years back, one of our KH-11 surveillance satellites went over the Soviet Northern Fleet base at Polyarnyi, near Murmansk. The satellite took photos of three Typhoon-class submarines in the harbor. Then a bad winter storm came up, and when our satellite returned on its next pass, the three submarines were in bad shape. Two were leaking air and one was bent in the middle. They were fake. Rubber duckies."

As Cissy was talking, I was extracting an old cover memo from the *Buran* task force from my file, and saw that one C. Manning was a member of the group, and my face was warm indeed.

"The second *Buran* was a fake," I said.

"Very good," she said, and even with those words, her tone wasn't mocking. "We like to think of those old Soviets as very dour, mean and sour sons of bitches. Which they are. But sometimes they also have a sense of humor. Think how funny it is. They spend under a hundred thousand rubles to make a fake *Buran*, and what do they get out of it? They get everybody in this building spun up, meetings are held and memos are rocketed back and forth, and we think they're bigger and better than we are."

"While in the process, we're wasting time, wasting resources and pulling people away from real situations," I said.

"Exactly. One big practical joke." Then she eyed my report. "One that's apparently still catching people."

I looked at her and she looked back at me with a steady gaze. I picked up the report and swiveled my chair and tossed it into one of our special wastebaskets, with a shredder on top. In a matter of seconds, about a month's worth of work was shredded, and by this evening, the shredded paper would become smoke.

"Thanks for the catch," I said. "And thanks for saving me from a major embarrassment."

Cissy laughed. "You're welcome, Lewis Cole, and you owe me one."

It only took a second. "Then why don't I take you out to lunch?"

She kept on smiling. "That sounds like a wonderful idea."

So we did, and that was the start of something short, sweet and delightful.

But something was wrong.

I looked back up at the stars. You didn't go deep enough. Not a mocking or accusatory tone. Just a statement of fact. You didn't go deep enough.

How about that.

Above me a meteorite seared its way through the atmosphere. This one was bright, with a long tail that looked like it had been shot out from a white-hot sparkler. A preview, maybe, of the Perseids. I kept on looking above me. The stars were as special as they always were, just shining on through, some of their light taking tens of thousands of years to reach here. Lot of distance, lot of time, and though the stars were wonderful and I never tired of seeing them, I wanted very much for the sun to rise and the day to begin. I had work to do.

Something was wrong.

I slept fitfully the rest of the night and skipped breakfast in the morning. I made three phone calls to Felix's house before I gave up. I knew he wasn't spending too much time there, and with today being the day of the exchange, I was sure that he was keeping busy. Checking his answering machine for phone calls from me probably wasn't high on his agenda.

One more try, then, and I called the Tyler police department. Diane Woods was not in. I tried her at home, and I got her answering machine. Lots of answering machine work going on this Friday morning. I wondered where everybody was. One thing, for sure, was that Felix and Diane weren't together. That was something I could bank on, like the sun coming up every morning.

I sat back in my comfortable office and looked around and finally accepted that cold little ball of high-grade steel that seemed to be working its way through my digestive system. This was one that I would have to take care of myself. No depending on friends or acquaintances or contacts. Just me. I picked up the phone and made one more call, and the person on the other end said, "Boston police department."

Then I spun a tale.

For such a short amount of time, I was rather proud of this particular tale. I explained that I was a columnist for *Shoreline* magazine, and that I needed to speak to a public affairs officer. When this gentleman came on the phone, I said I was exploring some story ideas that I would later pitch to my editor (avoiding the sort of trap that Justin Dix had earlier laid for me) and could I talk to him for a few minutes? Being a polite flack, he agreed. I said that I was thinking of doing a story about a Boston police detective, one Cal Maloney, who had died so suddenly and tragically about five years ago in a traffic accident in Newburyport, Massachusetts. The story I had in mind was a retrospective of this fine officer's life, and a look at what he might have done and accomplished if he had lived. The family he might have loved, the cases he might have cracked and the other officers and detectives he might have worked with.

When this spiel was over, I asked a few questions and there was a very long pause on the other end of the phone line. I think the public affairs officer thought I was loony, but after a moment or two he said, "I'll give it a shot. What's your phone number?"

I told him and hung up and prepared to wait.

And wait.

I sat back in my chair. I sat forward in my chair. I got up and looked through the windows of my office, to the ocean and to the Samson State Wildlife Preserve to the north. Then I went around to my bookcases. I cocked my head, looked at the spines and tried to recall the plot of every book that was in the case. I wondered if I should at long last alphabetize my books by author, then I tried to decide if the bookshelves should be segregated by hardcover and paperback. And if I did that, should I subdivide it even further, into category and genre?

And what about my magazines?

I looked at a tiny clock on another bookshelf. About five minutes had passed.

When the phone finally rang the morning was almost over, and I was busy scrubbing the tub in the bathroom adjacent to my office. I rubbed my hands briefly on an already soiled towel, and then I got into my office and answered the phone by the fourth ring at least.

"Yes?"

"Mr. Cole? Officer Wimmer, Boston police department. I have that information you were looking for."

Hang up the phone, a perverse voice inside me said. Hang up. You don't want to know.

But I did want to know. I uncapped a pen and found a piece of scrap paper on the mess that was my desk.

"Go ahead," I said, and he gave me some stuff over the next few minutes about Cal Maloney's life and his family and where he went to school and how long he had been with the Boston police department. Then the good officer paused.

"Well, one more thing," he said, and I could make out the sound of shuffling papers. "It took some digging but the man you're looking for is no longer with the Boston police department."

"He isn't?" I asked, trying to keep my voice neutral.

"Nope," Officer Wimmer said. "Cal Maloney's partner at the time of his death is now with the Massachusetts State Police."

"Un-hunh," and that was about the only intelligent thing I could say at the time. I was too busy praying that New England Telephone's long-distance service wouldn't pick that moment to have a system failure.

It didn't. Officer Wimmer's voice was clear and punctual.

"His name is Roger Krohn."

CHAPTER
TWENTY-SIX

Time is a marvelous thing. While I was waiting for Officer Wimmer to call back that morning, the red numerals on my clocks seemed to move with the speed of year-old motor oil. But when I was finished talking to him, I sat in my office, motionless, my hands behind my head, and from the way the sunlight was moving across the bookshelves, the polished hardwood floor and the white plaster walls in my office, I knew that time was going by quickly.

I looked over at the digital clock. Almost a couple of hours. I forgot what I had been thinking about in those one hundred or so minutes. I believe I was in shock.

Roger Krohn. I let those two words race around in my skull for a bit, and I refused to think any further. A lot of questions were screaming for attention, but I let them be for a while. I finally stirred myself and made two more phone calls, and neither Diane Woods nor Felix Tinios was answering. I got up and left.

A t Diane's condominium unit on Tyler Harbor, the two parking spaces in front of her town house were empty, but I knocked on the door anyway. No answer. A woman at the next unit, with short blond hair and wearing a white T-shirt and black tights, looked up at me. She was gently moving a baby carriage back and forth as she sat on the front doorstep to her unit. She wore only one earring.

"You looking for Diane?" she said, her voice a bit nasal. I knew her as a neighbor of Diane's, but I didn't know her name.

"Yes, I am. Do you know where she is?"

The baby carriage went back and forth twice and the infant inside gurgled. Diane's neighbor smiled. "She told me this morning that she was going to take a day off and drive south for a while, just get her head untangled. She even left her pager behind, she told me."

South. Massachusetts and Kara Miles and who knows where the two of them might go on this calm and sunny and marvelous day in August. The woman said something as I was thinking and I said, "Excuse me?"

She laughed. "I said, are you thirsty? I can get you a drink—iced tea or lemonade, or something stronger if you're in the mood."

Some mood. I gave her my best smile, not wanting to scare her. "Sorry. Maybe another time."

Diane's neighbor smiled back. "I'll still be here."

N ormally—which around here usually means off-season—the trip from Tyler Harbor to Rosemount Lane in North

Tyler would take only about fifteen minutes, but today it took twice that, because of the long lines of cars filled with impatient vacationers who were determined to squeeze out the last minutes and seconds of this summer.

I didn't expect to find Felix at home but I still felt a pang of disappointment when I saw the empty gravel driveway. This disappointment was also coupled with a terrible urgency to tell someone, anyone, about what I had found out about Roger Krohn. Oh, I probably could have gone to the Tyler police department and made a nuisance of myself, but I didn't have any proof, any evidence that linked Roger Krohn to what had been going on with me and Felix and Craig Dummer and the others over the past couple of weeks.

No, I had no evidence, but I did have a strong conviction in my gut that I was right.

Something was wrong. Sure. Just because Corelli had two cops in his pocket didn't mean that they were partners. Or that other cops weren't in his stable.

"Damm it, Felix, where are you hiding?" I asked, but no one was there to hear me.

I started up the Rover and left, feeling as if I was losing a race and I didn't know when it had started or how it would finish.

It was near dinnertime when I got home. There was a blinking green light on my answering machine. When I listened to the message, I had to sit down on the couch.

It was Felix, and the message was: "Lewis? You know who this is." There was a pause. "The exchange is on for eight o'clock tonight. Meet me at the Congregational church parking lot in York. Get there at seven and we'll go from there." Another pause. "Thanks." Then the click-click of the phone hanging up and there were no more messages.

I got up from the couch and replayed the message three times. Felix was telling me two things on the tape.

Where to meet him was the first thing.

And the second was something that scared me very much: for the first time ever, I listened to what sounded like fear in Felix's voice. Something was very wrong.

I looked at the time. About fifteen minutes away from six o'clock. I sat back on the couch and rested my head in my hands. I had this awful urge to unplug the phone and lock the doors and start working on the two six-packs of Molson that rested, cool and comfortable, in the rear of my refrigerator. The morning would come and things would be different, and I wouldn't have to do a damn thing. Just stay in this comfortable house and get drunk, as I had been doing almost every other day earlier in the summer after I had come home from the hospital. I was almost nostalgic with the memory of how I had been only a couple of short weeks ago, when I sat on the warm deck and drank all day long, reading old books and not worrying about anything, save for my thoughts about Paula Quinn and that nagging guilt that came from not completing a column for *Shoreline*. That period two weeks ago seemed as simple and childlike as a birthday party when I was six years old, and I longed again for that comparative peace.

It was not fair, not fair at all.

I looked back at the clock. Another five minutes had passed. The refrigerator was in the adjacent kitchen, looking white and clean and so available. I got up and started walking past the kitchen and headed upstairs. In my bedroom I went to an oak bureau, opened the top drawer and rummaged behind the socks and underwear. I took out a flat metal box. Inside was my 9 mm Beretta automatic, loaded, with two spare magazines.

From one of the bedroom closets I took out a lightweight blue warm-up jacket, along with a shoulder holster. I also went to the closet and from a bright red knapsack I took out a small pair of Nikon binoculars.

Back downstairs, I looked longingly at the phone, and then made one more call to Diane Woods's home. No answer. I had to force myself to hang up after fifteen rings. There was no rescue party out there, no U.S. Cavalry, nothing save for me and what I had. I almost felt sorry for Felix, having to depend on me for whatever was about to happen, but I didn't have the time. The clock said I was behind schedule.

I turned on the answering machine, and as I left, I tried not to look behind at my home. I didn't think I could stand it.

When I crossed over to Maine I pulled to the side of the road and checked my atlas for southern York County, where the town of York is located. In addition to the fear in Felix's voice, I also noticed something else that didn't make sense. The last time we'd visited York, we had parked in the Catholic church parking lot. It was a place we had been before, and I didn't think Felix would have wasted time sending me to someplace new. He wanted me to go the Congregational church lot, and in looking at the map, I saw that it was bordered on one side by a cemetery. A couple of side streets would get me to the other side of the cemetery, and that's all I needed. I put the atlas down and resumed driving. I refused to think any further about what was going to happen in the next hour or so.

When I got to York and was on a street called Barrows Lane, next to the cemetery, I found a parking place with no difficulty. I got out of the Rover, slipped the binoculars into my jacket, and went through an open gate into the cemetery. There was a black wrought-iron fence around the quiet plots and I remembered that stupid joke about fences and graveyards as I walked in. The land sloped up a gentle hill and through a grove of maples. I could make out the white spire of the Congregational church on the other side of the hill.

There were gravel paths for cars (or hearses, of course, although funeral directors—who could double as Pentagon spokesmen—always referred to them as coaches), but I stayed on the grass, working my way past the stones and markers as I went up the slight grade. The grass was well maintained, and at many of the graves tiny American flags were flying. Veterans, from the Civil War to the Persian Gulf and whatever new fights we got into, resting at last in this rocky Maine soil.

At this moment, I was sure that they had more comfort than I did.

When I crested the hill I felt slightly foolish as I hunkered down and worked my way down the opposite slope, hiding myself from view. The walk was an awkward one, made so by the growing feeling that I was getting myself into something awful and bloody, and also by the weight of the pistol in my shoulder holster. Unless you're a cop or a fool, carrying a weapon always changes the way you walk.

There were more trees and some bushes at the far fence, and I made out the blacktop of the church's parking lot. I took it slow then, thankful that there were no visitors or mourners in the graveyard at this hour. The clock was striking seven by the time I squeezed myself between a large headstone that said "Hanratty" and a bush that looked like it was holly. I sat on a mossy section of grass and took the binoculars out of my jacket. There was a light gray Lumina with New Hampshire plates in the parking lot, and when I brought my miniature binoculars up to my face, I saw that there was only one person in the car: Felix Tinios.

Next came that white-hot flush of embarrassment when you wonder just what in hell you've gotten yourself into, and which is best described as that feeling you get when you arrive in a clown's dress at a black-tie event, convinced that you were heading to a costume party. Felix was there, waiting for me, while I played Boy Scout in the woods. It seemed I was in the process of screwing up the exchange through my paranoia. From a nearby yard there came the sound of a young boy yelling at someone who seemed to be his sister. I thought it was time to get up and end this ridiculous wait, when I caught myself and brought up the binoculars again.

Something was wrong. I studied his face. Perhaps it was the way he was parked or maybe it was the lengthening shadows from the church spire and the nearby trees, but something was wrong with Felix's face. Parts of it looked dark. As though he had forgotten to shave, or had charcoal smeared on his skin, or he had gotten dirty.

Or he had been beaten.

The binoculars trembled in my hands, and I wished I had brought a stronger pair. I moved forward a bit, scraping myself in the holly, and adjusted the focus again. Felix was in the driver's seat of the car and there was definitely something wrong with his face. There were at least two dark patches, and his lips looked puffy. Both hands were on the steering wheel, and he looked uncomfortable, as if he were waiting for a dentist to arrive to give him a root canal in the front seat. His usually perfect moussed and styled hair was a mess, and there was a flickering about his eyelids that bothered me.

"Damn, damn, damn," I whispered as I brought the binoculars down and wiped my hands, and then brought the binoculars up again. On the other side of the parking lot I could make out the traffic easing by on Route 1A. It seemed so strange to see that ordinary traffic going by, to listen to the shouts of children in backyards only a short walk away, knowing that a few feet in front of me something horrible seemed to be happening to Felix Tinios.

I kept watch. Felix moved in his seat, and then something happened that was so odd that I raised and lowered the binoculars twice, just to make sure I wasn't seeing things.

Felix's lips were moving, as if he was talking to himself.

Was he going crazy? Cracking under some strain?

I looked again, and then I could look no longer. I knew what was happening, and I knew I was powerless to do anything.

Felix wasn't alone in the car, and he was talking to his tormentor.

The wait went on for at least a half hour, and in those thirty minutes I ran through plans and scenarios in my mind, trying to think of some way to get Felix out of that Lumina. Leaving to get the police was the one that came quickly to mind, but there was a good chance that while I was gone, Felix and whoever was holding him captive would leave. I was tempted to walk out of the graveyard and come at the Lumina from the rear, to surprise whoever was in the car with Felix, but that assumed that the parking lot wasn't being watched by someone else. I wasn't ready to make that assumption.

And while I was working on a scheme to get into my Range Rover and drive into the Lumina in a kamikaze-type crash—something as unexpected and crazy as that just might work—the decision was made for me. Felix seemed to shrug and bow his head. He started the car engine, and the Lumina left.

I ran all the way back up the hill of the graveyard, wondering with fear if there were any open graves along the way.

There was only one logical place to go, and it took me only a few minutes to get there. I parked the Rover on a side street away from Landing Lane and did the same cross-country trek that I had done some weeks before with Felix, and when I got to the safe house, sweaty and itchy from having moved through the brambles and brush, I sat down with an "oof" and wondered what I would do next.

The driveway was empty, and no lights were on at the house.

Jesus. So where did they go?

I sat against a pine tree and started gnawing at a thumbnail, and then shifted my seat, as the Beretta dug into my side. Where would Felix have gone, with someone in the backseat holding a gun to his head? Back to New Hampshire? To Tyler Beach and my house, to see why I didn't show up? Or a deserted potato field deeper into Maine, where Felix was now lying in the mud, bleeding to death.

It didn't make sense. Movies and television programs love to show segments of people being forced to drive for long distances, but it's not that easy. You've got to concentrate. You've got to keep a steady hand on your weapon. And you've got to make sure the driver doesn't do something to draw police attention, like speeding or even going too slow. Forced drives are usually short drives.

Dammit, they couldn't have gone far. It didn't make sense.

The sound of a car engine. I looked up. For once, sense had a tiny little victory.

The Lumina pulled into the driveway.

I was close enough so that I didn't need binoculars, and I was glad. Even from among the trees and brush, I was horrified at Felix's condition and what had happened to him. He got out of the car, Roger moving quickly beside him. His face was drawn and he walked with a shuffling gait. I didn't want—or need—to see that expression close up through the binoculars.

Roger walked right with him, smiling, holding a pistol against Felix's neck, all the way into the house.

My throat was aching from everything I saw, and as the two of them went into the house and the door was shut, I quickly got angry with myself.

Damn fool, I thought. There they were, Felix and Roger, going into the house and you had the drop on Roger. If you had gone out there with the Beretta, it would have been over. Right there.

Sure. My hands were shaking, and if Roger had looked over at me and said, no, I'm not doing a thing, would I have shot him? And would I have hit anything? And if I did hit something, wasn't there a good chance that it would be Felix?

Damn.

I got up from my hiding place and ran to the side of the house.

At the picture window I got a good view as Roger slapped a wide piece of masking tape across Felix's mouth. Felix's arms were already taped and part of me was impressed. Roger was good, dammit, to have taped up Felix's arms so quickly. And then I saw something that made my insides quiver. There was a black box in Roger's hands and some wires which led away from the box and to Felix. The wires disappeared up the legs of his khaki shorts. The side windows were open and I could make out Roger's voice easily enough as he talked.

"Well, we all have our setbacks, and the fact that your writer friend didn't show up is one I'll have to live with," Roger said, putting the black box down on a coffee table in front of the couch. "I'll just visit him tonight, maybe 2 A.M. or so, and I can tell you, Felix, I don't plan to discuss writing methods with him."

Roger sat down on the coffee table and I could see a side holster in the waistband of his pants. He leaned forward, elbows on his knees and hands clasped, and he said, "But you were trying to give me a problem back there, Felix, when you tried to flash your lights at that York police cruiser, and that's something I'm not going to tolerate."

And as casually as if he were turning a television switch on, he flicked a button on the black box and there was a muffled bellow, as Felix arched his back on the couch, his arms straining against the tape, his face red and eyes screwed tight. I thought I heard a crackling noise but I wasn't sure. I had to look away, and then the sound stopped. I forced myself to look back inside.

Roger was now standing, and Felix was slumped on the couch, his head bowed forward, his shoulders shaking. Roger was rubbing his chin, looking perplexed. "Learned this technique back when I was in a little desert adventure that never made the news. Against all civilized rules of warfare—hell of an oxymoron if I've ever heard one—but when you're fighting against a culture and religion that makes martyrs of dead people, and you need questions answered quickly, this box can work wonders. Of course, it doesn't look like you're a martyr right now."

Roger walked back to the couch and sniffed. "I'm afraid

you've wet the couch, Felix, but I don't think anybody will mind. Time for a phone call. The idiot of the evening is waiting at a motel just up the coast."

He went to the side table, where the phone was. Throughout the phone call, he kept his eyes on Felix. Despair started gnawing at me as I sat there, huddling next to a blueberry bush on a piece of property that was once owned by a now long-dead crime lord. I shifted a bit and my knees struck lengths of firewood that had been dumped here by the side of the house, and I tried not to gasp. Felix moved some against the couch, and I remembered the outline of the room. Two couches and a coffee table, an old television set and the glass doorways leading to the addition, off to my right. The draperies had been closed, hiding the sunroom and the paintings.

Roger murmured something on the phone and then hung up. He came back over and there was something else in his hands. He juggled it as he walked and I thought it was another black box for more torture, but when Roger sat down I saw that it was a VCR tape. Roger talked some more to Felix, and I couldn't make out what he was saying. While all of this was going on, my 9 mm Beretta was in my hand. I switched off the safety and waited, muscles taut and creaking, and I listened to the sound of a boat whistle, so quiet and peaceful out on the ocean. I could leave at this moment, and in ten to fifteen minutes I might have the York police department at this house, but the look and the actions of Roger Krohn made me wait. I couldn't do much, but I certainly could do something if he reached for the gun in his holster. If I went away, I didn't think I could ever come back, being too fearful at what I might find here later.

Roger Krohn. About as clear as a full moon at the end of a cloudless night, and I had missed it all along. Everything that had to do with the paintings started right after he came to Tyler Beach for the exchange program. That was a trigger I should have seen or heard. Instead, I had gotten sucked into his gladhanded approach and his interest—no doubt faked—in the police chief's job in Tyler.

Simple enough to figure it out. Once Tony Russo gets the necessary information about the safe house and the theft, Tony recontacts Roger Krohn, tells him that the man they want to deal with lives in North Tyler. Roger checks around, finds out about the exchange program in Tyler—just one town away—and he's here for the summer with a perfect cover.

Roger Krohn. Jesus.

The sound of a car engine, the crunching of tires on gravel and a car door slamming. I moved a bit from my position and looked in as a door opened to the house. Cameron Briggs strolled in carrying a slim brown briefcase.He walked down the short set of stairs to the sunken living room as if he were inspecting a yacht.

But tonight the well-tanned face looked troubled and his summer wardrobe of polo shirt and gray chinos looked rumpled, as if he had been sleeping in them. He got right to the point: "Where the hell are the paintings, Krohn?"

Roger had a grin on his face. If I had been Cameron Briggs, I would have been nervous. Roger had the same grin not more than ten minutes ago as he was sending jolts of electricity to Felix's genitals.

"In a moment, Cameron," Roger said, standing up behind the couch where Felix was sitting motionless. "It's time you and I had something we used to call a post-mission debrief."

Cameron look disgusted. "Spare me the old Army vet stories, Krohn. They get tiring." He glanced at Felix and looked away with disinterest, as if he had been seeing a mannequin heading to the dumpster. "Though you seem to be reliving them again tonight."

"Thanks for the compliment. I also relived them a couple of days ago when I took care of that leech Dummer for you. You should have retired him years ago, and not strung him along with those jobs of yours."

"He said he had evidence against me," Cameron said. "And even if he didn't, I didn't want the exposure if the shit went to the newspapers. Your partner should have done a better job of keeping his mouth shut back when you were robbing the museum."

"So you gave me a little extra to take him out. Because you didn't have the balls for it."

"That's what you get paid for, right?"

Another odd smile from Roger. "Sure. I get paid for the dirty work. Just like my days in the desert, doing what comes naturally, once you're told to do it. Now you're paying me again, for the paintings. Right?"

Cameron hefted up the slim case. "Here's the money," and then his voice got sharp: "But only half."

Roger's grin faded away. "You were supposed to bring full payment, Cameron."

It was Cameron's turn to smile. "Right. You show me the paintings and that's when you get this." He held up the case again. "Those paintings get back to my home, you get the other half."

"That wasn't the deal."

"That's right," Cameron said, his voice rising. "I made the deal with Corelli, and the deal was that you and your drunk partner were to steal the paintings. And once the heat decreased a bit and the newspapers went on to something else, they got delivered to me six months later. Little behind schedule, aren't we?"

"Wasn't my fault," Roger said. "The damn drunk was Corelli's number-one cop, and he was half in the bag when we did the job, when he was blabbing about stealing the paintings for some rich local hotshot. And how was I supposed to know that he'd wrap himself around a tree later that night?"

Cameron shrugged. "Right now, I couldn't give a shit. Right now, all I want to know is this: where are the goddam paintings?"

I shifted again, holding on to a length of firewood for balance. Then Roger did something odd. He started juggling that damn VCR tape again, and his rabid grin returned.

Roger said, "Still haven't done the debrief, Cameron."

It looked as though Cameron rolled his eyes. "For Christ's sake . . ."

The juggling stopped. "See this tape?" Roger said, holding it up. "This is all I've cared about, all I've been concerned about, ever since the night me and Cal Maloney stole those fucking paintings. When Cal took the paintings, he also took this tape. Said he was going to take care of it. You know what's on this tape?"

Cameron looked as if he was trying to control his temper. "Your sister being screwed by the Boston Celtics."

Roger went on, as though he didn't care what Cameron had said. "Nope. Me and Cal, getting into the museum. This was the main entrance surveillance tape, and it shows me and Cal, clear as day, getting into the Scribner. This is the biggest piece of evidence linking me and that theft, and it's right here."

"Fine. Now where are the paintings?"

That same grin, and even huddling outside, I could tell that his voice was changing, was becoming calmer. "One more minute, Cameron. Everything else was evidence, too, Cameron. Tony Russo, who you suggested I take care of, which I did. Craig Dummer, who I convinced to take down Tony, and who I visited later. That writer guy, who's on the list for tonight. This house and the paintings and Felix Tinios. This tape. Now it's all being taken care of. Now I'm in line for a chief's job, can you believe it? In one of the biggest resorts in New England, with a harbor and drug traffic and tourists . . . Man, the money I can make . . ."

"Krohn!" Cameron said, stepping forward, and it was as if Roger was snapping back to the fact that he was in this house in York, Maine, and Roger took a couple of steps to the opened sliding-glass doors and pulled the drapery aside. The lights were off in the sunroom and the three paintings were there, shaded some in the darkness.

Cameron let out a combination of a moan and a sigh. "My paintings . . . After all these years . . ."

Roger beckoned him, opening the sliding-glass doors wider, that smile back on his face. "Here they are, Cameron. All yours."

Cameron dropped the briefcase and strode forward, with a look on his face that seemed to be a mix of ecstasy and fulfillment. As Cameron went by him, Roger pulled out his pistol and shot Cameron in the back of the head.

CHAPTER
TWENTY-SEVEN

This time it was my turn to move fast.

After Cameron fell to the floor, Roger turned, pistol still in his hand, and started moving toward Felix. I stood up and I think I yelled, but I know for certain I fired off three rounds from my Beretta, the pistol bucking in my hands. The noise was deafening, louder than anything you hear in the movies. Roger might have fired back. I don't know. But when the shooting stopped he wasn't in the room anymore.

And then a length of firewood was in my hands and I smashed through the dining room window. In a matter of seconds I was standing there in the living room, pistol shaking violently in my hands, my left ankle throbbing painfully and blood running down my hands from where I had cut myself coming through the shattered glass. Felix looked up at me, eyes disbelieving. The room seemed to tilt and move around me, like an amusement park ride. The air was thick with the stench of burned gunpowder and sweaty fear. The cellar door was now open. Something gurgled from beyond the couch and I moved a few feet, breathing hard and fast, like a horse after a blue ribbon run at the racetrack. Cameron Briggs's left foot quivered slightly and was still. I tried not to look at the dark mush that used to be the back of his head. His briefcase was gone.

Things moved oddly. By now I was with Felix, and I tore away the wires from the black box and then pulled the tape strip off his face. He yelped and gasped and looked up at me and said, "We've got to get out of here."

I started tearing off the tape around his legs and arms. "Felix, wait, there's—"

"Lewis!" he said, his voice hoarse. "The man's got the place wired to blow up and burn. It's set in the cellar and that's where he just went. Move your ass!"

I helped Felix off the couch and he keened with some sort of anguished pain, but he moved ahead of me quickly enough, as if he was forcing each individual muscle and tendon to work together. Both of my shaking and bloody hands were now back on the Beretta as I kept watch on the cellar door, knowing that even if a shadow moved on those stairs, I would fire away. I remembered something the man had said back at his condo a Wednesday night ago: "You know what they say. There's not a problem in the world that can't be solved by explosives."

We got up to the kitchen landing and I took my aim away from the cellar stairs. The kitchen was still bright in its garish colors and plastic decorations, and I slapped the lights off. I moved in front of Felix, carefully opening the front door, not wanting to get ambushed. I hunkered down and Felix followed me out to the concrete steps. I turned to tell him that there was only the Lumina parked in the lot, that Roger must have left in Cameron's car.

But as I opened my mouth, the house exploded.

I didn't hear a damn thing, which means my ears must have refused to hear such a loud sound. All I remember is turning to Felix and forming the words in my mouth, and then a giant hand seemed to slap me in the back with a warm puff of air.

Darkness for a while, and then I was on my back looking up at the stars in a dreamlike state, wondering why there were trees growing in my backyard. Trees can't grow on beach sand. Then I blinked a few times and sat up and swore as I looked at the bloody mess of my scraped knees. I stumbled up, and Felix was a few feet away, opening and closing his mouth, looking like a fish out of water.

"What?" I said.

"Trying to clear the ears," he said, gazing straight ahead. It was hard to hear what he was saying, even though it looked like he was yelling. "You okay?"

"Beats the shit out of me," I said.

I turned and looked back at the house. The first and second floor had crumpled together in a mess of walls, plaster, shingles and jagged beams, and fire was burning merrily in two places. The lawn was covered with chunks of wood and broken glass. Felix called out to me, "We've got to haul ass. This place is going to be crawling in a minute or two."

"Just a sec," I said. "I've got to check on the paintings."

Felix swore and said, "Screw the paintings!" but I didn't answer him, as I went down the slight slope of land heading for the rear of the house. I went past the collapsed wall that I had dove into, what seemed like a few hours ago, and I watched where I was walking, the heat of the fire warming my skin like a midday June sun, stepping carefully over pieces of wood. It struck me as terribly funny at that moment that my tax dollars had gone toward training Roger Krohn years ago when he was in the Army, and had trained him so well in the art of killing that he had almost gotten me and Felix. I was afraid that if I started laughing, I might not stop.

At the rear of the house the force of the explosion had blasted away the beams that had been supporting the addition, and I realized why Felix and I had survived. Because of the way the foundation was set up, with a rear entry underneath the addition, the blast had been channeled away from the front of the house.

But the addition hadn't done so well. It had fallen upon itself in a confusing mix of floorboards, beams, draperies and broken chunks of glass. It was hard to figure out how the place had originally looked. I clambered up on one main floor beam, hearing Felix calling me again from the front of the house. I thought of those three Winslow Homer paintings, over a hundred years old and stolen away to this place, with their years of history and knowledge and skill wrapped up in the old oil paint, and I think tears came to my eyes at what I saw.

The three undamaged paintings, still hanging from the wooden framework, leaning against a broken wall, about a dozen feet or so away.

"There is a God," I whispered, and I moved again, and the beam gave way, almost dumping me into a chunk of wood that had a half dozen exposed spikes poking up, like a Viet Cong booby trap, waiting to impale me. I straddled the beam with both feet and tried again, and I got up a foot, the wood beneath me creaking and snapping. The paintings didn't seem any closer, and the dozen or so feet I had to navigate to get there were a treacherous mass of piping, wiring, broken plaster and wood strips.

I smelled smoke.

"Lewis!" came the call, and I grabbed at a length of something to haul myself up, and the sharp bite of broken glass made me fall back again. Damn. The smell of the smoke got stronger, and I could feel the warmth on my hands as I tried to climb again. Please, God. Just another minute or two. That's all I need.

There was now a smell of overcooked pork, of charred flesh. I didn't let my mind dwell on Cameron Briggs's final resting place.

I got up a couple of more feet, and then started inching my way across the ruins of the rear addition. My left foot slipped and was jammed into a pile of broken wood, and I started windmilling with my arms, trying not to fall on this awful mess. The paintings were getting harder to see through the tendrils of smoke coming up from the debris.

"Lewis!" Felix yelled again, closer, and I turned and shouted back, "Felix, shut up! I'm almost there."

But when I turned back, they were gone.

The flames from the burning paintings were bright enough so that I could see them char and curl up upon themselves, like old leaves in a campfire. I thought then of Winslow Homer and how his ghost must despise what was going on here. I turned away again and got down from the pile of trash that had once been a house. Felix was waiting for me, and he grabbed my arm.

"Let's go, you idiot," he hissed at me. "Do you want to explain to the York cops what the hell happened here?"

If I had been any brighter I might have said yes, but my mind was on something else.

Fog Warning. The fisherman alone in his dory, heading to his schooner, trying to beat a storm, trying to save his life.

Gone.

Eight Bells. Two sailors on the deck of a ship, wearing foul-weather gear and holding navigation instruments in their hands, a portrait of survival.

Gone.

The Gulf Stream. The lonely black man, on the slippery slope of his damaged vessel, looking for help, but the broaching sharks in the foreground tell of another ending.

Gone.

All of them. Three historic and priceless paintings, right before my eyes, almost within reach of my hands, just seconds away from being rescued by me. Gone. Just before I stepped in the Lumina, I saw something metallic on the ground. It was my 9 mm Beretta, and for whatever good it was, I picked it up and returned it to my shoulder holster. As I closed the Lumina's door, I felt like bawling.

Felix drove up the driveway out to the street, and people were coming out of the houses, looking at us, the expression on their faces demanding to know what was going on, but Felix didn't stop. There was a crack in the windshield and scratches on the hood of the car from the falling debris.

I took a deep breath. "Where'd you find the keys?"

"In my rear pocket," Felix said. "Idiot never bothered to strip them off me. Guess you and I know why, hunh? He never thought I'd be driving again tonight, would even get near a car, except maybe in the trunk."

"Felix, the paintings—"

"I know, and it's over, Lewis," he said. "We can't do anything about them. There's other stuff going on. We've got a lot to do, and the first thing to do is to dump this car. People back there are going to tell the cops and firefighters that they saw a Lumina haul ass away from a house that just blew up. Your Rover around here?"

I gave him the directions, and in less than a handful of minutes, he had pulled up behind my Range Rover. Felix got out and said, "Get your handkerchief out and wipe down the door handle, anything else we touched. Good enough crime lab might find something eventually, but that'll still give us some time."

While I was doing just that, he went to the trunk of the car, opened it up, and pulled out a black gym bag and a larger black zippered duffel bag. "Rented under fake ID, Felix?"

"Yeah," he said, slamming the trunk down. "One of the few bright things I've been doing here lately." With the duffel bag slung over his back and gym bag in hand, he went back to the front seat of the car and inserted the keys into the ignition and shut the door. "With some luck, some kid will come by and take this baby for a joyride."

I looked around the quiet street and the suburban homes. "Unless the Crips are vacationing here this summer, you're dreaming."

"Maybe so, but I'll still give it a try." Felix came up to the

Rover just as I opened the door, and then he stopped, head cocked. Just a couple of streets over, the sound of sirens.

"Time to go?" I asked.

"Time to go," he said.

We got in and got the hell out.

A s I drove, Felix zippered open the gym bag, pulled out his own automatic pistol and checked the magazine and action. As I headed south, toward New Hampshire, I said, "What happened, Felix? How did Roger ambush you?"

He reinserted the magazine, worked the pistol's action so a round was in the chamber. "He pulled me over."

I got stuck behind a dark green Saab that had a bumper sticker: "Think Globally, Act Locally." I wondered what the driver would have thought about the global and local actions that just happened up on Landing Lane. As I slowed down, I looked at my hands and wrists. They had stopped bleeding. Superficial cuts probably, though my knees still ached.

"He did what?"

Felix kept his head down, as if he was trying to hide his humiliation. "He pulled me over, Lewis. Easiest trick in the book and I fell for it. Same trick that killed those guys in the St. Valentine's Day Massacre in Chicago, except this time it wasn't a fake cop. It was a real one. Roger Krohn. I'm sorry to say, Lewis, he must have had your house under surveillance, because he caught up with me about twenty minutes after I dropped you off after our Boston trip. He pulled me over with his own car, which has blue lights in the radiator's grill, flashing headlights and siren. Being a well-mannered citizen—and not wanting to screw anything up the day of the exchange—I pulled over. I thought I had been speeding."

Then he looked up, his face haunted. "He opened the passenger's-side door and nailed me with a Taser, and when I was flailing around with thousands of volts going through me, he got me wrapped up. Then he got his black box working. The man likes his electricity, Lewis, and he made me drive to Maine, made me give up the house and made me call you."

"Felix, I—"

His voice got stronger. "I don't want to talk about that anymore, Lewis. All right? Not now and not ever. It's over. I just want to talk about now."

"What do you mean, now?"

"I mean we're going to hunt him down tonight and kill him."

I looked at the expression on his face and then I slowly pulled over and kept the engine running as we stopped by the side of the road. We had just crossed into Kittery.

"Say again?"

"You heard me." Felix pulled out a leather hip holster, and with his pistol in place, slid the pair into the side of his shorts.

"Felix, this has gone above and beyond anything that we can handle. We've got four dead bodies in the past couple of weeks—including your cousin—and we just saw millions of dollars of art go up in smoke. In case you've forgotten, your ass was about one minute from getting blown away by Roger Krohn, and both our asses got tossed out of a house by a firebomb. Now you want to keep on hunting? Forget it."

He rummaged around in the duffel bag, his face still dark and puffy. "Don't you think Krohn might come back for a visit when he finds out we made it out of the house? You got a better idea?"

"Yeah. Call the cops. That's what they get paid for."

Felix started rubbing his temples with his fingers, his voice low and even. "Lewis, I don't have time for this, and if you don't agree with what I'm about to say, then I'm stepping out of here and renting or stealing a fucking car and then I'm going to go off on my own, much as I owe you for what you did back at the house. Got that?"

"It's gotten."

"Great." Felix raised his head, looked at me, and I stared right back at him. "Lewis, we don't have time. The man's a cop, and cops stick together. You start spinning a story about what Roger Krohn's been up to, and the cops are going to take time to check the facts. They're not going to rush out to pick up a brother officer. And by the time they look at the records and figure out, yeah, the guy is dirty, he'll be working on a tan somewhere in the Caribbean. Right now, he's about fifteen, twenty minutes ahead of us, and each minute you and I have this discussion means he can be another mile away. We've got a window of opportunity here to take care of business—right this moment—and I'm going to get going before the window is closed."

I thought furiously for a moment and said, "One phone call. To Diane Woods."

For the first time in a long time, I thought Felix was going to strike me. It came to me that he wouldn't have to steal another car, he would just have to punch out my lights and take the Rover. Easy enough, and I don't know why I hadn't thought of it earlier.

But he surprised me. "All right. One phone call. But only if a phone booth's on the way. And you don't take more than a minute."

"Agreed," I said, and we were off, and I pulled over again after another mile, for I found my phone booth, in a Cumberland Farms parking lot. As I got out of the Rover, Felix said, "One minute," but I didn't answer and went to the booth and started dialing. The first call, to the police dispatcher, was a bust. Diane Woods was not on duty that night. I dialed her home number, and the ringing began.

"C'mon, c'mon," I whispered, but my demands went unmet. There was no answer at Diane Woods's. I looked over at Felix and his gaze was steady. I slammed the phone down, stalked back to the Rover and got in. Felix took out a blue Kevlar bulletproof vest and started undoing his shirt, and he said quietly, "You can let me borrow your Rover, and that'll be it."

"Really?"

"Yeah. I've got to do it, Lewis. I can't let Roger Krohn keep on breathing after what he did to me today. I wouldn't be . . . I wouldn't be me anymore, and I will not allow that to happen. But you don't have to come along, Lewis. You've done enough for tonight."

I held on to the Rover's steering wheel and heard myself say, "I've saved your butt once tonight, Felix. Don't be so eager to turn down my help."

I started the Rover up and we continued south. I looked up at the sky. It had become overcast, and it looked like rain.

W e got to the condominium development where Roger Krohn lived about a half hour after that last stop at Cumberland Farms. Along the way, and with Felix's help, I had put on a second Kevlar vest that Felix had stored in his duffel bag. The vest was heavy and constricting under my shirt, and I felt leaden, like I was moving through thick syrup. At the condominium lot I cruised around for a minute or two, and I said, "It's not here."

"What?"

"Cameron Briggs's Audi. The one that Roger Krohn stole. It's not here."

Felix looked stubborn. "He could have ditched the car, or parked somewhere else. We're going in, Lewis."

I didn't argue. It was now 8 P.M. and the parking lot was fairly full. People were streaming away from the cooling sands of Tyler Beach, which were just across the street from Roger's condominium. A light mist had begun to fall and I knew from experience that in a few short minutes the beaches would be as empty as they were hundreds of years ago.

The condominium building was concrete and balconies with black iron railings, and the roof was flat black shingles. After parking in the rear we went through a back entrance, Felix leading the way, his automatic in his right hand, close to his side. I guess I was more shy, since my own pistol was still in my shoulder holster. We took the concrete steps two at a time, and heard rock music from a couple of the units as we went up to the third floor. Just before the third-floor landing Felix raised a hand and looked back at me. The expression on his face was one that I would almost pay money not to see again.

"This is the set," he said calmly. "I'll go in first and you're just providing cover, Lewis. Nothing serious when we get in. This is a snatch, pure and simple, and we just scare him enough to get him down to the Rover. Then we'll do a drive to my place and I'll take care of business later. Alone. All right? But if any shooting starts, aim for his trunk and keep on pulling the trigger until you empty the magazine. Don't let up. This isn't a goddam arcade."

I nodded, breathing deeply, and I had my own pistol out by then and we went up to the landing. The corridor led off to the left. Roger's unit was right in front of us, and I pointed out the door. Felix motioned to me to get to the left side and he stepped back, now holding his 9 mm in both of his hands, fingers interlocked. He did a series of deep breaths, and I saw his face and muscles tense up, his skin turning red, and he did that for a couple of moments and then exhaled in a great *"paaaahhh!"* of air. Then he leapt forward, almost bounding, and kicked out his right foot and yelled something, and slammed the door open.

The damn thing nearly flew off its hinges. Felix got into the room, and I was right behind, crouching down. Felix moved so quickly that I had a problem keeping up with him. After a minute or two of going through the unit and popping open closet doors and looking under the bed and behind the couch and out on the balcony, Felix looked up at me and said, "Damn place is empty."

I reholstered my own weapon. "He's gone, Felix."

"Shit," Felix said.

We went out on the balcony and Felix started muttering to himself, saying, "Another hour to Logan, he might make it, but if I call down to Georgie, he and Bev, they might be able to check outgoing flights."

"Still chasing?" I asked.

"Yeah," Felix said. "He's out there, running, and I'm going to start making some calls here soon, throw out a net. Chances are the bastard's skulking back to Boston and will go to ground. This just makes it harder, Lewis. Oh, I'll catch up with him one of these days, because no one can hide forever, but I was hoping not to wait. I was looking forward to finishing everything tonight."

The view from the balcony showed the darkening and threatening sky to the east, where the lighthouse at White Island out on the Isles of Shoals was winking into existence. There were still some families on the sands below us, packing up under the mist, which was getting heavier with every passing minute. The view offered nothing to me, no thoughts of peace or serenity. Instead, I had that sickly feeling of relief, when you're approaching something awful that gets canceled at the last moment. Something like a high school math test you're not ready for, and the day of the test, school is canceled because of a boiler problem. Though you're relieved you don't have to take the test, you know that you still have to take it in another twenty-four hours and that those extra hours won't make a difference in how prepared you'll be. A postponement doesn't always equal bliss.

I had avoided Roger Krohn so far since we had left York. If I kept my mouth shut, I would be successful in avoiding him for the rest of my life, but I saw the tension and rage in Felix's face, and I couldn't let him live with that for days or weeks or months.

So I opened my mouth. "Felix?"

"Yeah?" Felix was leaning against the balcony railing, the skin around his wrists pasty white where the tape had torn away some skin and hair.

"I think he's still around here."

That got his attention, and he stood up. "You do? Why?"

"Think of who he is, Felix."

"A murderer and a torturer," he shot back.

"Yeah, but he's also a thief. He steals things. He stole the paintings, and just after he shot Cameron Briggs, he stole that briefcase with the money. So where would a thief go tonight if he feels he's been successful in killing you and me and Cameron Briggs, and in destroying the safe house and the evidence? Where would he go, Felix?"

Felix started nodding, his eyebrows coming together as he

realized what I was saying. "He'd have an opportunity for one more hit, and he'd take it."

"Right. Cameron Briggs's home. Full of antiques and paintings, and also holding the other half of the payment that Cameron brought to York tonight. He's probably right there at this moment, stripping the place clean." But by then I was alone on the balcony. I went after Felix. When we got out into the corridor, a neighbor opened the door. He was a thin, wiry man with a wispy blond beard and wire-rimmed glasses. He called out, "What's going on?"

Felix gave the man a brusque reply. "Police business. Get back in and shut the door."

I always knew that Felix's voice sometimes had a ring of authority, and this was proven to me again this evening. The door slammed shut as we raced down the concrete steps, and there were no more neighborly questions.

We were on Atlantic Avenue, heading north, and I turned to Felix and said, "Do you think he was telling the truth back there?"

"About what?"

"About becoming police chief. About running the town, getting mixed up with drug trafficking and the tourists. Not caring about the paintings, just seeing them as evidence."

"Absolutely," he said. "Roger told me, uh, when we were in the Congregational church parking lot, waiting for you to show up, he kept on repeating something, that it would all be worth it in the end. Something about running a department and having the whole town to himself, every summer. Having more money than he would know what to do with."

By now I had the Rover's windshield wipers on, for the mist had changed over to a steady rain. "He say anything else?"

Felix's tone was short. "Nothing else I'm going to mention."

Traffic was light, and when we crossed over the invisible line dividing Tyler from North Tyler, my legs started tingling and Felix drew out his pistol and laid it on his lap.

"We've got two options," I said.

"What's that?" Felix asked. "And don't tell me that one of them is calling the cops. That doesn't exist as an option."

I kept my eyes on the curving road, knowing that Cameron Briggs's home was coming up in a matter of seconds. "Two options," I said. "We either go in quiet or go in loud. We can park the Rover and snoop and poke our way in."

"Or we can go in hard-ass," Felix said, nodding. "I'm tired of being quiet, Lewis. Let's go in loud."

The curve straightened out and there was the open gate of Cameron Briggs's home, off to our left. I had another second or two of decision making, and a damnable voice said, skip it, just drive on and find a phone and call the cops. Felix looked at me with a gaze of fear and triumph and anticipation all mixed in, and I made the turn.

The Rover went up the gravel pathway and Felix called out, "Here we go!" and I saw the Audi parked off to the side, with the trunk lid open. I slowed the Rover down a bit, and then I didn't stop. I bumped right into the radiator grill of the Audi, and with the Rover shuddering some, I pushed the car into a brick wall in front of the house, and there was a metallic bang as the rear bumper of the Audi struck the brick.

After I switched off the engine, both of us bailed out of the Rover. I called out to Felix, "I want to make sure he isn't going anyplace," and Felix yelled back, "Take the rear and I'll get the front, and keep your head down!"

And I did just that.

I kept low when I went around the south side of the house, passing the windows and keeping a lookout so I wouldn't get ambushed. Shades and draperies were drawn, and I had gone several steps before realizing that my Beretta was now in my shaking hands. Past the putting green and across the stone patio, I got to the rear French doors, and I rattled the door handles. Locked.

Murmuring, "I've always wanted to do this," I smashed a pane of glass with the butt of the Beretta, and after reaching in to unlock the door I got into the rear dining area. I crouched down, breathing heavily, my throat feeling like the Kevlar vest was strangling me. Off to my left was the huge kitchen, with the stoves and walk-in refrigerator and collections of pots and pans hanging from the rafters. I slipped through, taking cover wherever I could find it, and remembering with great clarity a three-week course in firearms training I had taken in Quantico, back in my DoD days.

Training being training, I usually got killed during those sessions. That didn't help my confidence factor much.

There was an open door in front of me, and I remembered it led to a formal dining room. I made it through the door, near a long, polished table with dining chairs along the sides. It looked as if there were fresh flowers in the center of the table. I moved along the table to the far door, then the deafening thunder of two gunshots made me drop to the floor. So damn loud! I got up, hunched near the table, my breathing even more ragged, making my ribs hurt.

"Lewis!" Felix yelled from further inside the house. "He's—"

I didn't hear the rest because Roger Krohn came stumbling into the dining room, the door slapping open. His head was turned to Felix's voice, and I yelled, "Freeze!"

Roger turned, shocked, and then he brought his arms up, pistol in hand. He stood next to the long table, only a few feet away from me, pistol pointing at my head. My own hands were heavy but my aim didn't waver.

Roger said, almost in a conversational tone, "Looks like a bit of a standoff, doesn't it?"

"Not for long," I said, conscious that a weapon always feels heavier when you're pointing it at someone, and Roger said, "We'll see."

Felix came in, breathing harshly, his face bright red, pistol in hand.

Roger was quick. "Hold it there, Tinios. We're in a situation here, and you might succeed in wrapping things up, but your writer friend will be the first to go."

It was a terrifying tableau, the three of us in that dining room. Felix and I drawing down on Roger, and Roger drawing down on me. I blinked my eyes. The salt from the sweat trickling down my forehead made my eyes sting. My ribs and stomach hurt.

Felix, voice low and in control: "It's over, Roger. Drop it."

Roger stared at me and I stared right back, looking at the finger wrapped around the trigger, trying not to imagine seeing those muscles tense up.

"Do it, Roger," I said. "Drop the gun."

His eyes, unblinking.

"Roger," I said. Felix moved around to the other side of the table, arms extended, his own 9 mm pointing at Roger.

The pistol didn't waver.

I didn't move, looking at the man who wanted to be police chief, who wanted to fit in, who had been busy plotting and killing. I felt angry and scared and I felt despair, despair that I had not spotted this creature earlier.

Then he smiled.

And put both arms out, and the pistol clattered to the floor.

My chest ached so much, I realized I hadn't been breathing.

Felix moved in and kicked Roger's pistol away with a foot. Roger turned to him and started saying something, and Felix punched him to the ground with two sharp, hard jabs of his fist.

Then Felix muttered something in Italian and grabbed Roger by his shirt collar. Roger was groaning as he came back up, his legs and arms loose, blood streaming down his face. Felix spun Roger around and slammed him against a wall that was covered with gilt-edged wallpaper. Dishes on a serving table rattled.

Felix stepped back, nodding as if he was satisfied, pistol still extended.

"Pat him down, will you?" Felix asked.

I holstered my own weapon at the small of my back, and

moved in. Roger was against the wall, leaning on his hands. He turned his head as I came closer. Snot and blood were running down his nose. He noticed that I was watching him and he—

He winked. Roger winked at me.

"Felix—"

I was too late.

Roger spun around, quick as gravity, and slammed an elbow into my face, knocking me back, and I fell, my shoulders hitting the dining room table. More dishes rattled. Some yells. A door slamming open and then Roger was gone and Felix was almost as quick, stumbling past me and racing after him, and I followed, not quite believing what I had seen. The man had winked at me.

The chase was short, with Felix yelling back at me, "The bastard's gone upstairs!"

Felix raced up the sweeping staircase and I was right behind him, aiming over his shoulder at the doors that led off to the left. There was movement at the middle door and Felix fired, the enclosed roar making my ears hurt, and there was a splintering puff of wood from the doorway. We got to the upstairs landing and hallway and Felix went into the bedroom and then went out to the balcony. Both the bedroom and the balcony were empty.

Another Italian swearing session from Felix, and I said, "He's on the lawn, Felix."

And so he was. Running across the lawn in the swirling rain, and I saw him just pause for a second, as he grabbed something near his ankle, and then he resumed running down the gravel driveway, backup weapon in hand, heading out to the road and the ocean.

CHAPTER
TWENTY-EIGHT

Felix yelled out, "Not this time!" He shoved his pistol in his waistband and then leaped over the balcony, letting himself drop past the wrought iron and the trellis, grabbing and swearing as he tumbled down to the lawn. I looked down and looked back and ran into the house. Heights don't bother me all that much but controlled falls do.

When I got out to the lawn I was about a hundred feet or so behind Felix as we both ran down the soggy gravel driveway. I could just make out Roger in front of us as he ran past the open gate, and then Felix fired twice in his direction. Roger ducked and ran across the street, up the berm of dirt and rock, and then dropped from sight. Felix was there a few moments later, and then so was I, running across empty Atlantic Avenue and up the mound of sand and stones. Felix was below me, nimbly jumping from rock to rock, and Roger was farther up, about fifty yards or so.

On this part of the New Hampshire coast, there are no sandy beaches—just great lumps of rock and broken granite, jagged and sharp, with fissures filled with foaming sea water from the constant onslaught of the waves. Roger was running along, jumping about like all three of us, and we were alone on these rocks. The cold rain and evening hour had deserted the rocks of vacationers.

A sharp, popping noise, and I ducked. Roger was firing at us.

I looked up, breathing so hard it felt as though my lungs would collapse upon themselves from overwork, my face wet from the rain and the splashing spray from the sea. The rocks were a maze of hardness, and there were twigs and driftwood and dried seaweed and broken seashells all about. An empty beer can was at my elbow, jammed into a crack in one of the stones, the brand name having been scraped away by the corrosive salt water. I shook my head at the madness of it all. A gunfight occurring on one of the busiest coastlines in the world, within near view and distance of hundreds of people, and I was taking part in it.

Unbelievable.

Felix yelled my name, and I saw that he had ducked down some yards in front of me. He motioned to himself a couple of times, and then waved to the right. He pointed to me and held up his gun, making shooting motions, and I waved at him. I understood. I swallowed and my throat hurt. I eased up my head, seeing Roger still up there, moving slowly from rock to rock. In a few moments he would be far ahead of us, and I drew up my Beretta. I tried to swallow again, thinking of the lunacy of what I was going to do. Then I remembered what Roger had said, what he had done, and what he wanted to do, and I pulled the trigger, three times.

Roger fell. Felix started moving quickly, and then Roger poked his head up and I fired and he returned fire, but I think I spoiled his aim. This went on two more times. Felix edged closer, moving back and forth, jumping and scrambling over the rocks. Each time I saw a movement, saw Roger aim and fire, I shot at him. I was shooting at a person, at a man I had lunched and drank with, and all I could think about was that my wrists and knees hurt, and that even in August, it was getting damn cold out here in the rain and the dampness.

Then Roger started to run again, I shot once more, and he disappeared behind some rocks. Felix raced up and was over a boulder, and then there was no sound, no more shots, and nothing except for the cry of a few gulls and the rush of the waves across the rocks.

I t took me a long time to get to the place where both Roger and Felix had dropped from view. It was fear that was dragging me along.

I was afraid that at any moment Roger would stand up in front of me, ten feet tall and teeth bared in that hellish grin. I was afraid that I would find Felix dead among the rocks, alone. I was afraid that Roger had gotten away and that he would always be free, and that I would have to leave Tyler Beach and go away, because I would never sleep comfortably again knowing he was out there.

So I went from rock to rock, boulder to boulder, slipping some in the rain and noticing for the first time the faint stench of oil among the rocks. As I came over one rise of sloped rocks, there was Felix Tinios, sitting by himself below me, resting his head in his hands. His pistol was at his feet. He looked up at me, in utter exhaustion. There was blood around his lips. Then I noticed my own jaw was aching, from where Roger had struck me.

"You can put your gun away, Lewis," Felix said. "It's safe. Come on down."

I holstered my 9 mm under my jacket and came down to where Felix was sitting, trying not to fall. One boulder was particularly slippery and my hand was soiled as I touched it on the way down. It smelled of oil. An old gift from the *Petro Star* and the dead Cameron Briggs.

Felix was sitting on a piece of granite in front of a small tidal pool, and rocks and sand were at his feet. He managed a small smile and he said, "See that smear of oil up there?"

I got to the ground, my legs shaking. "Couldn't miss it. I got my hand in it."

Felix's smile got a bit wider. "When I got down here, Roger was grabbing his leg. I think he broke it. He slipped on that damn oil patch on the way down."

I sat next to Felix. "Cameron Briggs's revenge, I suppose. Where's Roger?"

Felix motioned out to the ocean, and I looked to where he pointed. I was not surprised.

Roger was in the water, gently moving with the swirl of the waves and the tugging of the tide, but I don't think he was in any position to enjoy the movements. He was face down, and his arms and legs bobbed with the motion of the water. I sat still and felt the rain strike my head and face. I was very tired, and a lot of bones and muscles ached.

My voice was quiet. "You said he probably broke his leg. But he hadn't been shot, had he?"

"Nope."

"And I didn't hear any more gunfire after I saw you go over the side."

"That's right."

"So what did you do, Felix?"

Felix nodded and kept his gaze out on the ocean, rubbing at his bloody mouth. "Thought it was fitting, he and I being here, at the ocean's edge, probably near the place where they dumped my cousin. Poor Sal, dead because of something I was involved with. It seemed fitting."

"So you tossed him in the ocean?"

Felix looked surprised. "No, I'm not that stupid."

"Oh?"

He picked up his pistol, looked at it as if he had just found it after a long search, and he put it back into his waistband. Then he wouldn't look at me.

"No, I'm not that stupid," he repeated. "I held his head down in that tidal pool until he drowned, Lewis, and then I dumped him in the ocean. I wanted things final. I had a chance to do it with my own two hands, and already I'm beginning to feel better."

I shivered and sat for a minute or two longer in the rain, and I watched as Roger Krohn's body tumbled in the waves. Some weeks ago I had gone out into these same waters to retrieve the mutilated corpse of a diver, and that one act had brought me down some hard roads and with some equally hard people. One act, one effort.

Right now, I was content to see Roger's corpse drift away.

"We should get out of here," Felix finally said.

"That's right."

We helped each other climb back up the rocks.

CHAPTER

TWENTY-NINE

It was Sunday afternoon, two days after Felix and I had that bloody trip from York to Wallis, and we were on the rear deck of my house, enjoying one of the few Sunday afternoons left in this summer. We were well fed, thanks to Felix, who had taken over my kitchen for the past couple of hours and had worked magic with my stove, coming up with a veal and fettuccine dish that rested fine and comfortable in my stomach. I was moving slower than usual, though, since my muscles and tendons were still aching from that awful workout on Friday. I do try to keep in shape, but it had been hard, after my sojourn in the hospital, and that hellish run across the rocks had stretched out fibers in my body that had been quiet for too long.

When dinner was done, Felix had kicked me out on the deck,

and I had gone with no argument, as he cleaned the kitchen and washed the dishes and packed away the food and utensils he had brought. Once he had given me a wide smile, saying it was a pleasure to sleep in his own bed again. It was good to see the healing process take hold. I had thought about that during the day, as his smiles seemed a bit too wide, his laughter a bit too forced, and I wondered what memories he would allow himself to keep over the years.

And I also wondered if he dreamed, if he dreamed about an evil cop with a sour taste for electricity. I knew I would have to ask him that, in a few months, for my own particular dreams had been with me for years, and I was resigned to the certainty that they would always be with me.

Out on the deck we sipped from tall lemonades, spiked with a splash of gin, and we said not much as we listened to a Red Sox–Blue Jays game on the radio. I had a sense of contentment for two reasons. The first was that on Saturday evening I had transmitted a column to *Shoreline* over my modem, and the words I had written had been an essay on the *Petro Star*, taking all of us to task for still relying on petroleum-based energy, which sets us up for such disasters. And the second was that the sky was clear and the weather prediction for the next few days was perfect. Tomorrow night was the first night of the Perseids, and I was eagerly anticipating their show. Earlier, while we were eating, Felix said, "You got those shooting stars coming up, right?"

"That's right. Tomorrow night."

"For how long?"

"Three, maybe four nights."

"Unh-hunh," he had said, spooning up a helping of fettuccine. "And what do you do?"

"I stay out at night and watch them."

"Do they make any noise?"

"Nope."

"Are there a lot of shooting stars? I mean, do they look like fireworks or something?"

"No, nothing like that," I had said, grinning at him. "You're lucky if you get a good one every five minutes or so."

Felix had shook his head at the insanity of it all. "Jesus, I think I'd rather watch golf."

As the afternoon wore on, we sipped our drinks and listened to the Red Sox and the Blue Jays duel it out for the American League East. We seemed to have an unspoken agreement not to discuss what had happened last week. However, as the afternoon got later and the innings of the game got longer, I was about ready to break that agreement.

I looked over at him. "We were lucky, you know."

Felix was back in his chair, eyes closed, glass in his hand. "Luck is where you find it, Lewis. Let's leave it at that."

"No, I don't mean what happened on Friday. I mean the aftermath. Cameron Briggs is missing and no one seems to know where he is, though it looks like—according to the evidence in his house—that he was the victim of foul play. There was a fire at a house in another state, and an unidentified body was found in the rubble, but so far, there's no connection between that body and Cameron Briggs's empty house."

"Which is fine," Felix murmured.

"Sure," I said. "And Roger Krohn has also seemed to vanish. He's just gone. Though I understand the Boston *Globe* did a piece on him the other day, based on an anonymous phone call, saying he's a dirty cop. They seem to think he's in Rio."

"Ocean's a big place," Felix said. "You've got fish, birds and lobsters, all of whom get hungry by and by, and the salt water can do a lot of damage. Don't worry about Roger."

"I'm not," I said as I leaned back. The sun felt good on my face and hands, and I was in a vaguely pleasant stupor induced by the sun, wine and good food. It made me wonder how Felix and his compatriots ever had the energy to do what they did for a living.

So now I looked over at his face and said quietly, "Felix?"

"Hmmm," he murmured in reply, his eyes still closed.

"Felix, where are the paintings?"

I kept watch. His face tightened and his eyes slowly opened and then he took a casual sip from his drink. Too casual.

"What paintings?"

Dumb answer. "The Winslow Homer paintings, Felix. Where are they?"

He turned in his chair, surprise etched on his face, but there was something cool and icelike in his eyes. "They're gone, Lewis. You saw them go up in flames yourself."

I raised my eyebrows. "Did I, Felix? Oh, sure, I saw three items that looked like three paintings get burned in York, but were they the real Winslow Homer paintings? Couple of things don't make sense."

Now his eyes were fully open and he was no longer relaxed. "Such as?"

"Such as your reaction, Felix. You've sweated and bled and went to ground and saw your own cousin get killed and your father get threatened over those paintings, and what's your reaction when they supposedly burn up? You say it's over, it's done with, and you never bring them up again. You don't curse your bad luck, or even show any sign that you're upset that those paintings you've worked so hard to make money off were destroyed. Hell, you didn't even go to the house to see if they made it through the explosion. I did that."

Felix's face was set, no expression. "Maybe I'm a guy who hides his emotions well."

"Right," I said, hoping there was enough scorn in my voice. "And maybe I'm a guy who belongs to the Flat Earth Society. One other thing doesn't make sense, Felix, and it took me a while to figure it out. They didn't burn right."

"They didn't what?"

I put down my glass of gin and lemonade on the round wooden table. "They didn't burn right, Felix. Supposedly those were the original Winslow Homer paintings, over a hundred years old and sturdy and painted on heavy canvas. It takes a lot of heat to burn canvas, and what I saw were three objects that went up in flames almost instantly, curling upon themselves like they were made of paper. Not canvas. Like they were poster reproductions you can buy at the Scribner Museum in Manchester."

For a bit we were both quiet, as over the radio Roger Clemens struck out his third Blue Jay batter in a row to end the seventh inning. Then Felix grinned and shook his head and said, "Damn, you are good, Lewis. Times like these, I wish you were working back at the Department of Defense. You'd be scaring people in other countries, that's how good you are."

"Thanks for the compliment," I said. "I would guess that when you took me to the safe house, those were the real paintings, and that you switched them later. Why the fakes? An insurance policy?"

Felix nodded, still smiling. "Absolutely. You know, those reproductions were so good that from across a room—if you weren't an art professor or something—you couldn't tell they were fakes. That's what I was counting on. The bad guys had the numbers, the guns and the money. A dangerous combination. I wanted to give up the address of the safe house, but then make it more difficult for the exchange to take place. Those fakes were just the bait, to get them to the house."

"And the real ones, Felix, where are they?"

He almost smirked at me, he looked so happy. "They're in a safe place."

"Felix . . ."

He shrugged. "Oh, all right. Lewis, they're in your house. Actually, your garage. And they've been there for weeks. You should learn to keep that garage door shut. It made me nervous."

Felix looked quite pleased with himself, and I was sure it was for two reasons. First was the knowledge that he had saved the paintings from destruction, and second was no doubt the sweet feeling of seeing me so shocked that I couldn't say anything. But I was going to return the favor in about one minute, which I did.

"My garage?"

"Yep. Figured it was as good a place as any, and had easy access."

I raised up my glass, finished my drink. "That's pretty good, Felix, and you know what? It makes sense to have them here."

His grin was still there. "Why's that?"

I winked at him. "Because I want them."

No more grin.

The discussion—which sometimes slipped into arguing— went on for a while until I killed it with this one reply. "Felix, those paintings are dangerous. Oh, they have a value—like a couple of pounds of plutonium—but they're too dangerous to keep. You try selling them to anybody out there on the fringe, and I might not be there again to save your tanned butt. Remember that. You owe me, and I want those paintings."

"Lewis . . ."

"Felix, you owe me. I know that Cameron Briggs's money found a happy home, right?"

Then his face clouded over and he squinted his eyes. He stood up and stomped over to the railing of my deck, looking down at the tiny backyard and my private cove, and the waves which crashed in on their monotonous journey. One hand was on the railing and the other was holding his glass. He shook his head a couple of times. Then he swore and tossed the glass over the side and the sudden outburst startled me, especially when he turned around with a big smile on his face.

"You know what, you miserable bastard?" he demanded.

"What's that?"

"You're absolutely right. I hate you for that, Lewis Cole, honest to God I do. If you had known me years earlier, I would have tossed you over the side, not that damn glass, for making such a demand."

"If I had known you years earlier, you might have been a defense contractor."

He laughed. "Could be, could be. Sounds like an intriguing job." He clapped his hands together and came back to his seat and sat down with a grunt. "So. They now belong to you. Are they going right back to the museum?"

I shrugged. "Eventually."

Felix looked surprised. "Eventually? What the hell do you mean by that?"

I sat back in the chair, closed my eyes. "Eventually. And you owe me a drinking glass."

He laughed again. "Why not. Today I seem to be giving you everything I own anyway."

After the Red Sox lost it in the tenth inning to the Blue Jays and Felix left, I walked out to my garage, which is really a glorified shack built next to my house. At one time, I think, it stored equipment for the Lifeboat Station that had once been here. Inside was my Range Rover, which took up most of the space. The floor was dirt, and I made my way to the front, where I had accumulated a couple of shovels, a rake and other odds and ends that seem to end up in a garage rather than a basement. There were some cardboard boxes back there that I was keeping, in the extremely unlikely event that I would ever move again, and behind those boxes, leaning against the rear garage wall and resting on some stones, was a large package.

The package was heavy and wrapped in twine and brown paper. I lugged it back to my house, bringing it into the living room. With a knife and scissors I carefully went to work, and in thirty minutes I had *Fog Warning*, *Eight Bells* and *The Gulf Stream* in my living room. I leaned the paintings against the cold and empty fireplace and stood there gingerly running my fingers across the paint and the old canvas. Tears came to my eyes.

"Winslow, old man," I whispered. "You certainly were one talented son of a bitch."

I went into the kitchen and returned with a glass of wine, finishing off the bottle that Felix had brought, and I sat on the floor for about an hour, just looking at the colors and the shapes, and appreciating how the changing light in my living room made them seem so alive.

But as I watched, a little cold worm started digging its way through my skull. I found myself thinking about keeping the paintings in my living room and study. No one would know, and if I ever had visitors, the paintings could go back in the garage. Three priceless Winslow Homers, resting in my home, and only I would know . . .

I finished off my wine and went outside. I tossed my wineglass in the general direction of the ocean, joining Felix's earlier contribution. I stood there until the clean salt air cleared out my head, then I went back inside and went to work.

Early on Monday evening I was working on dessert at Diane Woods's condo, having joined her and her companion, Kara Miles. Dinner had been beef Stroganoff and they had kept me in the living room while they cooked. There had been a lot of giggling and shrieking as the meal finally came together. Dessert was coffee and Famous Newburyport Cheesecake, which we ate cross-legged on the floor, with the dishes on a clear-glass coffee table. Diane and Kara looked like sisters, with white tennis shorts and dark blue polo shirts, and when I asked if they consulted each other on clothing choices, Kara had winked at Diane and said, "Only if she's on the pillow next to me in the morning."

Diane had giggled and kicked Kara at that, and Kara had rubbed her hair. Diane's eyes were bright. It was nice to see her in a good mood, though I knew other things had contributed to that mood on this day.

As I finished off the last of the cheesecake on my plate, I said, "So tell us again how you got the paintings."

"Yeah, Diane," Kara demanded. "Talk to us. You bore me with everything that goes wrong every day, might as well tell me when something goes right."

Diane still looked pleased. "Well, dispatch got a call from a male, at about 7 A.M. today. The message was for me and said that if I went to the St. Donna Cemetery on High Street and looked behind a gravestone at the intersection of 'D' and 'A' lanes, I would find some stolen property."

"What did it look like?" I said.

"Big package, all done up in brown paper. Opened it up and saw those three paintings, and I knew we weren't talking your standard over-the-couch artwork. Next thing I knew, the place was crawling with news media, and then the State Police and the goddam FBI showed up, and that's when I found out they were the Winslow Homers which were stolen from the Scribner Museum five years ago."

Kara looked over at Diane, admiration in her eyes. "Why do you think the guy gave them up, Diane?"

Diane looked right at me. "Guilt, maybe. Or maybe the guy got hold of the paintings and realized that they could never be fenced 'cause they were so hot." She shrugged. "Makes no difference to me," she added, smiling again. "All I know is that one Detective Diane Woods gets credit for recovering three of the most important paintings ever stolen in this country in this century. Not a bad way to end the summer."

"Not at all," I said.

Kara leaned over and kissed Diane and said, "Damn, I'm proud of you, hon."

Kara got up and started clearing the dishes. I looked up at her and said, "You've got four earrings in one ear, and three in the other. Aren't you running out of space?"

Kara giggled. "Maybe so. I've wanted to get other body parts pierced, but Miss Straitlaced here won't let me."

Diane kicked Kara's foot—gently—and said, "Stop gossiping, will you?" Kara just grinned in reply and went off to the kitchen, leaving Diane and me alone in the living room. I looked over at Diane and she gazed back at me.

"Understand the chief is doing better," I said.

She nodded. "He's in full remission, should be back in a

month. About time the old man let on what was going on, but that's the way he is. And the heir apparent, Mr. Roger Krohn, has apparently left town for parts unknown, and based on what I read in the *Globe*, I don't think I'll miss him. But, Lewis?"

"Yeah?"

"I don't forget."

"Forget what?"

"I don't forget that you've been snooping around the Scribner Museum about that five-year-old theft. It seems too much of a coincidence that you would be doing that and a couple of weeks later those paintings get dumped in my lap. Then, to cap things off, five minutes after I'm at the cemetery, your buddy Paula Quinn from the Tyler *Chronicle* stops by and gets an exclusive. What do you think about that?"

I was thinking of a joking reply, but the expression on her face gave me a better idea. "I think you're right. It's a hell of a co-incidence."

"It was your job, right? Start to finish."

There were a lot of things I could have said, but I decided the truth might just work. "Not from start, but to finish, yeah, it was my job."

"Anything else going to happen, or is it done?"

I thought about Roger Krohn and what had happened to him and Cameron Briggs. I closed my mouth and thought a bit more and said, "For you, Diane, it's done. I would just keep my press clippings and let the FBI and the Manchester cops sort everything else out."

Diane slowly smiled. "Then I have another amazing coincidence to report, Lewis, because that's exactly what I was planning on doing."

"Such a night for coincidences," I said.

She reached out and squeezed my hand. "Thanks," she said, and Kara strolled back in and jokingly told me to leave her woman alone, which I did. But Diane kept on smiling at me the rest of the night.

A few hours later I was on my back deck, resting on a mattress pad, happy that there was a warm female body snuggling up to me. Paula Quinn felt wonderful resting on my shoulder, and I breathed in her soft scent as we looked up at the stars. The ocean air this night was cool and there was a light blanket over us as we waited. Without the moon, the night sky was dark, the stars sharp and distinct. I could even make out the hazy swath of the Milky Way.

"Tell me why they're called the Perseids," she whispered, her hair tickling my throat.

I kept my own voice low. "Meteor showers that arrive each year are named for the place they seem to come from. These showers every August are named after the constellation Perseus, because they seem to radiate from that constellation."

"And who was Perseus?"

"A young warrior who saved the beautiful Andromeda from the sea monster Cetus. She had been chained to a sea cliff by the god Neptune."

"Oh," she said, not sounding very impressed. "Thanks for clearing that up."

"You're welcome."

She moved again and I turned my head and we kissed for a few minutes, gently and with a quiet passion, just exploring and tasting the texture of our mouths against each other. Both of us were content with this little step, and didn't want to push it any further. She sighed and squeezed my side and broke away, saying, "So how come I haven't seen any of these meteors yet?"

"Because we've been too busy."

"Hah," and I thought she was going to say something else, but a long, glittering flash of light streaked across the sky. It almost went across our entire field of view, a tail that seemed thick and wondrously bright, and Paula said, "Holy God."

"Not bad, right?"

"Lewis," she said, awe in her voice. "I've seen meteors before, but nothing like this before. It was huge!"

"Those are the Perseids," I said. "And this is probably the best night in years. Clear, no clouds and no moon."

Three more meteors flashed across, and it was almost like watching a Fourth of July fireworks show, except that they were random and not controlled by anyone on the surface of the planet. The tails were always thick and bright, and it was hard to believe that tiny specks of dust and rock from a long-ago comet were causing such a show. We lay in silence and watched the meteors streak across. Once I saw a bright moving dot of light that signaled a satellite or space debris, safe in its orbit around our planet. What lay above me in the sky was something so unique and wonderful I could not say a word, for fear that it would ruin everything. A few minutes went by and from the increasing regularity of her breathing, I could tell that Paula was sleeping.

Another half dozen meteors burned their way through the atmosphere before she yawned and said, "I dozed off there."

"So you did."

"Well, can you blame me?" she demanded. "I had a hell of a busy day. Up at dawn with a phone tip that those Winslow Homer paintings were at St. Donna's Cemetery, and my God, Lewis, when I got there it was just me and your cop buddy, Diane Woods. I got the particulars from everybody else who showed up and I got an exclusive, photos and everything else."

"Congratulations," I said, glad that in the darkness she couldn't see what my face looked like.

"Mmm," she said. "Not only that, but I got on the phone and started doing freelance, and I sold stringer stories to the Associated Press, the Boston *Globe* and a couple of radio stations. Even Channel 9 interviewed me."

"I saw you. I was impressed. If you ever want a career as a meat puppet, you can have it."

"Hunh," she said. "Not likely. Nope, I got bigger and better things ahead of me, Lewis. This afternoon I called up the head of security at the museum, some guy named Dix, and he was so happy to talk to me he was crying on the phone. I've got an interview set up with him tomorrow."

"You do?" I said. "Then tell him I said hello."

Paula squeezed me again. "You know him?"

"Just a little, but he'll know me. Tell him hello, and that I'm glad everything worked out."

"Hah," Paula said, nuzzling under my chin. "Anybody else at the museum I should say hi to?"

I remembered a long-legged woman on this back deck in a skimpy black bathing suit and the way she had looked at me, and how she had walked out, full of life and confidence. I smiled gently. "No one else, Paula. No one else."

She giggled slightly. "You weren't making any phone calls to the *Chronicle* this morning, were you? Seems like the cops got the same call. So one call was for Diane and the other was for me. And you know the two of us and the museum director. Pretty cozy, Lewis."

"Stop complaining," I said. "Just be glad you got called, and stop asking so many questions."

"Hmmm," she murmured. "All right, you secret-keeper you. And you know who else I called today? *Yankee* magazine. I called their articles editor and pitched her a story about the painting recovery, and she's interested. Can you believe that? Me in a national magazine!"

"Nice way to end up another boring summer at Tyler Beach," I said.

"Absolutely."

"So you're doing better."

"Yep."

I gave her a squeeze. "And how are we doing?"

"Hmmm," she said, gently kissing my neck. "I think we're doing better. We're starting over in a way, Lewis, and I think that's best."

"No arguments here."

"I'm glad."

The meteors went on, each one seemingly brighter than the one before it, and Paula kissed me and whispered, "Lewis, I should be going. I'm falling asleep here."

I thought about my response, and I carefully said, "You're welcome to spend the night. On the couch, if need be, Paula."

She kissed me again. "No, I should go home. And don't you get up—you'll ruin your night vision or something. You stay here and enjoy the show."

I squeezed her hand and there was the soft noise of the glass door sliding open. After a minute or two, she went out the front door and I could hear her walk up my dirt driveway. I waited until I caught the sound of her car engine starting and then heading away. Then I pulled the blanket up and lay back and stared up at the vastness of the evening sky, looking at my old constellation friends, running their names through my mind. Soon it seemed like with every passing minute meteor after meteor streaked across the sky, filling me with an ancient and wonderful joy, of being alive and breathing in such a huge and glorious universe.

I took a deep breath and my side felt fine and I smelled the clean air of the ocean waves, and there was no scent of oil, rot or decay.

The black tide was gone.